D1531919

COLLIERS ROW

COLLIERS ROW

Jan Webster

J. B. LIPPINCOTT COMPANY
Philadelphia and New York

First American edition

2 4 6 8 9 7 5 3 1

Printed in the United States of America

U.S. Library of Congress Cataloging in Publication Data

Webster, Jan, birth date
Colliers row.

I. Title.
PZ4.W38Co3 [PR6073.E2313] 823'.9'14 77-3961
ISBN-0-397-01228-4

For Drew, with love

COLLIERS ROW

PART ONE

♦

Chapter One

He never called her down in mid-afternoon.

Kate Kilgour smoothed down her skirts with hands that trembled. She noticed vaguely there were still little threads of flour under her cuticles from the morning's bread-making.

'Come in.' James Galbraith's voice sounded, deeply resonant, from the depths of his study, in response to her knock. He looked up uneasily as she went in.

'Mistress Kilgour, as from next month I am obliged to terminate your employment under my roof.'

He had always called her Mistress, because of the boy. Now the unbelievable moment had come, she looked at him aghast, no colour in her normally pink cheeks; a comely young woman, blue-eyed, fair of hair, with an air of calm order about her and an innate dignity. She saw he wore a clean stock, for once without her bidding.

'You know why I want you to go.' They had never so much as touched, but his look now was nakedly readable. A sense of loss twisted her inside, made her screw up in pain. He looked at her with some concern. 'They are talking in the toun.'

'What are they saying in Greenock now?' she burst out. 'That I have a bairn whose father wasn't man enough to marry me? No one points a finger at *him*. Am I to carry this stigma to the end of my days?'

'I am here to set an example in this parish,' said James Galbraith stonily.

'Why now?' she cried out. 'When you left the Church of Scotland two years ago and signed the Act of Separation, I came with you to the Free Kirk. I had the bairn then. The Free Kirk stands for the Gospel of forgiveness and redemption, doesn't it?' She pointed dramatically heavenwards. 'He forgives me, even if you do not.'

He stood up, a massive, forbidding man, rigid, rock-like, a lifetime of repression in his features. One of the things about the Church of Scotland before the Disruption of 1843 had been what someone had termed 'the great and offensive prominence of women' in it. He did not wish to see this repeated in the Free Kirk, and of late Kate, with her sermon-tasting and Sunday school, had been getting above herself. And it had been a mistake to let her take over the running of the prayer meeting on Wednesday nights. Now she had quite a following of her own and she was merely his housekeeper, after all, most of what she had learned passed on by him. Now she saw herself fit to argue, for instance, for St John against St Paul! As if she knew anything of Biblical Criticism. Talking about a just social order, about caring for the poor, even about being a missionary in Calabar. Well, it was maybe only to be expected from a woman from the West Highlands, where the christening bakes often furnished the marriage table and pride and loose morals abounded.

But his well-doing parishioners here did not take kindly to it and he had to consider their feelings, as Edith Gillespie never failed to remind him.

When he had taken Kate on as his housekeeper ten years ago in 1835, her child had been an infant in arms and he fresh out of university and full of Greek and Latin. Her mother, who had looked after the baby, had died of the flux and she herself had lost her job as a French polisher on the ships being fitted out on the Clyde. She had been commended to him as a hard worker and a repentant sinner and both were true. There was plenty to commend in her. Perhaps he had always seen too much. In the beginning, his nights had been furnished with visions of her yielding flesh. Even now he honed his mind on her sharp insights. He had thought all this would sort itself out as he got deep into his ministry and the philosophies of his faith, and partly this was so. Since he had become an Evangelical, with a desperate need to spread the Word, there had been much he had wanted to do.

It was all very well for some to say the Free Kirk were the new Puritans. But he was, he hoped, a man of intellect, and he looked to his Kirk to bring Scotland out of the sorry pass she was in since she had started aping the English. Where were the Humes and Scotts of today? The nation which had been the crucible of thought for the West, which had given the world the steam engine, through James Watt; the theory of heat, through Joseph Black; and the predominant political theories of the century, through Adam Smith, was being vitiated by neglect, drunkenness and emigration.

Braid Scots, the language of the philosophers, was now spoken only by the farm labourers. Plain living and high thinking had been tainted by industrial greed and exploitation; canny kindness and rough dignity by debauchery and loss of national certainty. Something had to be done about it and men like him had to do it, had to put kirk and nation above their own desires and bring the country back to a sense of duty.

He had recently been to preach in Glasgow and had seen a child without a nose – the result, his host had told him, of sexual disease passed on by the mother. Everywhere you looked there had been whisky shops and fallen women prostituting themselves in the street. He had been given a figure of nearly 3000 in Glasgow, while in Edinburgh, he had been told, even the domestic servants entertained men in the basements of the tall houses in the New Town, while more than two hundred brothels plied their evil trade. And as a country boy, well he knew the slack moralities of the farming communities, where labourers were actively encouraged to have unmarried followers who provided cheap labour and where immorality before marriage and traditions like bundling were regarded as very trifling.

He could not marry her. It was what part of him had wanted for many years, but how could he stand up for moral rectitude, for the reality of the Christian faith, if he made his heart's dearest a woman who had sinned? The moral struggle was wearing him down. Spirituality, holiness, heavenly-mindedness, superiority to worldly pleasures, these were the principles for which he stood.

And yet she could have remained a dear thorn in his flesh if it had not been for Miss Gillespie and her campaign within his congregation. She carried weight, as sister of an important ship-builder with an ever-growing yard, and she was on intellectually sound ground when she said that Calvinism should exert communal disapproval of anti-social conduct. She was not for bringing back the rigours of the kirk session, when miscreants had to confess their sins before their fellow churchgoers, but responsibility to the community was an issue that could not be dodged. He could see that.

There was another thing. Kate liked play-acting and enjoyed nothing better than discussing the fact that the Siddons had once appeared in *The Merchant of Venice* in nearby Greenock and that the Keans and the Kembles, the Macklins and Macreadys had all appeared there. She was one of those who thought Greenock, not Glasgow, the capital of the west. She had even been to dancing assemblies in the Tontine Hall.

Another thing. She did not agree with him over Sabbatarianism, arguing that it wasn't founded on Biblical truth.

She was altogether too commanding, considering her position. The fact remained: his middle-class, well-doing congregation was falling away because of his moral allegiance to her over the years. He could see himself parish-less and all his great plans for extending education to the toiling masses through the church would come to naught. If he courted Edith Gillespie, he would never know the joys he had hoped to taste with Kate. But a cup of water was better than nothing to a man dying of thirst in the desert. And Edith, with her sharpness, her standards, would help him to give up drinking. Not come in with a smile on her face, like Kate, and hand him a glass of claret. Then another. When the sons of the Covenanters were being described as the most drunken population on the face of the earth, he had a duty to uphold the rules of temperance; to work for the closing of the pubs on Sundays, for it was then the labourer spent his week's wages, leaving his family with nothing. God help him. His soul was damned if he did not try.

She was looking at him now as though he had struck her a physical blow. He began to weaken and bluster.

'There is no need for you and young Jack to leave immediately,' he said. 'You can look around for another position and I will vouchsafe that you are a good, plain cook and an exemplary housekeeper. When the time comes, I shall see the boy is apprenticed to a worthy trade.'

For a moment, she reminded him of the collie dog his parents had had on the farm. Ready to slink away with a look of livid reproach when kicked. But she broke through her humiliation and faced him:

'I have seen it coming! The Kirk is becoming famous for its narrowness. But I had thought better of you, James Galbraith. You don't have to tell me twice. I will go. I will go this very day and you can bring that thin-lipped barren Jezebel here to warm your bed!'

He thought briefly and forgivingly that reading the Bible had improved her vocabulary out of all knowledge. Now she had spoken, he knew some green spring had finally dried up in him and he was in a strange, broken landscape of the spirit. Yet there was exultation, too. What he had done, he had done in the Lord's name. Praise be to the Lord, in Whom all things were possible.

She went white-lipped to her room at the top of the house, and even as she packed their few belongings in a tin box, she did not cry. Not even when she packed the caricature handkerchief, with its design of the Manchester and Liverpool railway, that young Jack had given her as a New Year token, telling her to take care as the paint rubbed off easily. She was too angry to cry.

From down the river came the lonely sound of a ship's hooter. Young Jack would be by the river bank. He could spot a sail before anybody else. She resolved to fetch him in and give him a good meal of cold meat and fresh bread before they left.

'Will there be the sea at Glasgow?' demanded Jack.

They had reached Port Glasgow only and she was already weary, mainly from spent rage. Ever since the citizens of Glasgow had built this port, in opposition to Greenock, there had been fights and ill-feeling between the inhabitants of both places. Now all her anger was gone she saw that she had been hasty and ill-advised, but there was no question of going back. She had certainly burned her bridges. Her one comfort was the feeling of the guineas in her reticule, the knowledge that at least they would not starve until she found another position. The late August weather was warm, verging on hot, and if they had to sleep out on their walk to Glasgow, they would come to no harm.

She managed a bright smile for her son.

'There will be the same River Clyde that you see here. They widened the river so that the big ships could go up to Broomielaw. You know that as well as I do.'

He looked towards the river, grievance and uncertainty building up in him. When his mother had snatched him home for that hasty meal, he had been awaiting the *John and Maggie* in from Italy, with Sienna marble for baths for the gentry and, more interesting to him, macaroni, anchovies and liquorice paste, not to mention sweet currants. He was going to help her unload – well, watch her unload – and the master might have let him come aboard to explore. He was known as a willing, helpful lad, who could be relied upon to run vital errands. What would he do in Glasgow? They might not be near the river and anyway it would be narrow there. He hated Glasgow with the depth of the true Greenock native, who felt his town had been denied its birthright of trade.

A sadness that he might not be able to watch for his beautiful ships filled his whole being. Ships like the *Peter Senn*, that lovely barque of 195 tons with her distinctive carved figurehead. Or the big steamship *Britannia*, designed by the great Robert Napier, which could cross the Atlantic in ten days. (They had greeted her with cannon in Boston.) Or the full-rigged beauties that sailed across the periphery of the eye like something out of a dream – as though from another land that you had known a long time ago and wanted to visit again.

'Oh, my ships,' he blurted out. He had to keep shoving the tears from his eyes with the sleeve of his jacket. Kate pretended not to see and to divert him told him how she had sailed on the steamship *Comet*, coming to Greenock from Argyll to visit her mother's people as a child.

Although he had heard it all before, the magic worked.

'It wasn't the first *Comet* you came on,' he grumbled.

'No, the first *Comet* was wrecked at Graignish Point in 1820,' she told him. 'So that its name should live on, they built the second by public subscription and I sailed on it the year before it was run down by the *Ayr*, near Greenock, and went down with the loss of many lives.'

He gave a shudder. 'I'm glad you weren't on it. But I wish it *had* been the very first steamship ever built.' But although this was commonly boasted, he had spoken to sailors enough who knew differently. That had been the *Charlotte Dundas*, built at Grangemouth, and there were those who claimed for an American ship, the *Phoenix*, or even for some French vessels built over on the River Seine.

When she saw that he was more cheerful, she decided that she would tell him what she had in mind by making for Glasgow. First of all they should walk another mile or two, then she would select a spot where they could rest and eat the buttered scones she had prepared and drink from the bottle of cold tea.

In the event she chose a sheltered spot by the side of a

rutted track leading to a farm. The harvest had been early and the gleaners were at work, their busy figures lending a feeling of welcome companionship in a landscape that had become frighteningly strange and different.

Frail harebells grew where they sat and late bees visited the scented clover. From far off came the sound of a yellow hammer. The river was laid out in front of their eyes, about a mile off, and they could see a little brigantine make a stiff pace, like some pretty sea butterfly.

'John,' said Kate, wiping the moist butter from her lips as she finished her scone, 'we are going to Glasgow *for a purpose*.'

He knew she only called him John when she was being serious. He was an open-faced boy, freckled, tousle-haired, his interests almost exclusively male and maritime. Yet his sensitivity when it came to his mother was acute. The closed, secretive excitement on her face made his heart pound.

'There are records there, addresses and such,' she went on mysteriously. 'And I mean to find out.' She lapsed into a contemplative study, her face both sad and earnest, her mouth working. He held his breath, knowing better than to speak. Always afterwards he was to remember the smell of clover and cut corn, the brigantine painted on his memory hard as enamel.

'Your father,' she said at last, 'your real father, Jack. You must have thought sometimes about him. Have you?'

'Dunno.' He coloured. He had looked on James Galbraith as a *sort* of father, although his mother had made the relationship clear at all times. James Galbraith had sent him to church school, had helped him with his lessons and taught him a little Greek and Latin. It had even been suggested that Jack would 'follow' him into the ministry, but Jack had reserved his position on that. He was sure he wasn't going to read books all the time, like James Galbraith. He was going to sail all over the world, first to America, then to Africa where the Hottentots were, and after that he'd see. He applied himself when necessary to his lessons, because you needed arithmetic if you were going to sail the oceans, and you needed to know about languages if you were going to speak to foreigners. He might be a missionary, but so far he had not had The Call. He was going to think properly about God and The Call when he was older, but so far there just hadn't been enough time.

'Jack.' His mother prompted him gently. 'Your real father. *Have* you thought about him then, ever?'

'Well – ' He didn't know what to say. His mother had kept off the subject when *he* had wanted to ask a lot of questions and gradually he had pushed it more and more to the back of his mind. He knew it was tinged with something disagreeable, upsetting. He knew about bastards and bad women, but his mother had never seemed to him to be less than other women. Rather, more. She had soft, pink cheeks and her hair curled when the steam came from the big clootie dumpling over the hearth and it looked golden, real golden, at night when she tucked the bedclothes round his neck. She was not downtrodden, 'trauchled' like the poor women who came out of the whisky shops with their dirty, scab-marked babies carried in shawls and their hair streaking the sides of their faces. She treated James Galbraith like an equal, read the *Quarterly Review* and held her head up wherever she went. She was fiercely proud of being Highland and made 'Highland pride', indeed, anything Highland, sound like the original against which all other varieties were pale copies. But how you placed this mother, this person who, as she put it herself, was 'fit for anything and anybody', against the fact of his own undoubted existence, was something he had not brought himself round to coping with. So he stumbled again against the right words and said, 'I suppose I haven't, very much. Thought about him, I mean.'

She drew him to her then, sounding different, younger as she spoke.

'I had not long come from Argyll, my father having died heartbroken when the croft was taken from him and the sheep put to graze. When you are older, you will understand what the English landlords are doing to the likes of us, how they clear out the Highlands and put sheep where people should be. However, that is by the by. My mother – your grannie – and I came to Greenock, where she had been born, and we found a nice wee but and ben. She kept the floor well scoured and sanded. You have been brought up in the manse, son, and James Galbraith is ahead of his time with carpets on the floor and pictures on his walls, but this doesn't apply to most folk, you know. You have had advantages in book-learning, too. Give James Galbraith his due, he was a man o' parts when it came to book-learning and you and I are none the worse for having had the benefit of that.'

She broke off, and Jack prodded her knee gently with his balled fist saying impatiently, 'But my father – '

'Yes.' She sighed. 'Well, I got work as a French polisher, fitting out the ships. I was almost sixteen. We had some lovely woods to work on! Mahogany, walnut, oak. And one day I was working in this cabin when a young man came in. To see how he wanted his cabin fitted out, as he would be making the journey to Ameriky.'

'Americ-a,' corrected Jack.

'No matter.' She stopped, her roughened hands working in her lap, her face softened and alight. 'He was a handsome lad. You are like him, Jack. He wore a blue frock-coat, white drill trousers and a spotless stock, and gentleman was written all over him. I fell for his dark brown eye! "Can you recommend a quiet lodging in the toun?" he says to me, and I start to tell him about the big places when he says, "No, no, I want to be quiet, secret even." So I take him home and mother and I sleep with the fowls and he has the bed in the other room. He liked your grannie's barley broth and he said my bannocks were second to none.'

'Go on.'

'Well. We grew to have a regard for each other, although he stayed but for four days. He told me why he was seeking passage to Ameriky – America. It was because he had near killed a man in a fight – '

Jack's eyes rounded like saucers and his sucked-in breath hollowed his cheeks. 'Go *on*.'

'The man did not die but he was very sick and his brothers

were on your father's trail.'

'Why did he fight him?'

'I do not know. It was over land. Your father's father – your grandfather, that is – was a gentleman farmer. So Robin said – '

'His name was Robin! I never knew that before.'

'You do now,' she said tenderly. 'Robin Balfour. Whatever the cause of the fight, he had to flee the country.'

'Where is he now?'

'I don't know. He promised he would come back for me one day. I waited and waited. He may have made his fortune in Ameriky or, I fear, he may be dead. But if he is not, it is time we knew. He or his family must help me with your keep.'

Jack looked truculent. 'I don't want help. I can keep myself.'

'It is your entitlement. Perhaps you are entitled to a great deal. Anyway, it is what I mean to find out.'

She was glad he did not question her any more. As by common consent they got up and trudged on. Kate's mind was on that faraway seduction by Robin Balfour. Unprimed maid that she had been, she had not known what was happening to her. It had been the measure of his skill. All over in the dark. Afterwards that was what had shamed her. That she could have been left in such ignorance by her mother. But now Robin Balfour and James Galbraith were lumped together in an angry corner of her mind as betrayers both, in different ways. And now she wanted justice for womanhood. Justice for herself and Jack.

Kate's heels were rubbing agonizingly inside her boots when they decided it was time to stop for the night. How near they were to Glasgow, she had no notion. She knew who she must look for first when she got there: her friend Miss Marion Noble of the Missionary Society, a peripatetic lady much in demand as a speaker on the Church's role overseas, who had moved from Greenock to Glasgow at the time of the upheaval in the Church that culminated in the departure of nearly five hundred ministers from the Church of Scotland to the Calvinist-orientated Free Church. She was a clever, scholarly woman, as kind as she was dedicated, and Kate's hopes were pinned on her for advice not only on where to start looking for news of Robin, where to find a home and job, but also what to do about raw, blistering heels and the lost, pining look that seemed to be taking up permanent residence on young Jack's features.

In the lee of a hedge she laid her cloak and she and Jack curled up on it and soon slept from sheer exhaustion. They woke to early morning mist, like being entombed inside a pearl, with the sun already glaring pinkly through the pearl's skin. That day was their best. They covered many miles, not talking much, Kate's skirts brushing the pollen from the flowers and grasses, Jack's head down while he laboured over the thoughts of his newly-acquired father, of whom, with his freshly-laundered stock and merry dark eye, he was already faintly jealous.

If she – there was only one 'she' in his life and that his mother – if 'she' had a fondness for that man, after him bolting to America and leaving them both to it, then Jack had some reservations about having the least to do with him. I want to be independent, he thought. She has brought me up to be independent, and so I shall be. But he did not want to add to his mother's problems. He was vexed at the way her hair fell down from under her bonnet and at the summer dust that covered her boots and the bottom of her skirt and petticoats. Every so often she would give a desperate little sigh that rent him to the marrow. He tried not to think of the ships that would be coming into Greenock, about the friends he had left behind with their talk of storms at sea, and fires in the old wooden hulks and heroes who wouldn't leave till the ship went down, and of journeys round the Horn and to South America. But the deprivation rubbed his chest like a hair shirt and he grew more and more certain of his detestation for Glasgow.

They got a lift for a couple of miles in a dogcart and were even grateful to put their feet up from the ground for a short distance in a wagon going out to fetch in the last of the hay and the hay-makers.

'We must be getting nearer,' Kate thought desperately,

but there was nothing to indicate a place the size of Glasgow, no matter how many times she put her hand up to her eyes and gazed into the distance, willing the appearance of churches, quays, the horse-drawn omnibuses she'd heard about, the Broomielaw or even the hundreds of whisky shops she'd been warned about.

It was the hedgerows again for them that night, and the next morning she had a bout of retching that slowed them down considerably. While she sat resting on the edge of a field Jack made friends with some tattie-howkers working there whom he'd seen that morning emerging from a mean-looking, windowless building his mother referred to as a bothy.

They were mostly Irish, red-faced, blue-eyed, dark-haired One old woman showed him the long thumb nail she'd grown for scraping the cooked potatoes they ate for their dinner. Jack shared their meagre meal, but Kate turned down their kindly-meant offer of a potato, able only to sip at the last of the cold tea.

'Sure,' said the old woman with the long thumb nail when she heard they were making for Glasgow, 'that's a terrible bad place. There's a terrible amount of spirit shops there and you'll have to hang on to your money, if you have any, missus.' She cast a meaning glance at Kate's dainty reticule. She was drinking water with pepper in it, declaring she had grown quite addicted to it, milk, like bread, being something she rarely saw back home 'in the ould country'.

That night when she and Jack lay down to sleep against the wall of a ruined bothy, Kate was sure she heard footsteps and had no sooner shaken Jack awake than she was set upon by one of the men she had seen working earlier in the fields. Desperately she clung to her small fund of guineas and desperately, with tuggings and oaths, the man tried to get it away from her. Jack leapt on the man's back and rained blows down on his head with his hard, clenched fists.

One of Kate's kicks landed effectively on the man's shin and Jack leapt off his back and pulled him to the ground, sitting on his stomach and with a deft hand pushing back his chin. Hastily Kate stuffed the money down the front of her bodice, as far as it would go.

'Want more?' demanded young Jack. 'Just ask and you'll get it.' And he balled his fist meaningfully.

The man sat up, pushing Jack away from him, and to Kate's intense surprise broke into noisy weeping. Kate saw he was emaciated, frail.

''Tis the wife,' he cried. 'She has lost two childer already and now wee Paddy's going. She's got no milk for him at the end of the day. 'Tis a hard thing to have childer and see them die – ' He raised a pitiable face. ''Tis famine where we come from.'

Kate sat up discomfited and took a guinea from her bodice. She handed it over to the astonished man.

'Get some Godfrey's Cordial for your child and some meat for your wife,' she ordered. 'Take the money and go.'

Shame-faced, the man took the guinea and walked away, dusting himself down.

'We'll have to move on,' said Kate uneasily to Jack. 'We'll have the whole starving pack on us if we don't.'

Quickly and easily they moved through the night, fear lending them wings. Their eyes became accustomed to the cloudy moonlight and at one point they saw the Clyde, silvery and beautiful, and hearteningly narrow.

After several hours they stopped on the outskirts of a village and settled against the mossy, accommodating wall of a kirkyard. Kate's feet had toughened or else she had grown immune to the pain of broken blisters. After perhaps two hours' sleep, she woke to a fearsome red glow on the skyline, like something from Hades, with feeble twinkling lights around it in the gloom. Later she was to learn that the glow was from 'Dixon's Blazes', the ironworks at Govanhill, and the lights were from the oil lamps, mounted on wooden posts, or the more recent gas lamps, of Glasgow itself.

When Jack awoke and the daylight strengthened, it was soon obvious that they were indeed nearing Glasgow. There were many more people and carts about. Dirt roads gave way to whinstone and cobbles. Kate told Jack to stay by her side while she gradually got her bearings. A helpful 'Charlie' or 'Peeler' confirmed they were on their way.

The river seemed to draw them like a magnet. There was no mistaking when they came to the cobbles of the Broomielaw. The quay was crowded with people, a few unmistakable gentry, well-dressed and with handsome luggage; but most were less prosperous, anxiously shepherding children, dabbing their eyes, making farewells; and some dauntingly poor, pale and under-nourished, with wailing infants. A large ship was taking on its stores, all kinds of meat and provisions, live poultry, a panic-stricken cow. The bustle and preparations entranced Jack. He could come here every day.

One day he would sail the Atlantic. He could feel that day come so near he could touch it. He looked down at the racing waters of the Clyde and willed a promise from its muddy depths. When he looked up at his mother's weary face, it was almost as though the seas were already between them.

Chapter Two

He had left his mother conversing with Miss Marion Noble. The two women were cackling on to such an extent that it made his head ache, Miss Noble full of enthusiasm for the new Scottish Poor Law Act which meant there would be special places called poorhouses for destitute folk, whose only relief up till then had been the church poor-boxes and that confined, so said Miss Noble, to 'crukit folk, blind folk, impotent folk and waik folk'.

'These days, poor beggars can nae longer be lifted off the street by coal masters or manufacturers and made to slave for their meat and clothes,' said Miss Noble, with fierce indignation at the recent past. 'No more than they can be put in the stocks and burned through the ears with a hot iron, and their children bound as 'prentices till they're all of thirty years of age – thanks be to the Lord.'

They had found Miss Noble's austere rooms above the Missionary Society offices, and she had bedded them down, talking incessantly, on her floor with as many blankets as she could summon.

Two days had elapsed, and after what Miss Noble called 'much confabulation' they had tracked down news of his father from her church records. The name Balfour, it seemed, was well-known on the upper reaches of the Clyde in Lanarkshire, where the family had farmed for generations. Not only that, his grandfather had 'gone into coal' and owned several pits. He was a pillar of the Free Church and allowed no coal to be transported from his pits on Sunday. He contributed generously to missionary funds. But from what Miss Noble had been able to discover, his own father was given up for dead, the second son, Jeremiah, being regarded now as the sole heir, and the lost Robin's name, so she understood, never mentioned.

His mother's face had flushed at the news.

'He will be mentioned now,' she declared. 'When I see the old man, he will be mentioned. When he looks at my son's face, he will see Robin written there and Jack will get his due, at long last.'

Miss Noble's long, kindly face, with its protruding teeth and lightly whiskered upper lip, had taken on a look of horsy caution.

'I would advise proceeding with care, Mistress Kilgour. If we proceed with discretion, I am sure that as a good Christian old Mr Balfour will wish to provide for his grandchild. But if we rush in, we may have to prove the case, and that we could not do.'

He had left them arguing the pros and cons. Glasgow with its shops and people and busy streets distracted and fascinated him. He ignored Miss Noble's strictures and made boldly for the Broomielaw. Drunks didn't worry him – they had them in Greenock, too, after all, and he knew how to humour them with a jest and slip away from a detaining hand. He wandered through the foul slums of the Backlands and past the blocks of one-room houses in Gallowgate and Stockwell Street.

The immediate outlook did not please him. There was going to be a bath for him, new clothes, a haircut. Then he had been set to his lessons again by Miss Noble, with special emphasis on the Scriptures, so that when the confrontation took place with his grandfather it would be seen that he was indeed worthy of help.

He hated the whole idea. He was near enough twelve. His voice was breaking, and as the incident with the hungry Irishman had shown, he was as strong as a grown man. His hands itched to work and his brain to find ways of providing for himself and his mother.

What if they set him to farming? Or down the pit? As he neared the Clyde, his breath seemed to be coming in shorter and sharper gasps, the way it did when he had the bronchitis each winter, and he put up a hand to find tears on his cheeks, to his rage and humiliation.

''Hoy, there, if it isn't young Jack Kilgour!

He looked down from the Broomielaw, where he had been concentrating on not falling over hawsers, and saw a grimy little steamer with a tubby, red-faced sailor waving up at him from its littered deck. The boat he recognized as the *Jessie Grey*, which did business up and down the river from Greenock to Glasgow, and the sailor as Danny Macinch, for whom he'd fetched ale and 'baccy many a time in those good, uncomplicated days when Greenock had been his home.

'What you doin' here, lad?' demanded Danny.

'I live here.'

'Your good mother, too?' Danny's interest in Kate was genuine. He had attended the prayer meetings she conducted and seen, if not the Light, at least a sort of candle's glimmer. His good, simple face shone up at Jack, filled with consuming curiosity.

'You going back to Greenock?' Jack cut short his questioning.

'Within the hour.'

'Can I come?' His face reddening, for he was an unaccustomed liar, he added, 'My mother has left her best bonnet behind. I wish I could fetch it as she says she has nothing to wear on the Sabbath.'

Easily, Danny said, 'Come aboard.' The little ship was grimy with coal dust. Two calves bleated for their mother in the shambles of a hold.

Once it was under way, Jack's breath came more easily. He chatted freely to Danny, who was happy to find out where Kate was staying in Glasgow and whose mind was leaping ahead to his next trip, when he would seek Kate out with a gift of best tea, tied up neat in a packet, and who could envisage all sorts of happy possibilities arising from his befriending of young Jack and obligement of him over the Sunday bonnet.

As they neared Greenock, Jack began to keep a lookout for the larger ships in the river. He knew what he hoped to see, what he willed himself to see – the beautiful *Titania*, 'sail and steam', master Captain 'Carvie' Campbell, preparing for her voyage to New York. He knew the ship like the back of his own hand, had seen her built first for sails then for steam, launched, and also fitted out. He had watched her go out and come back on every voyage.

'Carvie' Campbell, so called for his well-known passion for caraway, or carvie, seeds spread on his bread and butter, was known as a man who could sail a teacup through a storm and bring it out right side up. He was vain to the point of ridicule, his jackets of the sharpest cut, his buttons polished, his cap set at an angle many copied but none could quite achieve and the tales of his seamanship, certainly not discouraged by him, were legion.

When in the past he had sneaked on board the *Titania* in company with other Greenock sparks, Jack had been careful to keep out of the captain's way. It had been a game then to dodge from deck to cabin, pitting your wits against the crew, but knowing that at the worst terra firma wasn't far away. Now it was going to be different. Now he knew from the resolution like a large, embedded boulder in his stomach that this time he was going to stow away for real. The promise the Clyde had made him was about to be fulfilled. He was going to New York to seek his fortune and nobody could stop him – not his grandfather, nor Miss Noble, nor Captain Campbell, nor even his mother. It was as though all his education on the river had been building up to this moment. And as though in answer to his prayer, at that moment a familiar lovely outline etched itself against the skyline. True to his calculations, the *Titania* was waiting for him at the Tail o' the Bank. He even knew the very corner that would hide him and where old Carvie would never find him. He had lied and now for the first time in his life, he also stole. He took some of Danny's ship's biscuit and a small hunk of cooked meat and stuffed them both down his britches' pockets as far as they would go.

'Come now, Mistress Kilgour, Kate, you must stop weeping some time. Where is your faith in the Lord?'

Kate dabbed each eye in turn. Blue as ever, they burned like pale sapphire lakes in her white face. She gave a quick intake of breath, pulled back her shoulders and tried for

Miss Noble's sake to be calmer.

'We know, from Danny Macinch, that Jack went back to Greenock. He wished to visit his old haunts again. He will be back here in a day or so, no harm come to him, for he is in the main a sensible lad.'

'No, he is gone for a stowaway. The lads do it for a game. He has the sea fever. He sickens for the river, just as I do.' She put out an apologetic hand and touched Miss Noble's arm lightly. 'Not that you haven't been kind to me, Miss Noble – Marion. But the sea is in our blood. All my brothers went for sailors, and my uncles before that.'

'What you will do,' said Miss Noble, kindly but firmly, 'is put on your bonnet and come with me to our meeting in the Evangelical Hall tonight. We have a brother from Lanarkshire who has saved more souls for Jesus than any I know. Findlay Fleming by name. He will have words of comfort for you and you will join our platform party as our dear sister from Down the Water.' As Kate made a deprecating gesture, she said, 'You forget I have heard you speak, Kate. The Lord was on your tongue.'

'I might as well come,' said Kate resignedly. 'If I stay here, I will only think of my child in peril on the sea.' But her movements as she got ready were automatic and the brave smile she gave Miss Noble as they both set out for the Evangelical Hall took every ounce of her courage.

She had not been out of doors for several days and the cool evening air was reviving. The hall was filling up already with people of every age and station, from decent old men and women with mittened hands to indescribably grimy urchins who hadn't seen water for weeks, and in some cases their mothers with regurgitating infants cuddled close in shawls. The smell of humanity, spirits, tobacco, milk, urine, faeces, sweat, permeated the air. A long trestle table had been drawn up on the platform, with carafes of water on it, and Miss Noble introduced Kate to several church worthies well-whiskered, sober and taciturn. There was no minister in evidence. Miss Noble had explained that Findlay Fleming was a working collier and radical preacher who would tie himself down to neither Auld Kirk nor Free Kirk but from a broad basis of theology attracted to him repentant sinners who afterwards were assigned to any church of their choice. Temporarily out of work at the pit, he was devoting all his time to preaching, expenses paid by Miss Noble.

James Galbraith would not have approved of her being there, Kate thought. For this she felt almost glad. What right had he to set himself above humble folks? There was a good feeling in the hall, a kind of rustling expectancy, of uplift, and even the little shawled infants held out their hands and squawked with joy at the music from the organ.

She was ill prepared for the effect of meeting the preacher, Findlay Fleming. He was a tall, upright man, with a shock of brown hair, his gaze steady, his eyes so kindled with warmth and fellowship, that she felt encompassed, swayed almost off her feet, by his compassionate presence and his firm, hard handshake.

He had all of James Galbraith's dignity but none of his cant. He was nearly as good-looking as she remembered Robin to be. And when he spoke or sang, his voice was strong and sweetly musical in its cadence, even if it bore traces of broad dialect and rough grammar. She knew that Lowland Scots did not speak the Queen's English with the same purity as Highlanders and especially as one like herself, whose father had come from Inverness. But it was a small thing in him, which could be quite overlooked in view of his luminosity, his fervour and his humanity.

'Who will stand up, stand up for Jesus?' he cried, after he had given a long discourse and many hymns had been sung with mounting fervour. Raggle-taggle creatures pushed themselves forward to shake his hand, while couthier citizens waited patiently for their turn.

'We are all brothers and sisters under Him who loves us,' he declared. 'Fear not, those of you who are hungry or in want. Fear not, those of you who are cast down through the loss of your loved ones, children, spouse, or parent. One day, the meek shall inherit the earth. The Good Book says it, and if the Good Book says it, it's good enough for me and it is good enough for you.'

'Amen,' called a poor woman whose exalted face was

streaked with tears. She grabbed Findlay Fleming's hand and looked up at him pitifully: 'Will I see my lad in heaven, mister? That died of the scarlet fever?'

'Be sure you will,' he said softly.

Two buns, some cheap sweets and an apple had been apportioned by Miss Noble and her friends into bags and these were handed to the poor as they filed out of the door and gratefully, not to say ravenously, received. Those who could afford it were asked to place coins in one of several tambourines and Kate found herself taking one of these round and then bringing it back to Findlay Fleming.

He took her hand between his.

'Miss Noble has told me of your concern for your son. I want you to know I shall pray for him, and for you.'

She could not take her eyes from his face. She saw the colour drain slightly from his features as though he laboured under some powerful emotion. Without letting go of her hand, he said in a low voice, 'Do you feel that the Lord has brought us together here for a purpose? I have had this feeling very strongly ever since I set eyes on you this evening.'

She could do no more than nod. From as though a great distance away she was aware of Marion Noble looking at her strangely.

'Is your work with the Lord?'

'It is,' she affirmed.

'Then you must listen to the Lord's voice in your prayers this night and if He tells you it is to be so, you must join me in my crusade. You know that as one door shuts, another opens. The Lord may have brought this calamity upon you, so that you will better be able to serve Him, to His great purpose.' He said gently, 'Can you see that this may be so?'

She nodded, again dumbly. Already, she did not wish to be parted from him. She knew that this strange night of heightened emotion, of Christian love in action, was a watershed. Unlike Lot's wife, she would never look back.

It was a thousand pities, Jack reflected later, that the third mate on *Titania* was big Archie Robertson, for whom he'd once refused to run an errand and who was as well known for his black bad temper as for his proclivity to ask boys to go for 'walks' with him in the fields behind Greenock.

Until Robertson spotted him, all had been going well. At first, under the tarpaulin, he had listened to the sounds of the ship getting under way. There had been a crack in one of the folds through which he was even able to discern a certain amount: the packing cases and portmanteaux being hauled aboard, the passengers sorting themselves out, rushing up and down like ferrets down a rabbit-hole, the women weeping, the mail bags being hauled aboard and finally, in a moment that nearly burst his lungs with suspense, Captain Campbell himself arriving, the shine on his boots all too evident a bare three feet away from his own hiding-place.

It would have been better had the master discovered him there and then, for Robertson wouldn't have taken it on himself to be his prime punisher and task-master. It all came from getting too confident. When the ship had first got under way, the pound of the engines and the quiet swish of the vessel through the waters had been as reassuring as being rocked in his mother's arms when he'd been a five-year-old with the toothache.

A joy and excitement so intense had taken hold of him that he felt sufficiently emboldened to get out and mix with the steerage passengers. One of his best friends back in Greenock, Percy Anderson, who had once stowed away to Quebec, and even got as far as the immigration sheds at Grosse Island, had done this, explaining that if you stood near a big family you were taken for one of them and if you were helpful to them and said you were a poor orphan going out to join an uncle you might even win enough sympathy to be able to confess your exploits and get them to smuggle you a crust and a piece of meat.

You had to keep out of the way when checks were made by the crew, of course. He'd got cocksure after two days, but had begun to feel the first stirrings of seasickness and even homesickness, and then, on the third day, when the ship was running into squally weather and he'd been crawling back towards the tarpaulin to sleep off his nausea, the big, red belligerent face of Archie Robertson had frozen into a triumphant rictus of recognition from the other side of the deck. He had been on him like a ton of coals and his big hammy hand had held Jack's neck in a vice while he dragged him off to the captain's cabin.

'Well, boy.' Maybe Carvie Campbell detected the fresh Highland looks, the open unafraid gaze of one of his own countrymen from the west. To be sure, he was none too fond of his third mate and had no intention of making a meal out of this almost routine incident just to meet the lascivious look of sadistic pleasure on big Robertson's face. But he had to go through the motions.

'Shall we hang you from the tops'l or throw you overboard to the fish?' he demanded. 'What makes you think we have foraging for the likes of you? This ship is provisioned for those who have paid their tickets, like honest citizens. Did your mother bring you up to take the bread out of hungry babes' mouths? Answer me.'

Jack hung his head. The mention of his mother had gone home. 'No, sir.'

'Well, since you have joined us' – the 'j' was pronounced more like a sort of 'ch' – 'you can earn your passage by working for us. Third mate, see he scrubs the decks, empties slops, makes himself useful.'

Jack drew himself up. 'I *want* to be useful. I am a good sailor, sir.'

'See you are,' said the master. 'Have you eaten these three days?'

The boy shook his head.

'See the cook. You will not starve. But see you work your passage. 'Twill be the worse for you if you do not.'

He wanted to please the captain. One day he wanted to be like him, with his cap at just such an angle and his feet planted in a noble stance on the bridge of some such vessel as the Titania. But his mother had never put him to any household task and he was clumsy and inept at almost everything he was given to do, even a simple job like swabbing the deck.

The weather, which had started off squally and cold, got steadily worse. The decks were practically clear of passengers, who were all below either being sick or lying down to recover from sickness. He made brief friends with a boy not much older than himself, who told him he was emigrating with his parents and brothers and sister because they had been put out of their croft.

'We owed nae a penny to anybody,' said the boy bitterly. 'But the landlords want the Highlands for sheep.'

'We should fight them,' said Jack angrily, remembering his own mother's case.

'What with?' said the boy. 'Stones? It is better to go to the States where a man is free.'

Big Robertson was never off his back. With a stupid leer on his face and a heavy rope's end, he laid into him whenever he stopped work. The rope cut and bled his legs but he would not let Robertson see his pain; only learned to dodge more quickly out of his way.

To his shame and chagrin he was horribly seasick. He, who had been up and down the Clyde to Rothesay and Tarbert and Helensburgh, who had only to see the curl of a sail to identify the ship that carried it, was reduced to the helplessness of any first-time passenger, able to keep nothing down, getting weaker and weaker, so that he scarcely felt the sting of the rope's end and did not want to rise when he lay down.

'What's this?' Carvie Campbell's foot stirred the boy's sleeping form. The decent clothes were torn and sodden, the boy's hair plastered to his head with the driving rain. 'Wake up, boy. Come to my cabin.'

Jack staggered after the master, his legs scarcely able to hold him up. The ship was rolling worse than ever, a gale coming up from the west and the seas rolling like blue-green mountains. Strangely, the nausea had at last left him, but he was as weak as a kitten, his head so light he scarcely knew what he was about.

'You would be a sailor,' said the master grimly. He poured some brandy into a glass and added water, handing it to Jack with the injunction to swallow it down fast. The fiery liquid scalded Jack's throat and burned his stomach, but in a little he began to feel wonderfully clear-headed. The master then bade him go to the cook's galley to have his clothes dried off and ask for some food.

The master's rough kindness made the boy his slave.

'The captain is a good man,' he told the cook.

'And may God help him – and us,' said the cook, who had heard the wind screaming and whistling through the rigging like this before. 'We are in for a rough passage.'

'I am not feart,' said Jack. As though the storm had taken note of his words, it seemed to abate for a few moments. Then the ship gave a fearful lurch and seemed to turn almost upside down. Jack grasped a hook that held ladles for the cook's work and held on grimly while all around him utensils crashed about, broth flew up out of its pots like fountains, crockery crashed and broke into a thousand pieces and cutlery jangled as though at the devil's tea-party. He could hear the squawks of terrified chickens and the fearful baying sound of cattle.

A flying ashet of potted meat had struck the cook a glancing blow on the head and he rolled about the floor helplessly, clutching his head with one hand, putting out the other to grasp something, anything, and in the end holding on to Jack's legs and almost pulling off his britches.

Screams of terror reached them from above and the sound of feet pounding from cabin to cabin. People fled from the saloon as the lights went out and water flooded in. The saloon sideboard and table were stood on end, then, as the ship was tossed again like a helpless cork, were dashed into a thousand splintered pieces. Luggage was pounded to pulp, swept overboard, and still the waves came at the *Titania* and pounded at her till the front of her poop stove in.

In a momentary lull, the cook let go of Jack's leg and the boy darted out of the galley and ran to the lee of the bridge hanging on to anything he could find. Looking up, he could see the master at the wheel, his cap still at the same jaunty angle, and as though under the reassurance of his hands, the ship seemed to be making a calmer passage, the seas seemed to be going down somewhat and a white-faced passenger peered from a cabin and shouted across to another, 'He's double-reefed the sails and put her under very slow steam.'

The master judged it safe to hand over to the first mate and came down to walk among the passengers and calm them.

'She's a stout ship, she's seen worse than this,' he said. He found his cabin invaded by passengers, sitting with the water above their ankles. Grim-faced, he made no comment, but ordered Jack to stay there and hand round brandy and water as necessary. The wind was roaring like a banshee and he made haste back to his bridge.

The men at the pumps were being washed about the main deck like corks. The bulwarks were torn away, the hen-coop with its drowned occupants slid into the sea, and like the denizens of nightmare, the soaked and white-faced passengers from second-class and steerage were led by the third mate Robertson into the forecastle.

Jack was coming up to the main deck, his weakness forgotten, his sea-legs established for good, prepared to fight with every last ounce of his puny strength to save the ship for the captain, when a huge sea rose and struck the bridge under the starboard side, twisting the horizontal railing upright like matchwood and tearing the planking up as though it were rice-paper.

The mountainous wave broke and its crest fell with a crash upon the leeward side of the bridge, snapping the stanchions, tearing up the floorboards. Then the merciless sea retreated, tearing two boats loose and breaking the main boom. Just out of reach, Jack saw the waters overwhelm the master and his first mate and sweep them into the sea as though they were dolls he'd seen girls make and play with in what seemed like the million-years-off days of his childhood.

'Captain Carvie!' he cried. The second mate and Robertson rushed to the taffrail and Jack sprang to help throw ropes and lifebuoys into the foaming sea.

The engineer was ordered to stop the engines. Hanging

for grim life to the taffrail, Jack strained his eyes into the hellish dark. 'Two specks!' he cried. 'Over there!'

Even though it was slowing, the ship seemed to be leaving the specks behind at a dreadful speed. The engines throbbed to a halt. 'Hopeless,' cried the second mate, into the teeth of the gale. *Titania* was paying off dangerously into the trough of the sea. He knew he had no option but to let the sea have her dead and order the engineer to start the engines again.

The ship drove before the wind. Frozen almost into insensibility, Jack returned to the galley. The cook lay on his bunk, not caring if he lived or died. Sobbing quietly, Jack relived the moment of horror when the captain and mate had been swept into the sea. The scene was engraved on his mind forever.

'There is no God,' he said to himself. His mother's face came to him, hovering sweetly over him as it did when she tucked him up at night. But he turned from her, saying again, 'There is no God. There is no God.'

Nine days later the battered ship sailed into New York. Jack saw more ships' masts than he had ever seen in his life before. Had all the world come here? It looked like it.

The morning mists cleared and he saw the quay with its capstans, its carts and coaches, its people and dogs, approaching with an alacrity he was suddenly unprepared to handle. America after the nightmare was as beautiful and unbelievable as a dream.

Chapter Three

The old woman sat by the chimney-piece, smoking a white clay pipe, her pock-marked face framed with a clean white mutch, her skirt and shorgin of a greeny-black stuff and her substantial lap protected by a sacking apron. Pinned across her chest with a luckenbooth brooch (that heart-shaped item associated with the hapless Mary, Queen of Scots) was a light brown shawl. Her breath made loud, wheezing sounds but she appeared to be accustomed to this and it did not seem to distress her.

She got up as Kate bent her head to enter the tiny grey-stone cottage and Findlay drew Kate forward to introduce her to his mother. The old woman gave Kate a shrewd, not unfriendly look, with something akin to friendly amusement in it that puzzled Kate slightly. Even before the smallpox had left its ugly traces, in the days before vaccination became available in 1840, she could not have been a pretty woman, Kate decided, but the eyes were Findlay's eyes, dark and alert with a native intelligence.

Old Mrs Fleming drew cups and plates down from a solid oak dresser and with a great deal of slow ceremony, which she seemed to enjoy, made a pot of tea when the blackened kettle on the hearth rattled its lid to indicate boiling point.

The journey to Dounhead, the small mining village about ten miles south-west of Glasgow, had been a chill one, with squalls of autumn rain, and Kate was glad of the refreshment. The first impression of the village had not been unpleasing. Some barefoot but happy-looking children were clustered round the brazier of an old tinker, who was mending their parents' kettles and pots. A woman had looked up from her washing bine outside her door and given her and Findlay a decorous only faintly inquisitive smile. Dounhead nestled in a gentle hollow of fields, with the river, shallow but swift, hurling by it on its way to join the Clyde.

Urging Kate to sample a scone, old Mrs Fleming asked her: 'Is there news of your poor laddie?'

'I have heard from a master of the Henderson Line that he was on the ship *Titania*, that lost its captain and first mate in a terrible storm in the middle of the Atlantic,' said Kate. 'I am assured my boy is safe, though when I shall see him again, I do not know.'

'He was young enough to leave you,' said Mrs Fleming.

Then, as though to distract Kate from her thoughts, which were casting a sorrowful expression on her face, the old woman began a monologue on her own life, in which she was word-perfect, having trotted it out regularly to the visitors Findlay brought to see her.

'I started work when I was eight. I was tied to a farmer and I went to him when it was just beginning to snow, and before I got there, it was a snowstorm. I wanted to lie down and die in it, but the big farmer came along on horseback, looking for this little lass they knew was coming, and he picked me up, light as a fly, and rode back with me to the farm kitchen.

'It was a good meat-house, that. We had saut herring every day, tea once a month.'

'Aye, and tatties and dip for your dinner,' interpolated Findlay.

'I scrubbed the big kitchen table every day,' went on his mother, 'then we'se emptied this great muckle pot of tatties straight on to it and the lads came in from the fields and ate them with their fingers, dipping the tatties in the salt. Tatties and dip, it was called. That and a good drink o' soor dook – soor milk – and you felt you had something. Eh, Findlay?'

'She's a proper-trained dairymaid,' said Findlay, with a fond look at his mother. 'She can make butter – '

'And cheese with the yellow lady's bedstraw,' added Mrs Fleming.

'And cure a ham and pluck a fowl, with the best,' said Findlay, with a look at the hams above the fireplace.

His mother preened herself. 'I wid nae ga down the pit,

like some of the women here. It near broke my heart to send Findlay down. In them days, he and his brother Tam went down on the end of the rope, cross-lapped they called it, one facing the other atop his lap, on the clatch-iron. Tam was only ten years old and Findlay here but seven. They used to come home so tired they fell asleep on the floor and I had to wash them and put them to bed.'

'And Tam died?' prompted Kate.

'Of a broken back. Once he opened his eyes when they brought him up and said my name: "Mither." George died of the fever and wee Ainsley, my last bairn, of the convulsions when my milk dried up from grief at my husband's death. The pit took him too. The week before he died, they stopped his wages because there was too much dust in his tub. Yet the week before that, when his tub had over the measure, he didn't get a farthing more. They broke his spirit before they took his life.'

'The price o' coal,' said Findlay. The low-ceilinged room had turned cold with the touch of memory and he rose and put more fuel on the fire, stirring it to life with the poker. He patted his mother's knee and said, with an effort at cheerfulness, 'But we are no' come here to talk about death, Mither. I mean to marry her – ' he turned to Kate – 'and we want your blessing on't.'

'Is it a case of needs must when the devil drives?' demanded Mrs Fleming, with a sardonic expression. Kate blushed at her perception. She had not told Findlay yet, but she was sure she was with child.

She had not meant it to happen but she had not been able to help herself. He had been tender with her, making it clear that it was nothing less than marriage he had in mind from the start, and her body had re-awakened and rejoiced to his touch as though all the choirs in Heaven were singing at their union. When he moved her, it was like a glimpse of eternity, like moving towards Heaven itself at a great pace. Sometimes, afterwards, she seemed to see James Galbraith's gaunt, guilt-ridden face in her mind and she wished for him . . . she did not know what she wished . . . perhaps that his life need not have been so joyless. In all those years they had lived together under the same roof, it had been there, a kind of tenderness seeking expression, never finding it. Now she had found it with Findlay, she wanted the world and James Galbraith to know it.

Findlay was looking at his mother with a startled sort of expression.

'You maun bridle your tongue, Mither,' he said, not un kindly.

'I can bridle it nae longer,' wheezed the old woman. 'I didnae want to say what I'm going to say, in front of your bride, but she maun ken what sort of a rake you are for the lassies.'

Kate paled.

'What's this?' demanded Findlay.

'They were here, a week syne, saying Nancy Paterson's time was near and the bairn was yours.'

Kate could feel a great uprush of blood that then receded from her brain leaving her faint and sick. She put out a hand and grasped the edge of the deep window-sill where the old woman had displayed two conch shells and some smaller knick-knacks.

'He will not deny it.' Mrs Fleming's voice came to her from a long way off. 'He went winching her at the back-end o' the year, soon after she moved into the farm with her uncle and aunt.' The old woman cast Kate a look of subdued mischief. 'He canna resist a bonnie blue eye, no more than a glimpse of white stocking.'

Scarcely knowing what she was doing, Kate sat down on the hard wooden chair near one of the two beds set into the cottage wall. Endlessly she chafed her hands. It was a judgement sent to her because she had been so happy. Happy even when Jack was across the ocean from her, facing the Lord knew what kind of dangers. And there'd been pride in her, too, at the thought of being Mistress Findlay Fleming, a married woman with all the status that involved and with a man who made heads turn and ears listen wherever he went.

She shivered, feeling a cold despair, deeper than any she'd ever felt in her life before. To fall once from grace was bad enough; twice placed her in the category of a fallen woman. So where could she go? Piteously, she looked at Findlay. He was seated with his head in his hands, unable to meet her eye.

'They put her out at the farm,' said Mrs Fleming relentlessly. 'The old uncle is an elder at the kirk. He cannae have immorality under his roof, so he says, though it's changed days since he wrapped the lassies in *his* plaidie.' She gave a wheezing cackle.

'Where is she now?' Findlay burst out.

'Staying in one o' the bothies,' said his mother, 'up by the big byre.'

'Go to her,' said Kate, between her chittering teeth. 'In the name of Christ, go to her and do what you can.'

He rose without another word. It was growing dark as he strode towards the farm and its out-buildings. He found the bothy his mother had spoken of, its entrance marked by the dim yellow glow of candlelight.

The village howdie, or midwife, a tangle-haired old woman named Mistress Simpson, looked up at him as he went in. She was wrapping a child up with what looked like rags. On a straw bed lay Nancy Paterson, her dark hair spread about her, her face a strange grey shade in the flickering light.

He went straight to her and took her hand.

'Nancy lass, I never knew.'

''Tis only the lass that does,' she said, between pallid lips.

'She hid it well,' said the howdie.

'It wasn't for want of taking the pennyroyal infusions,' said Nancy. 'I never wanted it. No' when I heard your eye was took elsewhere.'

He straightened up and held out his arms for the child.

''Tis a boy child,' said the old woman. 'He took a while to make a sound, but he's right enough.'

Findlay looked down into the small, almost watchful face. The baby had some fair down of hair. His eyes were open, blue and fathomless, and his crown crusted. He felt a surge of something near delight, or terror. The baby bore an uncanny resemblance to Tam, the brother with whom he had gone down the pit, cross-lapped.

Almost reverently, he said to Nancy, 'I'll pay for him. I'll not neglect you, or him.'

She said nothing. The old howdie hustled to her bedside, working with her under the tattered covers. To his horror, Findlay saw a bright red stain spread its way across the straw and on to the mud of the bothy floor.

'She's been at the bleeding, this while back,' said Mistress Simpson. He forced himself to look down at Nancy but her eyes were opaque and her jaw had fallen open.

'I'll get the doctor,' he said urgently.

'Dinna bother,' said the old woman, almost laconically. 'She sent word for me too late in the day.' Her wrinkled old face was unreadable as she turned towards him. 'She's awa'.'

He opened his jacket and put the child inside it for warmth. The night had come down as dark as pitch and he made his way stumblingly towards the greystone cottage.

'Nancy's awa',' he said to Kate, who had jumped up from the fire as he went in. He looked her full in the face. His own face was white, blank.

'This is my son,' he said, holding out the bundle of rags towards her. 'I acknowledge him. His name will be Thomas Paterson Fleming and we maun bring him up as ours. Yours and mine.'

Her arms unfolded automatically and she took the bundle from him. The baby turned his head towards her breast and began to make little mewing sounds, like a kitten.

He sat down then by the fireside and his body was racked with sobs, his head buried in his arms. Kate said nothing to him. Mrs Fleming held out her arms in turn and Kate put the baby into them. The old woman gave an involuntary sigh of pleasure.

'Have you some clean cloth?' Kate demanded. 'We shall need milk, for he seems hungry. And a drawer from your chest will do to put him in, till we can make or find a cradle.'

The two women busied themselves, saying little either to each other and nothing to the man who cringed at the hearth. Stretching in its rags, the baby howled.

The bowsprits of ships stretched across the footway at the waterfront just under Wall Street. Reading the names of ships as he ran, even in his haste stopping occasionally to admire a figurehead here, or gold lettering there, Jack put as much space between himself and Archie Robertson as he could. The third mate, stunned like everyone else at the deaths of the captain and first mate, had given up his bullying for the time being and, in company with the second mate, now in command, was talking of ways of getting Jack back to Scotland. The *Titania* would be in New York for extensive repairs and no one knew how soon she would be able to sail again.

Much to his embarrassment, Jack had come to be regarded by the now decanted passengers as some kind of hero. They were only too ready to talk of how he had rescued luggage, calmed children, helped mothers and never once shown fear, either during or after the storm. Men had pressed coins upon him and before disembarking the women had handed out a testimonial, begging the authorities to deal lightly with him in view of his bravery and youth. Because of this, *Titania*'s owners had made it clear, he would be brought back home in one of their ships on a free passage.

One way and another, they were in a fair way to ruining his own plans for himself, Jack saw. He'd be back in Glasgow before he'd had a chance to see what America was all about. And his mother was still back in the old country, talking about getting him money from his grandfather, as though he was some kind of pet goat that had to be fed.

It wasn't that he wouldn't go back, one day. But it had to be when he was ready. His confidence, his certainty that the world was in the main a good and kindly place, had taken a bruising knock with the death of Captain Campbell. Like some wee helpless bairn he had cried for his mother then, feeling totally forsaken in a universe that was merciless in its cold attrition.

But the sight of New York had bucked him up, so much so that his escape from *Titania* had been almost immediate.

Let Archie Robertson explain his departure as he liked: the fact remained that the third mate had been blind drunk and it hadn't been difficult to jouk him.

He was his own man. It was wonderful to feel the pavement of Wall Street under his feet. Every step made him feel better and better. He would remember everything his mother had taught him, about pride in himself and bowing the knee to no man. He slowed from a run to a brisk walk, and then to a confident saunter.

So this was New York! Not all that different from Glasgow, he had thought at first, but then, as the waterfront receded, its strangeness was borne in upon him. Wall Street was narrow, and hot. He was glad when he came to a place called Broadway, which was a great, wide street filled with bustle and people. He had to dodge gigs and phaetons spanking along at a great pace and even watch out for the more lumbering omnibuses.

He sat with his back to a wall, trying to sort out his impressions, to decide his next course of action. He watched huge blocks of ice being carried into a bar-room and the sight made him thirsty. He felt for the money in his pocket. Would they take it in the shops here? He decided to try his luck later, but putting the thought of pineapple or watermelon, so deliciously displayed, behind him for the moment, decided he would take in a few more of the sights of Broadway.

At one end he came to Battery Gardens. Turning back on his tracks, he wandered through the crowds till his head began to ache. He had never seen so many splendidly dressed ladies. His mother's douce clothes came back to mind. What would she say about the brilliant silks and satins the women wore here, with ribbons and tassels flowing from their brightly lined cloaks and the parasols blossoming like so many beautiful exotic flowers?

He must have walked three or four miles, he decided, looking in shop windows, his mouth watering at the advertisements for 'Oysters in Every Style' (although he'd never sampled oysters in his life), his eye caught by the splendour of the big Carlton House Hotel, by the glittering brass in the bar-rooms, the ready-made clothes in the tailors' shop windows and by the occasional large ugly pig making its way unconcernedly among the traffic. Broadway petered out at the other end into open country. He'd already become addicted to the city and turned back towards its bustle and anonymity. Soon he would have to see if his money would be accepted. Then he would look for a job. He could help carry ice into the bar-rooms and shops, or give other carters a hand with their loads. For a start.

He turned off Broadway, his bravado ebbing slightly with fatigue, into a less impressive street called the Bowery. They were lighting candles inside the cooked meat shops and in the eating houses where oysters were again for sale. He could hear the rumble of a railway. It was already getting dark and he hadn't ventured into a single shop.

Near one of the larger bar-rooms he became aware of a small raggedy figure, who, with a bundle of papers under his arm and his free hand cupped to his mouth, was shouting something he couldn't quite discern.

He went up to the boy and said boldly, 'What are you doing?'

The red-haired, freckled urchin, his face streaked with grime, turned towards him in a not unfriendly manner and answered: 'Selling newspapers.' He looked Jack over shrewdly. 'You just got here, then?'

Jack nodded.

'Scotch?'

Another nod.

'Thought so. I'm from Dublin meself.'

'I knew that. Why are you selling papers in the street?'

'Don't they do it in Glasgow or wherever you're from?'

'We don't have papers *every* day.'

'We do in Dublin. I sold them there, too.'

Obscurely needled, Jack said precipitately, 'The Scotch are better than the Irish.'

The boy put down his papers obligingly and went for Jack's waist. In a moment, the two of them were rolling in the dust.

Over and over they went. Jack became aware of the slightness of the other boy's frame, but his skinny, sharp-nailed hands could hurt, and did. Knowing his own superior strength, however, he felt slightly mollified. Sitting, but lightly, on the other's stomach, he said, 'Tell me where to get a job like yours and I'll let you go.'

'No jobs,' said the boy, gazing up at him without animosity. He got up and dusted down his rags. The brief wrestle had somehow established a kind of intimacy. Joe O'Rourke offered Jack half his newspapers to sell further up the street, on the strict understanding that he would come back to him with the takings, when Joe would decide what percentage of profit he could spare.

Within a short space of time, they were the best of friends. They did not sell all the papers, but Joe seemed satisfied with the night's takings and gave Jack enough to buy some food. Jack felt he could confide in his friend and Joe prompted him over and over again to re-tell the story of the storm and the death of the captain and first mate. In his turn, he revealed that he and his family had been in New York for nearly two years.

Things had not been easy for them. His two elder brothers had got jobs as navvies on the railways, but worked away from the city. His father had died back in the Old Country and his mother was still there, although they hoped to bring her out later. He lived with two sisters, whose occupation he did not disclose, and a brother who was too sick to work.

'Can you write?' asked Joe suddenly, as they ambled along Broadway taking in the sights. (Sometimes, to Jack's amazement, they were nudged out of the way by the snouts of huge pigs runting and grunting their way home.)

'Of course I can write,' said Jack.

'Will you come home with me and write a letter to our mother?' demanded Joe. 'Tell her we are well and happy and that Seamus and Michael are working for her passage. Tell her – '

'Wait till we get there!' cried Jack. He was more than a little relieved to be going home with Joe. The sights and sounds of the city at night were disconcertingly strange. He did not want to have to ask his way back to Wall Street and perhaps even to the battered hulk of the *Titania,* which he felt he was in danger of doing if left by himself.

'Where's this?' he demanded, in a subdued tone, after they had left Broadway well behind them and reached an altogether darker and different part of the city.

'The Five Points,' said Joe. They laboured up a muddy alley and along a dark lane. A Negro passed them, stumbling drunkenly and singing in a low, almost contemplative manner. Jack's heart rose in his mouth, for the only black people he'd seen up till then were occasional crew members on the ships coming up the Clyde. Tales of savage Africa which he'd heard at Sunday school came back to plague him as more Negro faces passed him.

'They'll not touch you,' said Joe scornfully, sensing his terror. Only slightly reassured, Jack stumbled along behind him. Sometimes, swing doors would part in one of the rackety buildings and there would be the sound of fiddle and tambourine. Once, there was a sudden loud jangling of bells and Joe pointed out a red glow in the sky that meant a house was on fire somewhere; an event, Jack gathered from his nonchalance, that was far from uncommon.

At last, thankfully, they seemed to have arrived, for Joe led the way up some uneven outside stairs and opened one of the doors on a dark uneven landing. The room beyond was candlelit, barely furnished, but the faces that turned towards them were welcoming and smiling, if a little anxious.

'Is it all right to bring him in?' Joe asked the elder of the two young women who were sitting at a table, sewing. 'He's a Protestant.'

'Holy Mary, Mother of God!' smiled Mary O'Rourke. 'He's one of God's creatures, isn't he? Come in, boy, and let's have a look at you.'

While he recounted his story yet again, Jack was able to take in the rest of the room's occupants. The younger sister, Theresa, was obviously getting ready to go out, for she was carrying out a rough sort of toilet while, like the others, she listened with oohs and ahs and exclamations of 'Poor souls!' and 'May God give them rest!' She was pretty and spirited, where Mary was cautious but kind. The older brother, Seamus, was a cadaver of a man with sunken jaws and a repetitive cough. Every now and then he spat into the blackened embers of the fire.

'Are you off out, then?' Mary demanded anxiously, when Theresa had put on her cloak and bonnet, To Jack's untutored eye, she looked every bit as pretty as any of the women he'd seen on Broadway. 'Take care!'

'Don't I always?' demanded Theresa. With a playful backward glance at Jack, she went off down the stairs. Mary looked after her in a sad and thoughtful way. 'May the Lord have mercy on us,' she whispered, as though to herself.

With memories of his mother's Highland hospitality, Jack had had hopes of a meal, but there seemed to be nothing but a few scraps of food in the room. It appeared that the girls shared a makeshift bed and the men lay on the floor on anything they could find that would soften the impact of splintered boards.

Mary snuffed out the candle and it seemed there was nothing for it but to go to sleep. Jack lay listening to Seamus's regular, repetitive coughing. No wonder he coughed. The air was foul enough. Like a kind of chorus, Joe coughed fitfully, too. 'Hush now,' said Mary, through the dark.

Later, as he stirred to find some kind of comfort on his hard bed, Jack heard Theresa come in. She had a whispered consultation with Mary before they both fell asleep.

The next morning, to his great surprise, Jack saw cold meat, bread and butter and a jug of ale on the table. Judiciously, Mary gave him a small share, but Theresa pushed more meat towards him, saying, 'There's more where that came from.' With her pink cheeks and beautiful, long-lashed blue eyes, Jack thought she was probably prettier than anyone he had ever seen. He began boasting to impress her, and when they got paper and quill together, laboured with all his might to make the letter home to Mrs O'Rourke as clearly-written and spelled as he knew how.

They were all delighted with the letter and with the beautiful curls he put on their mother's name, especially the 'R'. Joe insisted he was going to learn to write and then, to show that Jack wasn't the only one with worldly accomplishments, said he would take him down to the paper office and put in a good word for him for a job.

'He can read and write,' he told the man who portioned out the papers to a horde of pushing, shoving urchins.

'Just sell papers,' said the man drily, handing Jack a bundle. 'There's fifty rivals on the street, if there's one. So don't hang back. They'll buy from you. You look clean and smart.'

The other urchins shot him jealous looks. But the man was right. Carriages drew up and coachmen proffered him their money. Fastidious ladies held out their coins at the end of their finger-tips and business men hurrying towards Wall Street snatched the sheets from his hand and threw the money at his feet in their haste.

Euphoria took him. He decided he would work with the papers for a week or two, until he had time to look around for a better job and perhaps better lodgings. New York suddenly did not seem alien at all. He even began to recognize one or two of the people he'd seen yesterday – a burly man who ran a bar-room, a little girl with ringlets he glimpsed through the window of the brick-built houses, a young woman who showed a glimpse of pink stocking and appeared to work in one of the oyster places.

'I'll have one.'

A large hand was placed on his shoulder from behind. He turned, the paper offered with an already expert flick of the wrist.

He looked up into the grimly-smiling face of Archie Robertson.

'Don't struggle. You'll no' get away this time,' said the third mate. 'There's your poor mither in Scotland, no' knowing whether you're alive or dead.'

He struggled just the same, but the third mate's grasp was iron. As though he'd sensed something was up, Joe O'Rourke came running round the corner and did what he could by aiming kicks at the third mate's shins. It was useless. Jack saw a crowd was gathering and his innate Highland dignity came to the fore with a rush.

He turned back and shouted to Joe, 'I'll see you one day.' He was sobbing with chagrin and rage.

'Aye,' said Joe O'Rourke. 'Right enough.' He spat manfully on the dry street. There was blood in it.

Chapter Four

In the summer of 1846, the first child of Kate and Findlay was born.

The wedding had taken place soon after the advent of little Paterson (called by his second name because Grannie Fleming could not bear to use the name Tam). Kate had worn a black bombazine dress and a white lace veil, one of Findlay's uncles had come in from the country with his fiddle and there had been baked meats and black bun and dancing for those who felt like it.

Kate and Findlay had both been subdued. The death of Nancy had affected him deeply and for days he had wandered around saying little to anybody. He barely looked at the child, who was sickly and difficult to rear. At last he had asked Kate if she still wanted to go ahead with the marriage and she had nodded, placing her hands over her own rounding stomach.

'I have little choice.'

'That is not the way I want it between us,' he'd said soberly.

'It's the way it maun be,' said Kate. But after the marriage she had allowed him back in her bed and something of the old joy and comfort had slowly returned.

She could not feel that Nancy's bairn was her own, but that did not mean she wasn't fond of the child. She simply could not feel for him as Grannie Fleming seemed to do; the old woman adored the wailing infant and spent all her time making possets and trying out remedies for his vomiting and lassitude. Kate nursed the little boy tenderly and patiently but she wished all the while that the infant growing and kicking inside her had been the first. She saw well enough that with a sprig of her own, however, she was in no position of moral superiority. Findlay remained in a mood of critical self-analysis. He had not led any revivalist meetings since Nancy's death and this wasn't necessarily because he feared what people might say. Although some had criticized his behaviour towards Nancy, most felt that by taking up his responsibilities towards the child he had evened the scales.

It was Jack, returning at last from America, who helped the spirits of both to recover. The boy was in a mixed-up, emotional state, wanting to go back to sea immediately, and it was Findlay's job to mediate between him and Kate, something he did with great patience and kindness, thus laying a stable relationship between him and his stepson from the start. At last Kate's pleadings and weeping wore Jack down and he agreed not to go to sea, for the time being at least. She for her part agreed that she would not pursue the question of his inheritance just yet with old Mr Balfour. There was still the question of what he was to do to earn his keep and the pit seemed the obvious answer, although Kate fought against this too. Findlay promised to keep an eye on him and found him a job underground as a trapper. The sturdy camaraderie of the colliers caught at Jack's imagination and his initiation into the strange working world beneath the ground intrigued and held him, for a time at least.

When the pit owner built a row of cottages and they were offered one, Kate and Findlay seized at the chance. Grannie Fleming's cottage was too small for a growing family and the old woman had no space to herself nowadays for spinning or weaving when she felt like it.

She would have demurred at the separation, but the new miners' rows were only a few hundred yards away from the greystone cottage, and any time she wanted she could take Paterson to her own hearth and give him the spoiling and cosseting she felt he needed.

Kate was glad theirs was the end house of the row, even if the communal water was fetched from outside their back door. At least, the wet middens were set well behind the houses, and were emptied once a week.

She had her own room and kitchen at last! First she set

about furnishing the two set-in beds in the kitchen. It meant placing two under-mattresses of straw over the strong boards in each recess and then the prized feather mattress, that was her mother-in-law's wedding present, on top of one bed and a flock mattress on the other. A lace-trimmed valance was run along the side of each bed and underneath was some good space for storing oddments like Findlay's carpetbag and her own tin chest. Curtains on either side of the beds meant a feeling of great cosiness and security when you lay down at night. She picked white ones with a pink rose pattern on them, and her heart swelled with pride the first time she saw them draped from their brass rods and tied back with crimson tassels. Queen Victoria herself would have been impressed, said Grannie Fleming.

She hooked a rag rug for the front of the fire and Findlay made her a strong wooden stand to place her washing bine on. One by one the other houses in the row were occupied. Through the wall were the Irish family Daly, husband and wife and four children, going on five. Nellie Daly was vociferous and touchy, but bore no grudges after neighbourly arguments and was known for her generosity and sense of fun.

When Duncan Kilgour Noble (after Miss Marion) Fleming made his debut in the world, Kate was more settled and happy than she had been for a long time. He was a beautiful child, with a scud of dark hair and eyes that were almost a navy blue and he set to at the breast with a will that seemed to say: 'I'm in a hurry to grow, don't stop me, time is of the essence.' Findlay watched his son on many such ravenous occasions. Kate met his indulgent stare with a smile of pure contentment and the happiness in the new house was so evident you could almost touch it.

Young Jack held wee Paterson on his knee when the two stepbrothers met the new arrival for the first time. Jack gave Duncan his full approval, but the seven-month-old Paterson looked down on the newcomer with such amazement, not to say perturbation, that everyone laughed.

In her new bliss, Kate found an access of love for her

little stepson. With milk to spare, she put the ailing child to her breast, but he suckled with difficulty and even pushed the nipple away.

When, at ten months old, little Paterson was standing on his grandmother's lap and pushing his feet into her soft skirts in an effort to walk, it became apparent that something they had all suspected was indeed the case – the child had a hip out of joint and one leg less strong than the other. The old woman, more percipient than Kate, had been massaging the weaker limb for some time, with oil, but already the left limb was discernibly less strong and the little foot slightly wasted.

It did not stop Paterson from crawling, then walking, though in a curious, if nimble, hobbling gait. The doctor commended the grandmother's care and told her to continue on the same lines. Now taking meat and bread from the table, Paterson was growing physically stronger and with an active, enquiring mind was, as his worn-out stepmother put it, 'into everything'.

By 1847, Kate had another baby to care for – their first daughter, Jean. Paterson now shared one of the set-in beds with young Jack, Duncan slept with his parents and the placid Jean was rocked to sleep each night from a string hooked to her mother's finger, from bed to wooden cradle.

It was about this time that Kate began to see something of a change in Findlay. 'Wrochting' down the pit, the heavy endeavours that took him away at dawn and kept him underground till it was dark, were beginning to make inroads on his physical strength.

She always tried to have hot water in the big kettle when he came in and helped him to wash the cloying, filthy coal-dust from his skin, but the coal was winning and was embedded in his fingernails, the pores of his face and neck and under his eyes. Only his body, protected by the heavy, rough clothes, was miraculously white, and moving her hands over it while she washed his back filled her with an ineffable, painful tenderness.

Although they went to church each Sunday, he had no

time now for his own brand of full-blooded revivalism. Often in the long, light evenings of summer, she came upon him with the Bible open between his hands, his tired face wearing a look of puzzled stillness.

Once, with the younger children asleep, she took the Good Book from his hands and said deliberately: 'What is it that takes your mind up so?'

'I am thinking,' he said directly, 'that it's not enough for a man to praise God. A man has to do something to help his fellows here on earth.'

'Do what?' she catechized. 'We should walk in the way of righteousness – '

'Not enough,' he interrupted her.

She looked at him, amazed at his vehemence. He shook his head at her. 'I doubt,' he said, 'I doubt if the meek inherit anything but water in their boots and hunger in their belly.'

'Findlay!' she protested.

He looked at her with a smouldering apologetic anger, his expressive eyes flashing, and she thought again what a handsome man he was, how his depths and heights stirred new chords in her constantly as though he played her like an instrument.

'I have had enough of it,' he said at last. 'Enough of working in the bloody dark, no better than a beast, for a wage that wouldna' keep the boss in 'baccy for a week.'

'What will you do?' she asked fearfully.

He put his hand out and laid it on her knee. 'Dinna fear. I'll bring you in your pay. But we are going to fight them, for a decent wage and a shorter day. It's the least I can do, with our lad down there, ten hours a day, opening and closing a door to let the air in. We maun fight, Kate, for our rights. We are made in His image. We arena' beasts.'

One of the big influences on Findlay at this time was Walter Chapman, referred to as the dominie, who ran the local school sponsored by the General Assembly of the Church of Scotland. He was a fierce, volatile man in his thirties, with pale ginger hair and dimples, and the girl who worked as a maid for him and his wife reported that Mrs Chapman had special plackets made in all her nightgowns, so that intercourse might be made easier. This information did a lot to bring 'Wattie' Chapman down from his high plane of learning and make him accessible to other vulnerable vulgar folk. He was popular and respected except by the pillars of the Kirk, who kept a very steady eye on him indeed.

He had been that nineteenth-century Scots phenomenon, the 'stickit' minister – a theological scholar who had never quite made it to a pulpit of his own. He had been too poor to complete his studies, but in the beginning his superiors had thought enough of him to let him run a small school and then take over the larger one for Dounhead and district. Over the years, Wattie Chapman's studies had veered off in many other directions than the purely theological and there were those who felt now he scarcely rated the description Christian at all. Except that he was unfailingly kind and helpful, even to the poorest in the parish, and he was just with his pupils, the able and slow alike.

The men met more frequently as Findlay began to lay aside the Bible as his sole reading and took to getting other books from the church library, also run by Chapman.

When Chapman had taken the library over, the only reading material had been badly printed tracts or Covenanting histories by Howie and Cruickshank, but over the years he had managed to add Swift and Addison, Hume and Sterne, Scott and Gibbon, and even in the past year the controversial *Vestiges of Creation*, written by a bookseller called Robert Chambers, which set out disturbing new trends of scientific thought.

'Come up to the house,' invited Chapman warmly, after a lively discussion one day with Findlay on the library steps, and after that Findlay became one of the small coterie of village 'intellects' who foregathered several times a month at the dominie's dwelling and who, over careful tots of whisky, tried to sort out some of the problems of the day, while pale Mrs Chapman, she of the notorious plackets, retired to bed with a candle and the latest works of Mr Charles Dickens.

Ideas were food and drink to Wattie Chapman, and anyone with an amusing or open or imaginative cast of mind he seized upon and brought into the intellectual life of the village. In addition to Findlay, others who met regularly at his house included Alfred Maclaren, a lively, balding bachelor who had been a shoemaker and was now a journalist of sorts, with an ambition to start up a local press of his own (fully aware that the arrival of the rotary press was going to mean a mass of such speculative ventures), and Duggie Currie, a young ploughman anxious to follow in Burns's footsteps by writing pastoral verse.

A retired miner, Jimmy Watson, a vigorous-minded old radical, and Wylie, the grocer, a deeply sceptical man with a caustic wit, made up the little circle. Their talk ranged over many subjects. Chapman himself was obsessed by the straits of more than half the children between six and sixteen who still didn't go to school and by the persistent absenteeism of many who did.

'Come harvest time,' he said, 'they start bringing me handfuls of ripening corn as a reminder that lessons come second and they will be away working in the fields. When they come back, they've forgotten all they've learned.'

'They maun have food in their bellies,' old Watson reminded him.

'The day will come when school will be compulsory,' said Wattie Chapman sternly.

A living wage for the working man was something that occupied a great deal of discussion time. The older men had a great deal of sympathy for the Chartists and their determination to get votes for all, but the cynical Wylie pointed out that the Chartists were doomed now that half of their six million signatures, in a monster petition to Parliament, had been found to be forgeries. How could you respect people like that?

Wounded, the old miner Watson declared that peaceful revolution, as set out by the now ageing exponent of the New View of society, Robert Owen, was the answer, despite the fact that Owen's New Lanark experiment, which had taken place not far from where they all sat, had not been repeated.

'People aren't ready for co-operative living,' enjoined Wylie.

'It's their only defence against machines,' argued the young ploughman-poet, Currie.

Findlay drank it all in deeply. As the least well-read of the dominie's coterie, he started off by regarding the anti-religious Owen as a total infidel, but Owen's view on marriage as being only genuine when based on true affection was one that struck a chord of response in Findlay's own heart. He *could* have married poor Nancy, perhaps should have married her, but he had never felt for her what he felt for Kate. Surely Owen was right when he said marriage without love was a kind of prostitution? And would the day come when families would be limited by birth control? Hungry, neglected bairns in the Rows postulated that Owen could be right.

For fun, Maclaren would pursue the Owenite line that families could be anti-social, with their prudery, false shame, selfishness and secrecy, but as he was unmarried, nobody took him seriously.

When they were in a very weighty mood, the village philosophers would even get to grips with Hume and his views that our only true knowledge was what went through our minds in a stream of images and that God could not be proved to exist. Wattie Chapman brought up his big guns, quoting Descartes and Berkeley, and young Currie, a Romantic to the backbone, instanced the beauty and simplicity of Nature, as proof of a Divine Being.

Chapman was also greatly intrigued by the lengths to which society was carrying the Utilitarian principles of Jeremy Bentham and was fond of quoting, with a good deal of irony, Bentham's precept that the greatest happiness of the greatest number was the measure of right and wrong. 'What happens to individual independence?' he demanded, and was pleased when he found that such a liberal thinker as John Stuart Mill was asking the same sort of questions.

Old Watson was then sometimes heard to demand, 'What about Haiggle, then?' He had forced his untutored but formidable mind to tackle the works of the German philosopher, Hegel, and had grasped the concept that the state was as much 'an organ of nature' as the individual and that the individual had no rights except through the state. 'Dangerous nonsense,' Chapman would roar, made profoundly uneasy by many of the European thinkers of the time, like Hegel and Mazzini. On the other hand, he was drawn towards the cooler optimism of the Frenchman, Auguste Comte, who believed that human society itself could be investigated and regulated by the new 'inductive' method of scientific truth.

Often the waspish Maclaren would weigh in with charges against the Kirk of superstition and bigotry holding up true progress.

'You maun read *The Principles of Geology*,' he would declaim, knowing full well that possibly only Wattie Chapman and himself were capable of getting to grips with Sir Charles Lyell's famous publication. 'It postulates that the earth has grown and changed over an immense extent of time; and if that applies to geological change, it can apply to species. *We* could have developed, too, under the influence of natural forces. I once met a man, Alfred Russell Wallace was his name, who held this theory.'

'Go canny,' Wattie Chapman growled. 'Voltaire tells us that nothing that grows and lives has changed; that all species have remained always the same.'

'I'll back a Scotsman against the French any day,' answered Maclaren fiercely. 'You know what the ignorant are trying to say now – that the fossils examined by Lyell and his great predecessor from Edinburgh, James Hutton, were planted by the devil!' He exploded into ribald mirth in which they all joined, though Findlay was the least certain of the lot in doing so.

When challenged about the bedrock of his Christian beliefs, Wattie Chapman threw his lot in with the Church still, arguing that there was some Mystery which man, with his finite mind, could never grasp without the rail of faith. Findlay always threw the weight of his own convictions into the arena at this point, but more and more he was questioning his own religious feelings.

'I preached without knowing what I was about,' he confessed to Kate. 'It was nothing but a form of vanity.'

'You brought comfort to many a poor soul,' she told him. But it was a comfort he could not bring himself to offer now; he turned down all and every invitation to go back to his old evangelizing, and those who knew no better put it down to laziness and preoccupation with his own family to the exclusion of everyone else.

Meanwhile, a crawling terror was taking hold of Kate. It was that young Jack would come to some desperate end in the pit.

She worried about Findlay, but he was cautious, experienced, trusted. Young Jack of late had grown wild and truculent, attending illegal cock-fights behind the village bakery and walking miles to see a fist fight. He was already half-seriously courting a Dounhead girl called Tibbie Hallett, the boldest and cheekiest of the village girls, with a challenging brown-eyed stare and a tongue that wouldn't affront a navvy. And when she had threatened him with Findlay's pit belt, she had seen the aggressive young muscles rippling under his jacket and the pugnacious clench of his chin. Soon he would be too much for her. Soon there would be troops of village mothers beating a retreat to her door with reports that their daughters had fallen with child by her Jack. Soon in his temper he would strike a man dead, or in his new careless attitude not do his job properly down below and cost a man – or himself – his life. Findlay laughed at these fears of hers when she told him about them, but she could not shake them off. Her resolve to get in touch with the Balfours and try to make his grandfather take an interest in the boy was one that grew in her every day.

It took a bit of organizing. She knew that old Mr Balfour's estate – and his huge coal pits – were at Bellnoch, which was barely ten miles away from Dounhead, and a growing, flourishing county town. The more she looked at the pittance of a wage paid to her husband and son, and the more she thought about the money old Balfour must have at his command, the more justified she felt in her course of action.

Young Jack protested every inch of the way but in the end, concerned by the increasing generation gap between his mother and himself, and still wanting her love and approbation more than anything else, he gave in.

His first infatuation with the pit and the camaraderie of the colliers was wearing off, in any case. Even when he came up into the daylight, he could often hear in his mind the relentless drip, drip, drip of the dank hole where he worked now. They had made him a pony driver and the one warm and meaningful thing in his working life was Wee Sanny, the shaggy little Highland pony that was half-blind from its labour in the Stygian gloom but which knew his voice above all others and even where he kept his flask of cold tea. If there wasn't a titbit in young Jack's snap, the little animal was quite capable of taking the cork out of his flask of cold tea and slurping up the emptied contents before Jack could move a muscle.

Once, on night shift, the cage had got stuck in the shaft and it had been four hours until it was freed, four hours while the air had got fouler and fouler and the men, even the older ones, more certain that they were going to be entombed forever.

Clearly, what his mother and Findlay said about setting his sights above the pit was wise, was something he had to accept and act on. But what else could he do? Maybe it would make sense to see his grandfather. It would mean a day off the pit, a diversion, and for once he and his mother would be on their own, just like the old days, before a husband and demanding bits of weans had taken over her life and left him on occasions feeling like a Gulliver among the Lilliputians in the book by Swift that James Galbraith had once given him to read.

Findlay tried to take an unselfish view in the affair. It went against his pride that his stepson should go cap-in-hand to anybody, but Kate had persuaded him to accept her ideas in the matter. He saw that this was something that had been in her mind a long time and he knew, too, that her worries about young Jack's behaviour were not groundless, although he had done his best to reassure her.

Kate asked Alf Maclaren if she might borrow his horse and gig for the trip to Bellnoch, leaving him to imagine that it was some household errand that took her there. Young Jack sat up as driver and on a sharp, frosty autumn day they set off, with the sun a big orange ball over the brown fields and Kate's resolve tucked tightly to her, like the muff she cuddled against her lap for warmth.

Neither she nor Jack was quite prepared for the size of the Balfour estate. A tall grey stone wall ran all round it, with two great pillars surmounted by stone lions at the entrance.

Kate hesitated only momentarily before she indicated to Jack to go on. As though sensing the importance of the occasion, Maclaren's horse jogged freshly up the drive towards the great ivy-covered mansion of Bellinch.

Before her knees gave in, Kate took a breath and pushed Jack towards the front door, giving the bell a mighty tug. Almost immediately, they heard the smart clack of footsteps in the hall beyond and the heavy door swung open to reveal a middle-aged maid-servant with a quelling expression.

'Yes?' she demanded.

'We wish to see Mr Balfour,' said Kate firmly. 'Senior.'

'He disnae see anybody without an appointment.'

'Just tell him it is with regard to his son, Robin,' said Kate.

The woman's jaw fell. Her eyes went to young Jack and a sudden wave of red ran up her scraggy neck.

'Wait here,' she enjoined, shutting the door in their faces.

'You maun come in,' she said a few minutes later, her manner a good deal more flustered. She led Kate and Jack towards the open door of the front parlour and ushered them in without so much as asking their names.

The room had highly polished wood floors and excellent rugs. Heavily ornate furniture gave it an overpowering atmosphere, which was partly mitigated by the huge coal fire roaring and crackling in the enormous grate.

A big old dog rose lazily from the hearth and half-wagged its tail in greeting, and a bewhiskered man dressed in black broadcloth waited for them to come towards him. His face was almost port-wine in colour and was heavily fleshed, but his eyes were shrewd and alert and his booming voice not displeasing.

He waited till Kate was quite in front of him, looking her and the boy up and down slowly before he spoke: 'Well, young woman, I am told you have some news of my son Robin.'

Kate looked down at her shoes, a sudden wave of faintness overwhelming her at this moment of confrontation, her voice refusing to function momentarily.

It was Jack who spoke up, in his rough, assertive adolescent way: 'We have no news of him, this while back. We are here to tell you – '

And here, his confidence also running out, Kate had to finish the sentence for him, 'about *his* son.'

'About me,' added Jack, nodding vigorously.

There was a moment of heavy silence, while the big clock in the corner tick-tocked ominously. Mr Balfour's face seemed to shrink, his jaw to sag inwards. With a gesture that was almost weary, he indicated the heavy mahogany table, and Kate and Jack took a seat on one side of it while he took a heavy carver chair on the other.

'*His* son?'

'This boy here,' said Kate, feeling more lively now the chair rather than her uncertain legs was supporting her. 'Fourteen years ago, Robin stopped at Greenock on his way to Ameriky, and Jack, my son here, was the result.'

'Come to the window, my boy,' said the old man. He took Jack's face between his fingers and turned it round to the light. 'He has the Balfour nose,' he said, almost calmly now. 'Show me your hands, boy.'

Jack held out his hands. The fingers, though blackened and roughened with work in the pit, were long and sensitive. The old man looked at them for a long time, then sighed. 'They are Balfour hands.'

His manner became more purposeful. He took a decanter from the sideboard and poured them each a glass of port.

'How did you find me here, madam?'

'Through a good friend in the Free Church.'

'Tell me,' he said to Kate, 'all you can remember about that time, fourteen years ago.'

Kate did this as well as she was able, the old man alternately sighing and prompting her. When she had come to the end of her recitation, Kate asked carefully, 'Have you had any word of Robin, sir? I do not remember him unkindly.'

He gave her a long, measuring look, before answering somewhat abruptly, 'He has been seen, once in Boston, latterly in California. I cannot give you a good report of him. He seems to have lived by his wits. And to think that all this – ' he indicated the house – 'could have been his some day.'

Kate drew herself up with all the dignity she could muster.

'That is the true purpose of our visit, sir,' she said. 'I have cared for my boy all these years without help from anyone except the good man who is now my husband. But Jack here needs more learning. He is too clever to spend his life labouring for coal.'

'You want me to keep him?' asked the old man coolly.

'It is no more than his due,' said Kate directly.

'What do you want to do, boy?'

'Go for a sailor, sir.'

'I don't want to lose him to the sea,' interjected Kate. 'I've asked him not to think about ships. Not till he's fully grown and knows his mind properly.'

Mr Balfour rose and turned his back on them, facing the fire, staring into the coals for such a long time that Kate and Jack began to look at each other uncertainly.

Suddenly he spun round smartly on his heel.

'Will you be prepared to work hard, boy?'

'His name is Jack, sir,' said Kate firmly.

'I don't mind work,' said Jack, a little uneasily.

'I am not going to hand you a fortune on a plate,' said

the old man. 'You must help yourself. You have heard of Samuel Smiles, I take it?'

'No, sir.'

'A fellow Scot. Read him. You will see that any man can improve his lot, if he is determined enough. Determination, that's what's needed.'

'Yes, sir.'

'I am a capitalist, boy. Do you know what that means? You will have read your great countryman, Adam Smith? *The Wealth of Nations?*' When the boy shook his head, he went to a bookshelf and took down the volume, pushing it into Jack's hand. Then he tapped his own head. 'But my capital is here. Brain capital.'

Jack shifted from one foot to another, looking towards his mother for a word of intervention, but Kate was bewildered, too, by the old man's outburst.

He saw their expressions and went on more quietly: 'Britain is on the verge of great wealth. You have heard of the Repeal of the Corn Laws – two years ago? That means free trade, boy. Fortunes for the asking. But only for those dedicated to hard work and self-improvement.

'This is the age of the railway. My money is helping to build some of them. I have invested wisely, not like some of the fools who lost everything in the Railway Mania of 'forty-six. I can get you a job on the railways, boy. Are you prepared to work hard, if I do? To show your mettle?'

'Yes,' said Jack.

'Then you can start at the navvying. As soon as you like. I will arrange it.'

'But navvies are a rough sort,' protested Kate. 'He needs education. I want him to be a man o' parts.'

The old man looked down at her, not unkindly.

'You came here for my help. You must allow me to do it my way.'

He gave a broad smile in Jack's direction.

'You will not be treated soft, as your father was. It would not be a kindness to you. Now then, lad, tell me your name again.'

PART TWO

◆

Chapter Five

'Jack, what is a railway?' asked Paterson, at the age of four prefacing everything with 'what is?' or 'why is?'

The two boys were sitting on the steps of the room-and-kitchen in the miners' rows at Dounhead, while inside Kate was heatedly telling Findlay for the hundredth time why she didn't want Jack to take up his grandfather's offer.

'Wheest a minute,' Jack abjured his young brother. 'I want to hear what she's saying,' and he put a warning finger to his lips.

'You know what navvies are like,' Kate was declaring. 'Have you seen some of the bothies they build themselves? Some are of nothing but stones and some are even just damp turf. I wouldn't care so much, but they mix all sorts, women and children and men, and when the Irishmen have taken drink they would fight with their shadows.'

'The old man told you he wanted to do it his way. Having gone this far, I don't think you should hold back now. Let the boy stand on his own two feet. He'll not thank you for coddling him.' It was Findlay, the voice of quiet reason.

A slow smile of satisfaction spread across Jack's face. His stepfather was on his side! It looked as though they were going to let him leave home. His mother always argued most strenuously when she knew she was beaten. He was dizzy with the prospect of freedom from the pit, of working in the open air, of being associated, even at a humble level, with something as progressive and exciting as railway trains.

A lot of what his grandfather had said to him about self-help had sunk in. Maybe he could be rich and important, if he worked hard enough. Maybe one day he'd be able to sail the Atlantic again, go back to New York and see Joe O'Rourke. He knew deep inside himself that he wasn't going to accept the drab yoke of the pit, the 'what-can-you-do?' attitude of even some of his younger contemporaries. It was a funny feeling, heady and yet, in some way, also frightening.

Buoyed up at the way things were going, he pulled young Paterson close to his side and said: 'You know my wee pony down the pit? Wee Sanny? Well, he pulls the wagons on a sort of railway. You know that! But what I'll be helping to build might be the Glasgow-to-London. Four hundred miles long. Do you know where London is?'

The small boy shook his head, never taking his big, dreamy blue eyes off Jack's face.

'London's in a place called England where the Queen has her palace. It's big, bigger than Dounhead or Bellnoch or even Glasgow or Greenock.'

'Will there be trains on the railway?' asked Paterson. They had been over most of this before, but it was a subject of which he never tired.

'Trains with folk in them,' Jack assured him.

'Will they not fall off?'

'No, the carriages have proper sides to them and even seats to sit on.' He looked mischievously down at the small boy and said, 'Some day, folk'll even have beds on them, and go to sleep. And tables, so that you can eat your dinner in them. And even a place where you can go to piss.'

'Go on!' cried Paterson, falling about with pleasure. 'Tell me about signalling.'

'Well, at night they put up a red lamp for danger, and a

white light for clear and a green one for caution. And for during the day, there's these big boards, they're on pivots – ' he demonstrated with his arms – 'on a high mast, and they semaphore the messages.'

Paterson repeated the word 'semaphore' and moved his arms up and down like Jack.

'Draw me a train,' he pleaded, and in the dust under their feet, Jack drew a train of sorts, with splendid wheels and a big funnel and, best of all in Paterson's eyes, steam curling up in great profusion. The little boy sighed with unalloyed pleasure. In the days to come, he tried to draw trains with a stick like Jack, and even if they were not very impressive, at least the steam was always very satisfactory.

He made chuffing noises as he went about. He stuck out his stomach as though it were the great steam belly of the engine itself. Kate said he practically brought himself up, he was so little trouble at this stage. As for Duncan, a small, red-haired Daly, named Josie, had taken him under her wing, and the two played contentedly the day long. Which was just as well, as Kate was pregnant again, and tired easily.

Jack was put in the care of a ganger by his grandfather and put to work, to his chagrin, not on the Glasgow-to-London, but what would eventually become a sort of offshoot, running from Glasgow to the town of Bellnoch itself. It meant, to Kate's relief, that he would not be all that far from home and could join the family at weekends, which was the time that most of the drunkenness took place among the navvies, if they weren't actually working on the Sabbath.

The ganger's name was Molloy. He was an Irishman, like most of the men, of immense strength and presence, a stickler for perfection whose intelligence was sometimes overcome by his choler.

On the morning Jack presented himself for work, Molloy was waiting for him. 'Pick, spade, shovel, barrow,' he barked. 'That's how we build railways. Think about it! It's the sweat of our brows that carries the nobs. Sweat that cuts the banking, sweat that makes the tunnels. I'm going to make you sweat, son. Lift that pick!'

They were working on an embankment now, and as he looked at the lake of mud men laboured in, Jack's heart sank. But he set to with a will under Molloy's instructions, and after an hour or two began to feel the exhilaration of his own sheer physical strength. He was glad when they stopped to eat, however, and no bread and cheese had ever tasted so good as his did that day. The men made hot, fresh tea in their billycans and in this way were better off than the colliers, who made do with cold.

Molloy had a bothy which he shared only with his woman follower and their two small children, and Jack slept there at night, insensible practically from the moment his head hit the ground. Each day as he wielded pick and shovel or pushed barrowloads of earth, he puzzled over what his grandfather had in mind for him. Not labour like this for long, surely? It was Kate's notion that the old man might find him a clerical job once he had proved his mettle and that by degrees Jack would be able to work himself up to a well-paid white-collar position.

Sensing some kind of privileged arrangement in Jack's employment, some of the other navvies tended to bait him and pick fights. Usually Molloy's savage gaze was enough to quell them, but once when Jack turned on a man who had aimed a kick at him, a young navvy called Harry Spence stuck up for him, and on the Saturday night it was Harry Spence who took Jack drinking in a country ale-house near the railway.

Jack drank just enough to make his head buzz. But all around, his workmates were putting back whisky and gin as though there were no tomorrow, and the atmosphere became thick with a kind of inchoate, drunken torpidity, laden with oaths and a low keening sound meant to be singing but which was really the expression of something that cut Jack to the marrow – a desolate, sentimentalized hymn to the state of man as worn labouring beast, divorced from hope and family alike. He got up, stumbling over a prostrate Harry Spence, seeing Molloy turn to aim a brutal blow at his wailing woman, and against the whitewashed wall of the hostelry was suddenly and spectacularly sick.

He had been there almost three weeks when one day, raising his head in line with his upheld pick, he saw his grandfather watching him. The old man beckoned him and said curtly, 'Get your jacket. Come with me.'

The boy did as he was told, following the old man back to a jaunting cart. Taking up the reins, Mr Balfour galloped the strong piebald horse along the rutted country roads towards Bellinch, saying nothing the while.

'Wipe your boots,' the old man indicated at the front door, and after a lengthy process of cleaning mud off on scraper and mat, Jack followed him into the same room where his grandfather had interviewed him once before.

Again there was the glass of port, the lengthy silence, and then Mr Balfour said abruptly, 'I have arranged for you to go to school. You will have heard of Bellnoch Academy? It has not been open long but already it has a good reputation for learning. Your mother told me you already had a bit of the Latin and Greek. Well, what you study there is up to you. I will pay the fees and also your lodgings in the toun. You will stay with a Mistress Mackinnon, the widow of a minister, in Hunt Street. I want to see you every six months, when I will make you a small allowance for clothes, books and the like. Well, what say you to that?'

'I don't know what to say,' answered Jack honestly.

The old man's face reddened and he said angrily, 'Isn't it what you wanted? An education? Or would you rather stay with the labouring masses?'

'I want to be a sailor,' said Jack.

The old man turned away from him, his face working. When he faced him again, he said, more reasonably, 'What kind of a sailor, then? The kind that takes the end of a ship's rope, or the kind that stands on the bridge and gives the orders? What about owning your own ship, sending it to China for tea or America for cotton? I have friends who have their own shipping line. There's something to aim for, is it not?'

He brought his face to within an inch of Jack's young

one. 'You go to school and apply yourself to your books. You've proved yourself with a pick. Now prove yourself with the mathematics and the logic. Aim high!'

'I will, Grandfather,' said Jack, almost with a note of apology.

The old man laid a hand on his shoulder. To his intense astonishment, Jack saw that there were tears in his eyes.

'I have two sons. One, your father, broke his mother's heart. The other sits in my office, keeping figures. Dependable, but dull. He, Jeremiah, your uncle, is my heir. We'll see how you shape up. I see a bit of myself in you.' He shook his head thoughtfully. 'It might all have been so different, if Robin had but married your mother.'

Once again young Jack felt gripped by the nameless feeling. What was it? Ambition? Some kind of striving? He identified with his grandfather. It was a kind of exultation, yet it hurt.

'You maun go now, down to Mistress Lindsay in the kitchen,' said the old man. 'She has a light hand with the cream and treacle scones and she will give you your tea.' He handed Jack a sealed packet. 'Give this to your mother – she will administer your allowance. Six months from now, bring her with you when you come to see me. And let me have a good report of you, do you hear?'

'Aye, Grandfather.'

Mistress Lindsay was the maid-servant who had answered the door on that fateful day he first came here with his mother. She was grey-haired, bent, with the tidy look of the hard worker.

Now, on the old man's instructions, she plied him with scones and tea.

'Acknowledged you, has he?' she asked curiously.

'I don't know what you mean,' said Jack, his mouth full of scone.

The woman smiled at him. A kindly, almost reminiscent smile.

'He couldn't deny you,' she said. 'I knew the first time I saw you, you were Robin's lad. You're his spitten image. It's all right. I've been here too long, not to have learned how to guard my tongue. Mr Jeremiah won't like it, though, will he? He's got a fine son of his own. Will you have a bit of black bun now, then? I'd clean forgotten how a laddie can shift the comestibles!'

When Jack was settled to his studies at Bellnoch Academy, Kate felt as though a great weight had been lifted from her shoulders. At last her ambition for her eldest child had been realized and the jealous mental image of James Galbraith's chiding face conciliated. That earnest, early schooling would not now go to waste.

She had plenty to claim her attention once Jack had gone. Late in 1849, Isabella was born, then in 1851, a little son, Hugh, who died after a week. Kate was distraught and sad till another baby was on the way and in 1852 came a beautiful daughter, Tansy. It seemed to Kate she was either bearing children or suckling them, sometimes both, but in a way it became almost a natural state for her to be pregnant, and once an infant found its feet and began to toddle, she looked forward to the next, helpless and demanding, in her arms.

Isabella was not an easy birth. Kate was a long time in labour and then the baby appeared feet first. Discussing it afterwards with her neighbour, Nellie Daly, who produced child for child with her, Kate decided that the new chloroform they heard about, being used in operations, would be a valuable thing to use in childbirth, and was not at all surprised when later she heard Queen Victoria agreed with her and had, indeed, tried it.

Just the same, the two later babies were born without any such help and Kate prayed that after Tansy there would be no more. Even her strong body was beginning to feel the demands made upon it and, as a sort of rough birth control, she made Findlay sleep with the boys while she took Jean and Isabella into bed with her and Tansy.

Life in the miners' rows took on its own gentle rhythms in these years. If Findlay's wages were small, his mother found ways of helping out with eggs from her hens, kale from her garden and bacon from her pig.

Kate always kept out of the way the day the pig was killed. The travelling butcher was often drunk or, at least, tipsy and the poor pig often managed to escape before its throat was cut, its horrendous screams resounding through the Rows. It was normally set up on a bench so that it would bleed thoroughly and slowly and preserve the quality of the meat. There was a superstition in the village that if a woman with a period touched the meat, it would give it a peculiar taste. Kate hated the whole procedure of waiting for the first two quarters of the moon because a waning moon was supposed to mean shrinking meat, burning straw to singe off the animal's bristles, or pulling off the gristly outer coverings of the pig's toes and throwing them to the waiting, shrieking children.

Yet she knew her attitude was illogical, for the bacon, once cured and hung above the fireplace, was a valuable addition to their diet and supplemented the mince-and-oatmeal 'skirlie', the barley-laced broth, the herring, cheese, potatoes and sour milk admirably.

The children, once they could walk, were out from under her feet most of the day, playing with the other children in the Rows, the older ones looking after the younger. Jean, in particular, was very maternal and usually had a number of other small children under her wing, as well as her own brothers and sisters.

From the start Paterson was protective of little Isabella, who was like him in looks and temperament. These two never quarrelled with each other, and supported each other in childish pranks or when they got into trouble. Duncan and Paterson competed in everything they did, Duncan trailing behind his brother declaring, 'I can do it, too.' The volatile Tansy crowed from her mother's arms to be allowed down to join in the games or squabbles.

In the main, Kate did not find discipline very difficult. If they were naughty, they were threatened with their father's pit belt, but Findlay only had to hold this up in a threatening manner and the children were quelled into good behaviour.

While they played their games behind the Rows, there were sometimes itinerant musicians to divert them – the hurdy-gurdy man with his sharp-eyed monkey, or a sad-eyed Russian with his dancing bear. Tansy in particular adored these diversions and would try to leap from her mother's arms when she saw the others dancing. Kate would stand by the cottage door listening, thinking back to the days of theatre and music-hall in Greenock. No tramp was ever sent away from her door without at least a piece of bread.

Some day when the children were older she was going to ask Findlay to take her to the Hippodrome in Bellnoch, where they had plays like *All That Glitters Is Not Gold* and *The Factory Girl*. But meantime, she drew what amusement she could from listening to someone like the Wee Melody-Man, who played a sort of concertina and sang:

'Oh, the cuckoo, aye, the cuckoo,
Oh, the cuckoo's nest!
I'll bring you a bottle
Of the very, very best
If you show me the road
To the cuckoo's nest!'

She would meet the merry look on Nellie Daly's face and the two women would dissolve into laughter on their respective doorsteps, as much at the cross-eyed expression of lechery on the musician's face as at his saucy words.

Once a year the children were taken to the village fair, where there were more entertainments; tumblers, sideshows, quacks selling nostrums for all ills and where the more serious business of hiring farm labour was carried out.

'Try Pritchett's Vegetable Vermifuge,' said the quack. 'Not a particle of calomel, scammony, gamboge or other drastic article in it,' and the children would tug at their mother's skirts urging her to buy it and were greatly let down when they discovered it was only a cure for worms. Dr Hallett's Napolitaine Pills sounded good, too, but when the children asked what they were for, Kate pulled them away with a moue of disgust and would not specify what the 'certain disorder' was that could 'frequently be contracted in a moment of inebriety'.

Kate boiled up a big kettle and pot of water for the wooden bine, built up the fire, and then each Saturday scrubbed the week's collected grime from each child, starting with the baby and working up to Paterson, after which she bone-combed their hair, looking for lice or nits, and gave sulphur and treacle or cascara to any who looked a bit pale and listless.

On Sunday morning, she and Findlay took their brood to church and in the afternoon those who were old enough went to Sunday school, while she and Findlay attended evening service and Grannie Fleming came in to keep an eye on the babies.

There were plenty of activities connected with the church – weekday prayer meetings, educational lectures, Sunday school outings in the summer and soirées in the winter. A visiting minister came to tell them about the wonders of the Great Exhibition of 1851, in the Crystal Palace, the brainchild of the Prince Consort.

Alfred Maclaren, taking up his usual role of sceptic, thought it was a great hypocrisy to cover up the miseries of the poor. If Britain was such a great place, why were so many men selling up every last stick and joining the gold rushes in California and Australia? But Wattie Chapman argued that the Prince Consort was president of the Society for the Improvement of the Conditions of the Labouring Classes and had insisted that a model working-class house should be built for the Exhibition on a patch of ground near the Knightsbridge Cavalry Barracks.

The visiting minister turned down his mouth at both of them, for he, by great good fortune, had actually been to London and seen Joseph Paxton's fabulous glass mansion, as one of the six million visitors and thirteen thousand exhibitors.

So he lectured them assiduously about the moral purpose of the Exhibition, which was to bring the nations together in peaceful rivalry of industry and skill. And then he described the reaping machines from the United States, the cotton machines from Oldham, the pottery from France, the fine black lace from Barcelona and even the medal-making machine in which the Queen was especially interested, which produced fifty million medals a week. Leaving young minds boggling, he went on to describe the electric telegraph, the pyramids of soaps and ornaments, the sewing machines and Louis Quatorze furniture, even the Elizabethan-style sideboard made out of gutta-percha. He was greeted at the end with generous applause and scuffing of feet. Kate was 'black affronted' when she saw young Paterson tugging at the minister's coat-tails later, asking him to tell him 'more about the engines'.

The coterie chewed over their impressions of the lecture the next time they met. Wattie had come round to the view that much of it was a vain show and that the Queen and her Consort should have been turning their minds to the religious crisis under their noses, following the Pope's decision to divide England into Roman Catholic dioceses and restore a regular Catholic hierarchy, and the move from the Church of England to the Church of Rome of leading Anglican clergy like the Archdeacon Manning.

Maclaren declared that it didn't much matter anyway. Even at the risk of offending his friend Chapman, he had to point out that most folk, most working folk, didn't go to church anyhow, whether Catholic or Protestant.

'It's the Communist Manifesto we should be thinking about,' he argued. 'We've had a good harvest this year, but wait till we get a situation like the Hungry Forties again. Do you think the poor will accept their lot, when they hear about fol-de-rols like gutta-percha sideboards?'

As usual, he had reduced the argument to happy absurdity and when the other members of the coterie thought about the Exhibition afterwards, it wasn't the 'blazing arch of lucid glass' they envisaged, but that ridiculous rubber sideboard.

There was one unforeseen result of Findlay belonging to the coterie. From the modest dram that Wattie Chapman offered on occasion, he had developed a taste for whisky. He did not in fact give Kate all his wages now, but instead dropped in at the village pub for 'a couple of drams' or a measure of gin on pay day.

Kate pointed out, tight-lipped, that it was an indulgence that went against her own beliefs. She pleaded with him to join the temperance society, to give up drinking entirely. The evils of drink were apparent all around them.

He would look at her, a look compounded of apology and defiance.

'A man maun have something to take away the taste of the pit,' he would answer quietly, and she knew there was no reply to that. But she was glad when the law at last decreed that the pubs should close on Sundays and at eleven o'clock on other days. The level of drunkenness in the village terrified her – with brandy 16s. a gallon – and her nightmare was that the dram which Findlay took now would be the start of a long, slow slide into dissolution and poverty.

In the late summer and autumn she was able to earn a little extra money by fruit-picking and working at the harvest. She liked what she called a little 'reuchness' in the house (a Lallans expression she'd learned from Grannie Fleming) – the feeling that she had a few pence above the usual to spend on extra food or clothing. Jean, Duncan and Paterson went with her to Summerton's Farm, for they could twist the straw into bands and help her to tie up the sheaves.

She liked it best of all when Findlay joined them after his own shift at the pit and they worked together setting up the shocks, right into the gentle dusk, tired but companionable and part of the ancient bondage of the harvest field.

Old Mistress Summerton didn't mind the children coming to watch the cows being milked by the dairymaid and herself as long as they were quiet and well-behaved. Childless, she was known to take laudanum and opium to relieve some unspecified complaint. Wide-eyed and silent, Jean and Paterson saw the steaming milk being squirted into the pails, poured into the shallow earthenware pans and left till the cream had risen to the top.

Janet the dairymaid would later skim the cream off, and if the children were lucky they would be given some of the milk that was left before it was taken to the pigs.

Best of all, they liked watching the cream go into the churn, a large wooden tub mounted on a stand, with long blades inside that beat the cream into butter, and Janet was not averse to having their help at turning the handle. Sometimes they helped, too, with the cheese-making, fascinated by the whey dripping through the cloth and the big heavy wooden presses, worked by screws, that extracted the last of the whey from the curd.

The farmer's wife, a big, generous-hearted woman, would set up a harvest supper in the barn, on the first Saturday after all the harvest was gathered in, and there were fiddles and mouth-music, dancing and flirting, candles set in scooped-out turnips, eating and drinking. What alcohol was taken had to be in secret 'oot bye' behind the barn, for the farmer and his wife were ferocious temperance advocates.

Kate did not mind when the days drew in and the winter came upon them, for she loved the feeling of having her brood about her in the comfort and warmth of their own but-and-ben.

With a big free-coal fire in the grate and Findlay nodding in his chair opposite her, she liked to gather the children about her knee and sing to them or tell them stories about her Highland childhood, centred mainly about the gift of the second sight and premonitions that had come true. Sometimes she recalled the days in Greenock, days of great ships made by the Napiers, the cousins David and Robert, one the artist building a ship for its 'line', the other the greatest marine engineer of the age, according to James Galbraith. When she mentioned the latter, her face would grow serious as she held up the precepts he had taught her, of seeking education and knowledge for their own sake and so that the poor and under-privileged could be helped towards a better life.

It was Kate who taught them to put their hands together

and pray each night and who, simply and artlessly, read or related the Bible stories, while the younger ones played their own absorbed games under the valances of the set-in beds, half-listening but securely aware of the warmth and boundaries of the family.

Christmas and New Year were best of all. There was the Sunday school soirée to look forward to, with its buns and fruit and nuts for the children. And the sweet benediction of the Christmas story, as she read it to them from the family Bible:

' "Now when Jesus was born in Bethlehem of Judea in the days of Herod the king, behold, there came wise men from the east to Jerusalem,

'Saying, where is he that is born King of the Jews? for we have seen his star in the east and are come to worship him . . ." '

Duncan, solemn, brown-eyed, her first-born by Findlay, always listened the most intently. He would take the Bible from her lap and turn over page after page, print seeming to have an absorbing grip on his imagination. He was quickest of all her children to read, she having taught him his letters herself.

Sometimes Josie and one or two other red-haired Dalys would join Kate's 'congregation', Josie usually reminding everybody they were Catholic. 'It doesn't matter,' Kate found herself saying. 'There are many ways to God.' Catholic and Protestant alike in the Rows respected each other. The pit and poverty brought them together, if the Churches did not.

Chapter Six

Old Balfour had chosen well when he decided that Jack would stay with the Widow Mackinnon in Bellnoch, during his period at the Academy.

Mrs Mackinnon was a good housekeeper and an excellent cook. Her mutton pies and clootie dumplings were just the fare to put meat on his bones, as she averred, after the long walk home from school, often in rain, snow or fog and with his heavy books carried in a strap; and the big coal fires tonguing up the chimney a cheerful sight for someone who had several hours' homework by candle-light in front of him.

There was another reason why Jack's stay with Mistress Mackinnon was to prove pleasant: the last of the widow's family to remain at home, her seventeen-year-old daughter, Clementine, known as Clemmie.

Although she had been brought up to make herself useful in the house, Clemmie was 'accomplished' in the manner of young ladies in stations well above her own. She could draw, paint, converse in French and sing in a charming light contralto, as well as embroider most beautifully and tat with great skill and ease.

She was a slender girl, with a neck as delicate as a scrawny chicken's and a frail, sensitive face. Jack liked to raise his head from his books and see her, seated in her straight-backed chair, her fair ringlets falling forward, working over some sampler or tray-cloth with a calm, concentrated zeal.

This charming, accomplished girl with her transparent skin, under which every fleeting emotion registered like the ebb and flow of the sea; with her bird-like wrists and huge, innocent, dark-blue eyes, contrasted greatly with the robust Tibbie Hallett back in Dounhead, who had been only too ready with her favours had he had the wish to take her up on them. A certain fastidiousness had held him back. Now he was glad. Now he could fall whole-heartedly in love with Clemmie Mackinnon, something which he proceeded to do with a thoroughness that bordered on the foolhardy.

His wooing began in earnest during the second summer of his stay in the Mackinnon household. He accompanied Clemmie on evening walks over the Kenner Brae, a gentle, sloping area leading down to the river's edge, sprinkled with soft grasses, harebells and wild strawberries. He would put down his jacket for her to sit on and tell her what he hoped to do when his schooling was over, or reminisce over his brief visit to New York, or seek her comforting murmur over his recollection of the terrible deaths of Captain Carvie Campbell and his first mate.

He loved when she lay back and he could look down into that cool, near-perfect face with its flawless complexion, the very mirror of femininity, so void of experience, so innocent that he trembled with the wish to imprint himself there.

He was held back by the fear of his own passion, the thought that he could destroy her almost, and the conflict made him moody, unbearable. Till one evening, as they lay listening to the laverocks, she brought her gentle mouth to his and his passion broke over them both like a crashing wave.

He had thought she would resist, but in a way that filled him with a holy exultation, her passion seemed to match his own. 'Yes, oh yes,' she cried, casting her bodice open, helping his fumbling hands, guiding him, at the last, where he should go. After that, it was as though they had reached a plateau together, a place above ordinary life and folks, where bliss superseded anything as ordinary as happiness and heaven itself was the only synonym for what they felt and knew.

'You'll marry me, Clemmie,' he said with certainty. 'When I've a good position and can keep a roof over your head.'

'Oh yes,' she answered, with equal certainty. 'I would die

away from you.' She looked the same: calm, untouched, except for where her mouth quirked upwards in a secret smile.

He said nothing of all this when, emerging as dux of the Academy, he went to see his grandfather about the next stage in his career. The old man had not been idle; had, in fact, found him a position with a promising new shipping line in Glasgow which was planning to run a number of screw propeller steamers to serve the Californian Gold Rush.

'At the moment, the only way you can get to the Isthmus of Panama – and the quickest way to the goldfields – is by the Royal Mail Steam Packet,' the old man explained. 'But the mail steamers have to be wooden paddle steamers and everyone knows they use up far too much fuel. These new iron screw steamers will be of modern design, they'll take more passengers and less fuel.'

He looked good-humouredly at young Jack.

'You'll be thinking you'd rather sail on them than find out how to run a shipping line,' he said. 'Well, bide your time. Learn all you can. There are still too many good ships at the bottom of the ocean and I'm not risking all that good grey matter – ' he tapped Jack's forehead – 'sending you for a common sailor. You understand?'

As this was largely what Clemmie had been saying, Jack nodded.

'Clerking it is,' he agreed, matching his grandfather's good humour. Once he was installed in the shipping-line office he became fascinated by the planning that was going on to open up this exciting new commercial route. The firm had put out orders for two beautiful three-deck iron steamers, barque-rigged. Jack gasped in pleasure over the drawings. One ship was 266 feet long, the other 307, and they had simple, low-pressure engines, giving moderate speed. The first-class passengers would be accommodated in the poop, the gold-seekers in the 'tweendecks which, though bare, would be much more comfortable than similar accommodation in sailing vessels of a low freeboard.

His grandfather was soon proved right. He became so

caught up in the challenges presented daily to the new firm that in no time at all it seemed as though working in Glasgow had been his life forever. He was learning something new and valuable every day.

His salary was not a high one, but at least for the first time he knew what it felt like to have money of his own to spend. He found a modest room on the south side of the river, away from the worst of the slums and sewers and with a pleasant view of open fields.

He visited his old friend Miss Noble and found her in her own words 'thin as a whipping post' after some chest ailment which she blamed on the winter fogs, but exulting over the fact that her old friend, the missionary Hope Waddell, had been so successful, in company with his three Jamaican helpers, in Christianizing Old Calabar in West Africa that a sea captain had just brought back a letter from the King and chiefs welcoming more missionaries and promising them land. 'And they don't kill off his slaves any more when a chief dies,' exulted Miss Noble. 'Let's hope they've stopped killing off their twins as well.'

Much as he loved the old lady, he felt himself that the Church could be doing with cleaning up Glasgow before turning its mind to Calabar. Just up the street from where he lived, he discovered, was one of the city's five hundred 'houses of ill fame'. He had seen the mistress, a fat, waddling creature with three chins, and a young fellow-lodger explained to him that the customary four girls worked to this woman's instructions, with three 'bullies' or 'fancy men' keeping an eye on things.

From eighty to a hundred 'customers' dodged into the seedy shadows of the house each week.

'They pay the girls a shilling a time,' said Jack's informant, who had been there but took care not to disclose the fact. 'You have to spend about two bob in drink and they often take as much out of your pooch. The lasses only last about six years. After that, they're finished.'

'Why do they do it?' Jack demanded. He could not help thinking of his own beautiful Clemmie, so innocent and yet so passionate. Could she have fallen into a life of vice, had Fate been less kind to her? He knew from his reading of the radical *Glasgow Sentinel* that women and girls died on the Glasgow streets from hunger. If a girl was lucky she could get a miserable 1s. 6d. for sewing men's shirts, or work till midnight on Saturdays in a shop, but there were thousands who were unemployed. And if you wanted money for food . . . It was true what James Begg, the doughty leader of the 'Highland Host' section of the Free Kirk, said. The wealthy West End churches were full but the congregations cared little for the East End slums or the casualties of the mean streets and their stinking, evil-smelling cellars.

In one area the Church had perhaps been commendably zealous. Its campaigning had helped to get the pubs closed on Sundays and at eleven o'clock on other nights. (Hadn't James Begg disclosed that in the little village of Liberton, there had been 135 pubs to one church!) At least now the drunken brawling that characterized the Glasgow streets and sometimes ended in murder confined itself to Saturday night. And Jack decided to keep away from the centre of the city then. Dickens's latest, *Bleak House*, kept him busy reading it, for several Saturdays, and then he fell into the way of attending meetings held by people like Robert Buchanan, the socialist, anti-clerical free-thinker, some of whose views he agreed with, and some violently opposed.

He found it exhilarating to put his views against other sharp young minds of the time, to quote Pitt (when he rejected a Bill to fix a minimum of wages): let the price of labour find its own level. (Adam Smith again!) A fair field to all and no favour to any.

But he knew there was something in the other argument: that freedom of contract meant for the employer, in most cases, the liberty to do as he pleased; for the employed, the liberty to do as he must. And that wealth could be accumulated, in the wrong hands, at an appalling cost to human life.

It was at this period, living in Glasgow, that he stopped going to church altogether. It was not a conscious decision. He did not allow himself to think what his mother would say if she knew. He was only aware of the turmoil of moral conflict going on inside his head and he knew he would not go back to church until he had settled many questions, many doubts, once and for all.

Nellie Daly's child, her eldest, Cornelius, aged ten, came home from his last day at school, complaining of feeling unwell and the next day was dead.

This was how it began, the invasion of King Cholera in Dounhead. Doing her best to comfort poor Nellie, Kate looked down at the small, freckled features, composed, rigid and ageless in death, and felt a cold hand of terror grip her insides.

What if one of hers was next? Up and down the Rows the epidemic wandered, picking a random victim here, striking whole families there. She became almost hysterical in her vigilance for symptoms – the diarrhoea and vomiting, mild enough to start with, but then happening so often that motions became like rice-water; the raised temperature, the terrible thirst, the blue-tinged skin, cold to the touch, the weak voice.

Sometimes death was quick, in less than twenty-four hours. A man coming up from the pit, dropping in his tracks. A woman, struggling to get the baking done despite feeling unwell, dead before the bread reached the oven.

Up and down the country the epidemic that was to take 20,000 British lives raged, and the reasons given for its severity ranged from the wrath of God to vague talk of 'miasmas' and fog. No wonder Sir John Simon pleaded for a Ministry of Health! Meanwhile the clergy thundered from their pulpits that it would do a Godless nation no harm to fast, while Palmerston rose in Parliament to insist it was better to cleanse than fast.

Somehow Kate had never thought of Findlay being affected. It was the children who were her first concern, perhaps because of the death of Nellie's boy next door.

He did not make much of it at first, saying it was nothing, just an ordinary stomach upset, and set off for the pit in the ordinary way. In the middle of the morning, they brought him home, his face contorted by the pain of cramp in his legs and belly, his thirst unslakeable. The first thing the doctor ordered was that he should not be given water, as this further depleted the body salts already reduced by sickness and diarrhoea.

Grannie Fleming had her spare bed sent down from the cottage and they set it up for him in the 'front room', which was normally used only on Sundays or special occasions.

There he could be quiet and Kate could leave the younger children in the competent hands of Jean and Paterson, whose capability grew with their sense of importance.

Kate lived in a nightmare vacuum that had only the two-dimensional figures of herself and Findlay in it. She soothed him, washed him, propped him up to try a little of his mother's chicken broth, helped him lie down when his fever grew worse and his head turned from side to side in his delirium.

Dr Pettigrew had said, 'The patient has to fight this illness with his will and constitution.' He was a tired man, worn out with trying to convince the authorities that wet middens had much to do with spreading the disease and with watching that dusky purple mantle too many faces as urine dried up, skin shrank and voices weakened.

On the third night of his illness, Findlay called Kate to him and asked for a drink of water. She told him he was not allowed it but she moistened his lips with fingers dipped in the jug by the window.

'Bitch!' he called out to her, in a weak, husky voice. 'You filthy, rotting bitch. Whore of Babylon! Cunt! Water! I want water . . .'

She sponged his brow. The skin was dry, crackly, his eyes staring at some strange landscape of the mind. He raved and cursed her, trying to throw off the bed-covers, to get up, his hand going out to grasp some imaginary cup, his breath fast and light.

'Oh, Lord,' she prayed, on her knees to hold him and keep him covered. 'Spare this father, thy servant.'

After a little, he quietened. His colour was dreadful, like

the faded stains of brambles, and his pulse was scarcely there.

His eyes fluttered open. 'Kate,' he said, in a more normal voice, but so faintly, she could scarcely hear. 'I'm cold. Terrible cold!'

Her tears scalding her hands, she undressed to her petticoats and got in beside him. She held his almost lifeless hands to her warm breasts. She sat up so that his head lay in the curve of her bosom. She put her warm and living limbs close to his wasted ones. And so they lay through the night.

In the morning, he looked different. It was hard to decide in what way, except that the ghastly purple colour had receded slightly and his eyes were making some contact with an outer reality.

The doctor permitted himself a restricted optimism.

'It might be that he is on the road to recovery,' he told Kate, 'But we must be on the lookout for a relapse. It's careful nursing that will count now. Are you up to it, woman?'

Kate nodded. She had hung on so fast that if Findlay went now, she would surely go with him. Over the next weeks, it took all her strength and determination to keep going, because the illness had taken a heavy toll on Findlay's strength and his recovery was protracted and slow.

He did not seem to realize how weary she was and made endless demands on her, like a spoiled child, pushing away broth she had made, wanting pillows plumped, asking her to sit and talk to him when the children were crying for her attention in the other room.

She did not know how they would have lived if it had not been for Grannie Fleming. The old woman went back to toffee-making, something she had done when Findlay was small, and did a brisk daily trade from her cottage parlour window. The toffee was simply made, mainly from sugar, water and vinegar, and when it was ready she pulled it into long strips and cut it off into mouth-sized pieces, or 'cheughers', with an elderly pair of none-too-clean scissors. The tiny income she made from this she gave to Kate, as well as providing eggs, and kale from her garden. The children gathered firewood and in this way also made a few coppers, but food was of the barest and Kate had to keep the older children away from school as she could not afford their penny-a-week contribution.

Alf Maclaren had a whip-round among the coterie and brought Kate thirty shillings and some tonic wine for the invalid, as well as a copy of his just-launched weekly paper, the *Dounhead Clarion*. Findlay's workmates sent small sums of money and their wives sent the children with gifts of vegetables, home-made jam and canisters of soup.

People's kindness touched Kate deeply but she did not let others see the extent of her hard-upness. As soon as Findlay was sufficiently recovered, she brought out her Sunday clothes again, sponged them with vinegar to freshen them, and went back to kirk with her head held high and the overt impression that the Flemings were 'managing fine' in the face of adversity.

At the time of this family crisis, young Jack had not been near the Rows.

Unknown to his mother, he had been sent about the country on export matters – to Dunfermline to see about linen and to Edinburgh to interview the tanners about leather.

Back in Glasgow, he had been caught up in meetings, arguments and outings and had been altogether so intrigued by the many avenues waiting to be explored in his new mode of life that the family and even Clemmie had faded somewhat from the foreground of his thoughts.

After three months away, he found the atmosphere in the little house in the Rows vastly changed. Where there had once been stir and bustle, easy affection and ready hospitality, now there was strain, moodiness, the pall of sickness and his mother's thin face jealously watching every bite you ate.

He was sickened with himself for not having been in closer touch and of some assistance, but when he offered to give his mother a little money (he had not been saving anything at all of late), she rounded on him angrily and said, 'What makes you think we can't manage? Your stepfather is going back to work next month.'

He knew this was retributive, for when he looked round at his brothers and sisters they all wore the same look of silent, somehow disdainful, reproach. They had been through a bad time together and he had not been part of it. At the end of the unsuccessful visit, he placed a sovereign on the kitchen table, and ran.

Although the family weathered the crisis of Findlay's severe illness and after several false starts he went back to work in the pit, there were two results which were to be long-lasting in their effect.

The first was the change in Findlay's personality. It was as though a little of his manhood had gone, certainly a portion of his manly strength. He had to summon up each day enough will, enough courage, to go down the pit, to work among men whose health was as yet undiminished. They were good to him: they took some of the burden away from him, knowing that he had a wife and bairns to keep. But it was still his weary limbs that had to drag themselves from bed before the light and home again when the day had gone.

In his illness he had been like a petulant child and something of this remained: he reproached Kate for the slightest thing, criticizing her when the children were noisy or quarrelsome, sulking if, too desperately tired to listen, she did not hear his petty demands for a drink, a smoke or a candle to be lit.

In her secret grieving over the change in Findlay, Kate unwittingly brought about result number two – a sense of estrangement from young Jack. Although she knew it was neither consistent nor fair, she blamed her eldest for not being around when she most needed him, for leading his own life in Glasgow.

In other families around her, when the sons reached their early teens, they went down the pits like their fathers and the mothers reaped the benefit of their intact pay packets as well as the husband's. Then they doled a small sum out to the boys, but with more money at their command were able to buy more meat, fresh ribbons for their

Sunday bonnets and gee-gaws from the pedlars who came round the doors. The reward of big families was that you 'got something back' before they went off and started homes of their own. But what had happened in her case? By getting old Balfour to find work for Jack in Glasgow, she had cut off her nose to spite her face.

When Jack finally plucked up enough courage to bring Clemmie to meet his family, Kate was constrained and less than her generous, hospitable self. Did this little chit with her genteel manners have marriage to her Jack in mind? Did she think it beneath her to visit in the Rows? Kate had seen her look at the threadbare cushions and worn chairs.

She did not warm to Clemmie at all, noticing that the girl had drawn back her skirts when the baby, Tansy, approached her with sticky hands and that she and Jack had exchanged glances when Findlay made some grammatical error. Miss High and Mighty! She was driven to fall back on accounts of her own life as housekeeper in Greenock, building poor James Galbraith up till he sounded nearly as important as the Kirk Moderator himself, and embroidering on the social life and fashions she had seen till she half-wished herself she had never left the place.

Afterwards, it was more the old, gentle Findlay who teased her: 'From the way you spoke, Katie lass, I was beginning to think you wouldnae call the Queen your cousin!' The children giggled at this and Kate, pleased by his caring, smiled half-ashamedly and admitted she might have been a bit forbidding.

When the railway line was opened between Glasgow and Bellnoch and then continued from Bellnoch to Dounhead and beyond, it made it easier for Jack to visit his family in the physical sense, but the gap between his city life and their parochial one was widening. It seemed to him that his mother and Findlay were often warring nowadays over Findlay's drinking, and the children were argumentative, wild and disrespectful. He mistook his mother's deep physical fatigue for lack of caring, and reproached her in his mind for it. She seemed to spend a lot of time just sitting by the fire, while there were cobwebs in the corners and the children's clothes needed washing.

He hoped Clemmie would not get like that. She had developed a light, persistent cough and her mother had worriedly postponed their engagement for at least another year, scaring the lights out of him with talk of Clemmie going into a decline. He was sure it was nothing sinister, but his Clemmie would always be delicate and need taking care of, that much he knew.

One Saturday, when Clemmie had not been very well and was resting, he took his mother, Paterson and Duncan into Bellnoch by train, bought them their tea and finished off the outing by taking them to the play at the Hippodrome.

This outing was a huge success and brought animation back into his mother's pale face. She had seen two ladies wearing the new crinoline and pined one day to have one herself. Paterson could not stop talking about the railway, while Duncan had a hundred questions about the show they had seen. They took sugar mice home for the others and an ounce of thick black tobacco for Findlay. Kate invited Jack to stay the night and go with them to the church next day.

It was the moment of truth.

'I'll stay but I'll not go to the kirk,' he said.

Kate looked at him dumbstruck.

'I haven't been for a long time, Mother,' he admitted.

'You mean you don't believe there is a God?'

'I mean, I don't know.'

Findlay looked at her warningly, but she was pale with anger, the soft, smiling theatregoer lost in the vengeful matriarch.

'I have brought you up in the fear of the Lord. There will be no blaspheming in this house. That I should live to see the day!' She rounded on Findlay. 'It was you who sowed the seeds of this. With your socialism and free thinking.'

It was the first of several such scenes, each more bitter than the last. He had taken his obstinacy from her and could not give in. She saw her God as the Rock one clung to and felt that once he let go, the maelstrom of vice and drunkenness in the world would pull him down and down.

She wept and he went white-lipped as she scourged him with her tongue. But neither gave in. He knew he was struggling against firm matriarchal bonds and for the right to call his soul his own – or God's. She knew the faith of her fathers was slipping away from him and there was nothing to put in its place. The break between them could never be final, but he knew he could best show filial kindness by staying away.

In any case, the sands were shifting also in his mercantile career. The building of the splendid ships ordered for the Panama run was delayed. There was war in the Crimea and the Admiralty had first demand on the shipyards for warships.

The ships which should have carried prospectors in search of Californian gold, although finished eventually, were chartered as troopers by the French and carried men from Marseilles to the Crimea instead.

Faced with frustrations all round, Jack began to find his desk work tedious. More and more his steps took him towards the Broomielaw, where the river called to him with its old magic.

One night on his way back to his lodgings, he saw one of the girls from the bawdy-house down the street. He had seen her before. She had a dark, challenging stare and a face of sullen beauty.

'What are you staring at?' she demanded.

'No' much, when I'm looking at you,' he riposted.

She grinned. So he wasn't so high and mighty after all!

'Dae you no' fancy coming up the hoose?' she demanded.

He looked at her curiously. 'What's your name?'

'Jinty McGraw.'

'You're too nice a lass for this kind of life, Jinty.'

He saw that there were tears in her black eyes.

'Come up the hoose. We'll just sit and talk.'

Talk was all they did. She wanted to impress him – or anybody – with the fact that she could dance and sing and would soon be moving on to better things. He felt desperately sorry for her and, missing Clemmie, was sore tempted to pay for her services.

In the days to come, meeting her in the street, painfully warding off her blandishments, he found this one frustration more than he could take.

In a sense, he was running away to sea again. This time, he told his mother and his grandfather what he was going to do, not asking for advice or opinion. This time, he went with a grim determination to achieve what he had really wanted all along: his master's ticket and a ship of his own.

His grandfather paid twenty-five pounds and he was indentured for four years on the clipper *Bellharry*, a full-rigged wooden ship of nearly six hundred tons and as near as dammit the ship of his dreams.

Chapter Seven

'This wean should never have been sent down the pit,' said Dr Pettigrew. He looked up at Kate sharply, his face perplexed. He had seen her turn from a fine, upstanding woman, bonnie to look at, into a whey-faced near-slut, whose bairns ran wild all over the Rows. He could see she was exhausted to the point of collapse, her hair uncombed, falling in greasy strands from her cap, her eyes dull and apathetic, sunk in her face, like holes burnt in a blanket. Didn't it happen to them all?

He turned again towards Paterson, who was lying back on the sofa, the coal dust on his face streaked white where the tears had run.

'How old are you now, young 'un?'

'Thirteen, sir.'

'It's time they kept the likes of you out of the pits. Now, let's look at this cut. Get me some hot water, woman,' he addressed Kate. She rose and poured some from the hissing kettle into a basin. The fire was choked with 'clinkers' of old coal and ashes. Dr Pettigrew suspected that a chamberpot under one of the beds had not been emptied. The room was hung with damp washing and the bine cluttered with dirty dishes. He sighed. He had heard about Fleming's latest drinking bouts. No doubt that was the root of the trouble. What could you expect with brandy sixteen bob the gallon and conditions such as they were in a wet mine like Dounhead?

Paterson sobbed quietly as the doctor cleansed the gaping wound on the back of his head.

'How did it happen?' he demanded.

Holding the basin for him, staring with a sick fascination at the wound, Kate answered when Paterson would not: 'They told him I wasn't his real mother.'

'Who did?'

'The other young 'uns,' burst out Paterson violently. 'They said mine had been a witch and that was why I was born wi' a cloven hoof. Big Sanny Henderson knocked me down and I cut my head on a shovel.'

His face a grim study, the doctor went on calmly bandaging up the head, then removed the battered boot and dirty sock from the child's lame foot. Tenderly, he felt the wasted muscles, not trusting himself to meet the look of agonized defeat on Kate's face.

At last he said, 'You don't like it down the pit, laddie?'

The boy would not admit it. He looked up at Kate, who answered for him again, 'There was no bread in the house, else I would never have sent him.' In a gesture of unconscious dignity she put her arms round the boy and he wept quietly into her shoulder.

'He should have a boot for that foot, a special boot,' said the doctor, almost to himself.

'Where am I to find the money?' demanded Kate bitterly.

Pettigrew rose. Sometimes he found the poverty in the Rows overpowering. Too many children, too little space. He wished himself back home for his wife's tender steak pie and a glass of whisky.

Sighing, he said, 'Try to find a different job for him, or I won't answer for his health.'

Kate nodded. She could have argued that there were no other jobs to be got, but she had discovered that there was little point in trying to make people like the doctor understand. It wasn't that they weren't kind. It was just that, able to eat enough themselves, with clean clothes to dress in, they could not always understand that poverty wasn't always your own fault.

'I canna pay you, Doctor,' she said at the door. 'Not at the moment.'

'When you can,' he said briefly. She knew payment was not a prerequisite of his care.

Pale under his streaky grime, Paterson fell asleep on the sofa. Kate put a cover over him and took her own shawl down from behind the door. Once Friday nights had been good nights; when Findlay had brought her his pay unopened and she had been able to go to the grocer's and get a full basket of goods, with free packets of sweets tucked in at the sides, for Wylie the grocer knew her then as a good payer.

Now she could not go there, for she owed them money and Mrs Wylie passed her at church with her nose in the air. She owed at the butcher's too, and the draper's. Little by little her dignity, her Highland pride, was being stripped from her. *That* was poverty. Not the hunger pangs in your belly, nor the cold you felt from old clothes. But the loss of people's respect. (Not your neighbours', thank God, for Nellie Daly was often in the same straits.)

She rattled noisily on Nellie's door now and her neighbour's alarmed face appeared, above a guttering candle.

'Is yours in yet?' she asked.

Nellie shook her head.

'I'm going down there to get mine out,' said Kate resolutely. 'There's Paterson lying in there, his head cut open. The doctor's been to him and says he needs a special boot.' Her voice was rising in its hysteria. 'Nellie, where am I to get bread to put in their mouths, never mind boots for their feet?'

'Don't go, lass,' Nellie soothed. 'Come in and I'll pour you a glass of elderberry wine.'

'No,' cried Kate wildly. 'I'm going down there to get him. If I don't come back, look after my bairns for me. In God's name, Nellie, he'll either listen to me tonight or the river will get me.'

She made off down the uneven open gutter of the Rows. Nellie stood looking after her fearfully, then closed her door as she disappeared into the gloom. Kate passed the manager's house, brightly lit from one of the new paraffin lamps, and inside she could see his wife busy setting a table. Something good was cooking, meat with sizzling onions. The saliva flowed into her mouth unbidden and she began to sob from hunger. Since breakfast of a scrap of bread and dinner of a potato, nothing had crossed her lips that day.

When she got to Macqueen's Public House, she hesitated outside. Only low women had anything to do with pubs. She herself had never tasted spirits, nor even ale. A girl of about eleven in a torn pinny was waiting outside with a shopping basket, her eyes gleaming with tears, for her father to emerge. The sight of her somehow stiffened Kate's resolve.

'What's your name, hen?' she demanded.

'Annie Beattie,' said the child.

'And is you father in there?'

The girl nodded.

Kate pushed the door of the pub open. Inside, all was brightness and rough conviviality, in the yellow glare of the gaslight. There was sawdust on the floor and the brass rail round the bar had been polished till it shone. Miners, farm labourers, navvies stood or sat around, some just putting in first orders, others in an advanced state of inebriation but far from ready for the door.

'The man Beattie,' she called out with as much authority as she could command. 'Your child is waiting for you.' Her voice seemed weak, even to herself, and nobody appeared to hear.

She saw Findlay standing in a corner with one arm confidingly round Joakie Daly's shoulders. Findlay's face was flushed, owlishly concentrated as he tried to hear what a third man was saying.

'Findlay Fleming!' This time, she called his name out, good and loud. Every pair of eyes in the place turned towards her.

'Are you coming with me, or do I leave this life forever?'

A babble of protest and laughter broke out. A man near her touched her and asked for a kiss. She could feel her flesh shrink and scream, but she stood her ground. 'I will not leave here without you. Your bairns have starved for long enough.'

She turned to the rest of the jeering, jostling men.

'What are you, men or beasts? You have children and wives at home waiting for bread – '

Slowly and unsteadily, Findlay came towards her, the light

of danger in his eyes. Recently, as drink had got more and more of a hold on him, he had taken to striking her in temper. His hand was raised now, but she did not flinch.

'Strike me!' she dared him. 'And let your friends see what a man you are!'

There was a burst of maudlin cheering and he crumpled before it. In a quieter, slurred voice he said ingratiatingly, 'Kate, Kate, what are you doing here, lass? You maun go home.'

She seized him by the arm. 'You are coming with me.'

She dragged him outside with her, her puny strength battling with his spirit-clouded clumsiness. The little girl still stood there, crying openly now. Kate said, 'He's coming hen,' then gripped Findlay's arm more firmly and led him off down the main street.

How could she ever go back to the kirk now this had happened? She was aware of curtains twitching and faces peering as they passed. 'Her with the airs and graces,' they would be saying. 'Look at her now!'

He was at the stage they called 'miraculous', so drunk that he did not know what he was doing. His legs were all over the place and he was smiling and talking to himself. If only she could get him home before he reached the next stage, which was the one she feared most; that of black, raging temper, when the decent man she'd married turned into some evil monster who turned his fury on everything and everyone in sight.

The other children were back by the time they reached home. Jean had cleared away the ashes and there was bright new coal in the grate. They had used all their coal allowance, so the children must have 'collected' it from the loaded wagons or from the smouldering bing or slagheap itself.

They were eating bread and drinking milk.

'Where did you get it?' Kate demanded.

'From the farm. Janet gave us it when Mistress Summerton wasn't looking,' said Jean.

'May God bless her,' murmured Kate hoarsely.

Paterson was sitting up and looking better, Isabella,

whom they called Isa, by his side as usual.

It was Duncan who strode forward from the fire and stood before them.

'Is he drunk again?'

'You hear?' Findlay appealed to the heavens. 'Honour thy father and thy mother, that thy days may be long upon the earth.' His face crumpled into maudlin tears and he dropped like a stone into his chair by the hearth.

Kate bundled the younger children off to bed. Tansy fell asleep almost at once, but Isa lay staring at the scene by the hearth, her big, intelligent eyes missing nothing.

Kate knelt and went through Findlay's pockets while he snored. With a relief that was almost crazy she saw he had about half his pay left: at least tomorrow she could get some victuals. She would have to spare something for the old woman, her mother-in-law, for Grannie Fleming hadn't been able to tend her garden or hens recently, her poor old chest whistling like the wind in the barley.

It did not take much to kindle hope again. Her hunger forgotten she began to tidy up the kitchen. Would the day come when they would get out of this dreadful slough? Sometimes, it seemed to her, the old proud Kate who had told others how to pray, seemed to be standing aside, waiting, looking at this other, helpless Kate, tied to the hearth by bonds of sickness, poverty and weariness. She would not go away, this Kate. She would not give in. She knew there was a God, a loving Father, who in his mercy would not desert her. 'Underneath are the Everlasting Arms.'

'What are you doing, woman?' Findlay rose with a crash, sending the three-legged stool spinning. He rose heavily, unsteadily, feeling in his pocket, and when he knew the money was gone his dark brows darkened like thunder.

He picked the kettle from the hob and sent it across the room with its scalding contents. Some of the water fell on Jean's legs and she screamed like a little, trapped animal.

'Findlay, Findlay.' Kate tried desperately to soothe him. Her heart was pounding so loudly she thought it would burst in her chest. 'Don't, man. Don't.'

He looked at the dresser and picked up the milk jug that was her pride and joy, pink and white with a fluted lip. He crashed it against the wall. He took his arm and swept everything else off the dresser, cups, plates, candlesticks, Bible. Kate fell forward and began to pick them up, Paterson helping her.

He took the tongs from the hearth and picked up a blazing lump of coal, brandishing it high.

'I'll burn the lot of you!' he raved. 'You'll roast in hell!' He turned towards the beds and Isa jumped out, screaming, and ran out into the street. Duncan threw himself at his father and brought down his arm. The coal fell to the hearth and Kate kicked it into the grate, where it smoked and smouldered.

A figure appeared at the door. It was Wattie Chapman, with a sobbing Isa by the hand.

'By God, Findlay, what is going on?' he demanded. 'I was visiting down the Rows, when this wean of yours came screaming after me like something demented.'

Kate's arms fell to her sides. 'See for yourself, Wattie,' she invited hoarsely. 'You don't need to go to the temperance lectures. It's all here.'

He came in and closed the door. He stayed till all the children were finally in bed. Talking quietly and soothingly, he got Findlay to settle in his chair, and took off his boots. Finally, he went next door and got Nellie Daly to send an older child to his wife, saying he would not be home, perhaps, till the small hours. Then he settled by the table and talked to Kate.

'It's since he had the cholera, Wattie,' she said. 'He went back to work and his strength gave out and he took to having a dram to keep him going.'

Wattie shook his head. 'Men aren't meant to work in the bowels of the earth all the hours that God sends,' he said gently. 'Findlay knows what can happen down there. He's seen it happen.'

'He knows nothing else,' said Kate. 'It was the pit for his father before him and it looks like the pit for his weans.'

'I'm not giving him up to the drink,' vowed Wattie.

'I know the man there is beneath – all this.' And he indicated the broken crockery, the upturned stool, the spent coal.

'I have given up my wee dram, to please my wife. I have signed the pledge. If it's the last thing I do, I am going to get Findlay to do the same.'

There was a strange listening silence and they turned simultaneously to see Findlay looking at them both, his gaze different, ashamed, almost sober. Wattie went over and stood beside him.

'Findlay, lad, it can't go on like this. Can it?'

Kate's husband shook his head, put his face down in his hands, and wept.

After the weekend, Findlay went back to the pit on Monday without having exchanged a word with Kate. For once, she felt she had not been able to go to her kirk on Sunday, or even send the children to Sunday School. They had circled Findlay warily, like cats stalking round a sleeping hound. He had sat with his head in his hands most of the day and in the evening gone for a long walk.

Kate was tending Paterson's wound on Monday when there was a loud, commanding knock on the door. She opened it to see a portly man with a gold watch chain extended across his massive stomach and a disapprobatory expression on his fleshy features.

'Mistress Fleming?'

Kate agreed cautiously.

'Bertram Gilmour.' He looked as though he might extend a hand, but changed his mind.

'The doctor has had a word with me. I understand you have a crippled child here.'

'Not crippled,' said Kate hotly, for she never thought of the active, lively Paterson as such.

'A child in need of a boot.' He pushed his way into the house and Kate clicked the latch behind him. He saw Paterson and said, 'Is this the boy?'

'This is Paterson,' said Kate. 'What do you want with him?'

'Have you heard of Gilmour's Crippleage? It is a place set up for the unfortunate children of the poor, whose needs cannot be met in the paternal home. The doctor has suggested that a place might be found for your son – '

When Findlay came home that night, she was still simmering with so much indignation that she could not help breaking the silence between them and telling him the whole story.

She saw his face fold in lines of anger and outrage – and perhaps something else which she found hard to look at, compounded of a bitter shame and humiliation.

'So he needs a boot,' he said heavily. 'By God, he shall have a boot. How much would it cost?'

'About three pound,' she said fearfully.

'Aye, well, put me my dinner on the table, Kate, and afterwards I will be going out.'

She had made a good vegetable broth from marrow bones and there was a slice of bread to go with it. He ate without saying another word, his dark eyes sombrely on his first-born supping with his brother and sisters. Afterwards, Kate handed him his cap and he went out without telling her where he was going.

His destination was Wattie Chapman's house. He was surprised when Mrs Chapman let him in with a murmur of surprised approval. 'Wattie was just coming to see you,' she explained.

'Come in, man,' Wattie greeted him, leading the way into the familiar dark but cosy parlour where the coterie had their gatherings. A fire blazed merrily on the hearth and a bright, new, paraffin lamp with an edge fluted like a parlourmaid's cap gave a gentle light in the corner by the bookshelves.

'Lettie'll bring us a cup of tea, by and by,' said Wattie genially. 'I'm sorry, but you and I maun get used to taking nothing stronger.'

Findlay's face relaxed in a grim smile. 'You were coming to see me?' he queried.

'Sit down, man. I have a serious proposition to make to you. But first, I am in the possession of news that hasn't yet reached the generality. From Macnicol the pit-owner himself. You know Willie Armstrong, the secretary of your union?'

Findlay nodded.

'He's decamped. This very day. With every penny of union funds. Old Macnicol's rejoicing, for it looks as though this'll put the tin lid on all union activities now.'

'Where's he gone? Armstrong?'

'America, we think.'

'His brother's a miner in Pennsylvania.'

'Right. That's Tom. The first brother, Archie, got himself a farm on the Pennsylvania frontier. You mind what happened to him?'

'Indians?'

'Aye. They were sitting round the fire one night when there was a gentle tap-tap at the windows. His son went out and they got him. The wife went out next and they took her.'

'I mind now. They got him too, later, didn't they?'

'Not before he'd taken one life for each of his.'

They stared sombrely into the fire, each crouched in his chair, as though half-expecting to hear a ghostly tap-tap on the window right here in Dounhead.

'Do you know why I want to see you?' demanded Wattie at last.

'I can guess.'

'I think *you* should take over as secretary of the union.'

Findlay looked away uneasily from his gaze. 'I'm not up to much nowadays,' he said harshly. But he could not keep his eyes away from Wattie's intense look.

'What happened to all your fighting talk?'

'I don't know if – if unions are the answer. Folk don't like them. They don't like paying their dues or being chased up and intimidated when they haven't got the money to pay. Look what's happening in England – shooting and murder in Sheffield and rattening – that's what they call it, isn't it? taking away their tools.'

'Cloak and dagger unionism, the papers call it,' mused Wattie. 'I don't deny the rough element. You're bound to get it. Trade unionists aren't all like Robert Applegarth.'

'I've never heard of him.'

'He's the man they listen to in London. He's organizing the brickies to agitate for a nine-hour day. He tells the bosses straight that piecework is bad, that it makes men neglect their homes and education.' Wattie's homely face kindled. 'Like me, Findlay, he wants to see men and masters co-operating in voluntary understanding. But men can only bargain if they get themselves organized.'

'Maybe you're right,' said Findlay thoughtfully.

'You need a cause, man,' argued Wattie. 'Before you leave here tonight, you're signing the temperance pledge. I'm not letting you out of the house till you do. Put your mind to something else than drink, man. If you've gone off God, come to the aid of your fellow-man. The men'll come round when they see that they can give each other mutual support in the case of sickness or accident or death – it's worth giving up a copper or two for that kind of security.'

'It'll be a thankless job. Most of the folk think trade unionists are idle scroungers. We've got no standing. We might as well be back in the bad old days before '24 when we were totally banned. We're still regarded as 'in restraint of trade' and we can't even sue for recovery of funds from rogues like Willie Armstrong.'

Wattie drew his pipe from his mouth. 'You can either sit back and complain,' he argued, 'or you can get in there and fight for reform. We need another Alexander Macdonald, now that he's that busy in London setting up the National Miners' Association.'

Findlay was silent for a time. Then he said with a grave deliberation, 'When and if I become the secretary, one of the first things I'll push for is a stop to bairns under twelve being sent down the pit.'

'That's bound to happen soon,' said Wattie. 'A good thing, too.'

'My lad went down there, lame foot and all,' Findlay said. Hearing the emotion in his voice, Wattie looked up at him sharply.

'He needs a boot, a built-up, surgical boot,' Findlay went on. 'And I need the money to buy him it.'

'How much?' asked Wattie, going towards his desk.

'Three pound. I'll pay you back something each week.'

'When you can,' said Wattie quietly.

'Aye, well, I'll be going,' said Findlay, awkwardly pocketing the money.

'What about that other son of yours?' Wattie put out a detaining hand.

'You mean Duncan?'

'Aye, Duncan. He's been a bit sullen of late, contentious in the classroom.'

'He's a bit of a rebel,' said Findlay.

'Maybe with cause,' answered Wattie drily. 'Are you hard on him, man?'

'He shows me no respect.'

The dominie's eyebrows shot up almost to his hairline, and Findlay coloured and looked away.

'I would take him away from school if I were you,' offered Wattie at last. 'Maclaren needs a sharp youngster to help him on the paper. I've nothing more to teach young Duncan. He's the sort who must learn for himself. 'Prentice him to Maclaren, let him run errands and sharpen quills. He might make a journalist one day. He already writes and spells as well as I do.'

'I can't afford to pay – '

'Maclaren wouldn't take anything from you.' The dominie laughed. 'I know. I've asked him.'

Findlay managed a slow smile. 'You've decided between you, have you? Well, I've no objections. Better that, than down the pit.' There was still an edge of resentment to his voice, which made Wattie urge as he showed him to the door, 'Go easy on him, man. Don't break his spirit.'

Findlay did not tell Kate about the union position until he had been formally nominated for secretary and had accepted. Although she did not like the element of coercion about joining the union, and knew there would be trouble in the future, as there had been in the past, she was glad to see Findlay getting to grips with a problem outside himself and the new self-respect it had brought to him.

He did not tell her about signing the pledge or where he had got the money for Paterson's boot, either, but she guessed.

It was enough for her that four Sundays after that terrible weekend when she had thought their family life broken down and ruined for ever, Findlay put on his dark suit and white collar and came to church with her again.

She had a new ribbon on her bonnet and the children were neat and clean in the clothes she had laboured to make them from hand-me-downs and cast-offs. One day, she determined, she would have a gown in the new purple that was all the rage.

Best of all, Paterson had his new built-up boot and stood tall and proud in it, his slight body no longer forced out of true by the unevenness of his limbs. Beaming and scrubbed, his narrow face with its large, striking eyes and shock of fair hair was the one the congregation's communal gaze alighted on, with looks of genuine affection.

Not for anything would he have confessed that the boot was heavy and made his pelvis ache.

Only Isa saw, and knew. As always.

Chapter Eight

'Are you all listening?' demanded Jean, self-importantly. It was her Sunday afternoon off, the first since she had started in service at the house of James Tolley, the draper, in Bellnoch.

They were seated round the tea-table in the little house in the Rows – Kate's favourite occasion of the week. All except the two youngest were still in their Kirk clothes, self-consciously formal in their manners, aware of the good lace cloth and the cut glass jam-dishes with the Apostle spoons. Isa and Tansy were silently counting the scones and carefully-cut fingers of seed cake. Findlay was casting Kate reproachful glances about not being allowed to remove his jacket, but as it was Jean's first visit home Kate saw fit to misinterpret them and handed her husband the first cup of tea, saying graciously, 'You must be ready for this. It was hot in the Kirk today.'

'Well,' said Jean, biting into a potato scone, 'we've got a coachman, and cook says that makes us carriage-folk. Real gentry.' She cast rather pitying glances round the busy table. 'There's nothing like it in Dounhead. *All* the bedrooms have got carpets *all* over them, lovely soft Brussels carpets, all bonnie colours . . .'

She did not add that the small attic room at the top of the draper's house had no carpet and a grate so tiny there was room only for one lump of coal. Nor that she had wept from tiredness that first week, rising at five-thirty and dropping into bed, bone-weary, at ten. Up till now, it had been the boys and their jobs that held the limelight and she wasn't going to lose out on her brief moment of glory.

'I have to clean the dining-room and hall first thing, carry the hot water to the bedrooms, clean the lamps, attend prayers and serve cooked breakfast. Then we have our breakfast when the master has gone.'

Kate looked at her daughter. She was only thirteen, a strong, pink-cheeked, equable child who had seldom given her a moment's worry. But already her plump cheeks were thinner and her childish hands broadened and coarsened with rough work. Kate cut her own scone in half and put the larger piece on her daughter's plate. Jean looked back at her with a gleam of loving pleasure and returned to her account:

'You never saw so many settees and ottomans, Maw. Fancy mahogany tables, big gilt mirrors, pictures of bygone days.' She lowered her voice. 'In the mistress's bedroom, there's *two* dressing-tables, a big looking-glass that swings back and forrit, even dishes with roses on them for the toothbrushes and soap.'

She caught Tansy's hypnotized eye and went on, 'At night, I carry in the big zinc bath and in the morning I take in the hot water first thing and the mistress washes in front of the fire, with the towels all ready on a clothes-horse nearby.'

'She washes every day?' demanded Paterson incredulously. 'I don't believe it. She canna be dirty.'

Jean ignored him. '*Then* she puts on her lace-trimmed drawers, an underpetticoat three and a half yards wide, another petticoat all padded and stiffened with whalebone, *then* her white starched petticoat with the three flounces, her muslin petticoat and *then* her crinoline and bodice.'

'Has she a purple gown?' demanded Kate jealously.

'Several,' said Jean. 'And coloured silk stockings. Cook says when she goes to a ball she wears a wreath of flowers in her hair and carries a wee posy to match, or a fan. Cook says the second wife always comes off the best – '

'Aye, well,' said Findlay, who had not been altogether happy during the description of Mrs Tolley's underwear and who wanted tea to end so that he could doze off in front of the fire. But Jean was not to be stopped.

'*Young* Mr Tolley,' she said, 'him by the first marriage, he's a heavy swell. Cook says he's a young masher. He wears pegtop trousers, all big checks, and a yellow waistcoat and purple coat and yellow boots.'

'What does he *do?*' demanded Kate.

'Oh, loafs about,' responded Jean airily. 'Helps his father, I suppose. He's got an eye-glass with a black ribbon – '

Tansy picked up a spoon and held it to her eye and even Findlay joined in the laughter.

'And he's got an opera cloak and a cutaway coat,' cried Jean vexedly, trying to stem the tide of merriment. But it was no good. Paterson was giving an impersonation of a heavy swell, stroking his Dundreary whiskers, flicking a speck from his boots and Jean joined in the laughter, but a little reluctantly, with a catch somewhere in her chest. For young Mr Tolley was the best-looking male she'd ever seen and when he passed her in one of the corridors, giving her a warm, approbatory smile, her insides turned to water and she didn't know where to put herself.

Her mother's hand closed over hers.

'Don't let them run you into the ground,' she said quietly. 'Do your duty, but let them know you are a human being too. Is it a good meat-house?'

'You get pudding or tart every day,' said Jean enthusiastically. 'Cook sees to it we eat well.' She did not add that the servants' meals were subject to the running battle between her mistress and her insistence on servants' economy and the cook and her ingenuity at holding back some of the provender intended for upstairs.

When tea was finally over, Kate and Findlay retired to the front room, leaving the family to clear away and chatter among themselves.

Through paying into a weekly club, Kate had managed to get a small carpet for the front room, a rocking-chair for herself and a stiff-backed horsehair chair for Findlay. There were large pink vases with gilt lugs on the mantelpiece and handsome lace curtains at the window. Although the boys slept in this room, now that they were older, she still regarded it in the main as a sacrosanct place, and the children, when they were allowed in, apart from sleep, had to behave themselves.

Now she and Findlay sat themselves at either side of a

sleepy fire. He grumbled a little, declaring that the sleep 'had gone off him' because of Jean's chatter, but he lit his pipe and puffed away contentedly, while Kate, with her Bible on her lap, permitted herself some quiet reflection on her family.

Jean in a place; Duncan earning commendation from Alf Maclaren as a ready learner; even Paterson in a job to his liking, working at Dounhead Station, so that he saw his beloved trains every day. And young Jack, second mate now on the *Bellharry*, coming home soon, with the promise that he would take the whole family on a steamer excursion down the Clyde. She was looking forward to the trip almost as excitedly as the youngest and had already started planning what they should all wear and what food they should carry for a picnic.

'You look gey content,' said Findlay softly, from the other side of the fireplace.

Kate smiled at him. She had wanted to tell him how she felt about his giving up drinking, but her thankfulness was too great to talk about. Besides, he knew.

'I've got three bonnie daughters,' said Findlay expansively, 'but I'm thinking, Kate, you beat the lot.'

She blushed and laughed.

'Away with you, you old flatterer.' She was secretly delighted.

'No one will ever be as bonnie as you,' decreed Findlay. 'Not in my eyes, anyway.'

She put out the toe of her boot and gently touched the fire-irons. She wanted to find some words to give him back, but she could find none. Instead, she leaned over and gently touched his knee.

Into the companionable silence, he spoke a few minutes later:

'I have a bit of news.'

Her eyes flew open.

'Aye. News. They want me down in London for talks about the new Miners' National Union.'

'You? Go to London?'

He permitted himself a jocular smile. 'Aye. Even me. Expenses paid by the union. I'll not go if you don't want me to.'

'In the train?'

'I'm not walking it,' he joked.

She said agitatedly, 'You'll keep away from the pleasure gardens?'

'The Vauxhall's closed down. So Alf Maclaren tells me.'

'That's as may be. There's still the Cremorne – '

'I don't want to see fireworks or folk going up in balloons,' said Findlay scornfully. 'No more than polar bears in trousers.'

'Is that what it's like?'

'Well, there's music and dancing, theatricals, that sort of thing as well,' he said, with a little more interest. 'But I'll not go near it. What's the matter? Do you think some dancing girl's going to make away with me?'

'Away, you fool,' she said fondly.

They all went to the station to see him off. By dint of half-starving the lot of them for a couple of weeks, Kate managed to furnish her husband's stomach with an impressive watch and chain (and hoped nobody would miss her seed pearl brooch). Tansy wept because she could not go, too, and even Kate felt a strange restriction in her throat when the train gave a clank and a whistle and pulled away inexorably from their sight.

Findlay was impressed by the weight and tone of the union leaders he met in London. Here, argument was raised to the level of debate and if some of the speeches were a bit too long, he had to admit to the fluent persuasion of others. It put the crude arguments and even fights back at the pit into perspective. *This* was how it was going to be done: by a careful marshalling of the facts and a firm stand together against exploitation.

It wasn't only miners that he met. There were trade unionists representing bricklayers and dockers, the cutlers from Sheffield and cotton workers from Lancashire. He struck up a friendship with an open-faced young Jew from Leeds, who told him about the ghetto conditions there as more and more of his fellow-countrymen fled the pogroms in Russia.

Joe Levi's father had been a pedlar who had settled in Leeds many years before, but anti-Jewish feeling had only flared up with the more recent influx of immigrants, many of them arriving in long fur coats, fur caps and with bluchers round their feet, just as they'd left their frozen Russian or Polish villages. They were spat upon and vilified, especially on pay day when the pubs emptied.

With the coming of Singer's sewing machine from America and the 'divisional labour system' of making suits – that is, dividing the making of a suit into five or six different operations – the opportunities for sweated labour among Jew and Gentile alike were legion.

A red-faced Irish collier, named Deb Maclearie, from the Northumberland coalfield, usually sat beside Joe and Findlay at the meetings, and the three stuck together and explored the streets of London in their spare time. Maclearie had been embittered by the long strike in his county in 1844, when something like 40,000 men had come out for four months in protest against the yearly bond system, to no avail. Now he was fierce and vitriolic in argument, but away from the talks an amusing companion with a fund of diverting tales about boxing and horse-racing.

They all found the London streets noisy, with their omnibuses, four-wheeled cabs and hansoms; and smelly, too, especially near the meaner courts and the Thames itself. Miserable little crossing sweepers did their best, but the main streets often seemed ankle-deep in dung from the heavy horse-traffic and a visit to Parliament itself was half-spoiled by the odour that rose heavily from the Thames.

The friends tended to keep away from the centre of London and held their extra-curricular meetings in a small, friendly pub in Clapham. Under the circumstances, Findlay did not see how he could help taking a drink, but he confined it to ale, as much from a fear of being helpless and drunk in a strange city as from sinking back into the bad old ways that had caused Kate so much unhappiness.

On one particular evening, after the men had bought

their drinks, they became aware of a strange, heightened atmosphere around them. Men were gathered together in small groups, talking volubly but in low voices, their faces red with anticipation and excitement.

'What's up?' Findlay demanded of a potman who came to clear their table.

The man inclined his greasy head towards him with an air of conspiratorial unease: 'No pub in London will close tonight. That's what I'm telling you.' He winked and sketched a salute and made off before Findlay could question him further.

'Bigoad,' said Deb Maclearie, 'it's a mystery, so it is.'

He went up to the bar and collared the landlord, who, like himself, was an Irishman, and came back smirking happily.

'It's only the night of the world championship fight between Tom Sayers and the American, Heenan,' he said. 'What do you say we go to it?'

'Where is it?' demanded Joe Levi, his dark eyes lighting up.

'Aha! That's what all this conspiracy's about. The police have banned it, but it's taking place just the same. All the pubs are staying open till they get word of the secret venue and till they hear about the trains that are to be laid on to take folk there. Man, it'll be the greatest fight that ever was! Are youse game?'

Joe Levi nodded instantly. Findlay felt the money in his pocket, and although he wasn't reassured by what he found there, a mad sensation of recklessness was rising up in him, for the air of frenzied excitement in the pub was contagious. He couldn't be left out of it. He'd go and take the consequences.

Like three youngsters let out of school they stampeded with the rest of the clientele towards the station when the word finally came about the fight rendezvous. It was to be held on the edge of a wood at a place called Farnborough.

Sitting in the crowded train, his feet trodden down by the tramp of swaying drunks, his ears assaulted by language worse than anything he'd ever encountered in his life before, Findlay might have had second thoughts, but it was too late. Besides, this was Life, and God knew he had seen little enough of it to salt his old age.

'Heenan's got to win,' said Joe, who had been discussing form with a vociferous Cockney next to him. 'The man here says he's thirteen stone to Sayers's ten, and six foot one to Sayers's five foot eight.'

'Ah, sure, Heenan'll win. With a name like that,' Deb affirmed easily. At which the Cockney leaned over and took him by the waistcoat, declaring that Sayers was the bravest man who ever put up a pair of clean fists and that Heenan would be sorry he ever came.

The mob poured off the train and joined hundreds more gathering near the wood as the sun came up.

Findlay, although his sympathies lay with Sayers, did not see how the older man could win.

In the opening rounds, he was knocked down repeatedly, only to win the crowd's wild cheers for his gameness as he got up again and again and, with a smile on his face, advanced for more.

The hoarse cheering intensified as the blood began to pour down his face and yet round after round he stood up to the big American. Findlay began to feel sickened by the spectacle. The euphoria of the previous night was wearing off with the ale. And yet there was something splendid about this little gamecock who never even thought of giving in.

Heenan landed a blow with his great bare fist that reminded Findlay of the impact of a pit truck out of control, and game Sayers looked down at his right arm as though it were some wounded thing that didn't belong to him.

'It's all over,' opined Deb. 'His bloody arm's broke.' And it was clear from the way Sayers held his arm that Deb was right. And yet the fight went on, with the crowd out of their skins with excitement and Findlay held there by a mixture of disgust and admiration.

For two more hours the contest continued, round after round.

'Sure Simon Byrne lasted ninety-nine rounds then fell

down dead!' exulted Deb Maclearies. ''Tis going to be Simon Byrne all over again.'

The sea of humanity around the fighters began to break up into little, swirling eddies and loud voices ordering the mob to clear away made themselves heard, as the police, at last privy to what was going on, threw themselves furiously through the crowd and brought the contest to a standstill. Still the mob howled and still little Sayers stood there, sweat and blood running down his tanned body in about equal parts, that indefatigable expression on his face. Still undefeated! Heenan's expression was one of bruised bafflement that gave rise to loud cheers from the crowd.

The police were in earnest. It was the end of the match. Delighted at Sayers's magnificent performance, the fans began to move away from the wood, only those still inebriated or carried away by partisanship left to argue the case with the constabulary.

Findlay could not help recounting the famous fight when he got back home again. For a few days it made a hero of him in the Rows and even Kate listened with a kind of awed resentment to the telling of it.

In a few weeks, it and Findlay's visit to London were past history and the main source of excitement was young Jack's return from a long voyage to New Zealand and the prospect of the trip down the Clyde. He had written to his mother telling her he would like to bring Clemmie along on the outing with the family, with a view to them all getting to know each other better. Kate put two and two together and correctly surmised that Jack had marriage in view. She felt a strange, bittersweet tug at her heart, not wanting to part finally with her firstborn, yet acknowledging that with his master's ticket almost a certainty, Jack was now all the man he would ever be, fit and ready to start a family of his own. She would try to like Clemmie better, for Jack's sake, and to heal the rift caused by his lack of churchgoing. Once she had made this decision, she began to feel better, and to remind herself of Clemmie's lady-like skills that went along with her somewhat frozen-faced reserve.

On a day in early June, the whole family, picking up Clemmie at Bellnoch, set off for Glasgow and the Broomielaw. All the neighbours in the Rows came out to wave Kate farewell and admire the *purple* shawl which Jack had brought her back from abroad. And there was Jack himself, brown-faced, commanding in his uniform, bringing a real breath of sea air and excitement into the land-locked pit rows.

The younger children were in a fever of excitement and Tansy was sick before they even set out, but white-faced and determined she stumped along the road to the station with everyone else and in a little while was well enough to accept a peppermint from Grannie Fleming who, bronchial or not, refused to miss out on this great occasion.

At the Broomielaw two splendid Clyde steamers waited, the *Jessie June* and the *Rothay Castle*. Jack ushered them aboard the *Jessie June*, saying he knew its captain, Donnie Bell, and that he was a more dependable man than the master of the *Rothay*, one Peter Quick.

'Surely,' said Kate, with a twinge of apprehension, 'they are both dependable?'

Jack laughed and explained that Quick had a reputation for drawing other vessels into a race, a test of speed, a favourite Clyde sport of the time that could sometimes be unnerving for the passengers, but that Captain Bell was too sensible to do anything silly and wouldn't take Quick up on his challenge if he could help it.

'They are pleasure steamers, after all,' Clemmie pointed out. She was looking a little distraught and unsure of herself, Kate felt, not a bit like a girl who knows a proposal is on its way. A little stir of unease entered Kate's mind. Had the lovers had a tiff? She could see Jack appeared to be his usual jovial, forceful self, but was he putting on an act?

She decided it was pointless to worry, and besides there was too much else to attend to. She and Grannie Fleming found sheltered seats on the deck and the children leaned over the rails and savoured every moment of the casting off, while Findlay kept an eye on Paterson to make sure he didn't topple overboard in sheer enthusiasm.

The sun came out and the low-slung, delectable *Jessie June* straddled the gleaming river like a maritime version of the dear little Queen herself. A gentle breeze tugged at bonnet strings and lifted strands of children's hair. There was music from a German band, blending in with the pulsating throb-throb of the staunch little ship's engines, and there were titbits and delicacies from Grannie Fleming's wicker basket and the Gladstone bag Kate had borrowed from Alf Maclaren.

It was only Jack who was aware of the other ship dipping fast behind them at first. So Captain Quick was after a race after all, was he?

At Greenock, Kate went into rapturous reminiscence, pointing out this and that landmark from her childhood. When the *Jessie June* was leaving Greenock, the *Rothay* barged into the quay and almost immediately out again, so that it was clear that *Rothay* did want a contest of speed.

Jack looked up at the bridge where Captain Bell stood. The captain caught his glance and gave him a friendly wave, indicating that he wasn't interested in taking up the *Rothay*'s challenge. He slowed down indolently to let the other ship pass. *Rothay* passed and waited in her turn.

By this time, all the passengers on either ship knew what was afoot and there was a certain amount of friendly cat-calling and jeering. Grannie Fleming muttered into her bottle of cold tea that this wasn't what she'd come on an excursion for and Kate hastily agreed, although secretly she was quite enjoying the sport.

At last Captain Bell took up the challenge. He put the douce *Jessie June* at full speed and headed for Gourock. The *Rothay* tore through the waves, a bare two lengths behind. In the manoeuvering at Gourock the ships all but collided twice. Quick did not even let his passengers off there, but pursued the *Jessie June* down the river at a punishing pace.

First the *Rothay*, then the *Jessie June*, then the *Rothay*, took the lead. Often there was no more than half a length in it. The white clouds scudding across the summer sky seemed to join in the chase. The children dashed up and down the decks, wild with excitement, while Jack held Clemmie's hand and shook his head in indulgent amusement. It was all a far cry from the kind of sailing he did, when a man's life depended on his seamanship and the waves were always ready to punish the frivolous or the reckless.

At last, *Jessie June* established her supremacy by virtue of Captain Bell's superior skill and the other vessel fell back, broke off the race at the Cloch Light and returned to Gourock to resume its schedule. From then on the sail to Rothesay Bay was a thing of sheer delight, all sun and dappled water and scenery to enchant the eye.

The little town of Rothesay was in its sunniest mood. The shops attracted Kate and Grannie Fleming with their china gee-gaws, while the children raced about the beach throwing stones in the water, getting skirts and trouser-legs splashed, and Findlay kept a beneficent eye on all of them.

The young couple sauntered off together, and when they were safely out of sight and earshot Jack turned decisively to Clemmie and said: 'Now what is all this?'

Her chin quivered and she said: 'You have been gone a long time, Jack.'

'But we had an understanding. A firm understanding.'

'But a tacit one. There was no ring on my finger that claimed I was yours.'

'And so this dolt came back from India – '

'He was very brave and when he first returned, after the Mutiny, very sick.'

'And appealed to your sympathy.'

'A little, perhaps.'

'You will not marry him. You cannot.'

'I have promised him I would talk over my situation with you.'

'Can he keep you?'

'He has a pension.'

'But I will be a *master,*' he said urgently. 'I will be able to buy you a house on the coast. You can live in Gourock, or Dunoon, or in Glasgow itself if you like. You'll not be required to lift a finger . . .'

His emotions were so strong he had to turn away from her. He stood with his broad back to her, looking out over the sparkling sunny scene.

Clemmie hesitated a little then touched his shoulder. He turned and crushed her in his arms, smothering her with kisses. 'Beloved. My darling. You belong to *me*.'

She drew a quick, desperate breath, almost swooning in his arms.

'Clemmie, don't throw me over!'

She touched his face, her expression solemn. 'I *know* you are married to the sea. My dear Jack, if I asked you to choose between us, I know what you would choose!'

'Ah, so now we come to the real matter. I *knew* you could not love him.'

'But I don't know if I can face up to being a sailor's wife.'

'You could be proud of me.'

'But I could not look at you across the hearth at night.' She began to weep. 'At least Hamish would be there . . .'

'Clemmie, I can't give up the sea. I will soon have what I've always wanted – my own ship. You will be able to accompany me on occasion, although not on the harsher trips. It would not be all bad.'

He looked at her with his heart in his eyes and her mouth trembled piteously.

'I don't think I am strong enough, Jack.'

'If I don't marry you, I shall never marry.'

'That is unfair.'

'No,' he said angrily. 'I shall use any threat I can, to keep you.'

Still she would not commit herself. She dried her eyes and though still sad, was more composed.

'Don't let us spoil this day,' she pleaded. 'Let's go down to the family and see if it is time for tea.'

PART THREE

◆

Chapter Nine

On a cold, bright day in 1863, Kate was busy making scones on the griddle above the fire when she became aware of a commotion going on outside – the voices of children too small to be at school, the clip-clop of horses' hooves and the grind of carriage wheels. The wheels stopped outside her door.

Hastily wiping her floury hands on her apron, she lifted the latch and looked cautiously out. Old Mr Balfour was alighting from his carriage. He was a changed man since the last time she had seen him, his figure stooped, his face pale and lined.

He came towards her and removed his hat. Small children looked up at him, some giggling, some shy. Kate shooed the grubby, raggedy children away and brought the old man in to her fireside, her customary reserve towards him overcome by concern.

Her first instinct was to think that perhaps he had bad news of Jack and her heart began an uneven pounding in her breast.

He sensed her unspoken question and put up a hand:

'No, no, it's not young Jack I come about, mistress. It's his father, Robin.'

She said, dry-throated, clairvoyant: 'Is he dead?'

The old man nodded. His head dropped on to his chest and for a moment he could not speak.

Kate sat down as though she were suddenly boneless, a vivid flashing picture of Robin's youthful face, that morning he bade her goodbye, suddenly before her in dreadful clarity, and all the old sorrow at his faithlessness welling up in her as if Findlay and the children had never intervened.

The old man looked up at her and now he was not a ruthless, hard-headed money-maker, but a bereft father in desperate need of comfort.

'He was a reckless adventurer to the last,' he said brokenly. 'He considered himself an American and supported the Yankee cause in this Civil War of theirs. Do they not realize over there they are bleeding their country dry? How can anybody win, when it's brother against brother?'

Kate nodded, wordless.

'Well, it seems a certain Captain Andrews gathered a party of saboteurs about him in the North. Robin was one of them. They captured a Confederate locomotive at a place called Marietta, in the Southern state of Georgia, and they drove her north on a wrecking jaunt.'

He put his hand to his eyes and with a small shock Kate realized that there were overtones of pride overlaying the sorrow.

'They were chased by the Confederates, of course, over hundreds of miles. At first it seemed as though they would get away with it. But just short of the state line they were captured. Some of them were hanged as spies. Robin escaped only to fall to a Confederate bullet a day later.'

He drew a crumpled letter from an inner pocket. 'I have it all here, from a comrade in arms.' He handed the letter over to Kate. 'I want young Jack to have it. Let him at least know his father was a brave man as well as a foolish one.'

'I will do that,' said Kate simply. She put her arms about

the old man's shoulders. 'Let me make you a cup of tea before you start back,' she pleaded. 'It's a cold enough day to be out in.'

The old man straightened his shoulders. He was more composed.

'Thank you kindly,' he returned. 'But I shall be getting on now.' He looked at her keenly. 'He could have done much worse than marry you, lass. You would have been spared this poverty. But we maun both let his soul get to heaven without our regrets.'

He stood for a moment, as though weighing something up in his mind, then turned to her with a decisive movement.

'Would you like to move out of here? To somewhere better?'

'That depends,' she said cautiously.

'I can make that husband of yours up to under-manager at Dounhead.' He held up a hand at her start of surprise. 'This must be between you and me. I have become a major shareholder in the Dounhead pit and I am putting my grandson in charge here. Jeremiah's boy, Lachie. He will inherit my empire. He has had a university education. You understand, things must be this way. Young Jack will inherit something from me, but he can never be my heir.'

He looked faintly embarrassed. 'I would like to do something for you and I hear your husband is a good man, who knows the pit well from youth – '

Kate shook her head. She was trembling a little. 'It's a question of pride. I hope you understand.'

He gave a little bow, acknowledging the dignity of her stance. 'You could have had a better cottage – '

'I know you mean it kindly, but we could never take it. I have only ever asked for Jack's sake, and you have been more than generous towards him. Do not think you owe me anything.'

'I believe you mean it,' he said.

She opened the door to let him leave, watching his stout back as he heaved himself into his carriage, her emotions a strange mixture.

Then she wept a tear for Robin, behind the door where no one saw.

She did not know what Jack thought about his father. Like the others, he called Findlay by that name and she had always been thankful for the rapport that seemed to exist between the two men.

Jack was now captain of the full-rigged wooden ship the *Daniel Mackinlay*, a fast sailer built for the New Zealand trade and the China tea trade. Achieving his master's ticket had helped to make up for the bitter disappointment over Clemmie, who two years ago had married Hamish McNaughton, a survivor of the Indian Mutiny, and had set up house in Bellnoch a few streets away from her mother.

The fateful decision had been made that day they had all sailed to Rothesay. The young couple had been very quiet on the sail home, and although Jack had been solicitous and kind to Clemmie, as ever, his mother had noticed how their hands had not touched nor their glances met and knew what was coming before Jack broke the news to her.

He had not said much. But his manner had changed, become harder, more secretive. Kate had prayed for him to meet some other gentle, decent girl who would make him a good wife, but she suspected his heart was still with Clemmie, that a great many unresolved emotions still lay between the two and that Clemmie had chosen McNaughton because, perhaps naturally enough, she wanted a husband who would be there to talk to and not one sailing the Seven Seas for the greater part of his life.

Kate went back to her baking. Whatever happened, there were always hungry mouths to feed. She sometimes thought that the sorrows one's children had to bear were worse than your own, because the responsibility for bringing them into the world was yours. There was Jean, for example. She had started off in the Tolleys' big house full of freshness and enthusiasm, but now when she came home for the occasional visit, her eyes were sad and thoughtful and Kate could get nothing out of her. Something was amiss and Jean would not say what it was. Remembering how Jean had spoken of Harry Tolley, the son, with her eyes sparkling and her face vulnerable with the stirrings of love, Kate hoped that it would not turn out to be what she feared it might be.

Jean polished the brass stair-rods in the Tolley house, her cap askew, little beads of light sweat on her brow from the effort.

It did not take much to make her perspire these days, for she lived in a constant fret over Harry and what he would say when she told him she was pregnant.

She could not put it off much longer. She was six months gone. What was stopping her was the fear that he would no longer want anything to do with her. That his hands would no longer pull teasingly at her apron strings, then draw her into the pantry or the cloaks cupboard where he would kiss and love her, whispering endearments and reassurance and making her forget each and every time about the resolutions she had so painfully made not to be so weak and wicked.

She did not even hope that he would marry her. He had every kind of refinement and she had none. He travelled, went to musical soirées, wrote poetry (she had read it in his room) and dressed in the height of fashion. All she had to recommend her were her 'bonnie blue eyes' and her soft skin, but she had no confidence, no decent clothes (compared to the sort of things his stepmother wore) and her hands were rough and coarsened with harsh soap and cold water.

Even if he suggested marrying, which was unlikely, she would not have it. What a misery it would be to live his kind of life and pretend to be something she was not! She had a stubborn sort of pride in her own origins and did not really want to be other than she was. She could not bear his laughter when he corrected some turn of speech any more than she could stand his slighting references to colliers and their wives and the small airs and graces they allowed themselves when they were brave enough to enter the Tolley Emporium to buy a yard of lace or a new tablecover.

She did not know which way to turn. She could not tell her parents and see the look of shame on their faces, for although Kate had never denied Jack's illegitimacy, she had warned her daughters well not to fall into the same trap. Her warnings had not been very explicit or clear, but they had been definite enough. Illegitimate babies were common enough in the Rows, but a poor life most of them led, and hers would have, if she was unable to work to support it.

She had confided in no one, not even Bessie, the other housemaid, who had terminated a pregnancy of her own last year by means of pennyroyal and tansy infusions combined with jarring jumps from the kitchen-table. Bessie had no standards, would go out with any man, and Jean was sickened to think that some day it might be like that with her.

It was a good job that skirts were gathered at the waist and that bumps did not show, although she felt her breasts were swollen, too, and that it would be bound to show soon through the tight, black bombazine of her winter dress. When she undressed at night, her swelling shape was plain enough and when she passed her hand over her stomach, something kicked and moved, giving her the strangest feeling.

She had not felt like any breakfast this morning. The lumpy porridge and thick bread had turned her stomach. Cook had looked at her strangely, saying in an odd voice: 'Are you all right, lassie?'

She had said of course she was all right, but while doing the stair-rods the peculiar bearing-down feeling had returned. She looked around and no one else was about, so she climbed slowly to her own attic room and closed and locked the door. Water began to run down her legs and she was aware of this imperative need to bear down again. Quite calmly, she spread some newspaper over the floor and, removing her skirts and petticoat, took up a squatting position. The pains came fast and she held on to the iron bed-rail, clenching her teeth to stop herself from making any sound.

'Help me, dear God,' she prayed. 'Maw! Maw!' she

whispered, as though she was a little girl with a scratched knee.

The baby was born and she looked down at it, barely conscious. She drew in a juddering breath. It was a little girl. Very still and waxen. It did not open its eyes, or move, or cry. It was very small and wrinkled. Not fully grown, she realized, for she had missed only five of her periods. Dead, in fact. She put her head down to it, listening for any rasp of breath, for any pulse of life. She lay beside it for a long time, memorizing its face. The afterbirth came away and she left it beside the dead baby, getting up at last and moving away towards the ewer of water in the corner, to wash her hands and tidy herself up. Her overwhelming sensation was one of relief, of deliverance. She wrapped the baby up in newspapers and thought that she would take it into the country and lay it behind a hedge somewhere, with grasses and flowers over it. Only then did she sob a little. She felt light-headed and lay down on her bed. When Bessie came to knock anxiously at the door, she pleaded a severe headache. She did not tell Harry Tolley, nor her parents, then or ever, what had occurred. It was her secret. Between her and her Maker and the baby who had never moved.

When Kate heard that the Free Kirk minister at Dounhead was taking up a missionary appointment in South Africa, and that the new minister came from a church in Greenock, she had a moment of wild surmise that it might be James Galbraith.

Surely it would be too great a coincidence!

'What is the new minister's name?' she asked Mrs Chapman, who, as Wattie's wife, was privy to the information before the rest of the parish.

'Galbraith,' said Mrs Chapman. 'I understand he's a widower, with two daughters. His health is not very good, which is why he wants a smaller congregation. I believe he is a very scholarly man – '

Kate cut the conversation short and hurried home, her head buzzing. James Galbraith coming to Dounhead! Of course, he did not know she lived there and if he had known it probably would not have made any difference. But how could she go to his church when they had parted so bitterly?

She talked it over with Findlay, who declared that if she stopped churchgoing when the new minister came, it would only give rise to all sorts of wild speculation. Besides, she should exercise the Christian virtue of forgiveness and let James Galbraith see how she had risen above misfortune and made a new useful life with a husband and family.

Kate agonized over the position but found that once Galbraith had moved into the Free Kirk manse she could not keep away. She presented herself at the front door and a dour, elderly housekeeper showed her into James's study – a study furnished with the same heavy tomes, the same air of desiccated learning.

He looked at her long and earnestly as the door closed behind the old housekeeper.

'Mistress Fleming?' he vouchsafed. 'It is Kate Kilgour who once worked for me, is it not?'

She smiled and went forward and warmly shook his outheld hand.

'The mother of a large family now, Reverend.'

'How many, Kate?'

'Six, including young Jack.'

'Pray sit down.' He followed suit, putting his large, well-shaped hands together in steeple formation. He must be over fifty now, she thought, and both face and hair were grey, but the eyes were as fine as ever.

'I was sorry to lose touch with you,' he said. 'You gave me no chance to help.'

'Pride,' she said simply.

'Aha!' He smiled. He was genuinely pleased to see her, she thought. He said, 'I married soon after – soon after you'd gone. But my wife died ten years ago.'

'I am sorry. Miss Gillespie, was it?'

'Yes. Edith. She bore me two daughters, Honoria and Lilias. They have been a great comfort to me.'

The conversation that followed was one between old

friends. Kate told in detail most of what had happened to her since leaving Greenock, describing Findlay's illness, their struggle to keep their heads above water, the progress of her children.

When she rose to go, the minister held her hand between his. She saw that marriage and fatherhood had mellowed him, made him more human.

He said, with a note of sadness, 'You were a bonnie young woman when I knew you, Kate. And still are handsome! But I can see Care has laid its hand on you, and Poverty has stolen the bloom from your cheeks.'

'I am glad to see you again,' she responded. 'And I hope your own health will improve.'

He sighed heavily. 'I have failed to do much of what I set out to do, Kate. Since my wife's death, there has been a heaviness on my spirit – '

They stood facing each other, two people who could never be strangers to each other, and a current of warmth passed from one to the other. He touched her lightly on the shoulder, 'God bless you, my dear.' She gave him the bright, quick smile he had never quite forgotten, and left.

It seemed natural that she should go to James Galbraith when the worry over Jean became a problem that she and Findlay could not seem to solve themselves.

The girl came home oftener now, but there was a subtle change in her that neither parent could understand. She played a lot with the younger ones, sometimes as free and happy in their games as they were; but at other times sitting apart, her face shadowed and thoughtful.

When Kate taxed her, Jean simply said: 'I hate it there,' meaning the Tolley house and once, with tears streaming down her face, she pleaded to come home.

It was at a time when Findlay was laid off through strike action and Kate was half out of her mind with worry about money and food, so she persuaded Jean to remain in service, at least until she had found something else.

She half-hoped that the minister might take Jean into his own household, but he pointed out that his own two daughters were under-employed.

'Have you ever thought of arranging for her to emigrate?' Galbraith demanded.

Kate's face paled at the thought.

'It's only a suggestion,' said the minister reassuringly. 'It came to me because I have just arranged for a young orphan girl to go out on what they call a bride ship to a place called Victoria, off the west coast of Canada, and thence to another island called Salt Spring, where a young farmer wants a wife. She is quite prepared to face warlike Indians, like the Haida and the Bella Bellas, even cougar and wolves, not to mention the hazards of the crossing itself, because she wants above all a home and husband of her own. And you know that the Free Church has been largely responsible for the development of Otago in the South Island of New Zealand. Young female domestic servants are greatly in demand. In fact, many make good marriages and settle down to develop the land with their husbands. I could use my influence there.'

'I could never let Jean go,' sobbed Kate, upset by the very thought. But when the speaker at the women's weekly prayer meeting was a minister recently returned from Otago, she arranged for Jean to come over from Bellnoch on her night off and attend the talk with her. Even just to speculate over something as exciting as a new country might jog Jean out of her pale lethargy and, in the final analysis, if it meant a better life for her child, Kate knew she would find the strength somehow to let her go.

The two Galbraith girls welcomed the congregation at the prayer meeting. The elder, Honoria, was a solidly built, serious girl with her father's somewhat heavy features redeemed by an attractive smile; and the younger, Lilias, was a sprightly, fair-haired girl with an infectious giggle and a straightforward, friendly manner. Even though both possessed certain features and mannerisms that reminded her of their mother, Kate took to both girls and felt the need to encourage them in their new environment with a kindly word. In return, the girls appeared to wish to return this warmth and extend it to Jean and to Isa, who also came to the meeting.

'You know,' the speaker began portentously, 'that since New Zealand became part of the British Empire in 1840, we as a Church have been helping to colonize part of the South Island by transporting what we hope are whole communities, not just people of one station or one profession or one age or with one vision.

'It was with this in view that the Otago Association sprang into being, started by our founder George Rennie, developed by William Cargill, a brave veteran of the Peninsular War, and by Thomas Burns, a minister of our own Church.

'The first ships left Scotland for Dunedin in 1847 and Canterbury was founded in 1850. You may have heard of our Little Enemy in Canterbury! These are free-living Anglicans who have not always made our progress easy, but we have managed by the sale of land to found a system of public education which we hope will become a model for all New Zealand and *this*, I think, is one of our finest achievements.

'We have been very lucky. While Taranaki in the North Island was ravaged by war in 1861 and settlement there tailed off, in the South Island, Gabriel Read stumbled into a gully and scratched the surface of the great Tuapeka goldfield. Diggers came to this inhospitable part of the country, with its swift rivers, deep gorges, its heavy forests in some parts and deserted treeless wastes in other, and through the hot summers and bitter frosts of winter, they wrested the reluctant gold.'

He looked round at his listeners impressively.

'I repeat. We have been fortunate. Gold from the hinterland has meant spectacular growth in Otago. From an obscure Presbyterian outpost it has developed into the foremost commercial and industrial province, with plenty of land for settling, with wool fetching a good price, with all kinds of enterprises flourishing. We have settled many of our people there who would have been condemned to wretched drudgery in this country and who will have a far better chance of improving their lot by dint of hard work and perseverance than they ever would have here.

Young men who are willing to roll up their sleeves and build the roads to their own land . . . young women trained in the domestic virtues who will cook and clean and bring up the families . . .'

Kate stole a look at Jean's face and it was rapt, as though someone had just held up a beautiful picture before her from which she could not drag her eyes. As the speaker went on to talk of the sixty or so young single women whose passages were even now being arranged for the summer, Jean leaned forward with a look of such intensity and longing that Kate felt her heart swell and ache. She knew then that Jean would leave Scotland, that whatever ailed her could only be mended by a new beginning.

When it had been arranged that Jean would emigrate to New Zealand through the Otago Association, there was a pleasurable surprise in store for everybody. The ship in which she would sail would be the *Daniel Mackinlay*, Jack's own ship, and Jack was able to arrange for his mother to come down to Springfield Shed, South of Clyde, and see over the vessel while she was loading.

He deliberately made much of the elegant cabins fitted up to the taste of the few wealthy passengers who would be going out and not too much of what it would be like 'tween-decks for the other two hundred and fifty emigrants. With the single women like Jean aft, married couples amidships and single men forward, they would be packed like herring in a barrel. But he would naturally keep a wary eye on Jean who had refused his offer to travel out first-class. 'If I am going out to work like the other girls, I want to be with them,' she explained, and he had to admit the sense of that.

'Will the food be all right?' demanded Kate. She had seen the crude tins of meat and was doubtful that they would keep and she'd heard Jack say at other times that the firkins of butter went rancid after the tropics.

'We take on sheep, pigs and fowls for fresh meat,' Jack reassured her, again not revealing that this was mainly for cabin passengers and that in storms the livestock were sometimes lost. No point in worrying her unnecessarily!

But he showed her the casks which would carry plenty of fresh water and told her he had a good ship's cook who would provide an ample supply of biscuit.

'I'll tell you this, Mother,' he confided. 'All our passengers are well fed and after eighty or ninety days at sea, they arrive in New Zealand more robust in health than when they set out. Just look at me! Am I not a good advertisement for my own ship?'

His mother smiled. His cap was certainly at a jaunty angle and there was an exuberance about him that had been missing the last time she saw him. Maybe he was getting over Clemmie at last.

She went home a little more reassured about Jean's passage, but resolved to bake her plenty of good soda and treacle scones to start off with.

On a splendid summer day with a fast breeze, the good ship *Daniel Mackinlay* started on its voyage to New Zealand. Jean gazed at the Galloway Hills as they slipped away into the distance, remembering the feeling of her mother's lips on her cheek, the press of her father's hand. The younger ones had sobbed nearly the whole time and Jean's resolve had all but faltered when Tansy gave her a sampler she had worked, saying 'God Watches Over Us'. Under the 'o' in God was a little rusty stain where the child had pricked her finger and the 'us' was worked a little more unevenly than the rest, in the haste to finish.

In some ways, it was a relief to be under sail at last. Jean looked around the mixed bag of passengers. They were mostly Scots, with a sprinkling of Irish. She struck up an immediate friendship with a quiet girl called Nancy from the town of Hamilton, who like herself was going out to the Free Church hostel at Invercargill and hoped to get a good domestic post. Some of the girls were very boisterous and noisy and were courting the single males already.

Jack decreed that the steerage passengers should divide themselves into messes of ten. Each 'mess' had to keep its own quarters clean and tidy, get provisions, take the amount necessary to the galley to be cooked, serve it when ready and afterwards wash up. Jean and Nancy organized their 'mess' and the system worked well from the start.

During the first few days out, nearly everyone suffered from sea-sickness to some degree. After one very miserable day, Jean got used to the motion of the clipper and was never sick again, but it took poor Nancy longer and in the end she had to visit the ship's surgeon and get something to calm her stomach.

Quite soon, life on board the *Daniel Mackinlay* became not unlike life in the village of Dounhead – you got to know people and to like some and dislike others. It amused Jean to see the children go to school on deck, even sit exams and get prizes much as they would have done under Dominie Chapman.

When a young woman died in childbirth in the 'mess' next to hers, she was greatly upset, but Jack explained that on practically every voyage there were births and deaths and these had to be accepted and not brooded upon. The surgeon always hoped that births would outnumber deaths, as he got £1 a head for every soul he landed. Jack did not worry Jean by disclosing the fact that after the tropics, those with lung trouble (and there were always a fair number) sometimes found the high southern latitudes too cold and the sudden fall in temperature too much for their weakened bodies.

She deliberately did not see much of Jack, for there would have been complaints had she been seen to be treated differently from the other steerage passengers, but on several discreet occasions she visited him in his cabin and found his brotherly concern a great support.

It was she who mentioned Clemmie and the fact that he seemed to be forgetting her and it was then he made her privy to his great secret: Clemmie's marriage was not proving a success and he was meeting her again in secret, each time his ship put in to home port.

'She found out her mistake,' he said. 'She has got herself a husband in name only.'

'But it's wrong to see a married woman,' Jean protested, scandalized.

'She was mine first,' said Jack imperturbably. 'I regarded

her as mine always, and will do to the end.' And there the conversation ended, with Jack's insistence that Jean should tell no one and his statement that she was too young but would understand some day.

'I have been in love,' she protested, her face red.

Jack laughed indulgently. 'You'll find the right man some day, lass. But the man who weds my bonnie sister will have to be a good 'un.'

Good weather followed the *Daniel Mackinlay* most of the way. Crossing the Equator, the crew staged the elaborate ritual of bringing Neptune aboard and at other times there were concerts and music to keep the passengers amused. To Jean, sailing in the clipper began to seem almost a way of life, one that would never end. Days passed into weeks and the routine of getting meals, chatting with friends, talking about what New Zealand would be like, fell into a pleasant enough pattern, disturbed only once or twice by stormy weather when the meals from the galley went up in the air or overboard, and the children grew fractious. She had every evidence at such times of Jack's good seamanship and the way his crew respected him.

After eighty-five days, when the creaking rhythm of the ship, the sigh of its great sails, seemed to have entered blood and bone, land was sighted at Bluff Harbour, in the Southland, and a great wave of activity preceded disembarkation. Faces tensed with expectation, vows of friendship were exchanged and several couples who had met on board declared their intention of marrying, including Nancy, who had accepted a proposal from the surgeon's assistant.

Jean had fought off all attempts at wooing, although there had been plenty at the start. Her closed, alienated look and abrupt manner had taken effect and she had met all Nancy's gentle probings with a tight smile and a turn of the head.

Despite her apparent calm, the white showed through her knuckles as she stood at the ship's rail while the green fields and little buildings huddled round Bluff Harbour declared themselves ever more clearly. It was an alien land she was coming to and the day of disembarkation was a dull, cold one. 'Brief, reluctant summer,' the lecturer had said, she remembered. 'Cold, dark winters.' But the cold that was biting into her marrow was more than just the weather.

Jack had a quick word with her before he became too busy. 'We'll be taking wool on board for the return trip,' he reassured her, 'and that may take up to four months, for it comes in small schooners coastwise, and in wagons from miles inland. I'll be around, should you change your mind!'

She gave him that hard yet quivering look that had come to affect and worry him deeply.

'I'll never go back.'

'Write home.'

'I will.'

He kissed her. Her face was composed and tearless and he was dumbfounded to discover it was his throat that was dry. With a final hug and squeeze he had to leave her with her friends and attend to his own matters as master of the ship.

Everybody wanted to get off first, but Jean would not join in the crush and Nancy wanted another sight of her beloved before she left for Invercargill, so the two girls stood on deck and watched with fascination the hustle and muddle of disembarkation. A few families were being met by relatives or friends but many of the passengers stood on the quay looking helpless and lost, the enormity of their great decision to emigrate suddenly thrust upon them with all its force.

Jean had been watching a solitary figure on the quay, drawn to it by its stillness and air of being apart, and now she could see it was a red-headed man in heavy, dirty clothes, a cap at a careless angle over abundant hair, a red beard and whiskers tipped at an angle as the face scanned the decks of the ship.

'You there!' She realized he was looking and pointing at her.

Curiosity overcame her annoyance and she pointed to her chest with a 'moue' of interrogation.

The red-headed man nodded violently.

'I'm looking for a wife,' he called at her. 'You'll do. Will you marry me?'

Jean turned towards Nancy, her girl's sense of fun asserting itself, and the two burst into fits of giggling. Still the figure stood there, deliberate, immutable.

'You're the one I want,' it called up to Jean. 'I'll wait for you here.'

'Don't go to him,' Nancy said.

'Of course not,' said Jean, wiping tears of merriment from her eyes. Both girls knew that it was quite common for diggers to come down to the emigrant ships looking for wives. They had heard that there were only two women in the whole of Bluff Harbour at present and perhaps two hundred gold diggers fresh from the Hokitika goldfield.

Once on the quay, the girls discovered that transport which was to take them to the hostel was still on its way. They were to go to a house belonging to a member of the Otago Association and wait there for further orders.

Jean was never able to explain afterwards why she broke away from Nancy before they reached the house and ran back towards that lonely figure on the quay. It was, she tried to explain, as though a strong thread drew her, giving her no option.

Now she faced the man and saw that he was young, possibly about eighteen or twenty. His blue eyes in his grubby face were rimmed with dirt and fatigue.

'Will you come to the eating-house with me?' he begged her urgently. She found herself walking alongside him till they came to some rough-and-ready tea-rooms. Once inside, he asked her what she would like.

'You can have anything you like.'

She shook her head. 'Just tea.'

He began to speak rapidly in a hoarse but not unmusical Irish accent, dragging something from his hip pocket the while and spreading it out on the cloth before her eyes. She saw that it was gold nuggets and that other pockets about his person bulged with the same thing.

'There's plenty where they came from. Look, you won't

go hungry. There's land here for the asking – all you have to do is promise to work it. I want land, sheep, a farm. And a wife.' His blue eyes were suddenly pleading.

'I don't know anything about you,' she said.

'Does it matter? I knew the minute I cast eyes on you. I knew – that's her, I thought. The one I want. My mates have married girls from other ships, right ugly creatures some of them are. You're beautiful. You're right. We'll get married.'

As she explained it afterwards, a strange resolve was growing in Jean to do as he asked. She did not want to go back into service and clean other people's boots. She wanted the chance to become 'carriage-folk' herself. She wanted a challenge. She wanted to leave herself open to Fate. All the while, she was trying to imagine this man cleaned up, his beard trimmed, his clothes washed and pressed and his hair combed, and the end product, she realized, would not be unprepossessing, might even be quite handsome.

'What's your name?' she demanded.

'Pat,' he answered. 'Pat McGahey. And yours?'

'Jean. Jean Fleming.'

He looked as though he might fall down in a sleep at any moment, from exhaustion, but there was triumph and exultation on his face and a tender, proprietorial air that began to melt icebergs around Jean's heart. As she told it later, when his rough and calloused hand reached out and took hers, she could not bring herself to pull away. It seemed right, it seemed fateful, it seemed a desperate, breath-taking adventure.

She would go to Invercargill, as she had come out here with this intention.

But she would arrange to see Pat McGahey again and, if she became satisfied that her first impression of him was correct, she would throw her bonnet over the windmill. Challenge blew through her mind like a life-giving invigorating wind.

'So this is it,' said Jean.

They had found a rough, itinerant preacher of unspecified

denomination to marry them. During the service, the odour of rum had wafted over their heads. Pat had held her hand very fast, as though he were afraid she would run away, and at the last moment Nancy, her face long with foreboding, had come down from Invercargill to be best maid and had pushed a little posy of spring flowers into Jean's cold hands.

Now Jean stared at the small huddle of huts and tents that was to be her home, realization of what she had done thudding against her like a clout from her mother's hand when young. She had married a man she scarcely knew, a Catholic to boot, and this was what her dreams of being 'carriage-folk' amounted to as yet – three huts and two tents, grass and sheep, mud and rubble and a sharp, cold wind cutting through her shawl.

Behind them lay a rough track which Pat had filled in at the worst parts with stones and rubble. 'We have to make our own road,' he said, almost as though this were a matter of no account.

He saw her look of miserable uncertainty and said defensively, 'The sheep and the fences have to come first. But you will have a proper house.'

She pushed her way into the largest of the huts and looked around. There was a huge, ungainly stove and a truckle-bed. He led her over to the former and said with pride, 'It's got eight plates and a boiler on the side. Copper-bottomed.' He gave her a sidelong glance and said with delicacy, 'You'll be able to have a bath.' He did not add that the stove was murder to light, that it sulked on cold mornings and blew black smoke into the room unless cosseted and pampered with dry, precious wood.

A small wooden cross hung above the bed and in a corner she saw a blue-robed plaster Madonna. She said nothing. He had given her to understand that, like a number of the other Otago diggers who were Catholic Irish, he had left his faith behind in the cold, hard fight for simple survival.

Angrily he had told her about the farm back home in Ireland, the land broken up to share among succeeding children until the last plots were too small to grow much else but potatoes; about the stone and straw house no more than ten foot by ten, with one bed set in the wall and straw put out for visitors to lie on in their day clothes, then swept under the bed during the day till it was passed on to the animals. A desperate, poor life of 'champ' (mashed potatoes with scallions) and consumption, that he had been glad to leave behind forever.

At home she would have been alarmed by these evidences of Mariolatry, but here in this strange place they were oddly comforting, like going into the Daly household back home in the Rows. She smoothed the plaster folds on the Madonna's gown with her finger and asked, 'Who live in the other huts and tents?'

'The herds for the sheep and I've got three men on the fences and the road. They'll help me with the house. One's a good carpenter – he's made some doors and window-frames already.'

She stood, still not taking off her outdoor clothes. He said heartily, 'Sure you'll soon settle down. It'll take a wee while.' He came and touched her cheek with the back of his hand. 'I can't believe you're here. That I've got you.'

When they eased themselves into the truckle-bed that night, she realized with a shock that she was the more experienced of the two. His ardour was held in check by a dumbfounding shyness. The second shock was how much she wanted him. With his red-gold beard and his slender, strong physique, his clumsiness and pecking kisses, he aroused a passion in her she scarcely found acceptable. Overcome with a strange, fierce tenderness for his youth and ignorance, she passed on the extent of her own sexual knowledge.

It had been a mistake. In the morning, his blue eye next to her on the pillow held an accusatory stare that stopped her heart in her breast.

'Have you ever loved anybody else?'

Palpitatingly, she lied. 'No.'

Could he know, then, about the baby and Harry Tolley? Had he expected blood on the sheet, resistance, coyness?

She understood little about her body and its workings, only the promptings of her own wild, secret nature.

'Have you been with another man?'

He pulled her round to face him, but she buried her face in the bedclothes, crying 'No, no, no. There's been nobody, Pat. Nobody.'

Her fingers when she dressed were shaking. She had refused for so long to dredge up that anguish, so deep it could not be articulated. Yet she had been brought up to be honest and truthful and she was filled with a self-despising guilt that she had not told Pat the truth about herself. Well, of course he wasn't stupid. She had behaved last night like a wanton. He had guessed he was not the first and the fact that *he* was inexperienced made matters worse.

But there was a stubbornness in her, too. She had taken him without asking questions and he should take her, too, as she was. This hard country demanded hard compromise and no looking back. If he had wanted a saint, he should have said so.

With these thoughts in her mind, and a troubled truculence evident in his, they circled each other warily all the next day. Supper was taken formally, with the workmen brought in to share the meal, and afterwards in bed she took care that she would not make the first move. But it was a small bed, and they could not keep apart. Joyfully she knew him, his ribs, his curling beard, but she held her body in check as long as she could until he cried out, 'Kiss me! As you did last night.'

They would not go away, though, the question mark in his mind and the guilt in hers. They soured the days and there were nights when they lay like a bolster between them on the narrow bed.

She tried to please him. It was another mistake because he correctly read it as an admission of guilt. She cooked for everybody, she turned the lamentable hut into a spotless, cheerful haven; she even did men's work, hammering stabs into the unyielding ground, lifting and heaving stones to make the road more accessible to the carts and wagons bringing the materials for the house-building.

He was working hard, too. He rose early and was out with his men, absorbed in the hard, demanding work of getting the station on its feet. When he came in at night he was often too tired even to speak, but would sit after supper, smoking and staring into the hearth, every muscle aching with fatigue.

Catharsis came, not out of these moments of weariness, but forcing itself out of her troubled unconscious on a day when things had gone well.

The sheep-shearing was finished and he had taken the wool to Otago and got a good price for it. Elated, he came back with gee-gaws for the house and a length of sprigged muslin so that she could make herself a gown.

The muslin seemed to her very pure and beautiful, with its tiny sprigs of pale knots, and it was the first present she had ever had in her life.

'It'll suit you,' he told her, looking sideways in that way of his. 'I fancy seeing you in it in the summer.'

He had been thinking of how she would look when the warmer days came. The thought stuck in her throat, its tenderness too much for her to swallow. That night, sitting in the shadows, listening to him boast about buying the freehold for his land and becoming a station-owner, not a mere runholder, the muslin lay in her lap, soft and beautiful. When he bade her light the lamp, she found herself telling him, 'In a minute,' and then, soundlessly weeping, the tears slipping down her cheeks in silent torrents, babbling about her seduction in the linen cupboard in the big house at Bellnoch and the baby that had come and gone like a bad dream.

He said tonelessly in the dark, 'Why tell me now?'

'Because it had to come out between us. You had to know.'

'This was a good day. Now all the good has gone out of it.'

She appealed to him. 'You bring me presents. I can't take them and not have you know. It can still be a good day, Pat, if you tell me I'm forgiven.'

Silence. Then he said in a low voice: 'You had better go.'

'You don't mean that.'

He brought his fist down on the table, with such weight that the unlit lamp toppled over and they could hear the paraffin drip steadily on to the floor.

'Get out, I said. My God, I knew it. You had all the ways of trapping a man – '

'Calm yourself,' she said, 'before you say more you'll regret. I need never have told you. It belongs to the past, to a different me. Have you never done anything you're ashamed of? I came out here with the slate wiped clean.'

For answer, he strode round the room like a man bereft of his senses, lit a candle, picked up her clothes and the few other items she had brought with her and threw them into her bag with all the force he could muster.

'You'll think other of me in the morning,' she said, between dry lips. 'Please, Pat.'

He threw her shawl at her feet. She picked it up and put it round her shoulders, wandering to the door as though in a daze. She opened the door and her bag came sailing past her into the night.

She left it where it lay and began to stumble down the half-made road in the moonlight. She did not know where to go and she didn't much care. It was the movement away from his rage that was important.

Oh, why had she told him? She could not answer that question. Why had she thought that because he brought her a present, he would love her enough to understand?

Vaguely she knew the way to Otago. But once their own road petered out, she found herself wandering in unfamiliar fields instead of the wide track that would have taken her nearer town. How had she done that? She looked back and judged that a weak light she saw twinkling on the hill was from the station. It seemed immeasurably far away.

She was no longer weeping. Something of her true stoic nature reasserted itself. She even began to feel quite at home in the dark. She no longer waited to hear him pound after her on horseback. It was not going to happen. The best she could hope for would be a bush, a cranny in the landscape, a bothy, against which she could crouch till daylight. She found a bush eventually and drew her shawl about her. She was past feeling cold.

She awoke to a dull, grey light and the sound of slithering hooves beside her. Numb with cold, she tried to struggle to her feet and run away. But Pat had dismounted and caught hold of her easily. From his weary, distraught face she knew he had been up all night.

He rubbed her hands, without saying a word, then brought brandy from his hip pocket and made her gulp some down.

'I'm not coming back to you,' she said gamely.

'You're my wife,' he gritted. He pushed her on to the old grey horse and leaped up in front. Neither spoke till they got back to the station. One of the hands gave a curious stare as they dismounted.

In the hut, she stood defiantly, sagging with weariness, and said clearly, 'You'll never do that to me again. And I shall never apologize again for what I am.'

'So be it,' he said soberly. Then he added, 'You'll get used to my temper.' It was the nearest he came to apology.

In the days to come, she did not know if the marriage would work out. She saw less than ever of him and at the weekends he joined in hard-drinking bouts with the men, sometimes making love to her afterwards in a perfunctory fashion that she found humiliating.

She could get a domestic post somewhere. She might save enough eventually to go back home to Scotland. She pined for the shops of Bellnoch and for the warmth and closeness of her family.

Then, as on the day of the sprigged muslin, came an incident that changed things once again. It concerned the carpenter, Bill Lloyd, a taciturn, rude man who never answered when she spoke to him. The house was nearing completion and he brought a bill to the hut for Pat to sign, for materials to finish off the kitchen.

Jean noticed that as always when dealing with paper matters, Pat turned away and pored over them in seclusion. This time, some urgent matter took him outside and the paper was left behind. She saw with a shock that he had not signed his name but instead made a shaky, barely intelligible cross. His mark. So that was why he had signed the marriage papers after her, and hurriedly stuffed them into a pocket.

Something made her con the paper carefully now and she realized that Pat was signing for more materials than they could ever use. Lloyd was cheating him.

Angrily she told him what she had discovered. He tackled Lloyd and after an acrimonious argument the man left.

That night, she said without preamble: 'I shall teach you to read.'

His face coloured, and he spat into the grate.

'You'll get my supper,' he returned. 'You'll do what *I* say.'

She ignored his bluster. When he had supped and washed, she brought a paper and pencil to the table and wrote out the letters of the alphabet.

She edged her chair round till she was next to him, pointing out the letters one by one, printing his name, so that he became interested in spite of himself.

On the following nights, she read to him each evening, two lines only, from the local paper, and made him repeat them, word for word. He began to pick up a word here and there and sometimes she would catch him puzzling over a headline, his lips moving as he struggled to put the syllables together.

He had difficulty at first in differentiating between 'b' and 'd'.

'Look,' she explained. 'This one, "b", has a big balloon of a belly in front of him. Balloon and belly both begin with "b". Whereas this one, "d", starts to say "door". Look how he bends and pushes against that straight line, that door.'

He looked at the letters and saw what she was getting at. Then an irresistible, childish merriment rose up in him and he burst out laughing. She joined in and the sound of her laughter, girlish, light and innocent, dissolved some harshness he had still harboured towards her.

She kept him at it and the simple task brought them closer, almost as though they were children together. Each would reminisce about childhood and family and the dim outlines of each other's lives became filled in and coloured.

She would hold his big, balled fist and lead it over the outline of the words she was teaching him. When he had achieved something difficult, a freckled grin of satisfaction spread across his face and she would feel a catch in her throat that was close to a sob.

One night, into their closeness he threw the sudden challenge: 'What was he like, that one you were fond of, back there?'

'Nothing like as good as you.'

The next day, he said, 'If I had him here, I'd break every bone in his body.'

He came over to her, as she was dishing up his supper, and put his arms round her waist.

'He hurt you,' he said, his blue eyes so close to her face she almost drowned in their fierce and troubled expression.

The pain loosened inside her, dissolved.

She said steadily, shaking the bacon in the pan, 'It's past. It's you and me now, isn't it?'

'Come on,' she invited, after they had eaten. 'Read me something from the paper.'

He took the paper out of her hands and lifted her, pulled her, out of her chair and into his arms. They made love with all their clothes on, because they could not wait, and later in bed they made love all over again, and he was her master and husband and lover and family, all rolled into one.

It was the next letter home that finally eased the worry about Jean in Kate's mind. Joy in her new life fairly bounced off the pages and furled like a flag from her signature.

Kate read the letter to Findlay, her pleasure evident from the careful sheaving of the pages, the slow savouring of each sentence. With a mother's prescience, she knew what the next piece of news would be. Sure enough, with the house finished, the early prospect of Pat buying the freehold for the land, the drapes up in the parlour and a carpet on its way from Dunedin, came the information of a baby on the way, with all the usual hallmarks of parental impatience over whether it would be a boy or girl, red-haired or dark.

Kate had had many misgivings about her daughter's mixed marriage, misgivings shared by Findlay, but now the note of happiness in the letters was such as would take a harder heart than Kate's to resist.

She no longer worried quite so much about Jean. But she still missed that one bright face at the Sunday tea and she still thought she heard, occasionally, the sound of Jean's foot on the step and her young, eager voice describing the scope and grandeur of Mrs Tolley's petticoats.

Chapter Ten

'Here! Wash your hands!'

Isa met her brother Duncan at the door and pushed the rough sacking towel towards him. His look of bafflement increased as Tansy and Paterson burst out laughing and Isa indicated the water ready in the wooden bine by the window.

'Miss Nightingale says you have to pay attention to cleanliness,' she averred. She opened the window above the bine and a gust of cold air swept into the cosy room. 'And she says fresh air is important.'

'Who gave her that book?' demanded Duncan truculently, referring to the sevenpenny edition of *Notes on Nursing for the Labouring Classes* by the heroine of the Crimea.

'The dominie,' cried Tansy.

'Then I'll burn it,' teased Duncan, picking the offending volume off the dresser and pretending to throw it on the fire.

'Sit down and take your tea,' roared Findlay, above the hubbub. 'Your mother's had it ready this while back.'

Duncan took his meal from the corner of the table. He always ate as though half on the wing elsewhere and eating a necessary nuisance. The potatoes and meat had crisped up deliciously from keeping hot on the hob and although she had eaten earlier, Tansy eyed the plateful greedily and pinched half a potato when Duncan wasn't looking. It burnt her mouth and Isa went into fits of silent laughter at her efforts to conceal the fact. They were in what Kate called one of their daft moods, ready to giggle at anything, and Findlay's patience with them in danger of running out.

Duncan ignored the girls' silliness. He had other things on his mind and he had been hoping against hope that tonight he would find his father in a good mood. In the years since his father's worst drinking bout, when he had wrestled with him to get the hot coal away from him, there had been estrangement between them, born mainly of Findlay's humiliation. Sensing this, Duncan had known it was up to him to make friendly overtures and somehow rebuild his father's self-esteem, but it was not easy. He was tired of rebuffs and angry over the unspoken implication that he, Duncan, was in some way 'guilty' too. Guilty of what? All he had tried to do was protect his mother and the other children.

'I hear, Faither,' he began, 'that the men may be coming out again on strike.'

Findlay looked at him ironically. 'And where did you hear that?'

'The word is that Jamie Anderson was hurt in a fall last week and the men are pressing for a full examination of the seam.'

'And what would you know about pits?' demanded Findlay harshly. 'Sitting up in your fancy wee bit office all day, with your new-fangled pen and nib – '

'Findlay!' protested Kate.

'I know I don't know anything about pits,' Duncan conceded with controlled calm. 'That's why I'm asking you.'

'Gang down the pit yourself,' said Findlay. 'Find out what it's like to crawl on your belly. And then think yourself fit to write about the miners.'

The boy stood up, white-faced with anger. With his dark, curling hair and new moustache and whiskers, his piercing dark eyes, he looked somehow out of place in the rough homeliness of the miner's cottage. His boyish looks were turning into lean and thoughtful, near-elegant manhood and the strong force of intellectual vigour emanating from him was almost tangible.

'All right, I will,' he breathed furiously. His fists were clenched and Kate put out a restraining hand towards him.

'Your father's tired,' she remonstrated.

'He's always tired,' Duncan raged. 'It's become a habit with him. I have another name for it. Apathy. He doesn't care. He's forgotten everything he preached when he was younger. Just give him his beer and his 'baccy – '

'By God.' Findlay was on his feet, unbuckling his pit belt. 'Ye tasted this when you were a laddie, and I'm not too tired to let you have it again.'

'No good, Faither,' shouted Duncan, beside himself. 'If silence fails, try violence. No good. You'll listen to me. You listen to the coterie. You preach the brotherhood of man. Am I exempt from that brotherhood?'

Findlay sat down heavily. 'Calm yourself, man,' he growled.

'You do nothing but sneer at my ideas, yet when I try to talk to you about them you rise and go out. What is it about me, then? Am I a leper? Is it because I've never gone down the stinking pit? I thought you wanted to keep us out of it. But all right, if you want me to see what it's like, I'll go down. If you want an earnest of my intent, I'll go down. Will that please you?'

'Duncan,' Kate commanded. 'Take a hold of yourself.'

He threw her a blind, ignoring glance. This was between him and the man who had fathered him. For the moment, no one else existed for him in this room.

'What's brought this on?' asked Findlay. He was feeling his way across an abyss, tugged on all sides by a passion to strike, to curb, to conquer the wild young presence opposite him.

'You're supposed to run a lodge down there,' said Duncan bitterly. 'A union. Yet that greedy old man up at Bellinch – yes, I know, Mother, it's old Balfour I'm talking about, we all know he's bought out Macnicol at last, now his other pit's mined out – that greedy old man gets five thousand pounds a year while his men sweat in fear of the roof coming down on them, and take home less than a pound a week.

'Did you know he owns a chemical factory at Bellnoch, too, where the men and women work a twelve-hour shift with no meal-hour?

'And that he's talking about setting up a pit-shop and giving some of the wages in tokens so that you'll have to spend there and so that more and more money can flow into his bulging pockets?'

'Aye, aye,' said Findlay, more calmly at last. 'You tell me nothing I don't know already. And now you can listen to me. Jamie Anderson lost his job at the pit because he put too much into the union. Neither him nor his two brothers could get work for years, just because he once stood up to old Macnicol. I got him his job back and his wife knows what it is again to put food into her children's mouths. He doesn't want this strike, he wants work the minute he's well enough to take it, and I can guarantee he'll get it.'

It was Duncan's turn to sneer.

'Kid glove treatment,' he said. 'Where will the unions get, with kid glove treatment?'

'Everywhere,' replied Findlay. 'We'll make representation to old Balfour about that bad seam. He has his faults, but he's safety-minded. He'll listen.'

Duncan was about to interrupt but Findlay quietened him with a downward wave of his hand.

'Learn this. We don't want revolution in this country. It's not our way. We want change by constitutional means. Read your John Stuart Mill and learn how we have to guard individual freedom even while we seek collective security. A fine edge to tread. But it's the only way.'

Kate looked from one engrossed face to the other, feeling the beginning of a great content. They were so alike, these two, yet neither could see it. She hid a smile.

'You sent me to church,' Duncan was saying. 'You dinned the precepts of Christianity into me, but now I don't want to hear it preached any more. I want to see it practised. I want the communal and collective ownership of all the means of production, distribution and exchange. I want a *Labour* party that will truly represent the toiling masses, that will rejoice in the common man and not put on a smug, respectable Liberal face – '

'Aye, you want heaven in the twinkling of an eye,' returned Findlay. 'And it'll not happen that way. It'll happen when we get a Royal Commission into the trade unions, when we are legally recognized and our funds protected. It'll happen when working men get the vote in the towns and peaceful picketing is allowed by law. Mind, I said peaceful picketing.'

'Well,' said Duncan, 'you've made up my mind for me. I'm coming down the pit too, to see what it's like. You'll jeer no more about me being a writing man.'

'You'll do no such thing,' cried Kate. 'What about Maclaren? He's taught you all you know and now you're going to walk out on him. All for a silly whim.'

Duncan gazed at her. 'So you think it's a whim, do you? You don't know a point of principle when you see one.'

'Aye, aye, what's the principle, then?' asked Findlay, enjoying himself.

'Too subtle for some,' answered Duncan. 'But I'll try and explain. Listen, Mother, for I'll not set it out again. You know Maclaren's been pleased with my work on the paper?'

Kate nodded.

'He's been at Wattie Chapman about getting me into the university at Glasgow. Would you like a son who was a lad o' pairts, Mother? A son at the university?'

'We could never afford to send you, son. You know that.'

'There's ways,' said Duncan decisively. 'Wattie Chapman could find me a sponsor and I could go there and learn fine ways. How to flick my tail coat and sit down quickly before I crumpled it. How to kiss the ladies' hands and the bosses' arses.'

'Mind your tongue!' said Findlay savagely, while Isa and Tansy fell about, whooping with desperate giggles.

'But I'll not go, Mother. Now try to understand why. Because it would separate me from the people I want to help. I don't want elevating on my own. I'll wait till the time comes when every mother's son can get the same chance. Do you understand what I'm trying to say?'

Kate nodded. 'I'm not thick,' she reprimanded.

'Aye, well, much good you'll do down the pit,' rumbled Findlay. 'I doubt you'll have the stamina for it. It's not the same as pen-pushing at all.'

Duncan gazed despairingly at his father. The goading was deliberate. He knew well enough Findlay's respect for the written word. Pen-pushing? Was that all his father thought of his attempts to rally Radical thought through his articles in the *Clarion*?

The pain of rejection exploded inside his head in a primal rage and he let out a savage bellow of impotence. With a sweeping gesture he sent his dinner plate spinning off the table. He saw his mother put her hand up to her mouth apprehensively, and even in his fury, the rough, coarse skin of her work-worn hands touched him unbearably. This, too, was what the struggle was about.

The girls had stopped larking and were looking at him consideringly, as if he were a mad bull who might suddenly lower his horns and charge.

'You're a bunch of ingrates and heathens, the lot of you!' he yelled. He could scarcely see the door-latch as it rattled under his trembling fingers. He turned as he went out and sought Kate's face. 'I don't mean you, Maw,' he added. The door rattled behind him.

'Aye,' said Findlay laconically, the sparkle of the argument still lighting his face and making him look years younger. 'Aye, there goes a Christian for you. One who loves his fellow-man.'

As he reached the end of the pit row, past the Daly house, Duncan became aware of a shadowy figure standing up against the wall.

His present mood was to pass by without acknowledgement, but a sound from the figure stopped him in his tracks. It was a deep sob, the kind that grated the rib-cage. She'd always cried in that way, his playmate in many a childish game, but now someone he saw little of: Josie Daly.

'Josie?' he said experimentally.

So caught up in whatever matter was affecting her was she, that she had been unaware of anyone near. Now he saw pale wrists rubbing the end of her shawl across her face and heard another of those devastating, shuddering sobs.

'What's the matter?'

Sob.

'Josie? You in trouble?'

'Go away.'

At the fierceness of her bidding, he began to obey, but then turned back again.

'I haven't seen you for a long time, Josie. How's life in service?'

'What life?' At least she had stopped weeping. He peered into a tangle of red hair and shawl fringe and saw two pale grey eyes in a white, grubby face. Josie gave a mighty sniff.

'Your Jean worked for them, too,' she whispered vehemently. 'The rotten Tolleys in Bellnoch. She hated them, too. I think I'll emigrate as well. I hate this rotten country!'

Duncan almost smiled in spite of himself. Someone besides himself in trouble. He tugged Josie towards the gable end of the Rows so that they would not be seen if someone came out.

'You just left your job?'

She nodded.

'Frightened to go in and tell them?'

Another nod. 'Old Daly'll kill me.'

He made no comment on her strange way of referring to her father. If it sounded less than daughterly, it wasn't surprising. Old Daly in his cups knocked both his wife and daughters about.

'Why did you leave?'

'That rotten blackguard of a son won't leave the maids alone. I blackened his eye and the mistress sent for me. "We can't have violence in this house," she says.' Josie eyed Duncan's half-raised eyebrow, the beginning of an urchin grin tugging at her features.

'She looked in my apron pocket and found a scone I'd pinched. "This is the end, Daly," she says. "We cannot have dishonesty." So I said, "I was hungry. You don't give us enough food. And I know you buy the diseased beasts from the farm for us servants." "Leave at once," she says, and throws my tin box out the back door.' Josie gave a sigh. 'So here I am. What do I do next?'

'I've just had an idea,' said Duncan. He looked her up and down. She was thin, her clothes verging on the raggedy, and none too clean. But she had a sharp intelligence. Why should someone as bright as Josie always be consigned to serving others less worthy than herself? He saw himself as her benefactor and the thought softened some of the anger left in him from the confrontation with his father.

'Would you like to work in an office, Josie?'

'Would I what?'

'Listen.' He explained that he was going down the pit and that Alf Maclaren would be needing someone to help him on the *Clarion*. The idea was growing in him that he could still write for Alf – almost as much as he ever did, for writing was something that came naturally to him, almost as naturally as breathing. But Alf would still need practical help with the paper and he was sure that Josie with her quick, sharp mind was just the person for him.

Josie was willing. She began to try to talk him out of going down the pit, but he brushed her arguments aside.

'I'll see Alf Maclaren,' he promised her. 'I'll fix it up. Now you go in there and tell them you are not going back into service. Say it firmly, and that you've got another job in prospect. If old Daly tries to hit you, tell him – tell him you'll fetch me.'

For once, she could think of nothing to say. He thought she was probably going to start weeping again, so he pushed her hastily in the direction of the Daly doorstep.

'Go on,' he urged her. 'Stick up for yourself, Josie. You can do it. You know you can.'

'You shouldn't have taunted him, Faither,' said Paterson. He had been trying to read in the corner by the fire while the argument had raged. While he often fought with Duncan himself, he felt vaguely there was some imbalance, of love as well as hate, in Findlay's attitude towards Duncan, and the feeling made him uncomfortable, critical.

'He thinks he knows it all,' said Findlay. 'Just like you.'

'At least we're ready to learn,' retorted Paterson, still calmly.

'You see,' Findlay appealed to Kate. 'They would challenge a father's authority. By God,' he swore on a rising note, 'if they'll not listen to my word, they'll get out of this house.'

'I intend to,' said Paterson. 'I'm going to America just as soon as the war there is over. What is there here in this country but greed on one hand and blind ignorance on the other?'

He often adopted this tone of superior, scolding scorn, delivered in a quiet, half-jocular vein, and they did not take him seriously. But as he, too, rose and went out, carrying an exercise book with him, his heart was as full of a fierce, unspecified anger as was Duncan's.

He didn't tell them at home about his night-school work, for they never expressed any but the most cursory interest in 'Paterson's drawings'. No use trying to tell them that he was studying locomotive design, that he had taken some of his work to head office in Glasgow and they had expressed themselves as astounded over his grasp of technical detail.

But where was the company that would employ him, thin and undersized as he was, with his built-up boot and his shabby clothes? He spoke too quietly and diffidently, in a rough, country dialect, and he was never able to put his ideas over in the right words. Yet they were all there, simmering away, and if the railway companies in Britain employed too many bosses' relatives, maybe in America it would be fairer and more equitable, and there was bound to be a great expansion of railways there when the war was over.

He was going to the young people's prayer meeting in the church hall, taking his exercise book with its notes and drawings in it to study while he waited for everybody else to arrive.

He was half-hoping Honoria Galbraith would come and sit by him this week again and that he'd feel confident enough to show her his ideas. Last week, he had had a try at explaining railway gauges to her and she had picked it all up very quickly. This week, he'd try and tell her the difference between outside and inside engine cylinders and air some of his theories about larger boilers.

When she did come and sit by him he forgot about his notebook in the stir and excitement of his blood. He noticed the set of her broad bosom, the pale purity of her skin, the way her even teeth caught her lower lip when she laughed. And when she bent near him there was the faint, musky scent of lavender and rosewater.

'Where's your brother?' she asked.

'Gone off somewhere.'

'I think he's a very poetic young man,' said Honoria, blushing. 'It must be wonderful to be a writer – '

'I've brought my drawings to show you,' said Paterson.

'I write a little,' said Honoria, confidingly. 'Oh, just poems that I show to no one.'

'You're beautiful.' The words burst from him. 'You don't need to be clever.'

She looked away from him and then dropped her head and would not meet his gaze.

'What's the matter?'

'I'm *not* beautiful. If anyone has looks, it's Lilias. She's the pretty one. I'm supposed to be the clever one.'

'All wrong,' said Paterson. 'You're both. Pretty and clever. Can I walk you home tonight?'

She nodded imperceptibly, knowing her father would not approve. But they slipped away quickly at the end of the meeting, both a little overcome by this first excursion with the opposite sex and Honoria positively uneasy by the time they reached the manse gate.

'Would you show my poems to your brother?' demanded Honoria. 'I would like to know what he thinks of them.'

Paterson scarcely heard her. His blood was pounding in his ears and he wanted more than anything in the world to kiss her.

'I wish I didn't limp,' he blurted out. In the yellow light of the street gas lamp, Honoria saw the gleam in his eyes and said with simple truth, 'It doesn't matter, Paterson. It's what goes on inside that matters.'

He came closer and his strong young arms went around her. He had to tilt his head up slightly to kiss her because she was taller than he but it was still very satisfactory. Honoria moved away with a little gasp, her crinoline dipping in her agitation.

'Will you be my lass?' said Paterson.

'We're too young,' she protested. More firmly, she added, 'I asked you if you would show my poems to Duncan.'

'Do you like him better than me?'

'I don't know.'

'It won't be any good. You're my lass.'

'Paterson!' She was really scandalized now. 'My father would kill me if he knew we were standing here, talking like this.'

'All right. See you next week.'

'I'll bring the poems.'

'You're in danger of becoming a right young prig,' said Alf Maclaren furiously. He faced Duncan across his littered desk in the tiny *Clarion* office.

'I've made up my mind,' said Duncan sullenly.

'You'll risk your neck going down a rotten hole of a pit that from all accounts isn't safe – '

'Will you listen?' demanded Duncan, goaded. 'If I'm to be a radical politician and improve the lot of the folk I live amongst, I shall live as they live. It's not that I don't enjoy writing – I do. But it's a dangerous ivory tower. Can you not understand that?'

'I could understand if you were a young ox with no brains or education. But to be offered the university – '

'I'm not ungrateful. Maybe one day . . . It's just that as of now, I feel this is what I want to do. I won't stay down forever.'

'Why go down at all?' pursued Maclaren wearily. Duncan indicated with a brusque gesture that he wasn't prepared to go over it all again.

Alf Maclaren stared at him. He was often puzzled by this lad. A strange mixture. Brought up a Christian but genuinely convinced that churchgoing wasn't enough, bursting with radical ideas and a strange violent sensitivity, as though possessed of a skin too few. He had a powerful aura, too, that went beyond character or intelligence and made you listen.

Alf sighed. There was no doubt it would suit him in

some ways if Duncan worked for him on a voluntary basis, taking no money, and he took this Josie Daly girl on for half what he'd paid Duncan. The *Clarion* at the moment struggled from issue to issue. He'd pay Duncan for his contributions once things started swinging upwards again.

'All right. I'll go along with this new arrangement. But mind – I want your copy in by Thursday night at the latest.'

'Don't worry,' said Duncan. He gave a relieved grin. 'Is my copy ever late?' He moved restlessly about the room. 'I wish I could make you understand, Alf. I want to be *involved*. If I was in London at this moment, I would be out in the streets with the trade union junta and the people demonstrating against the Russians and the way they're trying to crush the Polish revolt.'

'Aye,' said Alf drily. 'Well, how about writing me something soon on the Master and Servant Act?'

'You mean, strikers being threatened with prison if they refuse to go back to work?'

'Yes. Strikes should only be undertaken as a last resort – you could say – but men should have the right to withhold their labour, in a just cause.'

'I'll do it now. Before I go home.'

'Tomorrow will do. Tell me, what does your father think about this decision of yours?'

'He's against it.'

'So?'

'So it can't be helped.' He wouldn't let Alf see the hurt in his expression, but the older man sensed it. He put a hand on Duncan's shoulder.

'Allow for a man's weariness, laddie. Not many men in their forties can still hew coal, as he does.' Alf donned coat and hat, ready to go home. 'And remember youth's the time for a bit of fun. Have you not found yourself a nice lass yet? What about this lassie Daly?'

'Josie?' Duncan laughed incredulously. But Alf had unwittingly struck home, and as the two men locked up then walked together down the village street, Duncan's mind swung away at last from the trauma of the past few hours and into his mind swam the fair, laughing image of Lilias Galbraith.

Josie was – well, Josie. Sharp elbows, spitfire tongue, one of the brood next-door with whom he'd fought and played and grown up. He would always have a sense of loyalty towards her, remembering the times without number he'd seen her shoved out of doors, her arm up to her head to ward off parental clouts, and the quick, invincible spirit that bounced back for more.

But Lilias was his star. He identified her with everything that was good and gentle and womanly. A far cry from Josie's gruff, defensive speech was her light, beautifully-modulated voice. No one said his name as she did. He played it over in his head. 'Duncan. Duncan.' As she said his name, so he wanted to be. He wanted to throw himself at her feet, gather her into his arms, place her on a pedestal and at the same time possess her utterly. As his metaphors grew more wildly mixed in his head, he thought despairingly that he would never have the courage to tell her his feelings. But how he longed to hear her say she understood him, in all his complexities and contradictions. He would be a giant with such love.

He had taken to walking past the manse at night, gazing up at the bedroom windows, trying to imagine which room was hers, and envisaging her plaiting her long, flaxen locks or writing up her diary. When they met at church or prayer meeting, he wished he could respond to her engaging, teasing manner, but so often his replies made him sound like some sullen country oaf, instead of the wit and intellectual he hoped.

If only she could know about the poems he had written to her! He carried them about with him always. They would show her what he was really like. Tonight, emboldened by the bravado of his decision to go down the pit and faintly needled by Alf's remarks about girls, he made up his mind he would try to get the poems to her.

He wondered if he could leave them in a safe place somewhere in the manse garden and then send an anonymous note to her, somehow, telling her where to look. He would not sign them yet. Let her puzzle for a while. And when the right moment came, he would reveal all.

At the low wall surrounding the manse he suddenly found that night the niche for the envelope of poems. A crevice between two large greystone boulders, overgrown with moss and primroses, provided a hiding-place of the right romantic calibre.

And having gone this far, he managed to scribble a brief note telling her where to look. Greatly daring, he intended to creep up the drive and put it through the manse door.

He had just finished scribbling but had not added her name, when a light breathless voice sounded behind him and he turned to see Honoria Galbraith.

'Duncan!' she greeted him. 'Did Paterson mention my poems, then? I happened to look from my window and saw you hankering about. Look, I've brought them for you to look at.'

She handed him over a package tied in blue ribbon and he saw she was wearing thin pumps and the lightest of shawls. As he put out his hand for the package, the note he had been holding fluttered to the ground from his nervous fingers. Honoria picked it up and boldly read it.

'You've written some for me!' she breathed.

Duncan stood, stricken to the spot, wondering how this disastrous outcome of all his plans had come about. What was the girl talking about? Paterson had never said anything to him about poems, but Honoria, he thought somewhat uncharitably, was just the kind of girl who *would* write bad sentimental verse and think it worth putting alongside Tennyson's 'Maud'. Now the infuriating female was running her hand along inside the wall and had found the poems intended for her sister. But how could he tell her that? Her rather plain face was glowing under the yellow street lamp and he felt a grudging start of feeling towards her, almost of understanding. She was transformed by joy, almost beautiful. So could it be that she had some secret sentiments towards him, just as he had towards Lilias? The realization made him kind.

'Will you tell me if you think they have any literary aptitude?' he said quickly. 'They were not written with anybody – anybody special in mind.' ('Please forgive me, Lilias,' he prayed.) 'They embody the sentiments of *any* young man when he meets the object of his devotion.'

Honoria held the packet to her bosom.

'Oh, I shall treasure your confidence in me, Duncan,' she assured him. 'I must fly now. Father mustn't know I've been out.' And lightly in her heel-less pumps she fled back towards the forbidding shadow of the manse.

Nonplussed, Duncan stumped off towards home. What a mix-up of a night it had been. And now for this to happen! It wasn't that he didn't like Honoria and he felt, obscurely, that she might be a better listener than Lilias, more perceptive and, perhaps, kinder.

But it was Lilias's laughing, teasing face that seemed to go before him on the dark road towards the Rows. Like a will-o'-the wisp. He wanted her gaiety, her laughter, the other side of his own serious and sometimes forbidding nature.

A hootie owl sent its melancholy notes into the murky night air. Duncan managed a small, rueful smile to himself. He was not alone, it seemed.

The Widow Mackinnon bobbed her way down the back of the Rows towards the Fleming cottage. She had walked from Dounhead Station in the fine, smirring rain and her petticoats were as damp as her feet, but she scarcely knew it, so great was her agitation.

Aware of faces registering an interest in her passage from the other cottage windows, she kept her gaze down till she came to Kate's home then gave a loud, peremptory knock.

Kate had been nodding over the fire, taking a rest before the younger children came in from school and she would have to start the business of the evening meal. She rose red-faced and sleepy, pushing the greying tendrils from her eyes as she went to the door.

'Mistress Fleming?'

Kate nodded.

'You'll remember me? I am Mistress Mackinnon, who was young Jack's landlady.'

Kate's face broke into a welcoming smile and she opened the door wide to the wall, as she had been taught by her grandmother as a little child. 'Come in,' she invited. 'You are very welcome. But what a poor day you have chosen! Come and warm yourself by the fire. I'll make you a hot cup of tea.'

The widow sat straight-backed on the edge of Findlay's chair.

'I would not say no. I am perished to the bone.'

Kate put the kettle on the hob, and stirred the fire. She looked curiously at her visitor. Her face was pale and the nervous working of her hands betrayed distress.

'Is there something the matter?' she demanded.

'Plenty the matter!' Mistress Mackinnon burst out. She broke down and drew a scrap of lace from her sleeve edge to put to her eyes. 'Your son has got my daughter in a fine pickle. I don't know what's to be done about it. Really I don't.'

'Well, suppose you start at the beginning,' said Kate, composedly enough, although her heart was racing.

'I don't know what went wrong between them,' said the Widow Mackinnon. 'I always thought that Jack and Clemmie would marry, after all the years of understanding between them. But he left it too late. He chose the sea to her. And she is a proud girl. That is why she married Hamish McNaughton in the end.'

Kate said, a little sharply, 'But this is all history – '

'That's not the end on it,' said Mistress Mackinnon. 'Hamish is a good man, but he is twelve years older than Clemmie, and too long tied to his mother's apron strings. He has made no sort of a husband to her.' Her face coloured up like a peony. 'We have both been wed, Mistress Fleming. Do I need to tell you any further?'

'No, no,' vowed Kate hastily. She was embarrassed too.

'The upshot is that Clemmie has been writing to your Jack, and he to her, and they have been meeting in secret every time he comes home.'

'He told me he would never love anyone else,' Kate said faintly.

'That's as may be. The fact is, she is a married woman, and she owes loyalty to her poor, sick husband.'

Kate made the tea. She was glad of the occupation, because she did not know what to say next.

'I do not see what I can do,' she offered lamely, handing the widow a steaming cup.

Clemmie's mother took a sip and said, with a calm that was rather more alarming than her previous tears: 'It will come to divorce and disgrace. She will be an outcast woman and I, her mother, the widow of a minister of the Church, will never be able to hold my head up again.'

'Does her husband know?' demanded Kate.

'There's the nub of it. He found a letter from your son. But you have not yet heard it all. There is a child on the way. I think I have said enough to indicate whose it may be.'

'You mean – ?'

'Yes. I mean your Jack.'

Now Kate's face matched the widow's in grimness. They sat in silence on either side of the fireplace.

'I have been to consult my lawyer,' said Mistress Mackinnon, a little more evenly. 'He says that in – in divorce matters, Scotland is ahead of England. I would not know. It appears that up till only six years ago, a woman needed a special Act of Parliament and about six hundred pounds in the south before she could be awarded a divorce, as Clemmie might have been, on the grounds of non-consummation, or any other grounds, for that matter. Here in Scotland, divorce may be granted after four years' desertion and the – er – infidelity of one partner is no obstacle.'

'So what, then, is to happen?'

'I can get no sense out of my daughter. At first, she was going to live in Jack's house – or such a house as he might buy her, rather – until the four years were gone and they could marry.

'Then, when poor Hamish took to his bed with malaria again, and was very pitiful, she cared for him as a wife should and in gratitude he said he would acknowledge the bairn as his own, on condition that she never saw Jack again. Yet again, she wants to come and live with me until she knows her own mind more clearly. But it's my opinion that whichever path she chooses, she will regret not taking the other.'

'She cannot love both,' said Kate vexedly. 'I don't know what to say to you, Mistress Mackinnon. I am deeply sorry for the worry my son has brought on you by his behaviour. All I can promise is to talk to him when he comes home, and get him to see the error of his ways. If Clemmie is sure he is the father, perhaps he could contribute a father's portion towards the child's keep.'

'Fornication is one thing. Adultery's another,' said Mistress Mackinnon, with the utmost severity.

'You know what Burns said,' abjured Kate. She quoted:

'Then gently scan your fellow man
Still gentler, sister woman –
Though they may gang a' kennin' wrang
To step aside is human.'

'He was another,' replied the widow. 'Kindly do not hold the poet Burns up as an example. I do not accept him.'

'I think you should go,' said Kate gently. 'I am sorry about your journey, about the rain and about what has happened.' She held out her hand and the widow took it. They stared hopelessly at each other, reading no answers in either face, and the widow squelched off dejectedly towards the station, her bonnet strings fluttering behind her like tattered banners. Outside the station, a poster advertised Tom Taylor's play, *The Ticket-of-Leave Man*, in a Glasgow theatre.

Chapter Eleven

Duncan had just completed his first week's work at the pit and it was with a weary thankfulness he lifted the back door-latch, looking forward to getting cleaned up and having his meal. He would give his mother his pay packet unopened, knowing she would give him whatever she could spare for his pocket-money.

He was totally unprepared for the spitting, raging bundle of fury that launched itself on him, in the shape of Paterson.

'You pig!' cried Paterson. 'You've been seeing her! Writing her poetry!' He thumped Duncan's sides and chest with his fists, knocking the tired breath from him. 'You knew she was mine!' He was sobbing from red-faced anger. Duncan's own aggression rose in him like a tide. With an implacable, hard strength he grabbed his brother's arms and pinioned them behind his back.

'Now what is this?' he demanded

Isa spoke up from the hearth.

'You took Honoria away from him.' As always, she was Paterson's ally. 'It isn't fair. He loves her.'

'Have you taken leave of your senses?' pleaded Kate, as the wrestling, grunting boys thudded into the kitchen table. 'If you are going to fight, for goodness' sake get out in the fields and do it. I won't have it here, do you hear me?'

She stepped between the boys and because they were afraid of her being hurt, they stopped fighting. Half-smiling, scarcely taking the issue seriously, Duncan sat down. Rubbing his scraped knuckles against a tear-stained face, Paterson returned glowering to the hearth, to sit beside Isa.

Containedly, Duncan washed the dirt from his face and hands, then sat down for his meal. He had been bone-tired, but now a steady annoyance was building up in him and he shot Paterson angry, intimidating looks. He didn't want anything to do with Honoria. Certainly, they'd talked about her poetry at the prayer meeting, and about his, and as Isa had been there, she'd clearly carried the tale to Paterson.

He was damned if he was going to give over a harmless friendship, just because Paterson said so. Who did he think he was? Duncan swallowed down the last of his dinner and went outside, indicating with a jerk of his head that Paterson should follow him. Silently, they made for the fields behind the Rows, and when they adjudged they were well away from the village scrutiny, lashed into each other like furious dogs just let off the leash.

Isa had followed them and shouted at Duncan: 'It isn't fair. He's lame. Mind his bad leg!'

Duncan drew a punch and Paterson, taking advantage, pummelled a sledge-hammer blow into his stomach. Literally seeing red, Duncan didn't care then about the rules of the game, but like a mad thing gripped his brother round the waist and the two rolled over and over on the buttercups, their clothes spattered with yellow pollen, their bodies crushing plant and insect alike. Paterson had always been favoured, Duncan was thinking, because of his lameness. While Paterson was hitting out at Duncan's dark good looks, the dramatic sort that drew a girl like Honoria.

From the edge of the field, Isa in her fright and half-pleasurable terror heard the sound of a horse galloping and turned to see a figure, tall in the saddle, coming towards them from the Bellnoch direction.

Propriety overcame fear and she screeched at both boys, 'Stop! Stop it! Somebody's coming!'

Paterson staggered to his feet and aimed a final punch at his brother's head. Just rising, Duncan was caught off-balance and fell over, striking his head on a flint sticking up through the grass, and passing out cold. White-faced, Paterson took one look at him and fled.

Torn by fear and indecision, Isa nevertheless remained with Duncan, lifting his head on to her lap and seeing with a great surge of relief that his eyes were fluttering open.

'What's all this, then?' said a lazy, cultured voice and Isa looked up as the horseman reined to a halt and peered down at the little tableau.

She did not answer him. She was aware of devastating, dark good looks in a pale face. Duncan struggled to his feet, groggily feeling for the lump on his head. From a hundred yards off, Paterson turned back to notice with relief that he hadn't finished his brother off after all. He began to limp back towards the others, full of chagrin and remorse.

'It's just a family matter,' said Isa at last, as the newcomer showed no sign of moving on.

The horseman indicated by a wave of his hand that it was no concern of his. He said propitiatingly, 'Can you tell me if I'm right for Dounhead Rows?'

'Down there,' pointed Isa.

'And a family called Fleming?'

'That's us,' said Paterson, coming up.

'I have news,' said the rider, 'for your mother.'

This was how Lachie Balfour was introduced to the family. And the news he was bringing to Kate was somehow news she had, in her intuitive Highland way, been half-expecting, remembering the sad dejection of old Balfour's shoulders on his last visit to her in the Rows.

The old man had died two days ago and his will, largely by-passing the now-ailing Jeremiah, Lachie's father, had left the bulk of his estate to Lachie himself. The packet he bore now to Kate was the old man's instructions regarding Jack, and made him the recipient of a lump sum of £5000.

Between Lachie's visit and the lump on Duncan's head, not to mention Paterson's red-faced contrition, Kate's little household developed into a state of noisy chaos that evening, but she remembered her Highland good manners sufficiently to offer the visitor some port wine left over from Hogmanay. She was intrigued by the fleeting family resemblance between the visitor and her own Jack, though this cousin to Jack was slighter, darker, more elusive in personality.

He was concerned for Duncan and suggested calling in the doctor, but Duncan pooh-poohed the idea and would have none of it.

'I see you work down the pit,' said Lachie, indicating the pit clothes that Duncan had not yet removed, and when Duncan nodded, he coloured slightly and said, 'I shall be taking an interest in Dounhead myself.'

Findlay's deep voice came from the fringe of the room, where he had been watching the activities with bemusement: 'Shall you be going down yourself, then?'

'Yes, sir,' said Lachie. 'To see conditions for myself.'

'You'll not like it,' Findlay baited.

'Do you like it?' Lachie deftly turned the question round to Duncan.

'You don't *like* mining,' said Duncan coolly.

'Why do it, then?'

'Because I mean to work for better conditions for the men.'

'Duncan's a writer,' piped up Tansy, anxious to be noticed by the newcomer. 'He writes for the *Clarion*. He's gone down the pit to find out the facts for himself.' Her small face shone with importance.

'Here's a sixpence for you,' said Lachie, fishing in his pocket.

'So,' he said to Duncan, 'you think there's a lot of room for improvement? Such as?'

Before Duncan could answer, Findlay rose and with a grim look of determination interposed himself between Lachie Balfour and his own son.

'Let me answer,' he said. 'And listen well, young 'un. That pit of yours is being mined too deep. The deeper you go, the worse the ventilation. One of these days, if you proceed with the west shaft, there's going to be an almighty fall and the whole pit will land on our backs.'

'You exaggerate,' said Lachie calmly.

With equal calm, Findlay proceeded: 'Your grandfather brought his own men into the pit; men that hadn't the knowledge *I* have, or the men like me.

'They have been telling us what we maun do. Well, I tell you now, let the miners pick their own safety men. And let every pit be inspected every day. It takes a man who has worked down there for years to know the dangers – '

'Do you agree with this?' Lachie asked Duncan.

Duncan nodded. 'My father knows what he's talking

about. But safety's only one issue. Men work far too long hours. You start in the dark, and you finish in the dark in the winter. It isn't a life. It's a hellish form of animal existence. Eventually, the eight-hour day must come – '

'Should *you* be working at the coal-face?' demanded Lachie. 'By your own account, you didn't start work as a miner.'

'I wouldn't be allowed down there, but for the fact that my father oversees my work. I wouldn't move a hand without his permission.'

Findlay looked at his son and the expression of love and pride in his face brought the roughness of tears to Kate's throat. Day by day she watched Duncan depart for the hated pit, and prayed for him to give it up. But it was the price he was prepared to pay for his father's approval and that, as she saw now, he had won in full measure.

Now there was so much going through her mind she wished the visitor would go. Clearly, the whole family were enthralled by him, from Isa, who had never taken her eyes off him, to Findlay himself.

But she wanted him gone so that she could sit down and think out the full import of Jack's inheritance. She remained up till Lachie Balfour had gone and the others had retired, one by one, to bed. Then she stirred the embers of the fire and with a quill and paper laboriously composed a telegram so that Jack would get it when his ship docked in London within the next few days, as it was due to do after the 100-day run back from Foochow, where it had taken on a load of tea.

'Mr Balfour dead,' she wrote. Would he realize from that about the inheritance, she wondered, and decided he would. She thought long and hard about her talk with the Widow Mackinnon. Then she added, 'Clemmie unwell come home at once Mother.' She counted carefully, for you could not telegraph more than twelve words for sixpence.

She looked at her other sons before she went to bed. Paterson's arm was thrown across his face, obscuring it, as though he had been crying. She held the candle aloft and saw that Duncan's colour was good, that he was breathing normally. She would forbid any more disgraceful exhibitions like the fight between the two, on pain of sending one or both away from home.

When young Jack put in at the Thames, he had one task to perform before all others. He had been entrusted with many thousand pounds' worth of gold bars and had kept them in his own cabin, under his bed. It had been arranged that as soon as he docked, he was to put the gold into a spring cart, cover it with a tarpaulin and drive it straight to the Bank of England, where the seals would be examined. The owner of the gold, a rich New Zealander, had already rewarded him well for his care.

He was thankful to have the gold put into safe keeping and he then turned his attention to his mother's telegraphed message, which had been brought on board to him by a clerk from the head office. He was shaken by his grandfather's death, having felt the old man to be next to immortal, and even more shaken by the news of Clemmie's illness. After a hundred days at sea, on a voyage that had been filled with incident and worry, what he wanted now more than anything was a few days' relaxation, to enjoy some of his hard-earned money and see some of the sights of London. Almost without considering it, he decided he would wait a couple of days before getting the train north.

On the voyage out, there had been the worst epidemic of measles on board he had ever known and seventeen children had died, all under five. Then they had put in at Bluff Harbour and he had heard the news that Jean had married a digger and made for the interior to farm sheep. From all accounts her husband was a rough man and there were many doubts as to her safety.

Going on from New Zealand to Foochow, they had passed through the tail of a typhoon and one of his best seamen had been washed overboard in heavy weather: a valuable man, who could be trusted to teach others how to splice rope, reef and sew canvas, furl sails and climb with ease to the masthead, night or day, 100 feet from the main deck. Now Jack had the unenviable task of calling on his widow.

With much of this seething through his mind, he sought distraction with the first mate, Thompson, in the sights of London. They ate a gargantuan meal, then went to a music-hall, after which Thompson, with an increasing sense of urgency, declared that he wanted to find a woman. His mind clouded with drink, Jack was still enough in command of his senses to know that he was soon accompanying his first mate and a little trollop with fair curls to a house of ill-repute.

There, a surprise was in store for him. The madame was none other than Jinty McGraw, who had once plied her trade in the sordid house down the street from his first lodgings in Glasgow. Now a prepossessing, full-bosomed, well-dressed woman, irretrievable sadness and disillusion etched on her face as though on a coin, she greeted him warmly and promised to find him 'a nice, fresh girl', by which he gathered she meant a young virgin, brought in from the country and primed for a life of prostitution.

Sickened, he left Thompson to get on with it and told Jinty he would rather talk to her in her own rooms. There, he saw every evidence of comfort and easy living, from the fussy furbelows of the dressing-table to the little maid who answered Jinty's every demand with a quick, bobbing curtsy.

Jinty was quite bold now about her profession. Hadn't the state given them its blessing, especially in garrison and seaport towns? The Contagious Diseases Acts meant they had to be medically inspected on arrest and kept in hospital if they were infectious, till they were cured. There was even an official prostitutes' register. They were, in effect, performing a public duty. All that irked her was the double standard, by which a prostitute had to be inspected but not her male customer.

'But these – these children you bring in – for they are nothing more than that,' protested Jack, 'where do you find them?'

'They are all over thirteen!' protested Jinty. 'They come to London to work, or we bring them in ourselves and give them lodgings. Our own women bring their daughters up to it. No need to look so shocked! We give 'em a drowse the first time, snuff or laudanum, even chloroform. I've a doctor client who takes a maid a week at ten pounds a time.'

'Jinty, Jinty!' Jack sighed. 'You would be better off in Glasgow, would you not?'

She shot him a look that said it all. 'In Glasgow, I would be dead,' she answered. She poured him another whisky from a handsome decanter, raised her own glass and with a laugh that curdled his blood, proposed the toast:

'Here's to us –
Wha's like us?
Damn few –
And they're a' deid.'

He left Thompson to the tender ministrations or otherwise of his prostitute and took a cab to the station. He wanted to retch, wash his mouth out, scrub his hands, so strong was his feeling of revulsion after meeting Jinty.

It was not that he had never paid for his pleasure in foreign ports, but it had seemed spontaneous and almost innocent compared to the organized vice which festered all over London. He remembered Jinty as a young woman still with scruples about her sordid trade, and compared her now, immune to all feelings of pity or guilt. Even so, more sinned against than sinning.

In the train, he fell into a mood of maudlin self-pity. He wanted human warmth, a female body, he wanted Clemmie. She was a sickness in him he often wanted to excoriate, but a sickness from which he would never be cured. She had humiliated him by marrying another man and then come back to him, expecting to be forgiven. Their stolen meetings had reached the heights of ecstasy and the depths of despair.

Now he was going to have to resolve the dreadful dilemma of their lives. He felt an unjust, murderous hate towards Hamish McNaughton, mingled with pity for the man's milk-and-water nature.

When he got home, even the five thousand pounds,

coming to him from his grandfather's estate, brought with it more worry than pleasure. He wanted to buy Kate and Findlay a house, away from the pit, perhaps on the Clyde near his mother's old home, but although Kate was clearly intrigued by the idea, everybody else was mutinously against it and determined not to be patronized just because Jack had come into money.

He saw, obscurely, that life in the Rows, narrow though it might be, had its own rough security and that he could not impose his own ideas on so many independent minds. He settled for placing five hundred pounds in the bank for his mother, so that she would have access to it whenever she needed, and for buying a piano for the front room so that Tansy, and anyone else who wished, could learn to play.

Then, two days home, and fully apprised by his mother of the nature of Clemmie's indisposition, he met Clemmie in her mother's house at Bellnoch. She was very pale but, in mid-pregnancy, more beautiful than he had ever seen her. With her fair ringlets on her stalky neck, she reminded him of a frail cream rose reached vulnerable perfection before a summer breeze bore away her essence. He did not know why, but the image of full-rigged ships, lingering at the Tail o' the Bank on a summer's evening, hovering on the edge of the world, came simultaneously to mind, and he knew these two were all the definition of beauty he needed.

He held her cold hands while in a contained, low voice she tried to set out what she felt. She loved him, she wanted the baby, but she was very afraid of sinning in the face of the world and of compounding her previous behaviour by leaving her husband for good.

'What are you saying?' he asked, cold to the centre of his being.

'That nothing has changed,' she whimpered. 'You are still a sea captain and for most of the year I would be alone with the child.'

'Then come with me. I can arrange it.'

Now there was command in her gaze, not his.

'No, Jack. You have told me of your inheritance. So why should you not give up the sea? I need you with me. If

I am to break bonds, defy society, I can't do it alone. You have no right to ask me.'

'You are asking me to give up my ship?' he demanded stupidly.

'Yes.' She walked jerkily up and down her mother's over-furnished parlour, observed by china dogs and grave dark paintings of Highland scenes.

He said in a broken voice, 'I wish I had never seen you.'

She came closer to him then, her pale face sparked into life, her eyes blazing with fury.

'Then you need see me no more. My husband will father your child.'

He grasped her wrists, pulled her to him, held her.

'Clemmie,' he whispered. 'My Clemmie. Never say you will not see me again.'

'You wished you had never met me.'

'I didn't mean it.'

She pushed him away, her strength astonishing.

'We will never resolve it. I am always second to the sea or your ship.'

She drew herself up to her full stature, her movements containing, forbidding. Her voice was harsh, full of unshed tears, but deliberate: 'Jack, we both know what is best. It's that you should go away – and not see me again.'

'Is this your final word?'

'It is.'

Without further ado, he spun on his heel and went out of the room. He picked his captain's cap up from the hall-stand, automatically setting it to its customary jaunty angle. He caught sight of his face in the hall mirror and it was a stranger's face, full of desperation and woe, turbulent as the ocean.

He couldn't face his family and so he took a train for Glasgow and drank until the edge of reality was blurred and one day much like another. The *Daniel Mackinlay* was to make a quick turn-round this time, but the day for reporting to his firm's head office came and went without his realization, and unable to find him, his company appointed another master. He did not care. Day after day, he sat morosely in his lodgings till he had the strength to go out and get drunk and if he did not have the strength, it did not matter. He lay on his bed, recalling the death of Captain Carvie, the death of his best man on the last trip, the death of babies from measles, the death of his grandfather.

He courted death, he wanted it, but still he had to go through the motions of living. After a couple of weeks, the unbearable receded and he took to shaving again, to eating, and to drinking just enough to blur the edges but leave him in command of his faculties.

It was then he realized that he had thrown away the command of his ship and, more than that, his reputation. He tried firm after firm, but could find no command, until by chance the master of a speculation-built wooden ship from Canada, the *Chancellor*, went down with fever, and he was offered the job as stand-in. There would be no long hauls to Foochow or Otago on the *Chancellor;* for the moment, she was mainly carrying coals to Europe. Her size was the only impressive thing about her and he thought longingly of the clean, pared lines of the *Daniel Mackinlay*, that had clipped so cleanly through the water, responding to his touch like a woman. But there lay dangerous fathoms and he turned his mind away.

To pass the time till he took the *Chancellor* out he looked up one or two of the people he'd known as a young clerk. The tigers of yesteryear were mostly settled young married men now, with several children. He wrote to his mother, to put her mind at rest, but left out the address of his lodgings so that none of the family could seek him out and offer him sympathy or help he didn't want.

The night before the *Chancellor* was due to set sail, he was having a last drink in a pub near the quay with the first and second mates, when he looked over the rim of his glass and saw Duncan.

Duncan came towards him directly, embarrassed by the smoke and noise of the seamen's pub, and said in his ear urgently, 'Come outside. It's important.'

Once on the quay, Jack held his arm fast.

'What is this? How did you find me?'

'You'll find out soon enough. Come with me to the station.' He pulled at Jack urgently. 'Come on! 'I've been into nearly every pub in Glasgow, looking for you. What the hell do you mean going off like that and leaving Maw worried out of her mind?'

'Why the station?' Jack demanded.

'Because she's there. Waiting. At least, I hope she's still there.'

'Do you mean Maw?'

'No, you fool. I mean Clemmie.'

In the gaslight glare, Duncan saw Jack's face freeze into something like terror.

'Clemmie!' His shout was nearer a groan.

'She came to the house,' said Duncan rapidly. 'She's left her husband and her mother would not take her in. Neither would Maw – no, Jack, save your anger; it's not her affair. Clemmie says she wants to be with you, come what may, so I agreed to help her find you. She's half out of her mind, Jack. Hurry!'

She sat on a bench in the station, oblivious to the looks cast her way by leering men and curious women, a small portmanteau by her feet. As always, she bore a look of natural gentility. When he took her in his arms, she was trembling from head to foot, and she could not speak.

'I've done my bit,' said Duncan relievedly. 'Look, if I don't sprint, I'll miss my train to Bellnoch.'

Scarcely aware of anything except the fact that they were together again, Jack and Clemmie threaded their way through the dark streets back to his digs. He approached his landlady, explained that a friend had turned up unexpectedly and asked her to provide Clemmie with a room for the night.

Unable to contain her curiosity, the landlady brought a sketchy meal and stared Clemmie up and down. When she went, they looked at each other and shared a muted smile.

'Eat up,' he said.

She tried. Her lips were still almost blue and she could

scarcely talk for shaking. Like Jack, after their parting she had lived in a hell of desperation and had at last come to terms with the fact that, sin or not, she could not live away from him.

'Look,' he said, 'you can come with me on the *Chancellor*. The cabin's fine and roomy. You will pass for my wife, no questions asked. Will you come, Clemmie?'

'I shall be a poor sailor.' She laughed without humour. 'I don't regard the sea as my friend.'

He took her point and looked momentarily downcast. Then he said bracingly, 'All that will change. You will be with me and the sea air will do you good.'

She nodded, gathering her resolution about her. When they had finished eating, he took her down to the quay and showed her the shadowy hulk of the big wooden ship. He felt a tremor pass through her, but she said staunchly, 'We shall be together.' Silently, they retraced their steps over the cobbled quay, silvery in the moonlight.

That night, although he had booked a separate room for her, she lay in his arms all night. She took his hands and placed them on her stomach, so that he could feel their child kicking. He remembered Kenner Brae and wild strawberries and the days when they had first met. Only now, it was even better. Now it was forever, just as he had always said.

Chapter Twelve

'Do you think Lachie Balfour is handsome?' Tansy asked Isa.

Isa gave the matter her full consideration. 'I think he is handsome enough,' she conceded, 'but there is a weakness between the brows and in the mouth.'

Tansy threw the pin-cushion she was making at her.

'You got that out of one of your novels. I wish I were older. I'd set my cap at him. Isa, do you know what Lilias told me? That he goes to Miss Johnson's Dancing Academy in Bellnoch to learn the lancers and quadrille. I'm going to ask Maw if I can go, too.'

'Ask Maw what?' demanded Kate, coming in with her arms full of washing. 'Help me fold these sheets, lassie.'

'It wouldn't cost much. For Isa and me to have dancing lessons.'

Kate did not need much persuading. Ever since the dancing assemblies back in the Tontine Hall at Greenock, she had longed to dance again herself, and this opportunity for the girls to learn a new accomplishment was more than she could resist. She talked Findlay round, vetted Miss Johnson's respectability, persuaded James Galbraith into letting his daughters go too and listened with a shining face to the girls' weekly accounts of their dancing lessons.

Lachie Balfour, it transpired, had private lessons, but when the redoubtable Miss Johnson gave her annual soirée for all her pupils, he was bidden to attend. The girls went into a twitter of excitement over what they should wear.

'You're not having new dresses,' Kate warned, but she allowed Tansy to buy new ribbons and lace to pretty up their Sunday best and they each carried a pretty fan, brought back for them by Jack from one of his trips abroad.

Since she had left school and was helping her mother at

home, Isa was allowed to put her hair up. Tansy arranged hers in a profusion of ringlets, achieved by torturing her fine brown hair up in rags. Two pink-faced girls met up with Honoria and Lilias, equally shy and formal, in the gaily-decorated dancing rooms, where a five-piece band played a lively version of the Snap Dragon Polka.

It was Miss Johnson who coyly matched up partners and Isa found herself facing Lachie Balfour for the Monte Cristo Quadrille.

'What strange names they do have for these dances,' Lachie protested. Twice he trod on Isa's toes before he got into the rhythm of the dance.

'My apologies,' he muttered.

'Think nothing of it,' said Isa gaily.

Later he partnered her for a galop.

'Are your family all well?' he demanded. At her nod, he smiled and recollected, 'You were not such a fine young lady when I saw you last. Your brothers had been fighting, had they not?'

Isa blushed and admitted they might have been.

'Do you help your mama at home?'

'For the present.' He whirled her round with a new-found confidence and she saw, briefly, Tansy's scowling face viewing her from the sidelines, with a fat, spotty boy by her side.

'You have other ideas?'

'Oh yes.' She found the words spilling out of her. 'I would like to see the world, like my brother Jack, and maybe help people.'

'In what way?'

She felt awkward and uncomfortable. 'I don't know yet.'

'Would you like to come to the theatre with me in Glasgow?'

She looked at him incredulously. 'I should have to ask.'

'Then do that,' he insisted, a smile quirking the corners of his mouth.

It involved a battle royal at home. Findlay did not want closer relations with the young pit-owner. 'Let him keep to his own sort,' he said darkly, 'and leave my lasses alone.

'They'll not be your lasses always,' Kate scolded. 'Let them have some enjoyment in their lives. What's wrong with that?'

'She has all the fun,' cried Tansy furiously. 'Just because she's older.' Kate had to placate her with the promise of material for a dress which, being nimble-fingered, Tansy could make for herself.

The play they went to see was *East Lynne*, adapted from the novel by Mrs Henry Wood. Lachie had booked the best seats in Glasgow's Theatre Royal and Isa felt her life was reaching a pinnacle of sophistication.

The play was unbearably sad, however, and when the distinguished Metropolitan artiste', Miss Heath, as the sinning wife, cried at the death of her child, 'Dead, dead, and never called me Mother!' Isa had to turn her face away so that Lachie should not see she was crying.

'It *is* only play-acting,' he reassured her. She turned her tear-stained face towards him and smiled at him gratefully. Emotion fluttered between them, so that she was momentarily afraid, caught up somewhere between childish uncertainty and a new, adult seeking.

'Shall I see you again?' he asked as he took her home.

'Not too often,' she responded guardedly. The arguments at home were only part of the reason. She could not explain the rest.

His face dropped. 'May I kiss you good night?'

She shook her head and held out her hand. When Tansy wanted to hold a grand inquisition later, all Isa would say was that she had enjoyed herself and did Tansy expect her to go on all night?

I wish I had a bed of my own, thought Isa later. I wish I had a bed of my own, and a room of my own, and books of my own. She remembered the touch of Lachie's hand as he'd helped her out of the railway carriage and the look in his eyes when the play had ended and he'd seen her tears. Then where lay her dissatisfaction? It was that play-acting and life were not serious enough for her at the moment. She wanted to be taken seriously. Lachie would be like the rest. He would not do that. Angrily, she fell asleep.

Kate watched with a quiet amusement as Paterson got ready to go out for his Sunday walk. In his Kirk clothes he looked tidy and grown-up. He was approaching nineteen, and all the man he would ever be. He was clearly head-over-heels in love with Honoria and all this preparation for the Sunday stroll was proof of that, if proof were needed.

Never before had he spent so much time slicking down his fair hair, just to go for a walk by the river. But then Honoria and Lilias would be allowed out for their Sunday walk, too, two sedate little creatures in bonnets and crinolines, unlikely to be accompanied by their father as a rheumatism in his back was keeping him indoors. Most of the young folk of the parish would be stretching their legs and a great deal of harmless flirtation took place on the river walk, while younger brothers and sisters provided an excuse for exercise and a buffer against indiscretion.

Soon after Paterson had gone, Duncan came in and went through the same procedure. Again, Kate watched in silent amusement, saying nothing. Let the young bloods have their way. When they came up against James Galbraith, it would be another matter!

When Paterson met the girls, he stopped in front of them but maintained a truculent silence. Lilias giggled but Honoria said, 'I hear you have been fighting with Duncan.'

'Who told you?'

'Isa, of course.' Was there ever anyone as treacherous as a younger sister, he wondered. But red-faced he looked up at her, 'Yes, and it was over you.'

Embarrassed, Lilias walked on by herself and Honoria hissed at him, 'You had no right. Duncan and I were merely exchanging views on poetry. You wouldn't know anything about that!'

Desperately, he said, 'Poetry is musical thought. I have been reading Carlyle on it. If you like, I will try to understand better, although engines are what I really care for.'

She was pulled up short. 'You read Carlyle?'

'Yes. I had him from the library.'

She gave a small sigh, almost of desperation. What an exasperating person he was! He would not take his eyes from her face, those large, luminous, blue eyes, so full of intelligence and of something else that set up a slow-burning sensation inside her. She had been half-looking out for Duncan but now it was Paterson who seemed to be annexing her feelings. She had not intended to fall in love with him at all. In no way did he measure up to the Romantic figure she had carried round in her head since reading the novels of Sir Walter Scott. But he was so powerful in some way. Not physically. Honoria believed in the soul and she recognized that this was where Paterson's strength lay.

'I think we should get married,' he was saying now.

She looked at him and laughed. Not without tenderness, but with incredulity.

'I can't get any peace, for thinking about you,' he protested. 'Why should we not get married? I earn enough to rent a single-end. Then when I'm ready, I'll take you to America. I won't go there without you.'

'You're impossible,' Honoria gasped. 'My father would never let me go to America.'

'He won't be able to stop you. You'll be my wife and I shall be the master.'

She drew in her breath. A scandalous vision of freedom was entering her mind. To be liberated from the thousand small domestic tasks of the manse! To put an end to the pin-pricks of being Lilias's sister, never 'the pretty one'. Paterson had the good sense to see she had her own good looks – he had even called her beautiful.

She looked ahead but Lilias had turned a bend on the river path, so she sat down on a fallen tree with Paterson beside her and allowed him for a moment to put his arm round her waist and squeeze her. There was wonderful comfort in it. He looked at her closely, stole a quick kiss and for the first time that day, smiled.

'America,' she postulated.

'I already have names to follow up there,' he said urgently.

'Just as soon as the war there ends, we'll be off. I aim to make my fortune on the railways, Honoria. You'll have a big house and servants. Wait and see.'

'My father had a visitor to the manse,' said Honoria. 'He had been to Ohio in America and there were people there called Free Lovers. They believed in affinities and also that you could get in touch with the dead.' She shivered deliciously. 'They went barefoot and men and women alike wore trousers, short gowns and straw hats and carried blue cotton umbrellas.'

'I met a man at work who had been there,' countered Paterson, 'and he said there are people called Mormons and the men may have as many wives as they like!'

'I'm not sure I could go there,' said Honoria primly.

'We'll go,' he said assuredly. 'I have it all thought out. When can I come and see your father?'

Lilias felt strangely bereft as she followed the river path without her sister. There was something between those two, Honoria and Paterson, and she felt desperately left out of things.

'Lilias!' Duncan had come to the path by a different angle and now he could hardly believe his good luck at finding her alone. 'Where's Honoria?'

She said vexedly, 'With Paterson, your brother, as you might think.' She looked back anxiously over her shoulder. 'I suppose I'd better get back to them. Father wouldn't like us to split up like this.'

'Not just yet.' He put out a detaining hand. Although strong and confident in debate, he had nothing like Paterson's assurance or practicality when it came to dealing with the opposite sex. And he was too aware of the gulf between life in the manse and life in the Rows.

Lilias said, a little jealously, 'My sister seems to be in great demand.'

He drew a packet from his pocket. 'Would you give her back these? They are her poems. Tell her they are quite good. Not bad at all.'

Lilias said stiffly. 'I will.'

He wanted to tell her not to make anything of it. He

wanted to tell her that Honoria meant nothing to him. But it might look presumptuous. Her nearness was doing devastating things to him, making him trip over stones, walk like someone who had just learned to put one foot in front of the other. In a way it was hell to be with her, for he scarcely recognized the red-faced, tongue-tied booby he had become.

But afterwards, it was a hell he delighted to remember. One of her teeth overlapped another slightly, he recollected. When she pronounced the letter 's' there was the merest hint of a lisp. Her little ears were the most delicate he had ever seen. And even her breath was soft and sweet. Like the scent of clover.

Clemmie had agreed to sail on the *Chancellor* with Jack, but he knew it was merely the lesser of two evils. She could not bear the thought of being separated from him with the child coming.

But she faced up to the heaving decks, rough weather, Spartan living quarters and ship's discipline bravely enough. And she turned their cabin into a comfortable haven where, while he was busy elsewhere, she busied herself making clothes for the baby.

Sometimes he caught her staring at the sea with a look that was half hatred, half fear. Then he held her to him wordlessly and she clung to him almost as though drowning, her lips pale and trembling even as they shaped into an apology of a smile.

It was a strange sensation for him, combining work and domesticity. If the crew envied him (a few were mistrustful of having a woman on board), in the main they were helpful and respectful towards Clemmie, and the big, lumbering *Chancellor*, taking coals and passengers to Galle, was an undemanding background for their first days together.

As Clemmie's time drew near, Jack tried to persuade her to go ashore for the birth, but she pressed her lips together and would have none of it. The *Chancellor* had its own surgeon, an elderly doctor named Mackenzie, whose drinking was tolerated by the company because of his skill, and in the event he delivered Clemmie of a perfect eight-pound girl as the ship approached home waters after her second trip under Jack's command.

Clemmie wanted an exotic, foreign name for the baby and Jack chose Alexandria. She was fussed and fêted by the crew and went to sleep contentedly enough to the lullaby of the rigging and the rocking of the waves. Half-heartedly, and knowing that not all journeys would be without storms and danger, Jack tried to get Clemmie to think of settling ashore, but she set her mind mutinously against it. 'Let me stay with you,' she pleaded.

If he missed the longer journeys and the sophistication of the Clyde-built clippers, he said nothing to her. Just yet, he no more wanted separation than she did. And so on the nights when he dreamt of the China seas, and of the exhilaration of racing the tea back to London, for a premium; or of nursing a good ship through the doldrums; or setting an elegant bow into great seas and being chased by waves from behind, on these nights only his pillow knew his thoughts. And if his face brightened when a clipper was sighted on the horizon, sailing over the edge of the world, Clemmie tried not to read too much into his look, or pay too much attention to the old, jealous, sinking feelings towards a rival she was beginning to understand.

The winter day on their fourth voyage out started much like any other. Clemmie placed another cover over the sleeping babe in her cradle and when she went up on deck for her 'constitutional', as Jack called it, wrapped a heavier shawl round her own shoulders. She did not mind the nip of sharp air or the fresh breeze, but on the contrary found it invigorating.

The first sign she had of anything amiss was when the chief officer came away from the forehold, a worried frown on his face. 'Steam and smoke down there,' he told her. 'I should keep away, mistress.'

'Why, is there any danger?' Clemmie demanded ingenuously.

The weatherbeaten chief officer wondered how much she knew. About the danger of fire on a wooden ship, the swiftness with which flames could take hold, the variability of rescue if no other vessel happened to be near you . . . He decided there was no point in worrying her and said reassuringly, 'No, no. No danger. I'll just alert the captain, though. We'll keep an eye on things, never fear.'

Clemmie went back to the baby, a little clutch of fear in her chest. She would keep out of the way; that would be the best way to help Jack. She forced herself to work calmly at her sewing, but even in the cabin she was aware of a strong sulphurous smell, growing more and more definable.

In an hour or so, Jack appeared and said comfortingly, 'We've been all over the coals in the forehold. There's no great heat there.' His face was streaked with coal dust and his hands were black. Clemmie followed him on to the bridge, with the baby.

'We'll bear south-west,' he told her. 'Might as well keep in the track of ships.'

'Might we have to leave the ship?'

His face was paler under the grime, his smile wavered. 'It's just a possibility. We have to be prepared. Don't worry, my love. I'll take care of you.'

They tried putting the hatches on, taking them off, shutting off all ventilation.

But the nightmare, far from receding, grew worse. Bringing stores up from the lazaret, some of the men passed out from the fumes and the old doctor tended them through his alcoholic haze.

Clemmie found she could no longer stay below. Wrapping the baby up warmly, she came up on deck. Smoke and smell both were increasing and she saw the ominous curls eddy and swirl through the poop and forecastle. Checking she was all right, Jack ordered the hands to get the boats ready on the davits. There were not many women among the passengers but those few gravitated towards Clemmie and her baby, looking for a lead. She put on a reassuring face she was far from feeling.

Jack nursed his ship through the night, while the breeze freshened and the barometer fell. Huddled together on deck, the passengers did their best to keep each other's spirits up. Just before dawn, sparks flew off into the darkness and the chief officer reported that the pitch was beginning to run out of the seams on the deck.

Clemmie left the baby in the charge of a woman passenger and climbed on to the bridge beside Jack.

'What will happen to us?'

He did not answer her at first. His eyes were straining into the lightening dark, desperate for the sight of another vessel.

At last he said grimly, 'It may come to the boats. If it does, I want you to be my brave girl and go with the baby. You know I cannot come with you.'

Chokingly, she said, 'We stay.'

He strove to make his voice as normal as possible

'Just as the captain has his duty to perform, so has the captain's wife.'

'I am not your wife,' she temporized.

'The captain's woman,' he said steadily, 'must show the way to the other women. You will get on that boat with Alexandria and make me proud of you. Don't worry. I won't take any unncessary risks. I've been through worse than this and never lost a vessel yet.'

She clung to him once again before making her way back to the baby, and although there were tears on her cheeks, her voice was steadier as she spoke words of reassurance to the others.

At last, as dawn strengthened, another vessel hove in sight, passed to leeward and then hove to the *Chancellor*. She was the *Punjab*, on her way to Calcutta, and after consultation her captain consented to taking on the passengers and crew from the *Chancellor*, as well as any stores and effects that could be salvaged in time.

Clemmie had only time for one last look in Jack's direction. He raised his hand in a sort of benediction and his face was grim with strain. The heat was becoming unbearable – just how unbearable she did not fully realize till she and the baby were safely on the cool, damp deck of the rescue ship. She was humbly glad not to be in a small boat, for her nervous horror of the sea might then have become too much, and she might have disgraced herself by screaming or fainting.

Captain Grey of the *Punjab* came up to her now, one of the passengers having pointed her out as Jack's wife.

'They'll not save her now,' he declared grimly.

'Then get my husband off,' cried Clemmie wildly. It did not matter now about proprieties. Her husband he was, in all but name, and should be. She screamed with all the power in her lungs, 'Jack! Jack! Jack!'

Captain Grey did his best to calm her, leading her away from the rail and handing her over to the anxious care of the other women.

'He will do what needs to be done, and get himself and his men off when ready,' he assured Clemmie. But he was obliged to put more distance between his own vessel and the dangerous *Chancellor*. The lifeboat awaiting Jack, his chief officer and two others seemed very small and frail. And still they did not come.

Clemmie broke away from the women dementedly and would have been over the taffrail had not hands pulled her back. Losing all self-control, everything but the blind need to reach him deserted her, and she screamed into the roasting abyss, 'My Jack! Save him, somebody. God, save him!'

As though he had heard her screams, Jack suddenly appeared on the deck of the old wooden tub, scrabbling with his men across the roasting boards towards the lifeboat. Just then, in a mighty, victorious leap, flames burst at last through the after-hatch, spreading with a dreadful, implacable neatness right across the deck and half-way up the mast. Even on the *Punjab* the heat was terrible. The *Chancellor* juddered like a paper boat thrown on a bonfire.

Straining desperately to see through the flames, Clemmie could just make out the lifeboat. Her heart almost stopped as she saw there were only two men in it. Neither wore a dark jacket like Jack. Where was he? She screamed again.

The boat was pulling away fast from the burning *Chancellor* and she saw now that there were three figures in it, one, in fact, in the process of being hauled aboard. He looked like a drowned rat but if he were Jack, she would know it. The terrible realization bit through to her. The figure was small, slight, not bearded.

She felt as though her whole body was torn in a desperate scream but she was making no sound. It was like dying, it was like tearing spirit from flesh. Then who was this left on the *Punjab*, staring across the crimson and yellow waters as the fire ate across the big wooden hulk and set her aflame from end to end? Who heard the awe-stricken gasps of the watchers on the rescue ship?

She burned like a great yellow tableau against the dark morning, all vivid flame now, smoke swallowed up in pure flame, dark edges of fleeing night consumed by flame.

'My husband?' As in a dream, Clemmie turned to Captain Grey. The kindly old Liverpudlian put his arms about her shoulders.

'If he's in the sea and swimming, we'll get him, ma'am.'

'In the sea?' she queried stupidly.

'He leapt overboard as the flames swept across in his direction. He had no time to jump into the boat. Then they had to pull away because of the heat.'

'He's a strong swimmer.' Now it was old Mackenzie, the sawbones, by her side, his eyes straining, like everybody else's, to pick up any human movement on the sea.

'I've picked 'em up from two miles off,' said the captain.

'I've picked 'em with their scalp broke open from t'gallant yard, fell from unfurling the main royal,' said the old surgeon. 'I've picked 'em up with broken thighs and legs, when they's been near an hour in the water. And they've survived.'

'The boats are searching for him,' said the captain.

'I can see nothing,' said Clemmie. She was deathly pale, her eyes cloudy. The old doctor was about to have her taken below when there was a loud shout.

'Albatross!'

The gaze of everyone on the *Punjab* followed a young seaman's pointing finger. There was a quick flurry of activity as another boat was lowered

'What does it mean?' demanded Clemmie. Her lips could

scarcely move to frame the question.

'It means the birds have seen someone in the water.'

'A dead body?' Someone put the precipitate question then covered a mouth. The boat pulled away in the direction of the circling birds as though the oars were worked by clockwork and not the straining arms of men.

There *was* a body in the water. Clemmie watched the scene, though she could never remember having done so afterwards, having obliterated it from her mind. They dragged Jack aboard and more willing hands lifted him on board the *Punjab*.

She could feel herself swim out to meet him, join him in some watery consciousness. The old doctor worked over him, a ring of anxious faces above. At last there was a small, convulsive movement.

'He's alive,' said somebody. Mackenzie looked up with a small, hovering smile of triumph and somebody handed him a glass of whisky. Jack's eyes fluttered, opened.

It was only then that Clemmie felt the deadly cold, that the horror of the night finally overtook her. As she swooned in a faint beside her husband, the *Chancellor* burned right down to the water's edge. And was gone as though she had never been.

James Galbraith moved quietly towards Clemmie's bedside in the lodgings she and Jack had taken at Gourock. He had been warned how ill she had been after the fire at sea – fever, congestion of the lungs, lassitude and a nervous debility had all taken their toll. Jack had suffered a severe chill from his immersion in the sea, but his strong constitution had warded it off after a couple of weeks and now he stood looking down at Clemmie from the opposite side of the bed.

'Here is the Reverend Galbraith to see you,' Jack said. Clemmie made a feeble, fretting motion, indicating that the older man should sit down. It appeared to be too great an effort for her to lift her head from the pillows.

'My dear,' said James Galbraith, taking her unresisting hand in his. 'I am sorry to see you thus. Jack's mother has told me you have things on your mind, and asked me to see if I can bring you some kind of comfort.'

'The Church cannot help me,' said Clemmie, through cracked lips.

'There is no one God cannot help,' said James Galbraith 'No one is beyond the help of Jesus, who died for our sins. Let us pray.'

Jack bowed his head and Clemmie closed her eyes. The rich, resonant voice which had boomed out from so many pulpits adjusted itself to the narrower confines of the heavily-furnished room.

'Our Father, you see here our sister in sore distress. Comfort her in her hour of need, strengthen her will to live, so that those who love her and need her may be sustained by her. Turn not Your Face away from her, but forgive her her sins and those who have sinned against her with uncharity. For Jesus's sake, Amen.'

Jack rose and went into the next room, where his mother stood, still in her cape and bonnet after her journey. He saw her lips tighten involuntarily as he went towards her and his own heart hardened.

'Mother,' he said formally. 'It was good of you to come.'

'How is – how is Clemmie?'

'Not at all well. Troubled in her mind.'

Kate turned towards the window for a moment and when she looked back at him, Jack saw her eyes were full of tears. Instantly he went over to her and took her hand, bidding her to take off her bonnet and cape, and sit down and rest.

When she had done so, she said, 'Jack, I will stand by you – the divorce. You may tell Clemmie so. Will she see me?'

His gaze slid away from hers. 'She thinks she has placed herself beyond her own mother's affection. And yours.'

'I am not surprised. I should not have turned her away that night when she came to me. I have shed many bitter tears over that, Jack. My reason was I cannot look lightly upon – upon adultery. I have to say it, Jack. But I have talked it over with the Reverend and he has shown me that my Christian duty is not to turn my face away. I may hate the sin, but love the sinner.'

'He has changed from how I remember him,' said Jack, referring to Galbraith.

His mother nodded. 'He was always an upright man. Now he is a good man also, and much loved in Dounhead.'

'He spoke kindly to my Clemmie.'

'Ask if she will see me, Jack.'

A few moments later, Jack led his mother to Clemmie's beside. Any doubts Kate might have had about making the long journey with Galbraith were dissipated when she saw the girl's frailty and pallor.

She took Clemmie's chill hand in hers and said strongly, 'Clemmie, we must be friends, for we both love Jack.'

'Can you forgive me?'

'I will stand by you. I believe you and Jack must marry after the divorce and that the true bond between you will bring you closer to our Maker. The family will never shut you out, Clemmie, if I can help it.'

The girl threw her arms round Kate's neck and wept, while Kate gently patted her back. Jack and Galbraith moved over to the windows.

'You are good to come here,' said Jack, his face working with emotion.

'When your mother asked me to make this visit,' replied Galbraith, 'I was pleased to come back to old haunts. Besides, I owed it to you both, for old times' sake.'

He strode over and looked down at Clemmie. 'And now will you haste to get well? There is a child in your landlady's care who needs her mother.'

Clemmie put a scrap of hankie to her eyes and did not answer.

The minister said, with a patience that astounded Jack, 'And what else ails you, then?'

'It is that Jack will go back to sea, and I will be alone.'

'I have told you,' responded Jack gruffly, 'that I will not set foot on a sea-going ship again, until the day you tell me I can.' He held out his arms to his mother and Galbraith in eloquent appeal. 'I cannot say fairer than that.'

'What will you do?' Kate demanded.

'Find work on the Clyde. The pleasure steamers.'

'That would content you?'

'To be with Clemmie and Alexandria, it would.'

'Then I don't see what your complaint is, madam,' said Galbraith, with a clumsy attempt at lightness. 'Now let me tell you something else. Something cheerful. My daughter Honoria is to marry this young man's brother, name of Paterson. They are quite set on it, so I cannot say no. And what do you think of that?'

When Paterson had declared his intention of seeking Galbraith's permission to marry Honoria, Kate had been certain he would meet with opposition.

James Galbraith had certainly made some reproving noises, but as Kate had noted, fatherhood had softened the edge of his bigotry and ill-health undermined his former arrogance. Honoria, besides, was prepared to make small daily scenes, and Paterson was ready to be dourly implacable in his intentions, so the old warhorse turned surprisingly away from the scent of battle and gave in to a wedding with remarkably good grace.

Sending for Kate and Findlay, he made it clear that his respect for them was partly the reason for his concession. He then disclosed that Honoria, like Lilias, would come into a small annuity from their mother on marriage and it looked as though this would enable the young couple to furnish their home and live in quite reasonable comfort.

So on a fine spring day, sunshine alternating with brief showers, there was a village wedding with a reception afterwards in the church hall, and James Galbraith even relaxed his strictures enough to allow dancing.

Lame foot or not, Paterson led his bride off to the strains of the fiddle and Duncan overcame his shyness sufficiently to partner Lilias. The bride's father made a speech that verged, for him, on the sentimental, while Kate mopped her eyes and Tansy was dispatched with a piece of wedding cake to Grannie Fleming, who never now left her bed.

When it was over, and the rainbow showers of the early day had cleared to make way for a balmy evening, Kate and Findlay went for a stroll together, away from the rumbustious young ones and their lively games.

It was not often that they had the leisure, or indeed the impetus, to walk together, and now it was strangely sweet to be in each other's company. Alone for the moment, they mulled over the wedding and the strong, powerful drive of Paterson's nature. To have overcome so much – his inauspicious birth, his lameness and now even the disapproval of his bride's father! He had looked so handsome and certain of himself – and Honoria had glowed with such happiness that only a churl would have called her anything but beautiful.

They leaned on a gate, looking into a daisy-spattered field where the Summerton cows waited to be taken home for milking, and Findlay said broodingly, 'We've come a long way, lass. Do you regret any of it?'

Even remembering the bad days, she was able to turn to him with a humorous smile and say softly, 'None. Do you?'

'I regret – ' He stopped and sighed, then smiled at her. It wasn't an evening for sad thoughts, after all. But he had been affected by the sweet simplicity of the marriage service and he wanted to tell her that *their* being together was one aspect of living that had never been less than good.

'Kate?'

'Yes?'

'You have been the joy of my life.'

She could not look at him. She was blinded by swift, painful tears, so that Summerton's cows jumped up and down in a haze of green and white.

'Silly old fool!' she said affectionately, and savouring the last of the sun, they took their time as they strolled contentedly home.

Now there was the problem of what to do about Isa. It had been taken for granted that she would go into service, but since leaving school she had prevaricated on the matter, and for a time Kate had been glad to have her help at home.

With Paterson gone from the household, however, there was less work and less money, and Isa's increasing moodiness and unpredictability forced a family debate.

At first, Isa would only reiterate that she didn't want to be a skivvy. Later she burst out, 'I want to be like Paterson. He does the one thing he wants to do.'

'Well, what do *you* want to do?' demanded Kate patiently.

Isa listed all the things she didn't want. She didn't want to be a household drudge. She didn't want to marry young and have hordes of children. She hated washing heavy woollen underwear, and cleaning out coal fires, and peeling stones of potatoes, and carrying buckets of water. Why did women always have to do such back-breaking, soul-destroying work?

'Miss Lah-di-dah,' said Kate, a little less patiently. 'We'll get you a carriage and pair, and a footman to run your errands for you.'

'Wait a minute,' interposed Duncan. 'Why shouldn't a woman lead a life outside the home, if she wants to?'

'Florence Nightingale did,' said Isa, encouraged at last by a breakthrough in family apathy. 'She nursed the sick and wounded, which is what I want to do. I want to be a doctor, or a missionary, or something great like that.'

'Aye, well, how about getting on with your sewing while you think about?' put in her father drily. 'You maun learn to do the work God sends you with a willing heart and mind.'

Kate, however, having seen how Isa's delicate, neat-featured face closed down mutinously at her father's words, decided to speak to James Galbraith about her daughter.

'She was smart at school,' Kate told the minister. 'Do you think she could go for a governess, or something like that?'

James Galbraith had a better idea. Lilias was missing the company of her sister, his old housekeeper had retired, so he suggested Isa came to live and work at the manse, doing the cooking and cleaning. He would pay her a small wage and would also instruct her in Greek and Latin, and supervise her in a course of reading. This would fit her for something other than domestic labours, although Galbraith was uncertain for what.

'You had a sharp intelligence as a young woman,' he told Kate. 'It would appear that she follows after you.'

Although the relationship was a finely balanced one, Lilias and Isa got on well together. Lilias was accustomed to following the lead from Honoria and now listened to Isa's strong-minded views with a great deal of tolerance. Quite casually, she corrected Isa's slips in grammar and pronunciation, all with such light good humour and kindness that the young girl scarcely noticed it was being done.

She also helped Isa to take an interest in her appearance, showing her how to set her ringlets with sugar water and soften her skin with oatmeal, as well as how to use a goffering iron, do drawn-thread work and scallop the edges of her petticoats.

When she had been at the manse for a year, Isa did a Latin translation of such subtle merit that Galbraith, reading it in his study, was moved almost to tears. His Highland Kate and her pitman husband had produced a scholar of rare mind. Delightful though they were, neither of his daughters had anything like these intellectual gifts.

But he did not know what to do about it. He was reluctant to deprive Lilias of yet another female companion, when she had already lost her mother and her sister. And Isa's mind was still developing, would be none the worse of a few years under his careful tuition. Then they would have to see about harnessing her abilities, perhaps in some church institution, or hospital, or school. He was reluctant to change a situation that was working out, for the moment, so satisfactorily for them all.

The new situation was one of rare opportunity for Duncan. On the pretext of seeing his sister, he was able to slip in at the back door of the manse, and, sitting in the big, warm kitchen, get to know Lilias better than he had ever dreamed. Galbraith, cloistered in his study with his books and sermons, knew nothing of these calls and the girls were always careful to remove any evidence of them, from the dust off Duncan's boots, if he looked in on his way home from the pit, to the tell-tale dregs in a teacup or crumbs from a plate of scones.

Mostly, Duncan cleaned himself up before visiting, sensing correctly that Lilias hated to see him in his collier's clothes. Even so, the filth of the pit was hard to eradicate, especially if there was no hot water in the kettle and he had to wash in cold. The coal settled itself round the rims of his finger-nails and in his knuckles, embedded itself round his hairline, pitted itself in his skin, so that sometimes he looked like some strange half-caste, neither black nor white but a pink-eyed version somewhere in-between.

The girls' avowed antipathy towards the pit only served to make Duncan put forward his support of the colliers more vehemently than ever.

'There's only one thing I care about in life,' he said roughly, on one occasion, 'and that's how to improve conditions for the men under the ground.'

Lilias put her reservations delicately: 'You are qualified above the average miner. You can write, address meetings.'

'And so why should I not use these abilities to help the men I work with? The best miners' leader Scotland has produced, Alexander Macdonald, who's carrying on the fight for us south of the border now – *he* went to Glasgow University when he was twenty-five, and worked down the pit in the summer months, the better to equip himself for the cause. He had started work, like my father, when he was about eight.

'I won't pretend I like it down there, but it's the only way I'll get the respect of the men and be able to lead them later.'

'Lead them where?' demanded Lilias.

'Lead them to fight for shorter hours, better conditions, greater safety. You know that maybe one in five of the men who go below pay for coal with their lives and the rest by injury and ill-health.

'How do you think the factories keep going, and the trains and steamships run, but for coal? The whole basis of our life is coal, yet our men have to fight for every halfpenny they earn, every concession that will make life more bearable. Do you know what I see? I see a day when there will be great baths at the pithead itself, where the men will be able to wash the dirt from their bodies, and change into decent, clean clothes, before they even start for home. And a day when machines will do the work of the pick and the pony. Even then, men will still have to go below, in unnatural conditions, and even then risk their lives from the unpredictable shifts of nature.'

It was at these moment that Duncan saw he had the interest of his listeners and Lilias's glowing-eyed attention was sweeter to him than the piping hot tea the girls made him. Launched on his hobby-horse, he told them how coal had been burned in the houses of the Scottish nobility long before James VI took the custom south – Elizabeth had hated the 'sea coals', but the dearth of timber and the coming of chimneys had made the 'black stone' acceptable – eventually.

'They talk about slavery on the cotton plantations in America,' he said, eyes flashing with passion. 'Well, until the end of the last century, the miners in Scotland, the coal hewers and bearers, their wives and their children, were bound to one employer for life. What was that but serfdom and slavery? They were the property of the landlords, transferable, like goods.'

'Poor creatures!' affirmed Lilias.

'They were so kept down,' said Duncan, 'they often hadn't the strength for protest.

'But I've heard tell that in Bristol, once, more than a hundred years ago, the miners rose up in a body, filled up the shafts of several pits, cut off communication with the town by carts and pack-horses, stopped the coaches, demanded money from travellers and burned down the inns, and wouldn't stop rioting till the troops were sent in. Perhaps they carried things too far, but at least they still had the guts to protest!'

Isa shook her head at him, her dark eyes brooding. 'I hear Lachie Balfour is building a house, no more than a mile from here. You'll be crossing swords with him, no doubt. Father says he is one of the old school and will not be dictated to by his men.'

'He will listen,' said Duncan grimly.

Lilias raised her head from her needle-point, her face faintly pink.

'I saw him ride by on his horse the other day,' she averred. Smiling at Isa, she added, 'He looked quite a Young Lochinvar. I wonder who he will take to the west?'

PART FOUR

◆

Chapter Thirteen

'Papa,' said Sandia (once Alexandria), 'I want to see the ships.'

Jack lifted his five-year-old daughter in his arms and kissed her. 'Get your coat, then,' he urged her, setting her down, and she launched her small, plump figure in its full skirts down the hall, crying, 'Mama, we're going to see the ships. Come with us. Bring the baby.'

Clemmie came out of the bedroom, putting a finger to her lips, and laying down her copy of *Household Words.*

'Georgie is sleeping,' she whispered, 'and Mama wants to rest.' She buttoned her daughter into her boots and coat and tied the strings of her bonnet. She watched from the oriel window as Jack and Sandia walked hand-in-hand towards the river. These two were never happier than when together. What would Sandia do when her father took command of the new China clipper *Hermione*? These years since the disaster of the *Chancellor* he had been content to sail paddle steamers for the joint companies of railways and steamboats, taking holiday-makers and day-trippers up and down the Clyde. He had trained Sandia to recognize the *Neptune, Sannox, Jupiter, Waverley* and *Mercury,* but much though he loved the Clyde ships, Clemmie knew where his heart lay. And now, with clipper fever at its height and Aberdeen, Dundee and the Clyde vying with the American yards to produce the fastest flyer, from out of the blue had come this offer to be master of the newest of them all, the elegant *Hermione*, her lines pared away till some said she was neither safe nor economical.

How the offer had come about was rather to Clemmie's taste, fond as she was of reading novels of adventure and romance. One day Jack had been approached on the bridge of his ship by a small, rotund figure, talking in a loud American accent and smoking a large cigar.

'Joe O'Rourke,' the figure introduced itself. 'And if I am not mistaken, Jack Kilgour.'

'How did you know me?' Jack demanded, after a hearty session of back-slapping and hand-shaking.

'Apart from the beard, you haven't changed all that much, since that night in New York when you jumped ship and I took you home and you wrote a letter to our mother for us. Do you remember?'

'How could I forget?' said Jack.

Joe's tale was a strange one. Selling papers in the New York streets, he had collapsed one day from malnutrition and a lung infection. Taken to a paupers' ward, he had been visited there by the philanthropic wife of an Irish-American shipping magnate and later taken into their household as ward and later still, adopted son.

Showing great business acumen, he had eventually inherited the shipping business, and now his imagination was caught up in this exciting business of the clippers. He was convinced his yard had built the smartest of the lot and that Fate had taken him on this magnificent sail round the Kyles of Bute so that he should meet up with Jack again, and so find the skipper for *Hermione* he had been seeking.

'What makes you so sure I'm your man?' asked Jack.

'Intuition.' Joe tapped his forehead. 'And I've heard a thing or two about your career before the *Chancellor* went down.' He laughed, and Jack glimpsed again the urchin who'd led him through the Bowery maze all these years ago, when they were both children. 'Besides,' said Joe, 'I love a gamble!'

'What do you think?' Jack had asked Clemmie, with great caution.

'I think you should take it,' she answered quickly. Then she kissed him. 'I want it for you, too.'

All this refinement of the clippers was dictated by the China tea trade. The tea, being perishable, had to be got to the London market as quickly as possible and the annual seasonal export from Shanghai had developed into a race, with a considerable premium going to the first ship to reach London. Sometimes the whole country bet on which ship would come in first, as when the Greenock 'sisters', *Taeping* and *Serica*, and the exquisite *Ariel*, also Greenock-built, were joined by the *Fiery Cross* from Liverpool and the *Taitsing* out of Connell's yard in the great homeward race of 1886. Only minutes had separated *Ariel* and *Taeping* at Dungeness. In pure sailing, *Ariel* had won the race. But *Taeping* got the better tug and reached Gravesend an hour ahead of her rival.

Clemmie had watched Jack's face when discussing these events with seafaring friends and had resolved that, if he were given the chance of a new command, she would encourage him to take it. It was the measure of her love for him, a love that had deepened through the trauma of her divorce, their quiet wedding and the birth of their son. You could not hold back fulfilment for someone you loved. It was as simple as that. She would bring up their children, wait for his leaves and pray for the day when the sea would relinquish him to her for good.

There were those who doubted the future of the clipper, but Jack was not among them. When the Suez Canal was finished, said the doubters, a good steamer would do in fifty days what a clipper took twice that time to accomplish. Jack instanced the building of the beautiful *Thermopylae* at Greenock and the wonder *Cutty Sark* under construction at Dumbarton.

Would the yards be turning out these vessels if there was

no future for them? For many years to come, there would still be the demand for sailing ships and the men who knew how to sail them. When the last sail was furled, then Jack would be prepared to hang up his cap, but the romance, the excitement, would have gone. Let him have his China clipper, Clemmie thought, before she sails in all her beauty into the history books that Sandia and Georgie will read.

She sighed. She would have liked to put her feet up for half an hour, but with a visit from her mother-in-law and Tansy imminent, she had to check with her little servant, Lettie, that the kitchen grate was well-polished, the cutlery cleaned and the stock-pot boiling for the soup.

In mid-afternoon, the visitors arrived off the train and were warmly greeted, with Madeira and seed-cake offered immediately in the parlour, to sustain them till tea-time. Kate's embrace of Clemmie was warmer than usual, but then the marriage and new baby had changed much, and Kate had sensed new vulnerability and spiritual growth in her daughter-in-law.

Tansy was charmingly turned out in a blue cloth dress with kilted cloth frills and blue satin band, bow and sash, an over-tunic of blue brocade and a blue bonnet with a white feather.

Basking in Clemmie's admiration, she averred the crinoline was on the way out and that the very latest device was a small whalebone cage that supported the skirt at the back, called the bustle.

Indentured to a Bellnoch dressmaker at two-and-sixpence a year, she of course knew what she was talking about.

'She must not marry during her apprenticeship,' Kate confided to Clemmie.

'And do you think you might wish to?' Clemmie teased Tansy, who turned a saucy look on her and said, 'It would all depend on the man.'

'We have enough romance on our doorstep,' enjoined Kate. 'Lachie Balfour seems to feel the need to bring Isa many trifles, such as a book from Glasgow or flowers from the hothouse at his grand new house. Or some scene he has painted – for he has some pretensions as an artist.'

'And Duncan is still silly over Lilias Galbraith,' said Tansy.

'Such is love!' sighed Clemmie dramatically, with a satirical look at the ceiling. 'But Duncan has gone to Fife, you told me.'

'He is seduced by the sound of the so-called Free Colliers,' said Kate with a note of exasperation. 'He was well enough as he was. My husband offered to stand down as secretary to the miners' lodge at Dounhead, so that Duncan could have the job, but that wasn't enough for him. He wants to be where the action is, he says, and in Fife they are agitating more and more for the eight-hour day. And he wants to be in on it. They have made him secretary of a lodge there and he will be in at the finish, as he says.'

'And what then?' asked Clemmie.

'Oh, then he wishes to stand for Parliament, like his hero, the miners' leader Alexander Macdonald, who has gone in as a Liberal, although Duncan maintains he should be called Labour, as he is the first working-class member.'

'He is a very determined young man,' Clemmie opined, impressed. 'And what does Lilias think of all this?'

'Lilias likes to sing and dance, like me,' cried Tansy. 'She wearies of Duncan being so heavy and serious all the time. He would be better suited with someone like Josie Daly, who blushes as the mention of his name, and worships him.'

Kate looked at Tansy reprovingly. Fond though she was of the vociferous, lively-minded Josie, there was a difference of religion between the two families, and her friend and neighbour Nellie Daly would be no more in favour of such a match than she herself.

To change the subject, she patted the settee next to her for Clemmie to come and sit near her and portentously announced: 'I have something of great interest regarding Isabella to tell you.'

'Isa?' queried Clemmie.

'She chooses to be Isabella nowadays,' put in Tansy, with a quick lift of the head to indicate her impatience with such foolishness.

'Well,' said Kate, with a propitiating look at her youngest daughter, 'Isa or Isabella, what you will, may be the subject of a great honour.'

She had Clemmie's full attention now.

'Go on,' she urged.

'They are giving consideration to the question of having female medical students at Edinburgh and Isa may be one of them.'

'Isa a doctor?' Clemmie could not hide her shock. 'Is it a fit job for a woman?'

Kate said, 'Women can do much more than they are given credit for. Look how you yourself have gone to sea, and cared for an infant there. We have brains, as well as men, and James Galbraith says Isa has an intelligence above that of most men and that he is determined she should make use of it.'

'Oh, it is just that that idea takes a little getting used to,' admitted Clemmie. 'It is most exciting, and I wish her well.'

Kate smiled and, changing the subject, brought a letter from her bag with a broad smile of pleasure.

'More news,' she announced. 'We have heard from Jean in New Zealand and, like you, she is the mother of a second child, another little boy. Would you like me to read you what she says?'

'Please,' said Clemmie, settling back against the crocheted cover of the settee. 'It is lovely to feel part of the family.'

Kate's hand touched hers for a moment, in understanding, before she launched into Jean's letter:

'Dear Mother and Father and All, You will be glad to know that Pat and I are the parents of a fine boy, a brother for John Findlay. We have called him Samuel, after Pat's father, and I have something to tell you. We are having both boys brought up in the Catholic faith. I am doing this for Pat, who is a good husband, the best. I have told you about the little blue Madonna who stood in a corner when I came here. We still have her and I have prayed to her in times of trouble. I don't know what that makes me, Mother. Halfway between Protestant and Catholic, I suppose, but a

Christian anyhow, I hope.

'Well, we have had our problems since Pat became a runholder, but I am glad to say we have bought the freehold at last, so call him a station-owner now. There are a lot of Australian runholders here now – we call them "shagroons". Until we got all our fences, we lost a lot of sheep to them, and the "scab" cost us a lot more. It is very infectious (scab) so although wood was not easy, as we are poorly timbered, Pat used it first for fences then for our home.

'I wish you could all come out and see the house! I've got it very comfortable and have a maid called Lizzie to help me. We have people to dinner sometimes, for Pat wants to get into politics and I'm behind him. We went back to one house for a ball and they had a military band playing – it was very grand. I might try it out next year, Pat says why not?

'I think of you all often, of your soup and scones, Mother, and everybody talking over Sunday tea. Must go now and see to Baby. Pat sends his best. Your loving daughter, Jean.'

Kate's eyes were wet as she put the letter back in its envelope.

'Perhaps Jean will send a daguerreotype of the children,' said Clemmie. 'It sounds as though they are getting up with the latest fashions, and are doing well. And have you heard from Paterson and Honoria?'

'Not a word.' Kate's manner was uncharacteristically abrupt. But then she had good reason to be annoyed. Since Paterson and his wife had left for America, not long after the cessation of hostilities, news had been sparse indeed, and her abruptness was a cover-up for very real anxiety that she and James Galbraith alike shared concerning the young couple. Even if Findlay reassured her, saying, 'He will write when he is ready,' she could not help her worries.

Now, however, she composed herself, upbraiding herself mentally for having so little faith in the Lord's goodness. She and Tansy had come to Gourock to enjoy themselves, and now there was the sound of Jack's deep voice in the lobby and the patter of Sandia's eager feet as she launched herself towards Grannie with visions of the sugar tablet sure to be given a good little girl. Kate held out her arms, and smiled.

Honoria lay back on the cane-bottomed chair and listened to the lazy waters of the Mississippi slapping against the sides of the flat-bottomed, side-wheel steamboat, *Eleanor Belle*.

With her eyes closed, and a determined effort of the imagination, she was back momentarily in a cool, misty morning at Dounhead, preparing breakfast with Lilias in the big manse kitchen, stirring the fire in the grate, listening to her father clearing his throat, ready for the delivery of his sermon.

She opened her eyes. How different it all was here! Heat, water-melons, Negro folk with their high, musical voices, gamblers with their fancy waistcoats and scheming eyes, hard women ready to spend the easy money that came their way. Not the America she had pictured at all. Pioneer wagons and Red Indians, yes. Gold prospectors and a melting-pot of nations, too. But to be stuck on a great vulgar floating palace among entrepreneurs, demi-mondaines and downright rogues and vagabonds was another matter altogether and gave her a strange, almost disembodied feeling. This was not what Paterson had promised her. In fact, nothing had turned out as she had expected and her faith was running thinner and thinner, like watered blood. She tried to hide her fear from Paterson, but the long months and years of worry and privation were taking their toll. She had lost one child and was carrying another. On this close, cloudy day she felt sick and unwell.

She had never said to him, 'Let's go back home,' but the plea was rising in her like a tide which she felt barely able to stem. He would *have* to swallow his pride. Their money was all gone, but they could get a passage back somehow, on a promissory note, if need be. It was no longer enough for Paterson to say in that weary, dogged way, 'Stick it out, Honny. Believe in me!' Her small savings had gone to the rogue who had brought them out here, with his plans for a railroad that never was, and since then it had been hand-to-mouth, selling watches, jewellery, even clothes and books, to keep going, and taking unskilled jobs, both of them, in bars and guest-houses, even, as now, working on the river-boats as cooks and menials. She could not write home while this kind of vagabonding was their life. There was this silent, implicit bond between Paterson and herself. Success or nothing. She had the distressing conviction that he would sooner die of starvation than go back home beaten.

'Honny! Feeling better, are you?' Paterson stood before her with a long, cool mint julep, and she took the glass gratefully from his hand and sipped.

'Sweetheart, look!' He pulled her to her feet, pointing ahead of the steamboat to a splendid bridge spanning the river in front of them.

'Do you know what will soon cross that bridge, dear? On this great day for Kentucky? Its first train. Soon these old so-called floating palaces like the *Eleanor Belle* will be a thing of the past. No more blazes on the mud-banks as their boilers blow up. No solid mile of steamboats along the levee, but trains doing it all, so much more quickly and efficiently. First the joining of the Union Pacific to the Central Pacific at Promontory Point, Utah, and now this. Railways all over America, like veins and arteries carrying life-blood.'

He stopped himself and looked at her guardedly.

'I am told there is a man from the Union Pacific in Louisville for the bridge opening. I hear that Gould of the Pacific is negotiating to buy the Kansas Pacific and there are those who say he will eventually tie up the Texas Pacific and even the Santa Fé. Think of that in terms of railway engines! I have to convince them that there is a job for me!'

She saw by the set of his shoulders that even his hard-edged confidence was under siege.

'You go,' she said stoutly. 'You go and see this man. Make yourself smart. Stick your chin out. Remember we are Scotch and not easily beaten.' But there were tears in her eyes as she spoke, and he turned and held her wordlessly before he took her empty glass and returned to his labours below.

In the sumptuous, almost decadent reception room of the big Southern hotel, Paterson, with his limp and thin, wiry body, moved forward to meet the big-framed railway man, Charles De Witt.

'British, I see,' said De Witt.

'Scotch, to be precise,' said Paterson doggedly.

'It was one of your fellow-countrymen, Alec Stephen, who built the *Shenandoah*, the most successful Confederate cruiser in our late, great Civil War,' smiled the big man, more easily. 'I have a great respect for the British engineering tradition. This is why I consented to see you. I must tell you, though, that I think we in America have the edge on you now.

'It took America to overcome the problem of keeping the old four-wheelers on the rail.'

'But Britain sent you the *John Bull*, on which the experiments were carried out,' Paterson interposed. 'And that was the most advanced engine of its day, with its outside coupling rods and inside cylinders. Though your Thatcher Perkins is a fine designer, I concede.'

'Needed only two small wheels to act as pilot and steer the driving wheels,' said De Witt, handing Paterson a large cigar and inhaling on one himself. 'Thus was born the four-wheeled bogie, then the enlarged version with four driving wheels and so the standard American all-purpose locomotive. Have you got any ideas with that sort of simple genius? That is what we are seeking.'

'Well,' said Paterson hurriedly, for he had no wish to give offence in the circumstances, 'the bogie *was* used by Chapman and Hedley in Britain in the days before Stephenson, but it took Americans to see its true worth. And I think you will draw untold benefit from your greater flexibility. You can have passenger coaches of greater length, for example, and will not be tied down by coaches mounted on one frame.'

De Witt looked at him with a dawning respect.

'Stephenson was right about the narrow gauge,' said De Witt. 'I concede Brunel was a man of great vision, but his gauge of seven feet is too heavy on materials. Mark my words, eventually Stephenson's gauge will be accepted as standard, not only in your old country but here also.'

'I agree,' said Paterson eagerly. His eyes were glistening with enthusiasm and soon De Witt and he were exchanging notes and ideas that grew more and more complicated.

The big man ordered several pots of coffee, and then drinks, and still there did not seem to be time enough for the two of them to say all they wanted to say about a subject on which they were both, they admitted, fanatical.

Paterson excitedly covered page after page of paper with sketches, showing his development of the single front wheel design with a coupled driving-wheel, his notions for better cylinder performance and his ideas for reducing the pressure of the exhaust steam by turning the exhaust from one cylinder into another, where it would give a second thrust, and even elaborating on a system of three or possibly four cylinders.

'You have not been anywhere – to Europe, I mean – where you could have been fed such ideas?' demanded De Witt curiously. 'They have all come out of your brain?'

Paterson nodded.

De Witt lay back on his seat for what seemed to Paterson like an eternity. He looked out of the window; he got up and strode about. Still without saying anything. With Honoria completely out of his thoughts for the last few hours, Paterson was suddenly struck with the near-frantic need to get back to her and make sure she was all right. She had looked so pale, so composed, only her eyes betraying her fear. No man could have asked for a more loyal wife. He felt his stomach contract with anxiety and his palms break out in a cold sweat.

At last De Witt sat down again opposite him.

'Brakes,' he barked, in his staccato way. 'You will start work on the straight-air brake. With the sort of loads our big transcontinentals are expected to carry, we must find a way of applying brakes by air pressure, without breaking the pipe if the train breaks. You know the problem?'

Joy working through his body like a re-birth, Paterson said with miraculous calm: 'You have a brake in every coach, with brakesmen walking along the roof giving extra leverage when needed and taking care of the hobos stealing a ride. Some passenger trains are using compressed air, but the problem is as you stated.'

'Want to take it on?' asked De Witt.

Paterson had already started sketching out something, but De Witt gave a loud, infectious laugh and instead held out his large hand and shook Paterson's.

'I think we can supply you with plenty of problems, Mr Fleming. It will be up to you to supply the answers. You will hear from head office as to pay, but I will arrange that you start work as soon as possible and for a while at least you will work directly under my jurisdiction. Will that be satisfactory?'

'It will,' responded Paterson, with what dignity he could muster from his racing thoughts. Then he added, before he could think too much about it, 'There is one more thing.'

De Witt's expressive eyebrows shot upwards.

'Would it be possible for me to have a small advance?'

He thought at first that De Witt was going to refuse. Not only that, but that he had ruined his chances of the job. Only the coming baby and Honoria's needs had forced him to speak up.

De Witt took a hundred dollars from his inner pocket and handed it over without a word, but with the straightest of searching looks.

Paterson's returning gaze did not quiver.

'I trust a Scotchman,' said the elegant Southerner, at last.

'I would not ask, but from necessity,' said Paterson. 'You have my thanks.'

He could not get back to Honoria quickly enough. His only thought now was to get her off the *Eleanor Belle*, that transient and rumbustious old river dowager whose days were now surely numbered, and safely installed in comfortable digs to await the birth of the baby.

When she heard his news, she burst into tears and threw her arms around his neck, sobbing quite immoderately.

'I knew you could do it,' she said.

'Well,' said Paterson, 'so did I.' He dabbed at her tears somewhat ineffectively and demanded in bewilderment, 'But why are you crying – now?'

'Because I like America,' said Honoria, beaming at him like the sun after rain. 'It is a most unexpected country, and I fear Scotland would be very dull, after this.'

Later that night he found her writing a letter home.

'What are you saying?' he demanded.

'Why, that you are making your fortune,' she said, with a slow smile. 'They need not know the rest.'

'Do you mean it, Honny? There may be hard times ahead. Are you sure you want to stay and fight?'

'We are not going to give up now. Whatever happens.'

Chapter Fourteen

'I want you to give up the pit,' said Kate to Findlay. 'You have wrocht long enough down there. The older I get, the more I worry about accidents.'

'I maun take my chance with the rest,' said Findlay.

Outside, snow was settling over the Rows in a sooty drizzle, as coal smuts from the busy domestic chimneys mingled with the freezing rain. In the village, snow blew through the shop doors with their jingling entry bells to mingle with the sawdust on the floors, and working over a wedding dress in her dressmaking mentor's chill parlour, Tansy blew on stiff fingers for warmth. Out in the fields, Summerton's cow-man brought his charges in for milking through a white haze of blinding snow. (Only now was the stock being built up again after nearly all the beasts had been killed off by the rinderpest plague.)

Findlay drew in his breath on a wheezy rattle.

'That's what the pit has done for you,' said Kate, on an anxious note. She stirred the fire to make the room warmer, and taking camphorated oil on her finger tips from a warmed bottle, began to rub his chest, finishing by placing a large, heated square of flannel next to his skin.

'That's easy, lass,' said Findlay, looking happier.

But Kate was not to be mollified.

'You've had that chestiness since the hard cold of 'sixty-seven,' she averred. 'It was fine for the young ones, with skating on the river and all the rest, but I hope it won't be another like it this year.'

'It doesn't get any easier, rising afore cock-crow,' Findlay confessed, stretching already-singeing socks towards the roaring fire.

'Well then,' said Kate decisively, 'now that your mother is gone, we can move into her cottage and you can work her wee bit of garden and I'll mind the hens.' She put the corner of her apron to her eyes, for Grannie Fleming had been taken to her resting-place in Dounhead Cemetery a mere month before. The good old woman had gathered them all about her on her deathbed and with a lucid mind left them her blessings, her home and the few treasures of her long life.

'I'll be useless as an old boot,' said Findlay dejectedly.

'You can still be secretary to the lodge,' Kate reminded him. 'If it's the men you're worrying about, they'll find a new safety man.' She went on wheedlingly, 'With more time on your hands, you can maybe get support for your idea of a miners' institute and library. A place the men ca go for relaxation.'

He could not help a smile.

'How you know me!' he acknowledged.

Sensing victory, Kate pressed her case home. 'If you are worrying about money for Isa, James Galbraith says there are philanthropic people in the Church who will help. He has arranged free lodgings for her and I can give her a little from Jack's money. She is a frugal girl, with no vanity over clothes as Tansy has. She is to go to Edinburgh next week, as she has work to make up.'

Findlay shook his head doubtfully, but Kate went on vehemently, 'I would rather have you and porridge for my supper, than let the pit have you and sit in a house filled with fal-lals. Our weans have gone out into the wide world and soon we shall only have each other for company.'

Findlay knocked the dottle of his pipe out on the grate, his face changing.

'I don't like giving up when there is still so much to be done.'

'Leave it to the young ones. You have done your stint.'

'Can you see me breeding canaries, lass?'

'What's wrong with that? Don't worry, the folk round about'll still come to you with their problems. Old habits die hard!' She looked at him beseechingly. 'I feel the need of you now, my jo. Jean in New Zealand, Paterson in Ameriky and Jack on the China seas. I sometimes think we mothers in Scotland do nothing but have bairns to lose to the Empire. Up and down the Rows it's the same story – so-and-so's gone to dig for gold in the Cariboo, such-and-such has gone for a miner in Pennsylvania. And what do we see of Duncan, now he's taken up with his miners in Fife? When Isa goes to Edinburgh, we shall lose her to grand folk with grand ways – '

'Well, we knew it would come to that. They have to grow up and go their ways.' But she saw he was softening. The suppleness was leaving his bones and she saw the weary effort it took each night to divest himself of his pit-hardened clothes. The coal had entered deep into his pores and lungs and neither soap nor cough lozenges could shift it now. She wanted to see him sit in the sun, in his mother's garden, to touch his hand or shoulder as she went about her tasks.

Suddenly, in the middle of their deliberations, came a loud knock on the door.

'Who's out on a night like this?' demanded Kate. She opened the door to reveal Josie Daly, snow lying thickly on her red hair and like fanciful epaulettes along her shoulders.

'Josie! You have a knock like a man!' chided Kate. 'Come in.' Josie stepped quickly over the threshold as the soughing wind blew a handful of rice-like snow on the mat.

'I've just come up from the *Clarion* office,' said Josie, her breath snared. 'Mr Maclaren said to tell you. Lachie Balfour is to take sixpence off the men's wages at the pit, to pay for the safety work you made him do, and other work in hand.'

Findlay rose like a wrathful god, his eyes flashing.

'By God,' he shouted, 'he cannot do that. A pound is little enough. He'll not grind us down more.'

'That's what I said,' said Josie. 'Wait till old Daly comes off the night shift. He'll go mad when he hears his drinking money will be cut.'

'Come over to the fire, Josie,' urged Kate.

'Don't feel the cold,' said Josie shortly. 'Must get back and get something written for tomorrow's paper. Wish Duncan was here – he's the man we need.'

'Aye, well, I'm here,' roared Findlay. 'By the harry, I'll get back to that pit the morrow and stop that whipper-snapper before he brings the whole coalfield out on strike.'

'You're not well enough to go back,' protested Kate.

'Dinna fash me, woman!' her husband shouted. 'There's men's jobs at stake.' He rose, looking for his cap and muffler. 'I'll go up there and see him myself, tonight.'

Kate placed herself in front of him and said with a furious, contained calm: 'You go out this night and you'll not live to help anybody.'

'I'll go,' offered Josie. Kate looked doubtfully at her wafer-thin soles and already-sodden clothes. 'Don't feel the cold,' Josie assured her, intercepting her look. 'What shall I tell him, Mr Fleming?'

'Tell him to come and see me this night, or I'll not answer for the consequences,' said Findlay. More calmly, he added, 'Mind how you go, lass. It's a wild night out there.'

Josie hastened along the dimly-lit main street, sliding with a child-like glee and satisfaction where the snow was closely packed outside the shops. At the far end, she met Tansy going home, her teeth still chattering from the chill of the dressmaking parlour.

'Just been to your house,' Josie explained briefly. 'I'm to send Lachie Balfour to your da.'

'I'll come with you,' Tansy offered. 'I've always wanted to see inside Dounhead House. Maybe he'll ask us in!'

'Not when he knows what I've come about,' said Josie darkly.

The long drive up to Dounhead House was laid with white and grey pebbles, scrunching unevenly under the snow. 'My boot's through,' cried Josie vexedly. She was limping behind on frozen, snow-logged feet while Tansy was already pulling the bell.

'We wish to see Mr Balfour,' Tansy told Lachie's house-keeper when the old woman came to the door.

'Who shall I say?'

'Miss Tansy Fleming and Miss Josephine Daly. May we wait in the hall?'

Before the housekeeper could protest, Tansy had stepped into the warmth, dragging Josie after her. A door opened and Lachie came forward, a paint-brush in his hand. While Josie babbled the purpose of the errand, Tansy walked calmly into the room behind, where a splendid log fire was burning and in one well-lit corner an easel stood with a half-finished canvas.

'Make yourself at home,' said Lachie ironically.

'We'll just have a warm then get back,' Tansy replied.

'Can I offer you a hot toddy?'

'No, thanks.'

'Did Mr Fleming specify why he must see me tonight?' Lachie asked Josie.

'Only that it's urgent,' said Josie briefly. 'And I'll take a toddy.'

Tansy was looking at the canvas. It showed a newly-ploughed field, with farm cottages in the distance and a great expanse of clouded sky. It was unlike anything she had ever seen before, not realistic, she would have said; yet that sky made her feel uneasy, as though she were in the ploughed field herself, waiting for thunder to break and the rain to come.

'What do you think of it?' said Lachie.

'I don't know,' she said, nonplussed.

'It doesn't tell a story, does it?' he teased her. 'But look, d'you see how I'm using flat colour here? Effective, isn't it? It's the relationship of colour to mass that matters. I'm trying to tell you how I feel about this scene, as well as how it looks.'

Josie looked at it disparagingly, and said nothing. Tansy went closer, then stood back.

'Oh yes,' she said. 'I find it very interesting.'

His voice warmed. 'Do you really?'

'Certainly.'

'Will you come, then?' demanded Josie sharply.

Lachie laid his brush alongside his palette.

'Yes, I'll take you back in the trap.' He gave the painting a backward, assessing glance. 'We'll get things sorted out, shall we?'

While the two girls were fetching Lachie, Isa arrived home from the manse to ask after her father's health. When she heard what Lachie Balfour was proposing, her face coloured pink.

'I don't think Lachie would do it on his own,' she told her father. 'But he told Lilias and I when we met him the other day that his advisers were worried. The pit is outstripping its profits.'

'Let him dig into his own pockets,' growled Findlay. 'He can find the money. It's either that or sending men down an unsafe pit.'

'He's not one of your wicked pit-owners, Father,' said Isa. 'He's genuinely worried about the pit paying its way.'

'Aye?' said her father, raising an eyebrow. 'Worried about profits, is he? But we're in a roaring boom. His leader Disraeli calls it a "convulsion of prosperity". Beer a penny a pint and eggs fifty for a shilling! Is it not more the case that your Tory friend objects to Mr Gladstone and the Liberal majority? And the vote for the working man? Is it not the case that he's shaking in his privileged shoes?'

'Why must you always have it Them and Us?' demanded Isa, her own temper now as hot as her father's. 'Lachie can no more help being born to money than you can help being born without it. He's not a political man. He is an artist, a painter, a thoughtful man in his own way.'

'Artist?' said her father scornfully. 'Did he learn these fancy ways on his trips to the Continent, then?'

'You are in danger of becoming harsh and narrow, Father,' said Isa, with unaccustomed boldness. 'Lachie does his best with the business affairs left to him, but cannot help being what he is.'

'A namby-pamby!' said Findlay contemptuously.

'It is attitudes like that which make Scotland a Philistine nation,' Isa said bravely. 'Attitudes which equate coarseness with manliness and an artist's sensitivity with feebleness. No wonder we are falling behind other civilized nations. We can fight and we can drink. Such commendation! All art begins and ends with Rabbie Burns!'

'I wouldnae know,' said her father, with sudden, vulnerable dignity. 'I have aye been too busy wrochting a living in the dark, to have time for more than the reading I needed for enlightenment. Reading that I hoped might help my fellow-man.'

Contrite, Isa went to him and kissed him.

'I know you are a good man, Father.'

There was a swishing and jingling outside as Lachie and the two girls rode the trap down the back of the Rows in the now-mushy snow.

Beating their arms to get warm, the trio entered. Lachie looked embarrassed and surprised at Isa's presence.

Kate brought Lachie forward hospitably to the fire, but Findlay looked up at him without preamble and said, 'What's this I hear about a sixpence off?'

Red-faced but dour, Lachie admitted: 'It's the truth.'

'Sixpence less for boots for the weans. Sixpence less for broth for their bellies,' grated Josie.

'Sixpence less for the brewer and distiller,' said Lachie, just as grimly.

'I thought you were going to be different,' said Findlay. 'I gave you full marks for what you did in the way of safety measures.'

'Well, it wasn't done without great expense,' Lachie responded, still blowing on blue fingers. 'I am asking for a period of retrenchment. I want the pit to be run on up-to-date lines, I want to extend it. That means taking on more men eventually, more work for the village. But we have to be an economic proposition. I'm no financier, but the figures speak for themselves.'

Findlay spat into the grate. He did not even bother to rise.

'Then you and I have nothing further to say to each other,' he said grimly. 'You'll not recant?'

Lachie looked quickly from Findlay to Isa, his face darkening.

'I won't go back on a decision made on the economic facts,' he said. 'I hope you'll use your good offices to make the men see sense. That's the only reason I came here tonight.'

He sketched a quick bow towards Kate and they listened without words as the cheerful jingle from his horse's harness died away incongruously down the Rows.

'A strike?' demanded Josie.

'Aye,' said Findlay, refusing to meet the misery on Kate's face. 'A strike it is.'

Josie Daly waited patiently at Bellnoch Station for the train to arrive from Glasgow with Duncan on it. Ever since she had heard he was coming back to take over union duties in the Lanarkshire coalfield, she had determined she would be a reception committee of one.

They were all looking forward to having him back at Dounhead, and saying that he would give Lachie Balfour a run for his money now the strike had started. But she waited like a disciple awaiting the evangelist: she wanted to tell him she was in the political movement now up to her eyebrows, women's suffrage and all.

Working for Alf Maclaren on the *Clarion* had been like a kind of re-birth for Josie. From the start he'd respected her intelligence, fed her books and pamphlets, taken the time to explain political theories. It had never happened to Josie before, and although some of the polemics were half-digested, she knew this was the kind of nourishment for the rest of her life, and it was all due to Duncan, putting her up for the job in the first place.

While she'd waited, she'd seen a weeping mother, poorly clad, wave her son off to Canada. 'He's gone to the Cariboo to dig for gold,' the woman had told her. 'He'll send for me when he's made his pile.' She had shambled off the platform, the soles of her boots divorced from their uppers, and Josie had felt the sharp prick of tears behind her eyes. She hated the station. There was always somebody going away and some heart-broken figure waving desolately as the train snaked out of sight.

At last he came. He was never well dressed, he wore working men's clothes, but in Josie's eyes he stood out in the crowd as though some special aura were pencilled round him.

He looked at her in surprise.

'Josie, you here? How're things going?'

'Your mother's in bed. I think it's the worry over the strike and Isa going away. That, and the erysipelas. Her face is awful red.'

He looked concerned. 'She'll be all the better for seeing you,' said Josie. 'We all are. Duncan, I want to help you. You should be standing for Parliament, getting women the vote . . .'

He smiled down at her absently. 'Alf been feeding you propaganda?'

They passed ragged children playing in a field near the station. Although the day was bitterly cold, most of them had bare feet and were filthy and scabby. Josie indicated them with a movement of her head.

'The propaganda's all round me,' she said drily. 'I was like these bairns. I never knew what it was like to have a full belly when I was young. I was always, always hungry. My mother was always on the borrow – sending me for a bawbee here, a bawbee there. I hated it.'

Duncan glanced down at her. Her face was pinched and angry.

'I used to watch better-off folk, going to the kirk or chapel on a Sunday, or into Bellnoch to the music-hall on a Saturday night, and I used to think, "The world is ill-divided." I couldn't see why things weren't shared out, that's if there was a God, which I beg leave to doubt.'

'You're bitter, Josie.'

She looked up at him. 'No. Determined. Thanks to you, I'm not in blind ignorance any more. You'll let me help you?'

He nodded. 'I need all the help I can get.'

Tansy opened the door to him, but her greeting had an edge to it. 'Come to make trouble, have you?' she said, only half-joking.

She led him over to Kate's bed and said in the dainty tones she adopted now to go with her smart clothes, 'Mother, sit up and take a sip of broth. And see who's here to see you!'

Her mass of grey hair escaping untidily from her bed-cap, Kate pushed herself up in the set-in bed and peered into the gloomy room. In this hour before dark, they made do with the light from the fire. Was it Jack? Paterson? How could it be? She knew full well they were far away.

A strong arm went round her shoulders and a dark, moustachioed face smiled into hers.

'Duncan!' she said feebly.

'Maw!' said Duncan concernedly. 'What's this I hear about you taking to your bed? Missing Isa, are you?'

'It's the erysipelas, but it's going down now. I had a touch of the brain fever with it.'

'Well, I'm back now, to keep you in order. You must get out of there, Maw. We've a fight on our hands in the Rows. We need you.'

Duncan had spoken no more than the truth. When the men came out on strike at Dounhead, it was in the hope of a quick victory. But Lachie Balfour's pride was involved. They had scarcely given him the benefit of a proper hearing and would admit of no point of view but their own. Backed up by other pit-owners, he felt that if he gave in to them this time, there would never be any dialogue between them and he might as well hand over the entire running of the pit to the miners' lodge. But even the most experienced member of that lodge, even Findlay Fleming himself, had no idea of the long-term problems that might arise if he didn't get things on a good economic footing now.

From weekly contributions, the miners had amassed enough funds to help them over the first few difficult weeks, and support came in from miners far afield. But it was not the same as a weekly wage and wives were soon in serious difficulties. It was then the strike began to bite and tempers grew ugly on both sides.

Duncan had come back from the Fife coalfields filled with the invigoration of triumph, for had they not established the eight-hour day there and set an example that would be remembered as long as there were mines and miners? It might take many years, but the whole country would inevitably follow. Now he was promoted area organizer for Dounhead and other pits and, blooded in Fife, a seasoned campaigner. He organized meetings to keep up the men's morale, with songs and speeches.

Attending one of these meetings on the banks of the Clyde, Kate could not help comparing it with the old evangelical meetings Findlay had led in his youth. There was the same affecting fervour, the same sense of kinship. She looked around and saw hungry children, thin-faced women, desperate men, but when Duncan got on his platform and held the mirror of his vision before them, it could have been a new Jerusalem they saw, for their faces were alight with something that transcended hunger.

Josie Daly, a small, striking figure in black clothes, with flaming red hair, soon made herself notorious at these meetings, but as she did not stick to the main argument, but brought up the small wage paid to women in the mines, compared to that of men, and campaigned also for that will-o'-the-wisp, women's suffrage, she was often shouted down with good-humoured cat-calls from the men and not-so-good-humoured heckling by the women. Nonetheless, Duncan supported her, and came to rely on the whole-hearted way she would tackle any job, no matter how depressing or menial, if it would help what she referred to, in mental capital letters, as The Cause.

It was Josie who organized the miners' band, raggedy in execution but fervent in intent, which marched round the Rows and brought the crowd to listen at the street-corner meetings.

And it was Josie who organized the soup-kitchens, as the strike dragged on week after week and the womenfolk grew gaunt in the effort to find something to put in their hungry children's mouths.

Kate and Findlay, in the meantime, had effected the move from the Dounhead Rows into Grannie Fleming's cottage, and in the big stone kitchen boiler there, Kate made huge quantities of soup for the hungry folk who queued with bowls and jugs and porringers. At night, she fell into bed, too tired for more than troubled dreams.

Anyone who had a garden gave what vegetables they could and Josie arranged a roster of women to peel and chop. One by one, Grannie Fleming's hens were sacrificed to the soup pot, until all that remained was one tough old rooster who attacked anyone who came near enough to try to wring his neck.

James Galbraith and Wattie Chapman both arranged for meat to be sent from the village butcher's, and kindly old Mrs Summerton at the farm provided turnips, potatoes, kale and any 'soor dook' or sour milk she could spare. (Not that the milk went into the soup, but the older miners especially enjoyed this drink and the women used any left over for the making of scones if someone had donated flour.)

After seven weeks of the strike, it was almost as though the village of Dounhead was dying. The pit itself, with its bing, or slag heap, covered in purple loosestrife (or saugh, which was the Doric name) lay like a slumbering giant, a sour menace emanating from its frightening silence. The Rows themselves declined into a wintry torpor, even the tramps and pedlars keeping away in the full knowledge that no house had so much as a crust to spare. The children were too hungry and fretful for games and hung about on the doorsteps, watchful and wary.

Women scrounged, ran up debts, pleaded with tradesmen for food, turned their faces to the wall in bed at night, sent their children after kindling wood and into the farm fields to steal turnips. The men crouched on all fours at the Rows end, playing shove-ha'penny with buttons, desperate for a smoke or a drink, ready to fall out with the unforgiving logic that hunger brings.

Then with Christmas and Ne'erday approaching and starvation staring them in the face, the miners' will broke. Even with sixpence docked, the wage that had once appeared a pittance now assumed the proportions of fairy gold.

The final strike meeting was held in Grannie Fleming's cottage. Josie Daly tried to stir up resistance. Duncan, swallowing the bitter draught of failure, acceded to the men's wishes to go back with bowed head.

And Findlay, disillusion etched into his face like acid, made his position clear. He would not work for Lachie Balfour again. He was finished with Dounhead. Duncan could take over the secretaryship, but from now on, his own role would be on the sidelines.

In Kate's eyes, this was the only good to come from the strike. She busied herself making the new home as clean and comfortable as she could and when spring came, she would get some new chicks and Findlay could work in the garden. All she wanted was for the burden of the pit to be lifted at last from her husband's back; to see him sit out in the sun, respond to the flowers and the birds. And why not. maybe, follow in the miners' tradition by breeding canaries? Set in their cages outside each cottage door, they made a lovely sound.

A consciousness of the brevity of life seemed to be with her always now. So much had been toil and struggle, parting and heartbreak. Was it too much to ask that they should just be together now, her and her jo, ready with advice for those who sought it, but clear of the fight?

As the men went back to work in time for Christmas and New Year, life pulsed through the Rows once again. Women whitened their steps on a Friday with rubbing-stone, distinguishing each doorstep by the individuality of the designs they made. Money passed over the village counters and good smells came again from the big pots over the range fires.

Children had a farthing for sweeties and men lit their clay pipes and put their feet to warm by the coal fires, and there was a twist of tobacco for the grandmothers who also enjoyed a puff. Once again came the pedlars with button-hooks and elastic, the tinkers with their soldering-irons and braziers, the bearded beggar and the penny-whistle man.

But the legacy was bitterness. Colliers spat when they passed Dounhead House, faces turned away when Lachie Balfour rode in his trap down the main street. Tansy Fleming was one of the few who did not cut him. When they met, they spoke of everything but the strike, and he was able to tell her he had finished some pictures, which would be shown at the Glasgow Institute of the Fine Arts. There was just one thing she wished for: that he would not speak so much of Isa, or say he missed her presence with so much fervour in his voice.

Chapter Fifteen

'Paterson,' said Honoria, 'I have been thinking.'

Paterson looked up from his favourite breakfast of smoked beef, potatoes, toast and coffee and smiled at her benevolently.

'What, my love?'

'I've been thinking I would like to see Lilias. Papa, too, of course, but Lilias is more important.'

'You were always close to her, dear.'

'Yes,' said Honoria reflectively. 'And now that Isa has left her, I worry about her.'

'Invite her out on a visit. I'll pay.'

'You know she won't leave Papa. No, I shall have to go back to Scotland. I could take Junior – '

'Perhaps next year,' said Paterson absently. He riffled impatiently through the papers at the side of his plate, then looked up and, seeing her face was downcast, gave her all his concentration for a few precious moments.

'I have a surprise,' he said mysteriously. 'A special, cheer-up Honny surprise.'

The little boy they called Finn (after grandfather Findlay) threw himself at his father's knee.

'What surprise, Daddy?'

Honoria drew him back, laughing.

'No, he won't tell us, Finn. Will you?'

Paterson smiled inscrutably. 'No chance.'

'Tell me I am foolish to worry about Lilias,' she pursued anxiously.

'You are foolish,' he declared. 'But I love you. I can't spare you, Honny, not even to see your sister. But we'll go back together, one day. That would be best, wouldn't it?'

He leaned towards her and she returned his kiss. She

knew that what he said was true, that he depended on her to see to the practical details of his life, to see his clothes were clean and pressed, his food prepared to his liking. Since Finn had been born, they had travelled extensively on railroad business, and she had made it her duty to turn chilly hotel rooms into something like home, to be on hand when guests needed entertaining, to keep Finn quiet when there was urgent paper-work to be done and, above all, to be ready with her love and reassurance when problems seemed intractable and Paterson restless and insecure.

They were a team and the simple fact was he would not function properly without her. Yet the travelling, the lack of a permanent home, the inhuman demands Paterson made upon himself sometimes as his railroad interests widened and diversified, were beginning to take their toll of her emotional strength. More and more recently, she had been indulging in nostalgic recollections of Dounhead. She could not own to these too often to Paterson. He liked her to be strong, cheerful, imperturbable and she hated to be anything less.

She looked thoughtfully out of the railway carriage window as the train approached New York. It was no ordinary carriage they were travelling in, but one of the 'palace cars' designed by George Mortimer Pullman and the acme of comfort.

It was De Witt's own private railroad car and a measure of his regard for Paterson that he had insisted he use it while De Witt himself was in Canada, engaged in some intriguing scheme that might one day take a railroad through the Canadian Rockies. With power drilling, that had now become possible.

It meant that business men like De Witt could live independently of hotels, and its eighty feet contained a saloon, dining-room, bathroom, bedroom and kitchen – perhaps the nearest thing Honoria had experienced to a home since for a brief time they had rented a place near Baltimore.

Finn, of course, adored this method of travel and the car attendants spoiled him. They had taught him to sing 'Tenting Tonight' and 'Oh! Susanna', and when they weren't around he played endless games with the reversible plush seats.

Honoria's mind went back to journeys that had been a good deal less luxurious. The time they'd been snow-bound, for example, on the Central Pacific Railroad. Paterson had supervised the placing of three more locomotives behind the main engine and they'd charged the deep drifts repeatedly. She'd been terrified of a derailment but eventually they'd battered their way through, as Paterson had sworn they would, but afterwards he had put his mind to thinking up some kind of snow-clearing apparatus that could be brought into play when the situation demanded.

Not long afterwards, he and De Witt had started talking about Bessemer steel. Paterson had been in a ferment of excitement because the new steel would not only mean far more precise specifications in locomotives, but also longer – and longer-lasting – segments of rails.

He had explaimed to her that something called the Kelly-Bessemer process, which heated iron ore together with coke and then had forced draughts of air applied to it, had been developed almost simultaneously in England and America and that because of this, a world market was opening up for those, like his fellow emigrant Scot, Andrew Carnegie, who had the wit and energy to bring all the functioning parts of the new process together.

De Witt had taken Paterson with him to explore the extent of the Mesabi iron deposits in Minnesota and then to size up the quantities of good anthracite coal in western Pennsylvania. He'd been quick to see that heavy-duty railroads, carriers and cranes would be needed to bring together the heavy raw materials. And he'd used Paterson to hunt down the men who had the necessary metallurgical experience and who would be the master foremen in this new, strangely delicate and demanding process. Many were Slavs migrating to the Monongahela Valley, but there were Scots, too, among the first generation steel-workers.

The only times Paterson had left her and Finn behind were when he had gone on locomotive test-runs on some recently-constructed tracks where the Indians were still likely to attack. Only once had she glimpsed Indians, riding hard on the horizon, and she had felt the same distant pity for them that she'd felt for the buffalo herds, inexorably split into northern and southern herds by the progress of the Union Pacific. Sometimes it seemed to her that everything had to make way, go down, before the railroad. Including herself and Finn.

Just of late, though, she knew Paterson had been asking De Witt to get back to the sole task of designing special engines for special jobs. He did not care for the over-loaded design of many of the locomotives, preferring, for example, a straight stack instead of the ornate capped chimney which many sported.

He came now and sat by her, relaxed and dreamy, as the train snaked its way nearer and nearer to New York. Finn had gone to sleep on his bunk, a toy locomotive clutched possessively in both hands.

'You'll see them soon,' he told her, expecting, as always, instant tuning in to his thought processes. Then seeing she was baffled this time, he added, 'The elevated railways, trestled over the street. Cheap and useful. Could have gone underground, but for the serpentine rock on Manhattan Island.'

She shook her head. 'You never think of anything else.'

'Special problems.' He looked blissfully pleased. 'The little tank engines have no time between stops for pressure by air brakes. They need something like the Eames vacuum brake. And then, the engines have to follow the sharp curves of the city streets. That means trailing radial trucks, I think – '

She laughed. 'You're impossible. What is my lovely surprise? Won't you give me a hint?'

'You'll have to wait till after my meetings. Tomorrow, Honny. You'll see tomorrow.

They'd taken a train from New York, then an overnight steamer, then a train again to Boston – a method of travel between the two places much in favour at the moment – and now she was sitting in a horse-drawn buggy, going up a dirt-and-gravel street on the ouskirts of the Massachusetts town, wondering just what it was Paterson had in store for them.

He stopped the horse, got down, tied it to a cast-iron hitching-post outside a large house screened by shade trees and held out his hand to help her on to the stone block that led to the wooden sidewalk.

'Go on,' he said. 'Through the gate.'

She took Finn's hand – even his chatter had subsided, for once – and walked through the pretty gate in the wooden picket-fence, past flower beds laid out in a formal pattern and ornamented with iron deer, and up the wooden steps to the front porch of the big white clapboard house.

'Are we visiting?' she demanded.

He shook his head. 'Not this time. Honny, it's yours.'

He put a key into the front door and in a daze she stepped into the front hall. Quickly she walked from room to large room on the ground floor, with Paterson walking behind her identifying them – 'Parlour, second parlour, dining-room, study.' With Finn racing ahead they went upstairs and looked at the bedrooms, and then they went outside and inspected the chicken coop and cowshed, the barn for the horse and buggy, the sloping cellar door leading to the big cellar with its stone walls and earthen floor. Everything was brand new, well-finished, inviting.

Paterson took her back on to the rough lawn to admire the effect of the scroll-saw on the roof lines and then indoors again to look at the stained-glass windows in the hall and the beautifully-carved banisters and fireplaces.

'De Witt has told me this is where he wants me,' he explained. 'He is opening brand new offices in the centre of town and I'm being put in charge. The same builder made this house. The rent is good and reasonable.'

'You mean – ' She looked at him, scarcely able to comprehend what he was saying to her. 'You mean we really are going to settle down for good?'

'It's what you want, isn't it? I may have to go away from time to time, but you shall have staff to help run the house, and if I know you, you'll soon know everyone in the neighbourhood.'

She was bustling from room to room now like one of his little steam engines. 'We shall need a lot of furniture. And drapes. A big, round table here, don't you think, with a nice cloth – and Paterson, we just have to have a family Bible, straight away.'

'Right,' he humoured her. 'It'll need to be a big one, for the names of Finn's brothers and sisters.'

She threw him a merry look. 'I want that John Rogers statuette of the checkers players. Oh, and over here a bookcase. With sliding doors.'

He could not get her to leave the house to return to their hotel in the hired buggy. Even as the light was fading, she was still going from room to room, planning as she went, burbling about wicker swings for the porch and a jardinière for the main parlour.

Finally they stood under the shade trees, with a weary Finn held against his father's shoulder.

'I know I shall be happy here,' she said softly. 'I could feel a welcome from the house, right from the start.'

He laughed at her fancy. It was a supremely happy and fulfilling day for both of them. He knew now there would be no more references to 'going home'. This was home, the country they had made their own, and the dusk threw back the resonances of excitement and possibility of a whole wide and lovely continent.

Wattie Chapman hurried down the street to the *Clarion* office. Christmas Eve, and it was snowing again. He reflected wryly that Christmas in Dounhead was nothing like Christmas as featured in the London periodicals. There was still this strong, Calvinistic antipathy to celebrating the birth of Christ in any kind of light-hearted manner, but come Hogmanay and it was quite a different story again . . .

The English wife of Wylie the grocer had a little fir tree in their parlour window, glimmering with candles, and children were gathered at the garden fence to admire it. They had Albert the Good to thank for such whimsicalities, Christmas trees and a rash of tartans emanating from Balmoral. And, of course, an improvement in public hygiene because it was suspected that the illness that carried him off had been caused by bad drains. It was time somebody did something about the drains in Dounhead. He wouldn't allow himself to think about those children back there, many of them his scholars, half-fed, poorly-clothed. He'd grown used to the sore of frustration.

Alf Maclaren, Duncan Fleming and his father, Findlay, were seated in the chilly office when Wattie arrived, and Josie Daly was trying to coax the stubborn stove into life so that she could make them all some cocoa.

Wattie shook Duncan's hand. 'So you're lodge secretary and area organizer rolled into one?'

'That's right.'

'That'll keep you busy. But you know why we're here?'

'To put me up for the by-election. I would rather have waited for the general election.'

'Aye, trust old Tolley to choose an awkward time to go.' The multiple draper, caught up in London society, had died in his mistress's house in Hamilton Terrace, St John's Wood; died in the act, said some of the more scurrilous Parliamentary gossips, but the papers had called it a seizure.

'He'll do it,' Alf affirmed. 'There couldn't be a better time. If Lachie Balfour stands for the Tories, he'll find out what sixpence off the pit wage will cost him.'

'The colliers won't vote for him,' Wattie affirmed. 'But he carries a lot of sway around here. There's still this feudal notion of owing allegiance to the Big House. And something in the Scottish nature that wants to look up to somebody.'

Findlay looked keenly at his son. 'He needs blooding,' he said. 'Up yonder in Parliament they'll bludgeon him with patronage and fancy talk. You'll need to gird your loins, my man. You should maybe have taken that university chance when Wattie got it for you – '

'Don't put him down, man,' said Wattie mildly.

Findlay looked at him in surprise, then turned to Duncan

with a strange expression in his eyes.

'It's like sending Daniel into the lion's den. I would be a poor parent if I didn't have my reservations.'

'Then that's just about made up my mind for me!' Duncan joked, but with a hard edge. 'I'm your candidate. I pledge my hand and heart.' In the hubbub of congratulation and conjecture, the men paid no attention to Josie, but she had given a start of delight at Duncan's words and her face was pink with pleasure as she poured the cocoa at last into the waiting mugs.

It was not as simple as that, of course. Duncan was sailing under the Liberal banner and the party had several other names in mind. But in the days to come Wattie Chapman indulged in some rail-roading. His political acumen was recognized well beyond the bounds of Dounhead and in the end Duncan's candidacy was in the bag.

At the end of the meeting on Christmas Eve, Findlay and Duncan returned to the cottage in the Rows to find Lachie Balfour seated in Findlay's chair by the fire.

'That'll be my chair you're in,' said Findlay. He glared at Kate for allowing this act of lese-majesty. Lachie leaped out of the chair quickly and held out his hand.

'Shall we let bygones be bygones? I've come to offer you your job back as safety man.'

Findlay refused the outstretched hand. He spat in the grate and turned on Lachie a bitter, laconic smile.

'And I'm telling you what to do with your job,' he answered.

'You know more about the pit than anybody. I don't want safety neglected.'

'Then pay a decent wage.'

Lachie had kept his hand ostentatiously outstretched all this time. Now he dropped it and his face darkened, but he said in a controlled voice, 'I've authorized extra coal for every house this night, and free tokens to spend on food at the pit shop. You'll not force me into the role of heartless villain.'

'No,' Duncan interjected. 'It's more a failure of the

imagination. You don't know what it's like to be on the receiving end of patronage. You can keep your free coal and sugar.'

'That's not what the rest of the folk in the Rows feel,' said Lachie. 'I came here in seasonal goodwill.' Again he held out his hand towards Findlay. 'Will you take it?'

The old man turned his back on him in disgust. As Lachie went out of the door, he looked directly at Duncan and added, 'Ask Miss Lilias Galbraith if I am a heartless man. She's a friend of yours, I believe.'

'What does he mean?' ground Duncan.

'He was telling me before you came in that he'd taken Lilias in a sack of presents for the Sunday school soirée tonight – ' said Kate.

'By God!' Duncan exploded. 'He'll not do it! Try to buy us out of our poverty with a few miserable gimcracks!' His rage carried him at a fine pace towards the church hall, where Lilias and a few helpers were decorating the walls with evergreen and laying the trestle tables out with food.

He stopped at the door to the hall. He had seen little of Lilias since he'd got back, everything had been happening so fast, but he'd been saving up a proper meeting with her like a child saving the last comfit in a paper bag. She did not see him at first. She was on a pair of step-ladders, attaching scarlet ribbon streamers to some holly, and he saw the familiar narrow hollow of her nape and heard her light, floating laugh. Her effect on him was as magical as ever – a floating in the head, a tightening in the loins, a wild, alarming happiness that she should exist on the same planet. She jumped down and someone indicated him waiting by the door. She came towards him smiling and blushing.

'Duncan, you've come to help?'

'If you like.' He gazed down at her helplessly. 'What would you like me to do?'

'Oh, have you a head for heights? The top of the walls look so bare!' She put a hammer and nails into his hands and dragged forward a hamper of evergreen.

'Lilias, did Lachie Balfour come here with presents for the children?'

'He did. Wasn't it good of him?' she demanded briskly.

'You'll not accept them.'

'Not accept them? Do you realize how little our village children have? These are things like scarves and picture-books. Can you picture their faces? They've never had more than some fruit and a few comfits.'

'You know what he did to their fathers?'

'Oh yes. He told me his side of things, too. I try to be impartial.'

He gripped her wrist, but dropped it as she looked down angrily.

'Send them back.'

'I won't.'

'Please.'

She shook her curls. 'Come on, Duncan, it's Christmas. Love thine enemy.' She brushed his shoulder lightly with her small hand. The touch, the nearness of her, disarmed him. There was a smell of fresh bread and buns from the table, the sweet, sickly scent of the evergreen, and a brisk tympany of sound as the band tuned up in readiness for the musical games. He succumbed to the Christmas magic and, careless of who was looking, brushed her cheek boldly with his lips. The first time. Happiness beat in him like a Christmas drum.

'Duncan!' she said, in a low voice. And held her fingers to the place he had kissed.

She wanted him to stay for the party, but although he had given in over the presents, he had no intention of staying to see them handed out. He took as long as he could over the decorations, and even then hung about just for the pleasure of watching Lilias, but at last he turned to go, and her wave and smile stayed with him as he trudged home through the snow.

Kate's anxious face greeted him as he went in.

'You'd better get down to the pithead. There's been trouble about supplies running out in the pit shop. Old Daly took his free sugar and threw it down the shaft. I think some of the men have been drinking.

Drink had put a number of the men into an ugly mood.

Although they had been forced back to work, the docking of the sixpence from their wages festered like an underlying sore. Led by a shock-headed member of the hard-living Donaldson family, which had provided generations of sons for the pits, they were breaking up the pit shop and there was talk of lying in wait for Lachie Balfour and 'giving him the hiding of his life', as Sheugh Donaldson put it.

Duncan tried to talk some sense into them, but Sheugh Donaldson for one wasn't prepared to listen.

'Come back to my house,' he invited Duncan. 'I lost a wean with the consumption during the strike. Do you know how many wee white coffin tassels lie in our sideboard drawer? I'll tell you. Four. Four weans under the sod. Somebody has to pay for it.'

'Aye.' Duncan placated the near-raving man. It was well known that Belle Donaldson spent what little money she had on ale and whisky and the horde of Donaldson children brought each other up in a state of near-animal squalor. 'Now go home, man, and I'll get my mother to send something up for your wife and weans.'

Late on Christmas Eve, Tansy was sent by the dressmaker to Dounhead House, with a parcel of finished garments for the housekeeper, Mrs Lindsay. The old woman drew the girl into the hall, her eyes dilating, and said in a hoarse, frightened voice, 'There's been fine goings-on here the night, Miss Fleming.'

'What happened?' Tansy demanded.

'The scum from the Rows, they've been thumping and banging round the back of the house, looking for the master. I heard them shouting and cursing. One of them was going to set fire to the horses and stable, but I cried out I would get the law on them, and they were falling over each other, anyway, they were that fu'.'

'Have they gone now?'

'I got the master's gun, that he has for the birds, and I let off some shot.' Mrs Lindsay gave an almost toothless grin. 'I put the fear of death in them!'

'And where is the master?'

'Out by at Bellnoch, at a ball.'

Thoughtfully, Tansy made her way back down the drive. She could imagine how Lachie must have looked as he set out. How she wished she had been with him! So intensely did she imagine the festivities he was attending, she could almost hear the music, the stomp of feet, feel the cool gloss on the women's dresses and the crackle of the men's gloves.

She would know so well how to behave in such circumstances. If only Lachie could see the real lady beneath her well-worn bonnet and cracked boots. One day he would. She had always felt like a visitor to the Rows. They existed like an outpost in the vast territories of her imagination. She did not feel the nip of cold through her mitts. For she was elsewhere, dancing.

The flat basin of field near the river, where the village children played in the summer and the travelling fair set up twice a year, was a natural gathering point for Duncan's open-air election meetings, and two or three times a week crowds assembled and waited for him to come and talk. They were often the same people and the arguments covered much of the same ground, but sometimes strangers interjected and the polemic flew fast and furious.

Tonight Wattie Chapman had brought down visitors from Glasgow, and with election day only a week away there was excitement in the air. When she had set up Duncan's platform, a glorified soapbox, no more, Josie busied herself handing out pamphlets she had run off at the *Clarion* office. One concerned conditions in the mines, demanding every pit should be tested daily by deputy overseers and that miners should have the right to appoint their own inspectors.

A second, a different colour, described conditions in overcrowded, insanitary 'coffin ships' and demanded action to change them.

A third called for a reduction of hours for railway workers, to reduce the toll of accidents, and a fourth for a union to protect the rights of agricultural workers.

Josie had written them all herself, grammatical errors unobtrusively put right by Alf Maclaren, and now she foisted them on the audience whether they wanted them or not. Not all the listeners were, after all, sympathetic to Duncan's case, and many took exception to someone like Josie Daly thinking she knew what was best for them.

'Her faither's old Joakie Daly,' said one woman to another. 'And he's a drunken old sot.'

'Aye, who does she think she is?' demanded her friend. They wrapped their buxom arms comfortably inside their shawls and subjected Josie to a joint, hostile glare. She'd even been heard to suggest they should have women in Parliament, after all. Maybe, as one suggested to the other, she was a bit touched in the head.

Wattie Chapman and his friends listened patiently while the more sophisticated arguments put forward in the past by John Stuart Mill and Robert Owen were brought down to the level of the unlettered men in the gathering, as they carefully weighed them up in relation to their own lives and work.

'I don't need unions,' one big man in the front challenged Duncan vigorously. 'I'm a free man, I can negotiate my own wage. If I work harder than the man next to me, I deserve more than he gets.'

'This argument's not about money only, friend,' Duncan assured him. 'It's about the conditions you work under, the kind of home you live in, what happens when you're sick and unable to work, and how your wife feeds your children if you die.'

'Aye, and it's about rattening and taking away folks' tools if they don't agree with the union,' a sharp-faced man cried out. 'The unions are a big stick to beat the individual with – '

The audience was breaking now into two factions with little interest in listening to the platform. In vain Duncan called for order and in vain did Josie push her way through the crowds demanding respect for the speaker. Shouts broke down into fist-fights and undignified brawling. What started out as a political argument deteriorated into the personal and even the pointless.

'The awakening conscience,' said Wattie Chapman to his friends dispassionately, and took them off home.

Not far away, in the church hall, Lachie Balfour was

tackling a meeting on a smaller, more sedate scale.

A lad who didn't look old enough to have the vote was needling him about education.

'Have the Tory party any need for shame there?' demanded Lachie forcefully. 'The Duke of Argyll's Royal Commission showed that about ten times more children have a secondary education in Scotland than in England, and six times as many go to university.'

'But still only about one child in a hundred and forty gets a full education,' the youth persisted. 'And what are you going to do about it?'

'The Compulsory Education Act will provide for every child in Scotland,' said Lachie. 'We keep our lead on England, where it is only the children of manual labourers whose education will be so protected.'

The youth could not think of anything else he wanted to say and the meeting petered out. There was despondency in Lachie's camp and the suspicion that Duncan Fleming might be rallying more support than they had ever thought possible.

Lachie was glad the meeting had finished early. A travelling company were performing *The Octoroon*, a play about slavery in America, in Bellnoch, and Tansy Fleming had reminded him when they met in the street the other day that he had once recommended it to her. He wasn't quite sure how it had come about, but he had heard himself asking if she'd like to see it. Maybe, if he was honest with himself, he was dismayed at a complete break with the Fleming family. At least, if he kept in touch with Tansy, he could hear something of how Isa was doing in Edinburgh. And that was what really mattered.

It was little short of a vision that awaited him on the station platform. How had she slipped out of the house in that costume, assuring her parents she was going to the prayer meeting? The broadcloth of her skirt and shorgin was a delectable, dull blue, trimmed with black velvet ribbon, and her little matching hat set at a rakish angle set off a face sparkling with smiles and animation.

Cheered in spite of himself, he said, 'You look good

enough to eat,' and she gave him a look of such innocent devotion that he smiled inwardly. Funny, though, how Isa's still, cool, intelligent image wavered before his mind's eye all the way to Bellnoch. He enjoyed Tansy's company, just the same. She was witty, entertaining, easily pleased.

The travelling players were handicapped by a leading lady of singular ugliness and a hero whose words were distinctly slurred. A noble-browed child actor gave readings from Shakespeare in the intervals and, struck by the glint of irreverence in Tansy's eye, Lachie found himself dissolving into stupid, juvenile merriment. It was like a tonic after the recent grimness, and he thought that if they could keep it from Tansy's obdurate old fool of a father, there was no reason why they shouldn't do this sort of thing again.

His cup was full when on the train going home Tansy spoke of Isa, the bodies she had to dissect, the books she had to study. He watched her speed lightly in the direction of home then took off up his own drive. He had not gone more than twenty yards when figures sprang from the shrubbery on either side of him. He was never to know who they were, except that before he lost consciousness he thought he detected Sheugh Donaldson's voice saying, 'Get him! Finish him!' They did not botch the job. A kick broke his arm, another split his head. A sobbing Mrs Lindsay found him an hour later, having set out to look for him with a lantern. She covered him with a blanket against the night cold till she could find help to carry him in.

By next morning it was all round the village that union thugs had beaten Lachie Balfour half to death. Feeling that had been running against him over the sixpenny strike now began to turn in his favour. His Christmas Eve gifts to the householders in the Rows and the sack of presents he had donated to the Sunday school soirée were magnified now into gifts of saintly munificence. His good looks and easy manner were adumbrated in his favour. Mrs Wylie recollected how he always swept off his cap when he met her and others on hearing how long it had taken the doctor to bind up his cuts, remembered pennies given to children and kind words extended to dogs.

It only took Lachie's appearance at the last two public meetings, head bandaged and face deathly pale, to convert the tide in his favour. Although he denounced them at every opportunity, Duncan was now bracketed with the 'union thugs'. Ugly rumours of a plot to overthrow the Queen herself went coursing round the village. It was generally agreed that people should keep their station, that someone used to authority like Lachie should retain it and that upstarts like the Flemings should be kept in their places.

When the votes were polled, it became clear that Lachie Balfour would be returned by a handsome majority. Some kind of local loyalty towards Duncan reasserted itself at the last, but it was too late. Those kicks at Lachie Balfour's head had won him the day. Josie Daly wept while Duncan swallowed his own chagrin and said patiently, 'There'll come another day.'

But Alf Maclaren boiled with fury. He brought Duncan a copy of the *Dounhead Advertiser* and showed him a slanted leading article in it, saying in half-hints and innuendo that Duncan had tried to bring about victory by brute force.

'By God!' Alf fumed. 'You'll have to fight these whited sepulchres as well as the ignorant swine round here that keep their noses in their troughs and see nothing.'

A few days later, Alf sent for Duncan and declared he was handing over the *Clarion*, lock, stock and barrel, for what it was worth, to him and Josie.

'I'm seventy, man,' he declared. 'If there's going to be a new Jerusalem, I'm not going to be around to see it, so I'm going to my sister's in Ayrshire. I can always help to muck out the byre.'

'You're disillusioned,' said Duncan. 'Don't be.'

'You'll never change human nature,' Alf said fiercely, and there was the glint of tears behind his spectacles. 'Man's life is nasty, brutish, short, There's an end to it.'

'You don't think that or you wouldn't give us the *Clarion*. I'll take it on, Alf. I can make a go of it, with Josie's help.

But there's one change I insist on.'

'What's that?'

'That we call it the *Miners' Clarion*. Then there will be no mistake about our intentions.'

Alf smiled reluctantly. 'Stick to the truth as near as you can make it. That's all I ask.'

Chapter Sixteen

'Miss Fleming, there's a visitor to see you.'

Isa looked up from her anatomy textbook at her landlady's flustered face. Miss Anderson was a good woman, according to her lights, and a sedulous worker for the Church, but the room which she had made available to Isa in Edinburgh was austere and sparsely furnished, and, like Miss Anderson's brand of charity, without warmth. Isa did what she could in the way of small tasks to show her gratitude, but Miss Anderson had remained distant, formal, almost as though she were afraid of human contact. Only when they talked about the new chances available to women to enter the professions like medicine did her pale, spinsterly features show any animation. 'We women have been kept down too long,' she would declare. For men, except the minister, her manner was one of almost supercilious scorn.

Now, red-faced and plainly discomfited, she came up to Isa's plain deal table that served as a desk, and almost hissed at her: 'I told him I did not allow gentlemen callers. But he is very persistent. Well-spoken, too. Name of Balfour. I suppose you may see him in the parlour for ten minutes. But I shall be watching the clock!'

Her dark hair falling down from its chignon, her face pale from study and inky from her pen, Isa hastened down the dark stairs with their turkey-red carpet and entered the mausoleum-like chill of Miss Anderson's parlour, with its stuffed birds and small animals, its heavy furniture and oppressive drapes.

Lachie Balfour turned towards her with a troubled face, but could not help a quick smile at her ruffled appearance. As the door clicked shut on Miss Anderson's disapproving features, he went forward and kissed Isa on the brow.

'Well, Lachie,' she said coolly, 'what brings you to Edinburgh?'

'I've come to see my lawyer, before I take off for London. And to see my picture which was picked for the Royal Scottish Academy.'

'Congratulations.'

'It doesn't please me. None of them do. The Academy is not cosmopolitan enough in its outlook. But never mind me. How goes the profession of medicine?'

'Quite well,' she answered composedly. 'The men are growing more accustomed to having us now. They no longer throw mud and filth at us. One would think they had never heard of Lister and antisepsis, wouldn't one? We are taught separately, of course, and supposedly do not have the same status – '

'You do not let that bother you?'

'Of course not!'

'Good, good.'

'You should not have come here, you know. My landlady forbids visitors.'

He looked at her broodingly. 'Don't you want to see me?'

'It isn't that – '

'Has the bad feeling between your father and Duncan and me altered our friendship, then?'

'It is bound to make a difference,' she burst out.

'Can you not see my side of it?'

'You brought the men to their knees. They'll never forgive you.'

'Sometimes I have had enough of Dounhead pit,' he said harshly. 'I never wanted the responsibility in the first place.'

She raised her head with a measured, taunting look. 'Only children avoid their responsibilities.'

'I've not avoided anything. D'you think Parliament will be a bowl of cherries? Hang it, Isabella, you are not going to be as intransigent as your father? You have left Dounhead and all that behind you. One day you'll be a woman of consequence.'

'I just want to be a good doctor.'

'And a doctor should know the right people. I can introduce you to some Edinburgh notables. I am not without influence. And I wish you would use your influence with your father. I want the goodwill of all the colliers, not just those who voted for me.'

'I am bound to say, I think Duncan would have made a better MP. Aside from politics, he is the more serious man.'

'You think I am not serious?'

'Only about your painting. It is what you should do.'

They faced each other, eyes trying to read each other's thoughts, then the corners of Isa's mouth turned up and Lachie gave a short, barking laugh with a rueful humour in it.

'Pax,' he offered. He took her inky hands, staring down at them, then raised them, one after the other, to his lips.

'I find Dounhead insupportable without you.'

'You have Tansy. She is also your friend.'

He raised his eyebrows expressively. 'True. She is you, turned outwards. Did you know that?'

'Lachie, you must go. I won't presume on Miss Anderson's good offices further. Meet me tomorrow after classes, if you like.'

When she came down the steps from the dissecting-room next day, he thought how pale she looked, how contained and determined. His mood, which had been buoyant and expectant, dropped imperceptibly. Her dress was of a hodden-grey material and her cape was the shabby one he'd seen her wear to church back home, many times. Everyone went to church to see and be seen. Not Isabella, though. Yet the face under the white-trimmed, grey bonnet was the face he wanted to see more than any other on earth. This moment and always.

They strolled through the Edinburgh streets in pale sunshine. He had arranged that they could use his lawyer's chambers for a private talk and when they entered a room there, a pale little skivvy brought them tea, as he had asked, on a silver tray.

'Please pour,' he invited Isa, and watched as her long,

tapering hands dealt capably with the small, domestic ceremony.

He began to speak rapidly, before his courage ran out.

'I have said I miss you. You thought I was not serious. I don't want to disturb your studies and I am prepared to wait, if you will give me some encouragement – '

She looked at him, her eyes huge and alarmed. 'Don't go on, Lachie,' she pleaded.

'But I must. When I spoke of missing, I meant that all other women seem – insipid, next to you. You open windows in my mind I never knew were there.'

'Stop!'

There was no brooking the authority in her voice. He could not see her face momentarily for the grey bonnet, but when she turned it towards him it was full of a distress and turmoil that tore at his heart. Yet he knew better than to make a move towards her.

'You must know, Lachie, where my duty lies.'

'Duty! "Stern Daughter of the Voice of God". Isn't that what Wordsworth calls it? Make it your duty to love me!'

She laced her hands together on her lap. He could not take his eyes off those hands. When she spoke, her voice was low and quiet.

'I made my choice a long time ago, Lachie. When I saw my brother Paterson, not able to run about like other boys. And my father, his strength sapped by the cholera. I can't preach, like James Galbraith, or agitate, like my brother Duncan. But maybe I can heal.'

She gave him a small, almost absent-minded smile.

'Marriage has never come into it, with me. I presume that is what you have in mind. When I was a little girl, I wanted to be like Florence Nightingale. She rejected marriage, too, because she said it did not provide for the promptings of a moral, active nature, which requires satisfaction.'

He said humbly, 'Marriage need not make you less than you are.'

'I am not very much,' she said matter-of-factly. 'I cannot spread myself too thin.'

'You are cold,' he charged her. But she had won back composure. She sipped her tea to the dregs then got up.

'You will find someone else,' she temporized. 'As the ladies say in novels, I am not insensible to the honour you have paid me. Let us be friends!'

Just for a brief moment, he detected a wild and fleeting uncertainty in her eyes. But it was gone before he could name it.

'As you like,' he said heavily and, with a brave attempt to put the world back on its bearings, added, 'Let me show you some of the sights of Edinburgh and at least buy you a new pen and nib. Doctors should disdain inky fingers!'

'What is the matter, Lilias?' demanded James Galbraith of his daughter. She had pushed the food around her plate and at last laid down fork and knife, having eaten next to nothing. 'Are you missing Isabella?'

'A little,' she admitted, her eyes half-lidded. She was not accustomed to giving her father her confidences. He was a remote, slightly forbidding figure, never less than kind or just, but living on a different plane, where the small hurts and grievances of everyday life had no significance.

She could not, in any case, put a name to her restlessness. It had something to do with Isa going to Edinburgh, and much to do with Honoria and her family being in America. If only she could afford to go to Boston, where Paterson was now working and where Honoria was mistress of a beautiful house and several servants.

Paterson had, indeed, offered to pay her saloon fare, thirteen guineas, but her father would have none of it, insisting she was needed for the smooth running of the manse.

If only some excitement would enter her life! It was not that she wanted to depart from the straight and narrow path laid down for her by the Church, just that she wished goodness was not so often compatible with dullness.

She had just been reading about the building of the Quarrier Homes for Orphans at Bridge of Weir. Now there was Christian endeavour she could identify with, even if

William Quarrier was a Baptist. A prosperous shoemaker, he had, it appeared, been crossing Jamaica Bridge in Glasgow one winter night and found a child crying bitterly because his matches had been stolen.

This had inspired him to start the Shoeblack Brigade for destitute boys and he had gone on from there to organize the children as newspaper sellers and parcel carriers, meanwhile opening a series of small homes where they were provided with decent food, clothing, Christian training and self-respect.

In some ways, she had to agree with Duncan Fleming in his increasing criticism of the Church and, by implication, her own father.

Surely deeds, not words, were what mattered? It was not enough to get up in the pulpit each Sunday and preach to a congregation, the women of which, at least, were more concerned with each other's gowns and bonnets than the content of the sermon. And though her father's sermons were magnificent, full of closely-argued Biblical criticism, scholarly and inspiring, yet she could not deny what Duncan called the 'sterile apathy' of most of his listeners.

'Why don't you get some stuff for a new gown?' James Galbraith broke into her thoughts, laying a hand lightly on his daughter's fair hair. 'Young Tansy Fleming would make it up for you. And Kate Kilgour will help you choose material.'

She smiled at him. 'Why do you always call Mistress Fleming, Kate Kilgour?'

'For that is how she came to me, as a young woman,' he answered. His expression softened and she had the feeling he wanted to say more.

'Was she comely?' she prompted curiously.

He gave her a smile that made his heavy face look years younger and said with unwonted roguishness, 'That would be telling!'

'Father!' cried Lilias, laughing. 'I do believe you had an eye for the lasses when you were young.'

He did not deny it. He made a little pantomime of being an irresistible rake, all the funnier for the sober dark of his clothes and the heavy imponderability of his craggy features.

Lilias squeezed his arm. She liked him best of all when he was being the human, funny father, but it happened seldom enough.

For his part, Galbraith made his way to his study with a lighter heart. It had been good to see Lilias laugh. This younger one with her delicate ways was dear to him indeed.

He looked out from his study window, down the douce village street, the gentle Lanarkshire slopes beyond, feeling a glow of affection for this whole Lowland scene where he was so much at home.

He was an honest man, about his innermost feelings as about everything else. Talking about Kate had sparked off old and, as he had thought, half-dead emotions. That she still threaded his days, bright strand on dark cloth, was one reason why earthly life remained supportable and his spirit never wholly put down.

Maybe he should have married her all those years ago, and let public opinion go hang. And maybe he should now prepare his mind for Lilias getting married, for that would no doubt give a purpose to her days. He thought of Paterson as Kate's son, although she had told him the circumstances of his birth, and he was not averse to having another of her sons as a second son-in-law. He found Duncan difficult to know, with his dour passion and uncompromising mind, but Galbraith had not missed the devotion in his look when it lighted on Lilias, nor her grave stillness when he was around.

As though spawned from his thoughts, Duncan was striding down the village street and had stopped at the manse gates. Galbraith knew he should go down and greet him, but he had his sermon to finish and he left the civilities to Lilias. It would be a diversion for her.

'I've brought you this,' said Duncan immediately, as he stepped into the manse hall out of the sharp wind.

'What is it?' demanded Lilias, leading him into the morning-room.

'A gift,' he said formally, shifting about on his feet a

shade uncomfortably, for he was accustomed neither to the giving nor getting of presents.

Lilias tore the wrapping off. 'Blackmore's *Lorna Doone*! Wattie Chapman said I should like it – '

'I heard him. I've never given you anything before. Do I get no token for my kindness?'

She came over and blushingly kissed his cheek.

'Thank you,' she said, and he laughed with pleasure.

'Will you sit down?'

'Lilias,' he began peremptorily, 'have you noticed my new cap? And the shine on my boots? I don't smarten up like this every day.'

'But you should,' she said gravely.

'I will, if it pleases you.' He stretched across the chenille-covered table and imprisoned her hand. 'I have to tell you how I feel about you. You must know already – '

'How must I know?' she demanded, a little sharply. 'I know you are great friends with Josie Daly.'

'She is a comrade. That is all.'

'No, I cannot see that that is all. She is a woman, too.'

'I love *you*.'

'But you have not said so.'

He looked at her, not sure whether she was teasing or serious.

'It must have been obvious to – to this very table. To the birds, to the trees. To everybody. I felt sure it was as evident as if I'd taken my heart out of my body and sewn it on my sleeve with red stitches.'

'Not all that evident,' she temporized. 'When you went to Fife, I did not know what to think.'

'That I would come back, of course.'

There was a silence that palpitated between them, throbbing with emotion.

At last he got up, picked up his new cap, examined it then threw it down again with a despairing gesture.

'The trouble is,' he said bitterly, 'that I've had nothing to offer you. Nor ever will have much. Throw in your lot with me and all you'll get is poverty and more poverty. Strikes and soup kitchens.'

'Surely things will be better now for the unions,' she said carefully, 'now that they are legal and their funds protected?'

'Struggle's only just begun.'

'It's not that I'm afraid of want,' she said, with dignity. 'Our Lord had little enough.'

She looked at him and saw the composure break up in his face. He indicated the heavy, dubbined boots and moleskin trousers with a sweep of his hand and said, 'I'm used to poverty. But you've had a delicate upbringing. Sickness and hunger and drunkenness aren't easy to live with, and that's what it's like in the Rows.'

'Yes, but it's families sticking together, too, and helping each other. And steps being cleaned on a Friday, and children dancing to the hurdy-gurdy man. Sometimes the manse seems so apart from everything – '

'Then,' he said, with an unbearable look of hope on his face, 'you would consider living in the Rows? With me?'

She didn't answer immediately. She stood over by the window with her hands clasped just under her chin and he saw that she was crying. He rose immediately and put his arms tenderly around her.

'What is it? Don't frighten me. Tell me.'

'It isn't easy.'

'Try.'

'Well, I will try. It's this: you are in love with an idea, Duncan, the idea of changing the world. And I know what this means, for I have seen it in my father.'

'Go on.'

'I do not say that people like you – you and my father – do not live with the realities. Part of the time, you do. But most of the time, you are living in a dream of the future. Living inside your own head. And nobody can be there with you.'

'Don't say that, Lilias,' he pleaded. 'I would never shut you out. You know that.'

'I was only nine when my mother died,' she went on consideringly. 'But I was old enough to know that life had become increasingly cold for her, that she was shut off from my father's inmost being by the Church. As I might be shut out from you, through politics.'

'You really think this?' he demanded. 'I had no idea.'

'I think this has held me back a little. From committing myself to you, in my mind.'

'Then worry no more,' he cried. 'You are first, last and always, the one star that shines always for me. All I want is to know you'll be there in the fight with me – '

'Would I have the stamina?'

He gazed at her reproachfully. 'You would just have to *be* there. It would be enough.'

'I think you put me on a pedestal. You idealize me. You should not. I am nothing special.'

He stood looking down at her, saying nothing. Then he stretched out his hands and slowly pulled her close to him.

'What if I told you that this was the happiest day of my life?'

'I have not said I love you.'

'Then pity me; say it.'

'I love you.'

'And you'll marry me?'

'Since you say so!'

It was the merriment he remembered afterwards, the pretty teeth, the dimple, that brought the sun out for him, whatever the circumstances. Later, he thought of the pallor, and the chill cold of her hands.

'What's up? What's up?'

Kate sat bolt upright in the set-in bed, wondering if she were dreaming or if she had really heard the thunderous knocking on the door. It came again. It was no dream. She stepped nimbly over Findlay's sleeping form, on to the hard wooden chair placed beside the bed for the purpose, and so across the cold kitchen floor, her heart thudding like a drum.

'Who is it?' she called.

'Galbraith.'

She could scarcely make out his face against the guttering lamp he carried. The neck of his coat was caught and crumpled, showing the haste with which he'd put it on.

'Kate,' he said, without preamble. 'Can you come? It's Lilias. I fear she is very sick. Will you come and sit with her, till I get the doctor?'

She was already pulling her clothes on over her nightdress. Scarcely knowing or caring what she wore, so greatly did his expression alarm her, and with Findlay calling out for explanations as she ran, she accompanied her old employer back to the manse.

She could hear the grating bark of Lilias's cough as they entered the front door.

'The croup,' she diagnosed. 'Get me a steaming kettle, balsam or camphorated oil.'

'No, it is more than that,' said Galbraith. He stood woodenly about in the hall, as though bereft of his senses. Gently moving him out of the way, Kate stirred the kitchen fire and put the kettle on.

She was aware of a figure behind her. It was Duncan, half-dressed, his hair wild.

'Mother, what's the matter? Can I go up to her?'

She turned and said soothingly, 'Now, now, there's nothing to get in a state about. You can best help by getting the doctor.'

He did as he was told without delay and Kate climbed the stairs to Lilias's room. The girl's eyes were wide and dilated, her brow clammy and her hands burning.

'There now, lass,' said Kate. 'We'll sponge your hands and face, get you a nice drink. And Duncan's gone for Dr Pettigrew.'

As she worked about, she continued to speak soothingly and the panic in Lilias's face subsided, although she continued to breath stertorously. When she had made the girl comfortable, Kate went on to the landing where Galbraith hovered.

'No, this is no ordinary fever,' she conceded. A dreaded word stabbed her mind.

'Diphtheria,' said Galbraith. 'I've seen it often enough in the Rows.'

So had Kate. Children dying black in the face as the dreaded disease smothered them.

'I thought she was not well,' said Galbraith, almost to himself. 'I put it down to missing Isabella. How could I have been so blind? She picks the infants up in the Rows, you know, no matter how filthy and neglected.'

'You could not have prevented it,' said Kate. She placed her hands over his, not caring now about status or anything else, only his human need.

Meanwhile Duncan had rushed to the doctor's portentous stone villa at the other end of Dounhead, to find a light on in the kitchen and the doctor's wife making herself a cup of tea.

'He's gone up to old Summerton at the farm,' said Mrs Pettigrew, referring to her husband, as always, in the third person. 'He's been gone an hour. That mad bull of theirs went for the old man again and this time I doubt there's no saving him.'

Duncan gave her a blank look and tore up the lonely track to Summerton's Farm. All he could hear was the awful sound of Lilias breathing. He had never sworn in his life before. Now oaths came to his lips at the ineffectual pumping of his own legs and at every jagged stone prepared to trip him.

Old Summerton was still alive, and with a promise to return in the day to see him, Dr Pettigrew urged Duncan on to the trap beside him and sent his wily black mare flying over the country tracks.

He examined Lilias's swollen neck, the greyish-white membrane in the throat which bled when his gentle probe touched it, and was in no doubt about his diagnosis. Mostly the disease attacked younger children, but was by no means uncommon in young adults. He knew he had a fight on his hands.

The struggle for Lilias's life went on for three days, days in which Kate's own family saw little of her, days where Duncan and Galbraith hovered jealously on landing or stairs, kept largely away from the patient by the doctor's insistence on quiet and rest.

It began to look as though Lilias would fight her way through, but Pettigrew knew that after the first battle had been won, secondary enemies lay in wait.

There was nothing that Lilias wanted she did not get: cooling drinks, a sight of her father or Duncan, the window opened now and then to let in the warm, sweet air. Village children, hearing the minister's daughter was ill, brought up bunches of wild flowers; Dounhead matrons exchanged bulletins between emptying ashes from the fire or buying matches and treacle from Wylie the grocer.

On the fourth day, Duncan was involved in some urgent business with the *Clarion*, but returned in the afternoon to sit with his mother in the Galbraith kitchen, while Lilias slept and Galbraith took a stroll. While his mother nodded in the rocking-chair, Duncan crept upstairs to peep round Lilias's bedroom door and see if there was anything she wanted.

It had been difficult getting reassurance out of Pettigrew, but surely now, Duncan thought, there was a good hope of the battle being won.

She was lying back on the pillows, her slender hands lying limply on the pages of a book on the counterpane, her fair, thick hair spread out fanwise, glossy from Kate's brushing.

She made a little gesture to indicate to him that she had been reading. That she had stretched, even if it was only to the bedside table, to secure the book, perturbed him. She could not realize how ill she had been.

He could not describe the joy that poured through him just to see her smile. She pushed herself up to speak and then he saw her start and fall forward, making a strange sound in the back of her throat.

'Lilias!' Even as he started forward, he knew nothing he did would be of any use, but he lifted her up and laid her body back against the pillows, calling out her name repeatedly, 'Lilias, Lilias, Lilias!'

The secondary enemy had gone straight for the heart. And won.

Chapter Seventeen

Everyone in the town of Dounhead mourned Lilias Galbraith: the children she had taught at Sunday school or handed conversation lozenges in the Rows; the Catholic mothers she had always greeted with a cheerful smile and an enquiry about the size of their families; those who had known her well or little.

There was a large funeral, which every family in the town turned out to watch and weep over. Yet Duncan could handle none of the eulogies that came into the *Clarion* office. He left it to Josie. It was all he could do to hold himself together, keep himself from breaking down completely.

He would not allow even his mother to offer a word of comfort and walked away at the mention of Lilias's name. He wanted to keep his grief to himself, as though it were valuable, part of her. Those who knew him best said that Lilias's death changed him greatly. He had an absent look, as though arguing with forces unseen, an interminable argument in which he was always bested. Certainly, afterwards, he never entered a church again. Organized religion seemed to be no help at all to him, till then a regular churchgoer. Any help had to be of the most unobtrusive kind, a mug of cocoa placed at his elbow by Josie, a tap on his shoulder from his father.

Kate grieved that there was no way her son would allow her close enough to comfort him, and James Galbraith was her further concern. His deep voice boomed out with thanks to all those who came with condolences, he was seen to smile and acknowledge.

But it was like watching a great edifice crumble. His bony, craggy face, full of wise and watchful intelligence, seemed to fill with lines, fall in on itself. The deep-set eyes were dull and unresponsive, the mouth set in bitter lines of unforgiving grief.

Kate found a quiet little woman, Miss Gint, to go in and keep house for him on a daily basis. She came and went like a grey ghost, shining the furniture, watering the plants, cooking him stews with watery gravy.

Kate herself saw to his linen, unable to bear that he should look less than immaculate, but his clothes began to look as though he had slept in them which often he had, and his noble grey mane, that set off that impressive head in the pulpit, looked shaggy and unkempt.

Another minister came to take the services for a month, but then the old man took the well-worn path to his pulpit once again, and preached as he had always done, with a clear, logical challenge and a burning assertion. But the voice had faded, the gestures that had set many a bonnet quivering and guilty heart louping were weary.

He spoke to Kate, tenderly and quietly, about what Lilias had meant to him.

'She had a quality, my lass, that I can only describe as simple goodness. I never heard her speak a word against anybody. She hadn't your vigour, Kate, but she was like you. Neither of you was ever able to turn away a body in distress.'

Kate swallowed her own emotion and pleaded with him to take care of himself, for the sake of Honoria, who would surely make the trip to see him one day, with little Finn and the second child now on its way. Obediently he showed interest. But many days as she went about Dounhead, Kate would glimpse his white head moving about the graveyard, as he tended the grave with its white headstone and an unequivocal message: 'Safe in the arms of Jesus.'

Summer came and went and the old minister's physical decline continued. He became more slipshod than ever in his dress and went out absently in biting winds without an overcoat, a muffler slung inadequately round his neck. Gifts of calves-foot jelly, cakes made to tempt him, lay untouched in the kitchen till he gave them to Miss Gint to pass on to the needy.

This was the winter when the legend of the lamp grew up, when some late homegoer from pub or prayer meeting, or a young couple trysting in the woods, would see the minister trudge the road with his lantern in front of him.

If they met face to face, he would exchange a word and blessing with them. But where was he going? To the humblest cottage in the Rows, where the need was greatest, where the children were sick, or hungry, or merely too many. If he heard of family rows, sons fighting and falling out, contentious daughters, the old man was there. No one ever had the will to turn him away when his knock was heard at the door. Dousing his lamp by the step, he went in and sat by the table, sometimes with no more light than that from the failing fire. Nothing put him off, neither the foetid smell of close-quartered humanity, nor the stench of infants, nor the dry, quiet cough of the consumptive.

He simply entered into the life of the people he visited, listened to their troubles, gave what help and consolation he could. Often a hard-stretched woman would find a silver coin at the place where he'd sat at table. Although his sermons grew more diffuse and laboured, and one or two grander members took themselves off to Bellnoch on Sundays, a great love for the old man grew up in Dounhead. Total trust existed between him and the inhabitants.

Kate saw what was happening and found it hard to reconcile this man of humility with the near-arrogant Greek and Latin scholar who had once put her outwith his door. But she loved him like the rest and when she could, brought him into her own house for food and rest. A warm and mellow relationship grew up between Galbraith and Findlay. The minister could still bring out the jewels and display-pieces of a well-stocked mind and, with his eyes now unable to decipher print, Findlay was only too ready to test out his own ideas and philosophies, not to say prejudices, which, he owned with a smile, he had gathered with the rest.

It only needed Wattie Chapman to stop by on his now rathery tottery legs and it was almost as though the old coterie had been revived on occasion. Kate listened while they argued the issues of the day: was it Disraeli who'd talked the old Queen out of retirement to open Parliament, and where would the bounds of Empire end, now she was proclaimed Empress of India?

As always, Wattie was more concerned with what happened in Scotland. How was agriculture going to survive, if farmers 'locked out' trade union labourers when prices fell?

And was the fierce chauvinism, mostly whipped up by those who had left Scotland forever, justifiable? Did past glories matter?

And if emigration continued at such a pace, with the Highlands already cleared of people to make way for sheep, what sort of future had Scotland in store?

Would there always be rich and poor? And was it the Government's duty to worry about the unemployed? Kate always felt a lift of heart when she heard pros and cons being argued with vigour. They were good for each other. Sometimes she looked at Findlay's face, in these days of his retirement, and saw it lit up with all the passion and enjoyment of a young man.

It was after one of these gatherings that Tansy came home one evening and dropped her bombshell.

Standing close to Kate and avoiding her father's eyes, she announced: 'Lachie Balfour has asked me to marry him, and I've said yes.'

The ensuing row went on all evening, swaying from one camp to the other. With her arms round her weeping daughter, Kate argued that there was no reason why the marriage should not take place. Findlay, who had been totally in the dark about the courtship, spoke from an angry and wounded heart, but with Isa gone, Tansy had taken to winding him round her finger and he had known well enough from the first fat, well-rounded tear that he would give in.

'I'll never take to him,' he told Tansy. 'You needn't expect it.'

She kissed him. 'It's me that's marrying him.' She gave an April grin, soaked with tears.

On the following day, she ushered Lachie into the front

room, where Kate had the wax fruit on display on a glossily-polished table and Findlay groaned under the harness of a stiff collar.

The old man growled when Lachie made formal application for Tansy's hand, but he took the port wine and shortbread and warmed slowly to the looks of animation and delight on the faces of his wife and daughter.

'You watching the safety factor down that pit?' he demanded of Lachie.

'I've a good manager, Mr Fleming,' returned Tansy's suitor. 'With Parliament and the rest, I have to leave the pit to others these days.'

'A good owner knows what's what,' said Findlay stubbornly. 'My lad Duncan tells me yon's a fool you have in my place. Go elsewhere and find a better man, that's my advice to you.'

It was doubtful if Lachie heard. Tansy was seated at the piano which Jack had bought and beckoning him over to take the tenor line in a Stephen Foster song. Their voices blended, soared; their looks locked. Kate felt a desperate sensation of loss, centred on her stomach. Her bairn gone.

Duncan took the news to Josie next day, when he dropped in at the *Clarion* on his way to the union offices. A change had come over Josie recently. She was actually darning the holes in her clothes and, although not very well pressed, they were quite clean. She'd made attempts to tidy up her red hair, but as there was too much of it, it still escaped in wisps and strands all down her face, especially when she was busy.

She sometimes hummed as she went about her work, little absent-minded tunes that occasionally disturbed Duncan's concentration. He would glare at her and she would smile in return, saying 'Sorry!' She still had probably the most deplorable fingernails he had ever seen, bitten down to the quick. And there was nothing she liked better than a row with an outraged reader or a little tussle with a contributor.

She had said nothing at all when Lilias died. Her eyes had followed Duncan around, watchful and wary, like a spaniel's. But she'd shielded him from the worst worries for as long as she could, worries about the paper's finances, and when he'd taken over again he'd been surprised to find his affairs in reasonable order.

Also, she talked. About anything and everything, as long as it was not important. Still that wary eye. She could tune in to his mood in a second.

Now he said, 'Tansy's getting married. To Balfour.'

'I'm not surprised. But it was Isa he wanted, was it not?'

'Maybe. It's Tansy he's getting.'

She came over close to him, so that he could see the glints in her hair and the scrappy freckles on her short nose. She cleared her throat and said gruffly, 'Maybe we should do the same.'

He looked at her in astonishment. Her face was mantling with red and he thought he detected the gleam of moisture in her eye.

'You know,' she explained. 'I could look after you.'

He placed his hand on the back of her scrawny neck and said evenly, 'All right. You can take me on.'

In the years to come, there was no doubt that, in her way, Josie did look after Duncan. She turned him away from himself and forced him back into the battle to help those in need. There was plenty of scope for action – to improve, bit by bit, conditions in the pits; to fight for better wages and compensation. They joined the growing co-operative movement and, seeing the misery drink brought to many of the miners and their families, took up the temperance cause. Josie, with her magic lantern and vivid description of what alcohol did to the body, never mind the soul, was a great crowd-puller. Their home became the committee rooms of the Rows, the place where anyone with a problem went for help or advice.

They had a pit cottage in the Rows, a concession from Lachie since, although a union leader, Duncan no longer actually worked down the pits.

It was from this cottage that Josie now carried a pail with potato and turnip peelings out to the midden that morning in the year 1879, a scrap of newsprint already lying in the midden catching her eye with its headline about the Zulu War. What a long way away that was! She turned in the sunshine to go back indoors, feeling a sharp, involuntary tug of happiness at the blue and gold day.

Duncan was working at the kitchen table, the usual forms and papers strewn round him. She stood by him for a moment and he put an absent-minded arm around her waist.

'I think I'm having a wean,' she announced, without preamble.

He looked at her uncomprehendingly.

'You know,' she said sharply, 'one of those things you wrap in a shawl and put in a cradle.'

Stammering with surprise and shock, he got to his feet and laid his hands on her shoulders.

'Josie, are you sure? You've had alarms before.'

She gave a tight little smile.

'This time I waited. This time I'm sure.' Perhaps hoping for another reaction from him, she added, 'And I don't know if I want it.'

'Sit down,' he commanded. He took her over to the rickety wicker chair by the untidy fire – Josie could not be accused of being houseproud. He put his hands over hers as they lay in her lap.

'Josie. Josie Daly,' he said softly. 'You bonnie wee fighter, you. You were always the bane of my young life.' He added, still incredulous, 'Having a bairn, are you?'

'At my age, I should know better,' she said, turning her head from his. 'It'll be naught but an encumbrance.' And putting her red head into her thin hands, she wept.

Duncan stood up dazedly. 'How could our bairn be an encumbrance?'

'At meetings, and things,' she sobbed. 'I'll not be able to come with you – '

He fisted the tears from her eyes.

'Listen. Listen, will you? This child will come everywhere with us. On the platform, in the co-op halls, to the pithead if need be – '

Josie did not seem to hear him. Once embarked on her weeping, it seemed she could not stop. He put his head close to hers to try to make out what she was saying through her sobs. 'You don't care for me. Not the way you loved your Lilias. She should have had your bairns – '

He held her very gently then, his own tears damping her red hair, although he did not let her see them.

'Josie,' he crooned, knowing full well how much of himself he had held back from her, penitent but somehow cleansed by the knowledge. 'Let the past go. I love you, Josie Daly. What would I do without you? This bairn has come because we love each other. Is it not so?'

She looked at him tremulously. 'It's the first time you've said it.'

'I know,' he admitted humbly.

'Maybe it was hearing about your Jean's sixth out in New Zealand,' she said, more gaily. 'They do say it's catching!'

'That's better.' He gave her a slow, burning smile that seemed to take her whole being with it. 'Now, you just sit there.' He brought a battered old milking-stool and placed her small booted feet on it. 'What would you like? A cup of best tea and an Abernethy biscuit?'

Perhaps the caller had knocked once before, and they had not heard. Now it came, very loud and commanding, and Josie flew from her chair to answer it while Duncan was still settling the kettle over the fire.

A young collier she knew as Con Berry stood there, blue eyes huge in his coal-blackened face.

'Is Duncan in?'

Josie nodded.

'Would he come to the pithead? There's four men down there and there's been a fall – '

Just then the pit hooter went and doors opened all down the Rows. Men who had been on the night shift stumbled out from their beds; women ran, pulling shawls over their heads; children raced ahead or toddled behind.

In their cottage, Kate and Findlay heard the sound and looked at each other. Without a word, Findlay rose and put on cap and muffler.

Caught in an old terror, Kate detained him.

'Don't go down there. I had a dream last night – a warning.' In the past he might have hesitated, superstitious as she. Even meeting a red-haired woman had once been enough to make him turn back.

'I maun see what I can do,' he said firmly, putting her hand away from him. To comfort her, he said, 'It might be nothing much.'

Most of Dounhead had gathered at the pithead. At the foot of the bings, the purple loosestrife waved, and in the fields stretching away, the farm-workers bent their back to their job.

As Findlay reached the spot, Lachie Balfour galloped up like a mad thing on his grey mare.

'Aye, so it takes an accident to bring you,' said Findlay drily. He knew Parliament was in recess and that Tansy and her husband had just returned from a painting holiday in France.

Lachie ignored the jibe. He drew both Duncan and Findlay into the urgent talks that followed. It seemed that work had been re-started three months before on an old shaft. Although it had been well-tested for fire damp, it was the general opinion that damp must have occurred. There had been an explosion, followed by a heavy fall and the men were trapped with the pony and trucks in an area that must be getting more dangerous by the minute.

Findlay did not let Lachie off the hook. 'I told you to get yourself a decent safety man,' he growled.

Duncan said pacifically, 'There's always a margin of human error, Father.'

'But there shouldnae be,' retorted the old man stubbornly

'Never mind all that,' ordered Lachie. 'It's what we can do now that matters.'

The first batch of volunteers were coming up from underground, their faces rimed with sweat and effort, their backs aching unbearably. They had been tearing the coal away by hand and pick. Duncan watched the next lot lining up and said, 'I'm going down with them.'

Josie had been saying nothing. Now she looked at her father-in-law in alarm. 'Don't let him go, Mr Fleming.'

Findlay looked acutely from one to the other.

'I'm having a wean,' Josie whispered.

'No before time,' the old man grunted, but he grasped Duncan's arm and squeezed it so hard that it hurt. 'Stay up here, man. Let me go down.' To Josie, he pointed out Kate, who had followed him more slowly to the pithead and now stood with a little knot of women on the periphery of the crowd. 'Go you by my Kate, lass. You'll be all right with her.'

Duncan's face flushed. He waited till Josie was out of earshot then said to his father, 'I'm going down, Paw.'

'Aye,' Findlay gave in. 'Go canny then, lad.'

When Duncan had disappeared with the second batch of volunteers, Lachie approached Findlay and said urgently, 'Listen, I've got the old plans out. I want you to look at them. You know this pit better than anyone.' Findlay made grim acknowledgement. Lachie pointed: 'See here? Do you remember the old workings at this point? I thought – if we went down from this angle, we might be able to break through to them more quickly.'

Findlay studied the map, but he had no need of it. He nodded his agreement.

'Could it be done?'

'Needs must,' said Findlay. 'But I maun go down first and test for the damp. No use risking more men.'

As though she had sensed his intentions, Kate had come over to Findlay and now she cried sharply, 'Let somebody else go!'

He shook his head. 'The fireman's down below. One of the trapped.'

'I'll go with you,' said Lachie. He was glad that Tansy had gone to Bellnoch for the day. There were enough anxious faces around.

Cautiously, the two men let themselves down the old shaft. As they crawled along on hands and knees, a strange, eerie sound came to them.

'It's them!' cried Findlay jubilantly. 'They're alive. I can hear them singing.'

'By God!' said Lachie. 'They're near. Can we get at them, do you think?'

Findlay said cautiously, 'It's worth a try. It'll take too long the other way. Get the men down here!'

Scrabbling along in the dark and damp, Lachie did as he was told.

Not knowing if he would be heard, Findlay shouted encouragement: 'We're coming, men. We're coming.'

In a short space of time, four more volunteers appeared behind him. They had refused to let Lachie come down again with them, on the grounds that he would only be in the way when there was work to be done. Under Findlay's instructions, they began to work away at the coal. The singing stopped and a voice suddenly shouted, 'You're nearly there.' Suddenly there was a gap and a hand came through. A voice said in the dark, 'Thank God.'

Three men scrambled through the hole and then there was a pause and the sound of sobbing.

'On your way,' Findlay ordered the others, rescued and rescuers alike.

One of the rescued men said, 'It's young Wilson. He doesn't want to leave his pony.'

'Pat,' cried Findlay commandingly, remembering a cheeky lad who'd hung about the pit long before starting work there, asking the men for the remains of their 'chuck' as they came up off shift. 'Pat! We'll get the animal later. Come on, man.'

The only response was the harsh sound of the boy's weeping.

'On your way,' Findlay urged the others again. 'I'll wait for the young 'un.' The men did as they were told, recognizing his authority, those who had been entombed rasping for breath and staggering with weakness in any case and leaning on the others for help.

'Come on, laddie,' wheedled Findlay. 'Your maw is waiting up there for a sight of you. Be a man!'

'Nell's leg's broke. She's lying here with her head on my lap.' More weeping.

Findlay felt his way cautiously through the escape hole. His body had thickened in the years of retirement, but he was still muscular, active. From the old shaft, something that was not light yet not total darkness helped him to locate boy and pony. The little animal kicked out at him in its distress and he made soft, reassuring noises: 'Here, moshie, here.'

'She's near human,' said Pat Wilson. 'She takes the top of my tea flask off and drinks my tea.'

'Aye, I had one once that did that,' said Findlay. He placed a firm hand on the boy's arm. 'She'll have to be put down, son, with a broken leg. Come on. Time's short.'

At last the boy disengaged himself from the pony. Findlay pushed him towards the escape hole, hearing from a distance voices shouting for them both to hurry. Then it seemed that the whole earth reverberated above his head and in the darkness there was nothing but soft, inevitable noise and the flurry, flurry of something falling.

He pulled Pat back and felt him stiffen momentarily in his arms. Something he knew to be blood flowed from the boy's head. Findlay felt through the hole and knew that the old shaft had collapsed ahead of them. No way out there now. The boy groaned and said, 'Where are we?'

'We'll have to wait till the other lot get through to us,' said Findlay. 'Don't move. Save the air.'

At the pithead, Kate flew at the men who came up, demanding, 'Where's Findlay? Where's my man?'

'Coming,' they said. 'With young Pat Wilson. He wouldn't leave his pony.'

'Mother Fleming,' said Josie tenderly. 'Come home with me, will you? They'll tell us the minute there's news.'

The hours passed. The blue and gold went from the day. Kate insisted, dry-eyed, 'I will wait here.' They put tea and bread into her hands, but she did not know what she held.

When it was dark, they took her home and she sat in

Grannie Fleming's cottage, refusing to let anyone light the lamp. James Galbraith came in and sat with her hand in his.

It was two days later when the weary men working from the first approach finally broke through. They had held on to the hope of finding Findlay and Pat alive to the last. But it was not to be. The air had run out and the two bodies were carried forth before a silent crowd at the pithead.

They all came round her then, her family and her friends, showing by their many acts of kindness their love and respect for her.

She did not hear the exchange between Duncan and Lachie.

Duncan: 'Make yours a safety pit now, man. If you value him that's gone.'

Lachie: 'Could I have done more? He could have got out. Do you think I don't wish that he had?' His look was tortured, for he had had to take the news home to Tansy, his wife.

Kate heard little. She sat with a scrap of paper between her hands, refusing to eat, sipping cold tea, until the day a week later that Josie told her about the coming baby.

She smiled then, a pale ghost of a smile, and showed them what was on the paper they had found screwed up in Findlay's right hand.

The stub of pencil had been faint and the air nearly used up, for the last word was barely decipherable.

'My dear Kate,' Findlay had written. 'I leave you.'

Dounhead village was a greystone village, except for the red pit rows, and James Galbraith's kirk was of grey stone, but panelled and pewed inside in a warm, honeyed oak.

The congregation rose now as he ascended the pulpit and as one voice sang the opening hymn. Everyone was aware of that vacant space next to Mistress Fleming. Although no one looked directly at her, every man, woman and child was aware of the straight-backed figure in black.

It was only a week since the burial. They had all pleaded with her to stay at home and rest, but she had risen that morning and laid out all her Sabbath clothes, and the silk parasol that Paterson had sent her from America. She remembered that other nadir in her life, after Findlay's drinking, when somehow or other she had gathered her family and her self-respect together for that walk to the kirk through her neighbour's curious glances.

Those who were in the congregation afterwards said they had never heard James Galbraith preach a finer sermon. Always of late the old man's voice had faltered, his preaching had become diffuse and hard to follow.

There was no Old Testament thunder, just comfort from the well-loved Psalms: 'I have been young, and now am old; yet have I not seen the righteous forsaken, nor his seed begging bread.'

His strong voice overlaid with emotion, he looked directly at Kate as he said, 'Thou makest his beauty to consume away, like as it were a moth fretting a garment: every man therefore is but vanity.' Then he added softly, as the women in the congregation dabbed their eyes, 'Weeping may endure for a night, but joy cometh in the morning.'

Kate did not weep. She looked up at her old friend and mentor, and knew that he spoke nothing less than the truth. She believed in her God more passionately in her hour of greatest deprivation than she had ever done in her life.

The service finished with the singing of the twenty-third psalm and as the familiar words rang throughout the kirk, and soared away over the Covenanting hills beyond, Kate knew that she was not alone. But only waiting.

'Yea, though I walk in Death's dark vale
Yet will I fear no ill:
For Thou are with me and Thy rod
And staff me comfort still.'

Chapter Eighteen

In the year of 1880, Dounhead House, home of Lachie Balfour, Tory MP, was en fête for the birth of a son. Big trestle tables, covered with white cloths, were set up in the grounds, and the villagers poured in, dressed in their Sunday best, to sample the jellies and ginger beer, the fruit bun and the french cakes. Some of them brought gifts for the baby and all of them took the chance to stroll round the beautiful ornamental gardens or wander through the conservatories admiring the black grapes on the vine. There was music from a three-piece band, and decorous races for the children, and the sun was so warm it stilled any carping or envious comments.

Lachie's wife had properly persuaded him that it was a good excuse for a celebration on the grand scale, for was not everybody in need of cheering up after a summer like last year's, the worst in modern times, with the harvests blackened in the fields and three million sheep dead of rot. And even now, people were still talking about the dreadful Tay Bridge railway disaster, which had happened just before the Christmas of '79, and of the two hundred men killed in the Blantyre pit disaster.

But now things were bound to get better, Tansy insisted cheerfully. And although he had his reservations about that (there was a lot of talk at Westminster about an economic recession), Lachie indulged his wife fondly, for the birth of a child after six years' marriage and two false starts was indeed something to be happy about and Donald Darwin Balfour was a splendid, crowing boy of equable, sunny temperament, whom everyone loved.

He was going to be in at the start of a new era, this child, an era of people talking to each other by the telephone, of incandescent gas mantles giving a vastly superior light to the old jets, even of wonders like electric light, which now illuminated London's Waterloo Bridge. An age of scientific marvels.

All in all, Lachie reflected, with a certain cautious complacency, it was a good marriage. If she verged on the extravagant, his wife was nonetheless an excellent, out-going hostess. She dressed with style and flair, knew how to accept a pretty compliment graciously, could play the piano, sing and generally be the life and soul of any gathering. He had been lucky, allowing for the fact that some stubborn, mourning part of him had longed instead for Isa. Tansy had turned out to be a wholly delightful helpmate to him, clever, adaptable, fiercely loyal. And now she had given him a son.

If she wished she could fill the house with her relatives. Let them all come. Had his father-in-law lived, would he have relented sufficiently to join them on this happy day? Maybe not. But Kate his mother-in-law was here. He looked over at her straight-backed figure with respect and affection. It was from her that her daughters got their spirit. And he got on well with the rest of the family too, even his blood-cousin, Jack, and with Duncan, who was too large-hearted to carry grudges even though their political stances were poles apart.

It was Josie and Duncan who came towards him now, Josie holding some carefully-wrapped gee-gaw for the infant. He always thought she looked half-starved, but paintable, with her high cheek-bones, flaming red hair and customary black outfit. He could not deny she had a certain proletarian dignity.

For a time after Lilias had died, Duncan had looked as though he might slip into melancholia, but the need to keep the *Clarion* going and organize the union on a steady footing had gradually pulled him back. That, and Josie. If they said Tansy had made a dead set at him, Lachie, Josie had probably done the same for Duncan, and last year the union had produced a daughter, called Caroline, or more often Carlie, whom he could see now being shown the 'pretty flowers' by attentive older children.

Even now, Duncan wore a grave and solemn look, as though a shade unhappy at being in the midst of so much extravagance. Lachie had watched how everybody spoke to him as he walked through the grounds. He was winning a great deal of respect nowadays for his level-headed approach to politics. Next time he opposed him, the answer might be quite different.

Lachie would not mind, he found. He would enjoy staying at home with Tansy and the child and getting on with his painting.

'Aye, Lachie,' said Duncan, with a smile. 'Yon's a bonnie wee pit boss you and Tansy have.'

'He'll have more sense than his father,' teased Josie.

'He'll keep away from politics,' Lachie decreed. 'I fancy him for a scientist, maybe.'

'Have you not had enough yourself?' Duncan joked. 'By the time young Donald there is a man, Labour will be sweeping the decks. It has to come.'

Lachie rose to the bait, enumerating his argument on his fingers. 'Look,' he said, 'what Dizzie's done. One, shortened work hours in factories; two, given workmen legal equality with employers, three, guaranteed savings; four, cleared slums, improved sanitation and ended the pollution of rivers. And passed the Plimsoll Act to protect seamen in the so-called coffin ships – '

'So there's nothing more to be done?' said Josie, with contained ferocity. 'No women dying of lead poisoning, or farm-workers without the vote?'

'Aye, it's a fine day,' said Duncan deadpan, looking up at the ceiling, and the others realized he was mocking them and changing the subject in his own droll way.

Tansy bore down on them now, looking delightfully pretty in a cream voile dress with peacock blue ribbons and lace at the neck and sleeves. She kissed Josie and said, 'Come and talk to Clemmie. She sees so little of you.'

Clemmie was seated on the horsehair settee with her feet on a petit-point footstool, watching the servants close up the big french windows now that the actual christening ceremony was about to take place. She had grown plumper with the years, perhaps not surprisingly as she and Jack now had a brood of six.

She laughed up at Josie and reintroduced them now: 'This is Sandia and George, Mabel, Andrew, Kate and Alistair.' The girls curtsied and the handsome boys bowed from the waist. Clemmie patted the space beside her and said, to Josie, 'When will you and Duncan find the time to come and see us?'

'It's not the time, it's the money,' said Josie frankly, and Clemmie shifted a little uncomfortably. She did not understand half of what Josie and Duncan talked about. She did not like to see the poor, either, but really, what could anybody do about it? She, Clemmie, passed on all her own and the children's clothes to needy families. There was no need for Josie to be so prickly.

She could see that the situation between her Jack and Duncan was equally discomfiting. She could tell from the red on the back of Jack's neck. Duncan would be needling him again about the money he was making from the refrigeration of ships. The first cargo of frozen beef had just arrived on the Clyde from Australia and it was clear that a great new trade in beef and mutton was under way.

Why should not Jack put the money he had earned so hard and dangerously into any venture that would guarantee them comfort and security? To Clemmie, it was heaven to have him at home with her for good. Josie should understand that poverty was not the only form of suffering. To be parted from the man you loved, for years, and to know that every voyage might be his last, that too was hardship, and had to be borne.

'Don't you miss your clippers?' Duncan was saying to Jack. 'Man, you used to wax so poetic about them!'

'The clippers, yes,' admitted Jack. With his ruddy face and clear eyes, he could have been nothing but a sailor, even now looking marginally out of place on dry land. 'But the steamships, no. It is all too easy nowadays. They've got condensers to give them all the fresh water they need. Tinned food is so much better. The captain and the surgeon inspect the passengers' quarters daily, and once a week all the luggage is dragged up from the hold so that anyone may take out anything they want. We had no time for all that in the old days.'

'But the steamship still has not superseded the sailing ship,' said Duncan.

'No, but it will come, in the name of progress,' admitted Jack sadly.

'What about this freak ship they're building on the Clyde, the *Livadia*? It's for the Tsar, isn't it?'

'Designed by one Admiral Popoff! A kind of square, floating palace. It's just a passing wonder – all the bairns have *Livadia* on their sailor caps. But it's not every day that a yard gets an order worth three hundred thousand pounds.'

'You don't sound very enthusiastic.'

'Well,' Jack demurred. 'These are difficult days on the Clyde. The old craftsmen, the carpenters, won't work in iron and they're having to train up Irish labour as platers, riveters and hole-borers.' He looked carefully at Josie. 'With all due respect, they're a wild lot.'

'We'd have no roads or railways without Irish navvies,' interposed Duncan mildly. 'Like it or not, I'd say they make up about a sixth of the population round here – or soon will do. Mind you, some historians argue that we Scots in the South-West and the Irish were all one race, in the old Kingdom of Dalriada.'

'They're a flashy lot,' said Jack, 'when they have a bit of money. All hard hats and gold rings.'

Duncan laughed. 'Good luck to them. They've had little enough in the past.'

Lachie broke into the conversation. 'That was a splendid trip you recommended for Tansy and me,' he told Jack. Turning to Duncan, he recapitulated. 'You know, we sailed to Gibraltar, Algiers, Malta, Tunis and Alexandria last year, a round trip for the artist and scholar, as they put it. And all for thirty pounds a head.'

He saw Duncan's look harden. No doubt he was working out how many children could be fed for the sum. Losing patience slightly, he turned away and was just in time to see Isabella come in at the door. The old alchemy turned his blood rapidly to water.

'Lachie.' She took his hand. Again that slight tremor, change of colour, that indicated she was no more made of stone than he. At least, so he fancied. She had filled out slightly; the word for her now was handsome. And he had to admit, she looked fulfilled, content.

'How goes the ministration of the sick?' he demanded.

She gave that slight, secret smile of hers. 'It goes well, Lachie.'

'Is it enough?'

She knew what he meant. 'Oh yes. You must come through my wards with me some day. I'll show you my children.'

Tansy came towards them now, a slight wariness in her look. But she kissed her sister warmly and Isabella said, 'Now where is this wonder child? I must see him.' They went off to look at the baby.

In a little while, Tansy made her way back to her husband. Giving him a speculative look, she thrust her hand through his arm, gave him a little shove, and seeing this was not enough, kissed him. Nothing and yet everything was said by the gesture.

Isabella went over to her mother and sat by her, holding her hand.

'This is a great day for you, Mother. See how your grandchildren grow!'

Kate gave a gentle smile. 'It would have been nice, if Jean and Paterson and their families could have been here, too.'

'We should have needed the kirk hall!' joked Isabella.

Kate wanted to hear all about her daughter's work in the infirmary. She could not believe that this dignified, contained woman with her great skill and compassion was the same little girl who protested about carrying in the water and doing the other manual chores about the house. She was, if anything, a little in awe of her, but deeply proud.

'Dr Isa!' said Clemmie, joining their group and kissing her sister-in-law. 'How well you look!'

'I must see the Greenock clan,' Isabella said, bustling off to chat to Clemmie's brood, and Clemmie moved up to her mother-in-law with a purposeful expression.

'Mama,' she said, 'there is something Jack and I wish to talk to you about.'

'To me?' asked Kate, dragging her eyes away from the lively tableau of Isabella and the voluble, excited children.

'Yes. Please listen, dear. Do you remember that time when the *Chancellor* went down and you came to see me when I was so ill? Do you remember what you said to me then?'

'I'm not sure I do,' Kate admitted.

'You said, "You will always be part of the family, Clemmie, if I have any say in it," and you cannot know, Mother, what that meant to me then. I have never forgotten it.'

Seeing that Clemmie was moved almost to tears, Kate patted her hand reassuringly. 'My reward has been to see you and Jack so happy.'

'Well, what we have to say now, Mother, is this: we want to take you into *our* family. We want you to come and live with us at Greenock. You shall have the big front room upstairs so that you can watch the ships go up and down the river. You'd like that, wouldn't you?'

It was Kate's turn now to dab her eyes, so unexpected was the proposition. She could not deny she was attracted to the idea, for even after all these land-locked years at Dounhead, she had sometimes missed the Clyde.

She remembered now the day she had left Greenock with young Jack, her heart full of hurt and fury against James Galbraith and the sobs bursting from Jack's chest as he'd cried, 'My ships! My ships!' She had felt the loss of the river as a sustaining element. But it had taken much away from her, too. Its broad current had carried Jean and Paterson beyond her reach and taken Jack from his family for a large chunk of his life. She knew if she accepted the offer of the big front room, she would spend many days brooding on the mystery of these dark and restless waters, giving and taking like life itself on their way to the open seas.

'Think about it, Mama,' pleaded Clemmie now. 'We

worry about you being on your own in Grannie Fleming's cottage.'

'I will,' Kate promised. 'It is good and kind of you to think of me.'

She looked up and James Galbraith was staring at her from across the room, as though he sensed the burden of the conversation she had had with Clemmie. Whenever it was feasible, she rose and went unobtrusively across to his chair. Always there was something naked and vulnerable in his look that disarmed her. She wondered how much he remembered. She had never told him of that long walk to Glasgow, the terror she had felt when Jack disappeared. Nor, of course, of that feeling she had had when she first saw Findlay, so handsome, so exuding that warm humanity, that her life was sealed.

'Kate?' he said questioningly.

'Clemmie has asked me to go and live in Greenock,' she said. There was a silence, while she looked down on his snowy locks and bent back in the old black coat that was almost green with age. She could not help it, she could feel only compassion for him. Compassion and love. She knew now whose loss had been the greater, that day so long ago when he had shown her the door.

'And shall you go?' he asked carefully.

She knew for sure now there was only one possible answer.

'Oh no. I shall stay at Grannie Fleming's cottage. You and I have too many memories, James, ever to leave Dounhead.'

It was the first time she had ever used his Christian name and she saw his back straighten and stiffen.

'I shall come to the kirk on Sunday and listen to your sermon, for as long as you care to preach it.'

'You always were fond of a bit of sermon-tasting, Kate.' He turned full towards her now, with a splendid beaming look on his face. 'And shall you argue for St John, against St Paul, as you did in the old days?'

'I might,' she twinkled. 'I shall keep you up to scratch, never fear.'

There was a murmur in the room now which indicated that the actual christening was near. Donald Darwin Balfour's nurse brought him forward to the centre of the room, in all the glory of his many petticoats, his long, fine lawn christening robe, his be-ribboned, ruched bonnet and filmy silken veil covering his small, puckered face.

James Galbraith rose to conduct the ceremony. His voice was calm and musical, the mature instrument of his faith. Donald Darwin Balfour seemed lulled by it, and behaved, after an initial token protest, in exemplary fashion.

Seated at the groaning dining-table afterwards, his grandmother was permitted to have him on her knee, and so did less justice to the meats and jellies, the blancmanges and cakes, than did the others, especially the small guard of the Greenock brigade.

But Kate was happy. This small, wriggling bundle on her lap. born after the waiting years, was a symbol that life always began anew, hope was never in vain.

What was it Findlay had said to her, on the day Paterson and Honoria got married? 'You are the joy of my life.' She had never forgotten that. Never referred to it again. But had worn it like the most precious of jewels in her breast.

And this, a day crowned with such jewels!

The baby held a rosebud fist up to her lips, and she kissed it. And while his fond mother was looking elsewhere, she popped some celebratory blancmange into his waiting mouth.